# Emerald Buddha

Russell Blake

First edition.

Books@RussellBlake.com

ISBN: 978-1517585846

Published by

Reprobatio Limited

# Prologue

*1431 A.D., near the Laos-Burma border*

Birdcalls echoed through the hidden valley as the jungle awakened to a new day. Twenty Khmer warriors stirred to life on the riverbank, blinking in the dense fog that had seeped through a nearby pair of towering karst formations overnight. A team of fatigued oxen grazed a dozen yards from the water, where a ranking member of the royal court sat atop a wooden cart, deep circles shadowing his eyes from many sleepless hours on the long journey into the uncharted wilds.

Inside the ungainly conveyance rested chests containing the Khmer Empire's treasure – holy relics, gold cups and icons, and gems of immeasurable value. But the most priceless possession was wrapped in a thick blanket: the legendary Emerald Buddha, whose smaller twin resided with the royal family in Thailand, now at war with the Khmers.

The Khmer Empire had been no match for its rival from the south, and only weeks ago the elaborate temple complex of Angkor Wat had fallen to the Thai army, which had sacked it and taken its inhabitants captive. King Ponhea Yat had made a summary decision when he'd heard from his spies that the Thais were approaching the beloved landmark, and had entrusted the nation's riches to his deputy, Chey, as the rest of the Khmer court retreated north to safety.

A tall man in battle-scarred armor stood and approached the cart, a perpetual frown creasing the hard lines of his face. Sihanouk was one of the fiercest fighters in the entire kingdom, and clearly resented having been assigned to this duty when there was battle to be joined against the Thai invaders. It had not been his choosing to skulk around in the jungle like an old woman. But orders were orders, and he had followed them, whatever his feelings. He had escorted Chey, the royal appointee, deep into unfamiliar territory, and they'd finally arrived at a suitable location, where they would hide the king's riches until it was safe to return it to the royal court.

"This valley is as well concealed and desolate as any I've seen," Sihanouk began. "But I'm not sure that the treasure will be any safer at the end of the earth than it would be at home, surrounded by loyal warriors."

"Our job was to find an auspicious location. From here it is out of our hands," Chey said.

"Fate has been kind to us so far," Sihanouk agreed. "Let's hope that the cursed Hill People leave us be until we're able to finish our work."

"Have faith that all will turn out well."

Sihanouk eyed Chey skeptically. "While I appreciate your optimism, I'll still keep my sword close at hand."

Chey nodded. "I would expect nothing less."

There was no love lost between Chey, widely considered by the soldiers to be a schemer and sycophant, and Sihanouk, who had distinguished himself with valor. The king's choice of confidants was irritating to the warrior, but in the end Sihanouk served at the king's pleasure, and if he had to comply with Chey's instructions, he would. But the slimy royal court eel gave Sihanouk doubts, and he would be glad when this mission was over and he could defend his people honorably.

"Do you have a location in mind?" Sihanouk asked.

Chey offered a sly smile. "I have some ideas."

"We will be hard-pressed to find anything in this soup."

"It will lift before long. Have the men do something useful while we wait. Set out lines and see if there are fish to be had for breakfast. We will go in search of a suitable spot after we've filled our bellies."

The fog burned off by late morning, and Chey led Sihanouk along the river's course in search of an auspicious cave. As he'd hoped, there were several; though the water's erosion of the limestone had been inconsistent over millions of years, and all but one proved too shallow for their purposes. But the final depression was perfect – a narrow opening practically impossible to see from the river's present course, with a passage into a larger cavern that fed into several smaller chambers.

A month went by, the days long as the men carved the soft stone to suit their needs. On the final morning, Chey supervised the unloading of the cart and the placement of the chests inside. The last item to be situated in the newly created temple was the Emerald Buddha, which glowed in the torchlight, its golden robe dazzling even in the dim light of the cave.

The following morning the soldiers retraced their steps. The cart had been dismantled and its beams sent adrift down the river to obliterate any trace of their passage. Chey followed the column rather than heading it; he'd discharged his obligation and found a haven for the treasure, and was happy to trail the men as Sihanouk led the way.

They spent the evening at the base of the mountain they'd descended to enter the hidden valley. After eating his fill of the fish they'd packed for the return trip, Chey stood near their small fire and removed a cask from his bag.

"My friends, congratulations. The king authorized me to offer you this, the Khmer's finest rice wine, as a reward for a job well done. Gentlemen, I salute and honor each of you for your part." Chey broke the seal on the cask, took a long draft, and then handed it to Sihanouk to pass around to the men. In no time the vessel was drained, each man having eagerly taken a brimming mouthful and savored the liquor's pleasant burn. Chey excused himself and went to relieve himself in the brush. When he was finished, he rejoined the men, lingering at the edge of the small clearing, watching the dance of the orange flames.

Half an hour later the fire was little more than glowing embers and the soldiers were passed out, the sleeping agent in the wine having worked its magic. Chey had taken an antidote before he'd drunk, but the rest of the men were lost to the world, sprawled around the fire pit, snoring.

Chey approached Sihanouk and drew the warrior's sword. He paused as he inspected the wicked blade, and then, without hesitation, thrust the point through his throat. Sihanouk stiffened as his appendages twitched, and he gurgled a strangled moan before falling still. Chey stepped back from the lifeless body and repeated the act with the others until he'd slaughtered all the men in their sleep. He glanced around at the corpses, his face impassive, and nodded once to himself before he retrieved Sihanouk's belt and scabbard and cinched the wide leather strap around his waist.

He moved to the bag with the provisions and tested its weight. It was heavy, but he could always jettison food if he tired of carrying it. Better to have too much than too little, he reasoned, as he shouldered the sack and set off by moonlight for the trail that would lead him back to an uncertain future and to his king, who'd authorized the murder of his loyal men in order to keep the treasure's hiding place secret.

Now, only Chey knew the truth. And Chey was a survivor. Whatever awaited him in his homeland, he would fulfill his oath and bring to the king the location of the temple, for which he was sure he would be rewarded lavishly.

All he had to do was make it back alive.

# Chapter One

*Islamabad, Pakistan*

Stars glimmered through a light haze of smog over Rawal Lake. Traffic had slowed to a trickle from the city, the raucous noise of poorly muffled vehicles fading as darkness fell. Now the air was filled with the sound of televisions blasting from open windows and the dissonant keen of polyrhythmic music from radios as the suburb of Bhara Kahu settled in for the night. Largely working class, the area was only five miles from Islamabad, connected via a highway that skirted the lake.

A garbage truck rumbled down a dusty street on its way to the communal neighborhood dumping spot, piled high with contributions from local residents and passersby. A lone dog trotted stiffly behind it, a hopeful look in its haunted eyes. Lights glowed behind the iron-barred windows of small homes encircled by high walls topped with broken glass.

Four local men sat outside a tiny café at a circular glass table, playing cards and smoking strong cigarettes from which serpentine coils of pungent smoke corkscrewed into the air before dispersing into the light breeze. A boy no older than ten carried out to the men a red enamel tray loaded with four cups of coffee the consistency of crude oil. He set each down carefully before scuttling back inside. The men laughed at a joke, toasted, and resumed their betting, insulting one another good-naturedly as they traded coins back and forth.

A battered Nissan sedan with glass tinted so dark it was nearly opaque crept down the street and slowed as it approached the café. The men visibly stiffened, and one reached beneath his baggy shirt; and then relaxed when the passenger-side window rolled down and one of his friends waved and called out a greeting.

Jack Rollins watched the exchange through night vision goggles from the second-floor window of a house at the end of the block. He was wearing a balaclava and head-to-toe black, invisible in the darkened interior. Next to him lay a Kalashnikov AKM with a collapsible wire stock and a satchel that housed six magazines. Beside it was a .50-caliber sniper rifle with a compact night vision scope – a weapon that fired hand-loaded explosive rounds that would vaporize a man's head at a thousand yards.

He tapped his earbud and waited for a click to signal that all was still well. The answering pop came a second later. The target hadn't shown himself since returning from the nearby mosque for Isha salat, the last prayer of the day, intended to carry the faithful from dusk until dawn. Jack had wanted to take the man out right on the street, but that wasn't the mission, so instead he was waiting patiently.

"See anything on that side?" he murmured. A voice crackled in his ear almost immediately.

"Nothing's changed. Lights are on inside the house. Couple of goons outside with assault rifles. AKs, of course."

"Of course." AK-47s were ubiquitous in the Punjab area of Pakistan, as common as flies after decades of nonstop warring in nearby Afghanistan – something Jack knew all too well after two tours of duty there. The Afghans were mean as striped snakes and lived to fight, most having grown up battling the Russians and then the Americans.

*Not my problem*, Jack thought. *We all do what we must to survive.*

"Any signs from the surrounding houses?" Jack asked.

"Negative. All's quiet. Except for Saddam, of course. He never sleeps."

Saddam was the nickname they'd given the shooter on the roof of the adjacent home, part of the target's security precautions. Hamal Qureshi was a moderate voice in the debate with more extreme interpretations of the Koran, a devout cleric respected by many – so much so that his views on the non-orthodoxy of the latest terrorist groups disrupting the Middle East were shaping the dialog on whether they were legitimate or a false-flag operation for Western imperialist interests. Dangerous questions to ask, which would be rewarded with a death sentence.

"Probably has a guilty conscience," Jack mused, "or he's daydreaming about those fifty-five virgins."

"I think the number's seventy-two."

"Whatever." Jack checked his watch. "We go live in twenty minutes. Got the flash bangs and the ack-acks ready?"

"You bet. And in this outfit I look like Omar the Tentmaker, so they'll never see me coming." Jack's crew had been outfitted with local garb, in keeping with the clandestine nature of the assignment. They were to look like locals, terrorists out for a vocal dissenter's blood. The assassination would create outrage in the community and hopefully dampen enthusiasm for criticism. Whether it would work or not was above Jack's pay grade; he was just the hired help. And good at his job.

"All right. Let's maintain radio silence until we're ready to rock. Won't be long now. Watch your backs."

Jack signed off and watched the decrepit Nissan roll away, trailing exhaust from inadequate combustion. He'd been in town for three days with his crew, reconnoitering. Finally it was time – the waiting was the hardest part. He knew from experience that once the shooting started it would be over in a blink; hundreds of thousands of dollars of preparation, arms, fake papers, all for the two minutes he'd estimated it would take to neutralize Qureshi's guard and take out the great man himself.

The four card players were accounted for – if they tried to get in the mix, he'd off them like a bad habit. Collateral damage was unavoidable in these sorts of incursions. Nature of the beast, Jack thought, and he silently wished them winning hands and the good sense to duck for cover instead of trying to help the cleric.

On the table beside him the satellite phone's display pulsed, indicating an inbound call. There was only one person who knew the number, and Jack moved swiftly to answer.

"Honey Badger," he answered softly. The line hissed like a cobra, and then his superior's unmistakable voice rang from the speaker.

"Abort. Repeat, abort."

Jack's eyes narrowed. "Why?"

"You've been blown."

"Blown? How?"

"Just get out of there. It's over. Someone leaked the details on the web an hour ago – we just heard. Clock's ticking. Expect the Pakistanis to be serious about nailing you. Do whatever it takes to get away clean."

"Are you running interference?"

"Yes. That's why you're still alive. But we can only stall them so long. Move. Now."

"Roger that. I'll call when clear."

Jack hung up and thought for a moment, and then tapped his earbud again and relayed the news. At the far end of the block a car started its engine and pulled away. Jack didn't wait to see anything more. His crew were all big boys. They had their crisis-contingency plan down pat, and would each make their way out of the country using different routes.

Thank God he overthought every mission and was hyper-paranoid. Many would have just stuck with the default protocol rather than take the time and money to set up an alternative known only to them. But Jack wasn't one of the many. The shrapnel and bullet scars were a reminder of that every time he showered.

He quickly dismantled the .50-caliber Barrett that he'd modified for easy disassembly and packed it into a black nylon duffle with the AKM and the magazines. Last to go in were the goggles and the balaclava.

Jack was down the stairs and out the door in twenty seconds, and he rushed to the iron front gate as he heard the steady beat of helicopters approaching. So much for stalling. It would be close.

He pushed the gate open and moved hurriedly down the crumbling sidewalk, all subterfuge abandoned. He needed to get out of the area before some bright Pakistani officer established a cordon around the perimeter of the neighborhood to stop anyone from leaving.

At the corner he turned down a gloomy street, the streetlights long ago burned out, and jogged to a Toyota Hilux truck. He slid behind the wheel and tossed the bag onto the passenger side. The cab was dark, its interior bulb removed as a precaution.

It was the little things that could mean the difference between life and death, he knew.

The motor started with a cough, and he dropped the transmission in gear. He was two blocks away when he saw the aircraft in his rearview mirror: two helos, their spotlights blinding, beams sweeping over the rooftops of the area he'd just left.

"Damn," he muttered under his breath, and fought the urge to floor the gas. If it was his lucky night, he'd make it. If not, well, he couldn't allow himself to be captured. His hand brushed the grip of the pistol in his belt and he scowled. He hoped it wouldn't come to that, but there were worse things than death.

Sirens blared in the distance, and he tried to estimate where they were coming from. If the local cops were in on this, his odds dropped precipitously. Jack's mind raced over the abbreviated discussion with his control. Someone had posted the details of a top-secret black op nobody knew about. What did it mean?

That they had a leak was obvious.

But how could their network have been compromised?

It was impossible.

The howl of a nearby siren insisted it was all too real.

A police truck rounded the corner and accelerated toward him. Jack debated his options as he watched the vehicle draw near in his side mirror, and he was about to stomp on the brakes and put the Hilux into a controlled skid when the police truck screeched onto a side street, its tires howling in protest.

"Easy, Jack," he whispered. He suddenly wanted a drink more than anything in the world, despite having been dry for a decade. In his mind's eye he could see the warm amber of the bourbon, smell the tang of the sour mash, taste the searing pleasure as it slid down his throat and warmed him with well-being. "Old habits die hard," he said under his breath, and continued at a moderate pace, ears straining for any indication of pursuit.

On the outskirts of the town he eyed the fuel tank. It was half full, which would easily get him to Peshawar, where he'd lie low for a few days before crossing into Afghanistan. Driving at night in the region was borderline suicidal at the best of times, but he didn't have much choice.

As reluctant as he was to do it, he stopped by a dumpster and jettisoned his weapons. They would incriminate him, and there was no point in making it easy for those after him. That there would be a manhunt was a given, but nobody would report the guns, instead selling them on the thriving black market and pocketing several months' living expenses.

With a final look at the road behind him, he climbed behind the wheel and pointed the truck west, toward the Khyber Pass – and hopefully, escape.

# Chapter Two

*24 hours later, Xishuangbanna, Yunnan Province, China*

Christine Whitfield glanced up as the front door of her boyfriend's apartment opened. She could immediately see that he was agitated, and something else. His normally placid expression had been replaced by one of fear – an emotion that was out of place on his unlined, twenty-something face.

"What's wrong, Liu?" she asked. "I thought you were in Guandu till tomorrow."

"We have to leave," he snapped, moving to his laptop computer. "Now."

"What? Why?"

"I got a tip from a friend. Something went wrong. Grab your computer. Leave nothing behind. I've got a taxi waiting downstairs."

"But where are we going?"

"Thailand. We can disappear there. At least long enough to figure out how bad this is. But assume it's the worst."

"At this hour?"

"I called my brother before I got on the road. He's arranged for a private plane."

Another look at Liu's face convinced her. He was dead serious, his eyes wide with alarm. She leapt to her feet. "Who's after you?" she asked.

"MSS – Ministry of State Security. Or somebody else. Could be anyone. Doesn't really matter what the initials are, does it?"

"But how?"

"I have no idea." He paused as he finished stowing his computer, and fixed her with a steady gaze. "We can figure that out later. What I know is that if they get us, we'll never be seen again."

"But you haven't done anything wrong to the Chinese. Why would MSS cooperate?"

"That never stopped them. They'll invent something. You know how the country works. Anything's for sale for the right price."

She shook her head. "Have you told me everything?"

"We can talk about it on the plane. Pack whatever you can, and don't forget your passport."

Five minutes later they were on their way to the airport, the taxi driver uninterested in the odd pair – a tall blonde and a local. They watched the buildings fly by as he navigated the empty streets, the radio playing a popular Chinese pop song that had caused a sensation due to its risqué lyrics. Christine was sorely tempted to interrogate Liu, but a glance at him convinced her to wait. She trusted him implicitly, and if he felt they were in danger, right or wrong, she'd follow his lead.

The main section of the airport was closed and the huge glass terminal dark. Only a few security guards prowled the grounds. They pulled onto a side access road and through a gate that stood open, and drove to where a half-dozen small prop planes sat on the tarmac. At the far end an ancient Cessna 172 waited with its running lights glowing. As they drew near, they spotted a slight Chinese man standing by the fuselage – the pilot.

The taxi coasted to a stop, and Liu and Christine got out. The driver stepped from the car and moved to the trunk, lighting a cigarette as he did so. Smoking was the national pastime in China, and despite the health consequences, the population had one of the highest rates in the world. He opened the trunk and they retrieved their bags. Liu handed him a few bills, and he smiled and offered a small bow before heading back to his vehicle and driving off.

"Wasn't it a risk to take a cab?" Christine whispered as they approached the plane.

"We had no choice. I couldn't use my car. They may be looking for it by now."

"And you have no idea why the MSS would be after you?"

"I do. But there's nothing I can change at this point."

She stopped in her tracks. "What have you done, Liu? Is this related to our thing?"

"Only tangentially. I think I underestimated the sophistication of their tech people."

"What does that mean?"

He explained in a few terse sentences. By the time he was done, the blood had drained from her face.

"Liu…"

"Too late now, Christine. But do you see why we need to get out of here?"

"That's the understatement of the year. You really think we'll be safe in Thailand?"

"We can disappear, Christine. There are thousands of places off the beaten path."

"What about money? After you run out?"

"Least of our problems. We could survive for a year on that in rural Thailand. Even cheaper in Cambodia."

She gave him a skeptical look.

"Don't worry. I have ways of getting more."

"We're about to take a secret night flight over the Golden Triangle, and you're telling me not to worry? Are you serious?"

Liu stepped nearer. "Keep your voice down. For all we know, the pilot speaks English, too. A byproduct of your capitalist-run dog-lackey television shows."

She couldn't help but smile, reminded why she'd fallen so hard for him. He was blindingly smart, loyal, handsome, and charming in a roguish way. Tall for a Chinese, due to his family's northern blood, he stood six feet, with a slacker mop of longish hair and stylish Western clothes. At twenty-nine he still looked like he was barely out of his teens, and she marveled again at how brilliant he was, as well as how unassuming – a powerfully attractive combination, Christine thought.

They neared the plane and Liu greeted the pilot. After a brief discussion about discreet destinations in Thailand and the route they'd fly, they agreed on Chiang Rai, near the Laos and Myanmar border, in northern Thailand – well away from the madding crowds. The pilot loaded their things into the small hold and they climbed aboard, Liu taking the copilot's seat and Christine in the rear. After a few moments, the starter groaned and the engine burbled to life.

The pilot requested clearance from the tower and then taxied to the runway and accelerated along the smooth strip, rising into the sky before they were halfway down its length. They bounced from turbulence as the plane gained altitude, and eventually settled into a droning cruise at eight thousand feet.

The mountains and jungle beneath them were pitch black, no trace of humanity to be seen to the horizon. The pilot altered course to skirt pendulous clouds to the east, heavy with rain, and Christine leaned forward and yelled to Liu over the engine noise.

"How long will it take to get there?" she asked.

Liu translated and the pilot shrugged, tapping the air speed indicator. "Maybe two hours, maybe a little longer. There's a headwind, so probably more."

Liu relayed the information to Christine and turned back to the pilot. "Do you fly this area often?"

The pilot's expression turned cagey. "From time to time."

"No problem with Chinese or Myanmar airspace?"

The pilot shook his head. "No. At this altitude we're unlikely to raise any alarms. The locals are used to unidentified flights around here. There are many dirt airstrips due to the drug trade. The governments destroy them periodically, and within a week new ones are cut from the jungle. It's been going on forever."

"Sounds like you know what you're doing," Liu said.

"As much as anyone. What we'll do is drop to no more than a thousand feet off the canopy as we near the border. Safest bet if you don't want to announce your arrival. Laos is largely unpatrolled, but occasionally Myanmar will have choppers around. Although I've heard lately that they're so broke they can't get parts, so who knows? And the section in our flight path is controlled by rebel forces, so the chances of anything but us flying around there at night are nil."

"What about Thailand?"

"Oh, they'll have us on radar, more than likely, but a few baht handed out to the right people on the ground will ensure no questions are asked. Thailand is sort of a live-and-let-live place. I filed a flight plan for Chiang Kham, but will claim that I had engine issues so had to land in Chiang Rai. Nobody will care as long as palms are greased."

"And customs?"

"That can also be a matter of money. Depends on how badly you want to stay out of the system."

Liu stared into the dark night. "Perhaps it would be best if we did."

"Then get your wallet out. Anything's possible, but nothing's free." The pilot paused. "We're just crossing the mountain range that runs along the border. We'll be out of Chinese airspace in a few more minutes, and then we'll begin tapering off our altitude. Highest point along this course is six thousand feet, so we're actually still pretty close even at this height."

The plane bucked when it hit some rough air, and the pilot peered through the windshield at a line of thunderheads ahead. Their outlines stretched high into the heavens, blocking the stars from view. He eyed his compass and banked to the right while dropping. Flashes of lightning pulsed in the clouds, and he stabbed a finger in their direction.

"We're better off giving those a wide berth. It can get ugly quickly."

"There's no problem going off course?" Liu asked.

"Adds a little time, but are you in a particular hurry?"

"Better safe than sorry, right?"

They watched as the pilot took them down before settling at a thousand feet above the mountainous terrain below. From that distance they could make out the tops of the trees in the faint moonlight, punctuated by barren patches and the occasional peak of a rocky outcropping.

The pilot was adjusting a knob when a loud explosion shook the plane. The windshield cracked from metal shards and the engine alarm sounded as the prop pinwheeled away into the night. The pilot's eyes widened in shock, and he battled with the flaps as the plane pitched downward.

Liu's hand flew to his face, where blood seeped from a laceration in his forehead. His voice was a strangled cry when he managed words. "Oh, my God! What happened?"

The pilot gritted his teeth and yelled, "Something on the engine blew. We're going down."

"No…," Liu said as flames licked from the engine compartment and smoke poured from the ruined fuselage.

"We can glide, but it's going to be a hard landing," the pilot warned, eyeing the altimeter, which was unwinding as the plane dropped toward the earth. Christine gripped the seat, her face frozen in speechless fear.

"Do you see anyplace we can set down safely?" Liu asked, and then a second explosion rocked the aircraft, and it pitched toward the rapidly rising landscape.

"Hang on," the pilot screamed, and twisted the yoke at the last minute when he spotted a stream below.

The last thing Christine heard was Liu's alarmed yell as they crashed into the rocky riverbed, the impact instantly destroying most of the cockpit.

Water flooded the cabin.

# Chapter Three

*Two days later, Malibu, California*

Drake sat atop his longboard in the gentle swell off Malibu, basking in the warm morning sun as he waited for the next set of promising waves to push their way toward shore. He brushed a lock of unruly hair from his brow and glanced to his left, where three other locals bobbed, their spring wetsuits lending them the appearance of overfed seals. Off in the distance several fishing boats worked the outer rim of the kelp line, and hopeful seagulls wheeled overhead in anticipation of lost bait or human charity.

Drake had been living on the beach for two and a half months, ever since taking the suggestion to look at the area; he'd fallen instantly in love from his first encounter with Malibu. Unlike Northern California, where it rained a substantial chunk of the year, the weather in Southern California since he'd moved had been cool mornings with a marine layer that burned off by nine, followed by idyllic days of warmth and limitless sunshine.

He'd leased a two-bedroom beach home on the sand, largely because it was small and unassuming amidst neighboring houses that looked to him like monuments to garish opulence. That wasn't his style, and in spite of the massive wealth he'd come into overnight, he still felt out of place among the Hollywood directors and famous actors who called the stretch of beach home.

His days consisted of surfing in the morning for two to three hours, from dawn until he'd worn himself out, followed by a breakfast of four scrambled eggs and a pitcher of fresh-squeezed orange juice he got every evening at the local market, and then a slow three-mile run along the waterline before lunch. Afternoons were spent in front of the computer, answering emails and researching promising accounts of lost civilizations or tenuous rumors of hidden treasure.

Drake had developed a taste for the game on his trek through the Amazon, and now that he was a celebrity adventure hunter, he figured he might as well do something constructive with his life – and with the money. He'd always loathed the TV reality stars whose only talent seemed to be whining over broken nails or the difficulty of dealing with the paparazzi, and he had resolved not to add himself to the clutter of human flotsam. He would work at carrying on his father's legacy, and earn the respect that he still felt he'd gotten purely by accident.

His current project was another Inca site in Peru, hinted at on the document he'd discovered in Paititi, and he was actively debating mounting an expedition to look for it. Part of the reason for his sense of urgency was boredom and a sense of days rushing by wasted, but another was to see Allie again. Their rendezvous in Texas hadn't gone as he'd hoped; she'd been visibly frazzled by dealing with her father's estate and the funeral arrangements. It hadn't helped that within days of returning to the world, several suits had been filed by strangers claiming to have had handshake deals with Jack, and therefore felt entitled to a portion of his estate, which turned out to be considerable – not by Drake's new standards, but the property the old man had quietly accumulated around Texas and California was worth almost ten million dollars, which along with the breathless media accounts of Allie's newfound super wealth was enough to bring out the parasites.

She'd apologized and begged off spending time with him until she could get situated, but what he'd hoped would be a few weeks had stretched into months, with all too infrequent phone calls to maintain their connection. His last trip to Texas had been met with a distant attitude, and he hadn't known what to think about her preoccupation. She insisted that this was just a road bump, but he wasn't so sure. He'd toyed with the idea of hopping on a plane and sitting on her doorstep until they could have time together, but had discarded the idea after talking it over with Betty, who had transitioned from the office manager at the now-defunct bail bond outfit where he'd been working before striking it rich, and was now working as his assistant from her home in the Bay Area.

"Give her some space, Drake. She's been through a lot," Betty had said.

"I know. I was there, remember?"

"But she lost her father. That's hard at any time, but it affects some more than others."

"The legal pressures and trying to clear up all the land issues can't be easy," Drake conceded.

"Look, Drake, I know that it seems super urgent, but in the scheme of things, what's a few weeks one way or another? If the lady says she needs time, give her what she asks for, or she'll resent you for it. That's my advice."

"You're right. But I want to do something."

"Then send her a bouquet of roses or buy her an island. But don't smother her."

That had been a month ago, and since then they'd spoken three times. Which wasn't at all what he'd had in mind.

He was pulled out of his pity party by a nearby voice. "Looks like a good set," his new friend Seth called out from twenty yards away.

"Cowabunga," Drake agreed, nodding and squinting against the sun's glare on the water.

The waves neared, and Seth caught the first. Drake waited for the second and was rewarded seconds later by a larger twin. He paddled furiously, caught the curl just right, and pushed himself to his feet. The ride lasted only ten seconds at most, but Drake felt the same sense of exhilaration as he had in the old days up north, when he'd had to don a full neoprene body suit with a hood to catch waves off of Santa Cruz using a short board. The warmer water here helped him feel more relaxed, as did the easy camaraderie of his companions, which was unlike the standoffish competitive attitude he'd experienced on surfing forays further south in Huntington and Newport Beach.

When the wave had exhausted itself, he dropped into the water beside his board, glanced at his waterproof watch, and waved to the others.

"I'm pooped. You guys hang loose," he called. Their rides also over, they returned the wave, and Drake made his way against the pull of the surf to the golden stretch of sand. He unzipped his Rip Curl spring suit and shrugged the top loose, and then retrieved his board before padding toward his bungalow. Even after only a few months he'd already decided he liked the area enough to want to buy property, but he couldn't get past the embarrassment of being a snobby pretender whenever he looked at the listings online. And the numbers seemed astronomical to him for a collection of rooms. Even though he was now wealthy, it seemed insane to pay seven to ten million for fifty feet of beachfront with a neighbor jammed up against each side.

As he approached his wood-shingled house, its small deck a postage stamp compared to the adjacent homes, he saw a tumble of blonde hair poke over the blue-tinted glass railing of the home to his right, followed by a waving hand connected to a stunningly beautiful young woman – Kyra, the daughter of a movie mogul, staying at her father's place while she tried to make a name for herself in the business. Twenty years old and a product of genetic perfection, she would have stopped traffic anywhere in the world. He noted that her bikini was little more than string, and that she'd been sunbathing topless as she struggled to tie her top, failing to protect her modesty in the process – whether by accident or design, he couldn't be sure.

"Hey, Drake. Looking good, surfer dude," she called out, her voice musical on the light breeze.

"Thanks, Kyra. How's it going?"

"My agent got me some more auditions. I really feel like this is my year, you know?"

Drake ran his hand through his hair and tried not to gape at her flawless, tanned skin and blazing sky blue eyes. "Yeah, it could be. I hope so. It's been a pretty good one for me so far."

She eyed him like a cat eyeing a baby chick, her gaze lingering on his chest and abs. "Understatement of the year."

"I'm sure you'll get something that makes you famous, Kyra. It's only a matter of time." Which it was. She could read lines with all the conviction of a rock with a painted face, but with her dad's connections, she'd eventually be a star, he was sure.

"Easy for you to say. You already won that lottery. You should write a book or something. Ooh, or maybe a reality show! Right here, on the beach!"

"I'm afraid my life isn't all that exciting, Kyra."

"Oh, don't worry. It's all BS. They just make stuff up and you play along. Hey – I could be in it! Playing the struggling actress! It would be awesome. Let me make a couple of calls…"

"Not on my account. I moved here to get away from all that. But thanks anyway."

She gave him an appraising look. "See? That's why you're one in a million. Anyone else would be totally sucking up to have their own show. You? You couldn't care less."

"I probably just need more medication," Drake joked, offering her a grin. She feigned a pout and then beamed at him.

"You should come over later and have a margarita or something," she said, her voice all innocence but her expression making clear that she had definite ideas about what the something might entail.

"Cool. Thanks. I might take you up on that," Drake said, and then his attention was drawn to his house, which he habitually left unlocked – he had nothing worth stealing, and half his neighbors did the same, he knew – just another reminder of how different Malibu was from the real world over the hill. He spotted two men in suits standing inside his open glass terrace doors, watching him, hands folded, stone-faced. "What the hell–"

The tallest of the pair stepped forward. "Mr. Ramsey, sorry for the intrusion, but we knocked and it was open. Probably not a good idea to leave it unlocked," he said, his voice as welcoming as fingers on a blackboard. "Please, come in. We need a moment of your time."

"And you are…?"

"Someone you'd do well to speak with," the second man said, glancing over at Kyra before lowering his voice. "We're from Washington."

"Drake? Is everything okay?" Kyra asked, turning toward his house as he mounted the stairs to the deck.

Drake regarded the pair, who stepped further into the gloomy interior so they couldn't be seen by her, and nodded. "Yeah. But if I'm not back in ten minutes, call the cops."

# Chapter Four

"I can assure you that won't be necessary, Mr. Ramsey," the first man said as Drake leaned his surfboard against the rickety wood railing. "I'm Collins. This is Ross."

Drake squared his shoulders and faced them. "What do you want? And what gives you the right to barge into my home?"

"You and my boss had a discussion a few months back. Perhaps you recall it?" Collins said, ignoring Drake's indignant question.

Drake nodded, his heart sinking. He remembered as though it were yesterday. "Sure. Like a bad smell."

"I'll cut to the chase. We have a situation we could use your help with. Step inside and we can talk about it."

"I kind of like being out here, if you don't mind," Drake said.

"Ramsey, do us all a favor and get off the high horse, will you?" Ross growled. "Come in, have a soda or whatever, and hear us out. Then we'll leave. No strings attached."

Drake's right eyebrow rose. "No strings?"

"You heard right," Collins confirmed.

Drake sighed, pulled off his spring suit, and draped it on the railing. "Make it fast. I need to hose all this gear off."

Drake entered the living room wearing only board shorts. He looked at the sofa and shrugged, and then sat down, ignoring the soaking he was giving the white fabric. Collins walked over and sat in the easy chair. Ross remained standing by the dining room table.

Collins cleared his throat. "We could use your help. We have a delicate situation, and we need someone with your pedigree."

"My...pedigree?"

"Yes. You're a famous treasure hunter. You have access to places our agents wouldn't."

"Your agents," Drake repeated flatly.

Collins nodded. "Two days ago, a private plane went down somewhere around the border of Laos and Myanmar. Thai radar had a fix on it until it disappeared. There was a storm in the area, and we're afraid the worst has happened."

"I'm sorry," Drake said, his expression puzzled. "But what does that have to do with me?"

"The plane was carrying a woman named Christine Whitfield. She's the daughter of Senator Arthur Whitfield. Perhaps you've heard of him?"

Drake shook his head. "I don't pay much attention to politics."

"He's a veteran lawmaker who some say has as much clout as the president," Ross said.

Collins sighed. "The senator is frantic over his daughter going missing, Drake. He's pulled strings. A lot of them. One of them was to the director, who is also a friend. The director promised to help. Which is where you come in."

"I'm still not getting it."

"We need you to mount an expedition to the area immediately. We'll get permission from the appropriate parties, but we need someone visible, someone known, to look for her. They'd never approve it otherwise."

"Why not? I thought you guys ran the world."

Collins smiled for the first time, and the effect was chilling. "I'm afraid YouTube overstates our reach. We may be able to hide aliens and plot a new world order, but we can't get the Laotian government to allow us to poke around their territory. They're still a little sensitive about certain regrettable incidents during the Vietnamese war."

"And forget about Myanmar. They hate us more than Iran and North Korea's love child," Ross added.

"But they'll let me tromp around in their jungle? Why, exactly?"

"Crap, kid, you're famous. And very high profile right now. Of course they'd never let you go looking for a plane…which is why you won't be."

"What will I be looking for? Assuming I decide I'm interested?" Drake asked, curious.

"Have you ever heard of the Emerald Buddha of the Khmer Empire?" Collins asked, his gray eyes drilling into Drake's.

Drake shook his head. "No."

"You can Google it. When the Thais overran what's now Cambodia, legend says that the Khmer king hid the country's most precious treasure in a distant land. We have reason to believe that's near the Laotian and Myanmar border, which is coincidentally where the plane was last observed."

"Lost Khmer treasure? Who exactly were the Khmer? I've only heard of the Khmer Rouge."

"That name was taken from their ancestors. The Khmer people were at one point the most powerful empire in the region. They built extraordinary temples, were renowned for their advanced civilization, and were as close to a superpower as you could get in the Middle Ages. Angkor Wat is the most famous of their temple complexes. They ruled for centuries before Thailand ate their lunch in the fifteenth century."

Drake's eyes narrowed. "How do you know where the treasure is?"

"Well, truthfully, we don't. I mean, not exactly. But we have reason to believe we have a fix on the rough area."

"Right. But the question is how?"

"If you sign up for this, we'll give you a classified briefing. Among the items you'll be privy to is an interrogation with a guerilla commander who worked the region during the Vietnam conflict. He had valuable information that could lead a skilled adventurer like yourself to the hidden temple where the treasure's stashed."

Drake snorted. "Are you making this up?"

Collins stood. "Mr. Ramsey, we're on a short fuse. As I said, it's been over forty-eight hours since the plane vanished. Whitfield is distraught, and he needs closure. And if there's any chance that she's alive…well, you'd be doing your country, the director, and the senator an enormous favor they won't forget. It's never a bad idea to have people like that owing you one."

Drake considered it. "How long do I have to decide?"

"Now would be good."

Drake shook his head. "It's too little time. I need to think about it first."

"So think," Ross snapped.

"Mr. Ramsey, this is really simple," Collins said, his tone matter of fact. "You fly to Thailand. You go on an expedition accompanied by whomever you like, and one of ours. Maybe you find a treasure that will solidify your standing and show that Paititi wasn't a fluke. You also keep your eyes open for a plane. In doing so, you earn the gratitude of some of the most important people in the nation. How is that anything but good for you?" Collins hesitated, gauging Drake's reaction. "If nothing else, think of the girl. If she's still alive now, in that jungle she won't be much longer. And you could be the deciding factor in whether she lives or dies. Tell me, Mr. Ramsey, what do you have going on this week that's more important than potentially saving a girl's life and discovering a legendary treasure, all at the same time?"

Drake licked crusted sea salt from his lips. "I'd have to discuss this with my team."

"We'd need you to be in the air tomorrow. It'll take at least a couple of days to cut through the red tape and get you permission to mount an expedition in Laos and Myanmar."

"That may not work. Let me make some calls and see." Drake stood. "Assuming I decide to do it. Give me some breathing room to decide."

"I'd like an answer now."

"I'd like to ride a unicorn to Oz. What's a number where I can reach you?"

"We're not playing a game here, kid," Ross said, taking a step toward Drake.

Collins raised a hand to silence Ross and fished a pen from his pocket. He looked around the room and moved to the breakfast bar, where he scribbled a number on a pad by the phone. He tore off the sheet and handed it to Drake. "Can you decipher my scrawl?"

Drake read off the number. "Give me a little time to digest all this."

Collins shook his head in frustration. "We don't have a plan B, Mr. Ramsey. You're the senator's only hope. If it will help you decide, we can call him right now and you can speak with him. Perhaps hearing a father's desperation would sway you?"

"There's no need. I get it. Let me think it over and research what I can of your story. I'll call with an answer later today. That's the best I can do."

Collins nodded. "Sorry to barge in."

"Don't let the door hit you..."

The pair of CIA agents strode to the entry while Drake stood by the couch, the note in his hand, until Ross pulled the door closed. Drake covered the ground quickly, twisted the deadbolt, and then moved to his computer, lost in thought. He typed in Christine's name, and then looked up when Kyra's voice sounded from outside.

"Drake? Everything okay?"

He twisted and called out to her. "Yeah, Kyra. Thanks. It's all good."

"Okay. Remember about the margarita."

"I'll let you know."

Drake watched as his search engine listed page after page of entries for Christine, and clicked on her Facebook profile. A picture of a pleasant-looking young woman stared back at him with startling intensity. Drake tried to imagine what it must be like to have a daughter and not know whether she was alive or dead, and shivered involuntarily.

Next, he ran a search on the Khmer Emerald Buddha and read about the legends, as well as about the smaller twin at the royal palace in Thailand. That one was considered a holy relic by the Thais, who believed that the safety and well-being of the nation depended on its sanctity. An entire ceremony was involved in the Thai king dressing it in gold at the changing of each season. The term 'emerald' was a misnomer, apparently, and described the color, not the gemstone – the Thai statuette was carved from green jasper, which he assumed was the case for the Khmer Buddha as well.

The legends claimed that the royal Khmer treasure was secreted in a hidden temple whose location had been a mystery for almost six centuries, the exact spot lost to history due to a garbling of the accounts in a war-torn land. Multiple searches had been mounted by hopeful Khmers, and later, fortune hunters of many stripes, but none had found it. Over the last hundred years the area thought to be the correct one had become progressively more dangerous, and as war, famine, floods, storms, hostile governments, and roving gangs of drug traffickers had claimed the territory, it had been impractical to continue to search for it.

Drake studied Christine's Facebook page and read her public postings, perused the selfies under her images, and then returned to the photograph that had stopped him cold.

He looked at the photo for a long time. With a shake of his head, he swore softly under his breath and moved to the phone to call Allie and see if she was game.

But he'd already made up his mind.

He was going to Thailand.

# Chapter Five

*Beijing, China*

Two large personnel carriers rolled to a stop in front of a six-story chrome and glass building on the outskirts of Beijing, followed by a heavily plated mobile headquarters van with run-flat tires and gun ports dotting its sides. A squad of police in SWAT gear emptied from the vehicles and formed two columns on the sidewalk. Pedestrians paused and quickly detoured to avoid whatever was happening. Three men in neon emergency vests set up bright orange cones in the street and began waving traffic around them.

A black SUV pulled to the curb and the men stiffened to attention. A diminutive man in a black suit stepped from the vehicle and looked over the officers, and then nodded to the lieutenant at their head as more SUVs arrived.

"Let's do this," the little man said.

The lieutenant nodded and called out an order. The assembled gunmen chambered rounds in their weapons and prepared to storm the building.

~ ~ ~

Huang glared at the telephone on his desk and then back to the pile of paperwork he was plowing through, the phone's ringing as insistent as an angry wife. He dropped his pen on the contract he was reviewing and reached for the handset.

"Yes?"

"Sir, there's a group of men from the government on their way up. At least twenty of them. Armed." It was the security guard in the lobby of the building headquarters for Moontech – Huang's creation, a thriving technology firm that was bravely forging into the new world of global capitalism, hosting tens of thousands of websites and developing myriad programs and apps.

"What? Are you serious?"

"Completely, sir. They'll be there any moment."

Huang hung up and pushed back from his desk, alarmed. He operated his company honestly, paid off all the right people so he wouldn't be disturbed, didn't engage in piracy or any of the other schemes that had been the undoing of so many of his competitors. In other words, he was clean.

He moved to his door in time to see a squad of police carrying assault rifles tromping across the office floor, led by a suited man with a lupine face. Huang's workers froze at the sight, nobody daring to move. The officers dispersed and rounded them up at gunpoint.

Huang stepped through the door and confronted the little man, hands on his hips. "What is the meaning of this?"

"Huang Qi?" the suited official demanded.

"That's correct."

"You are under arrest." The man turned to the two officers behind him. "Cuff him."

Huang's expression was shocked. "For what? I haven't done anything."

"We will be the judge of that." One of the cops worked his way around Huang and twisted on handcuffs.

"This is an outrage," Huang said. "My company is known for its honesty."

"Save it. Where are your servers located?"

Huang blinked in surprise at the question. "In…in the basement. Why?"

The official withdrew a phone from his jacket pocket and made a call, ignoring Huang. "Send the tech team to the basement. Hold the workers until we've interrogated them all."

The blood drained from Huang's face. "I don't understand. Please. Why are you doing this? All our permits are in order, our accounts are audited, we–"

The little man's hand snaked toward Huang like lightning. Huang's head snapped to the side from the force of the slap.

"You don't ask questions. I do," the official hissed, his whisper more menacing than if he'd screamed. He looked over Huang's shoulder at the officer behind him. "Take him to headquarters."

Huang bit back his outrage at being struck in full view of his employees and allowed himself to be led to the elevators. The expressions on his people's faces were all the information he needed to grasp how dire his situation was. He didn't understand how he could have gone from a leading member of society to a prisoner in seconds, but he knew he was in serious trouble. That the man in the suit hadn't shown him any identification told him that this was an irregular operation. And in China, irregular meant more dangerous than a black widow.

The cops led him downstairs to an unmarked van and shackled his cuffs to a steel bench in the rear before closing the door. His alarm intensified – this was not how the police operated. Eventually, another man in a suit arrived, slid into the driver's seat, and started the engine.

"Where are you taking me?" Huang asked.

The man ignored him. Huang tried again and the man called out over his shoulder through the heavy steel grid that separated the cargo area from the cab. "Shut up or it will go worse for you."

Huang didn't pursue it. He'd find out soon enough what had happened. He searched his brain for anything that could have prompted the raid, and kept arriving at the same answer: somehow, one of his competitors had exerted leverage on cronies in the government, and was using the police to shut Moontech down.

~ ~ ~

Jiao Long watched silently as his men removed server after server from the racks in the icy-cold basement and carried them to the freight elevator, where they would be taken to headquarters and dissected for any hint of information that could aid him in his search. This was an issue of national security, and as such was of the highest priority, his superior had made clear. He was free to use whatever means at his disposal that would deliver results, including detainment and confiscation.

Jiao was a twenty-two-year veteran of China's MSS – the equivalent of America's CIA, the clandestine arm of the government responsible for espionage and countermeasures, as well as protecting the nation's secrets. There was no higher authority, and it answered directly to the premier, who routinely gave it carte blanche to conduct its affairs however it liked. That imbued Jiao with the power of a god over the citizenry, and he was never more in his element than when running an operation like the one against Moontech.

That subversive elements in the company were at work was a given; at least, that was where all the current evidence pointed. If that turned out to be false, it wasn't his concern. There was no redress for his victims, no court to complain to. He was effectively untouchable, and could and would ride roughshod over anyone in the way in his quest for answers.

"Notify me when the servers are at headquarters. Put the interrogation team on the workers. I want answers. Is that clear?" he instructed his subordinate, Deshi.

"Yes, sir."

"I'm going back to headquarters to learn what our friend Huang knows. I'll leave my cell on."

~ ~ ~

The interrogation rooms at MSS were grim, the walls gray unfinished concrete, the temperature frigid by design. Huang was shackled to a steel islet mounted to the wall, forced to stand as he waited for whatever was to come. A steel door with bubbling anthracite paint stood at the far end, and he tried to ignore the slight slope in the floor that fed into an oversized floor drain in the center of the room – he didn't want to contemplate what purpose it might serve.

The bolt on the outside of the door slid open with a clank and it opened. Jiao entered, followed by a pair of guards, one carrying a metal box, the other pushing a red mechanic's rolling cart. An array of power tools lay on the black rubber top, and a deep-cycle solar battery rested on the bottom tray.

Huang swallowed hard at the sight, and prayed that it was all intended for intimidation rather than actual use.

"You've been a naughty boy," Jiao said in a reasonable tone, as though chiding him for a traffic infraction. "You are accused of high crimes against the people's republic. Treasonous acts that are punishable by death. It would be best if you admitted what you've done, and who's in this with you, so we can take corrective measures. If you don't, I will get it out of you one way or another."

Huang's eyes widened and he shook his head. "I swear I have no idea what you're talking about."

"I knew you would say that. Subversives never admit their sins when confronted. It's one of the perennial truths of my job."

"I am telling the truth. I don't know anything. What am I accused of? Investigate it and you'll see. I'm innocent of any wrongdoing. I'm a loyal citizen," Huang protested.

"I'm disappointed that you've decided to go this route. I'm always hoping to be surprised by an honest man. But don't worry. My methods are highly effective, if agonizingly painful. You will confess."

"There's nothing to confess. I swear…"

An hour later Jiao confirmed that Huang had indeed been truthful in his declarations of innocence. Too late for Huang, but that was the job. Jiao regarded his two companions and wiped a fleck of gristle from his forehead with a handkerchief.

"Hose it down. We'll chat with his second-in-command next."

# Chapter Six

Drake hung up the phone as a low growl rumbled from the driveway in front of the house. Allie had been reluctant until he'd made her go to Facebook and look at the photo that had affected him so profoundly. She'd tried to explain that she was overwhelmed with the estate and the lawsuits, and that what he was asking would be a major disruption in her life.

"Allie, I know that, and I understand. But you're the archeologist. I wouldn't recognize a Khmer temple if it bit me. You're the expert, not me. I wouldn't ask you to do this if it wasn't important."

"How do you know they aren't BS-ing you about that part, just to give you a pretense for looking for the plane?"

"We'll get a complete briefing tomorrow. If it sounds like an invention, we'll bail. That simple."

She had paused for several moments. "I think you're kidding yourself if you believe anything involving…those guys…is ever simple."

"Allie, I don't trust them as far as I can throw them, but I verified the legend of the temple. It's as solid, or more so, than the Paititi account, and we did pretty well on that."

"If you don't count getting kidnapped, almost killed a bunch of times, and losing my father."

Drake had sighed. "I'm sorry I called, Allie. I…I just wanted you to be part of this. We worked really well together, and I can't imagine going on another expedition without you."

Her tone had softened. "Let me do some digging. I'll call you later when I decide."

"I miss you, Allie."

"I miss you, too, Drake. It's just that everything's so complicated right now…"

"It doesn't have to be. Between us."

"Easy for you to say."

That had been two hours ago, and Allie had just called back to say she reluctantly agreed and would be on the first flight out in the morning, arriving at nine at LAX.

"Take a charter flight, Allie," he'd said. "I'll have one waiting for whenever you want to take off. It's on me."

"If you think plying me with luxury is going to work, it might."

"That's my hope. I'll arrange it and send you an email. You sure you don't want to come out tonight?"

"It'll be a miracle if I can get everything done by tomorrow. Have them at the airport at seven a.m. And if they have croissants and good coffee, that would definitely earn you some points."

"I'll ensure they do. As well as mimosas and anything else you want."

"Coffee's more than enough." She paused. "I'll see you tomorrow."

"I'm glad. Thanks, Allie. You won't regret this."

"So you say."

The sound of a high-performance exhaust was unmistakable, and Drake approached the entry with puzzlement. When he opened the door, he was surprised to see a canary yellow Lamborghini Aventador LP 750-4 Superveloce parked in the driveway.

"What the hell…" he whispered to himself, and then the V-12 motor shut off and the driver's door rose.

Spencer's tanned face grinned at him as he climbed from the car. "Hey, buddy. How's it hanging?"

"Spencer! Haven't seen you for…forever. Is this yours?"

"Yup. Thought I'd take it for a spin up the coast. Trying to be low key and all."

Drake eyed him skeptically. It was a little too coincidental that Spencer would appear out of nowhere minutes after the CIA departed. His suspicions about Spencer immediately returned, but he didn't voice them. "How many tickets did you get? It looks like it's breaking about a dozen laws just sitting there."

"None today. But don't ask how many I've had since I took delivery." Spencer neared and gave Drake a slap on the shoulder. "What are you driving?"

"Oh, I've got a lifted FJ Cruiser. Not quite on par with the space shuttle here."

"Probably gets better gas mileage, though."

"Yeah, and I can occasionally hear the radio."

Spencer took in the exterior of the bungalow and shook his head at Drake. "Didn't anyone tell you that you're rich?"

Drake shrugged. "What? It does the job. It's just me, so what do I need with a castle?" He grinned. "You want the tour? It takes about ten seconds."

"Sure."

Drake led him inside, showed him around, and then offered him a drink. Spencer opted for a diet soda, and Drake a bottle of water. Spencer admired the view from the deck, and then caught sight of Kyra going into her house. When Drake arrived with the drinks, Spencer gave him a knowing look.

"I see why you like the place. Nice view, huh?" he said, a leer in his voice.

"Oh, that's just Kyra. The neighbor."

"Damn. I knew I lived in the wrong area."

"What? Last time we talked you were in escrow on a house down in Corona del Mar, weren't you?"

Spencer grimaced. "Laguna Beach."

"Right. Oceanfront, ritzy neighborhood, new development, mega-expensive?"

"That's the one. I closed a little over a month ago. I'm suing the developer. It's a piece of crap."

"What? How can it be crap for twenty million bucks?"

"Twenty-seven all in. The soil isn't compacted correctly, the foundation's cracking, the sheetrock is buckling – it's a nightmare."

"But you'll get out of it, right?"

"Turns out half the other owners are also suing him."

"Didn't they have to disclose that?"

"Sure. They just didn't. So now it's up to the courts. And the prick countersued me for damaging his good name."

"That's a nuisance suit."

"Turns out the developer knows some judges, because they froze a bunch of my money as potential damages."

"But you have a ton left."

"Yeah, but I have a big burn." Spencer took a long pull on his soda. "Did I tell you I bought a plane?"

"No. What kind?"

"A jet."

"What do you need a jet for? Why not just lease one or something?"

"To get to my boat."

"You bought a boat, too?"

"Yup. That's what rich guys are supposed to do, right?"

"I suppose…"

Spencer withdrew his phone from his pocket and thumbed through the menu until he had a photograph on the screen. He handed it to Drake, who whistled.

"Wow. That's sick. How big is it?"

"Hundred and eighty. You and Allie should use it sometime. It's in the Mediterranean right now, at a boatyard. They're doing maintenance. I bought it from a sheik for a song."

"What's a song these days?"

"Thirty."

"Million?"

"Actually more like thirty-five, with the work they're doing."

"Easy come…" Drake grinned. "Do I even want to know how much the plane cost?"

"I got it from the bank. The guy who'd owned it went bankrupt. Another land developer. Crooks, all of them."

"So a good buy?"

"For a Gulfstream, sure."

Drake's mouth fell open. "You bought a Gulfstream?"

"I know. But it sold new for fifty-eight. I got it for thirty-five, three years old, only four hundred hours on it."

"Kind of like a car, huh? Depreciates thirty percent when you drive it off the showroom floor?"

"A little like that." Spencer set his can down. "The problem is that it's eating me alive. The boat crew is about three quarters of a million a month, including the mooring cost and the maintenance. The jet costs three mil a year. And the attorneys are burning cash like it's going out of style."

"At least you still have most of your money. That's not terrible. It's rich-people problems."

Spencer frowned. "Well…I invested most of it with a hedge fund. The other day I asked for fifty mil back, but they only allow redemptions once a year, and I just put it in last month."

"Ouch. That's a lot of money to tie up with one group."

"I know. And the front page of the *Wall Street Journal* last week broke that they're being investigated by the SEC and the Justice Department."

"But your money's still there, right?"

"Oh, sure. They just can't give it to me for a year."

Drake tilted his head. "Can you at least verify they have it?"

"Well, they said yes, but when I asked for proof, they started shuffling. All about how they don't divulge trading positions because it could jeopardize their moves, and that a lot of it's in currency and derivatives and hedges and credit default swaps…"

"I'm getting a headache."

"Yup. I have another attorney clipping me for five hundred bucks an hour working on that one."

"Yikes."

"And then there are the other lawsuits. A guy I used to hang out with is suing because he says he had a deal with me that I reneged on. A woman claims I gave her an incurable social disease. Another claims she's my common-law wife from Peru. The cockroaches come out of the woodwork." Spencer sighed. "And to top it all off, my gardener claims he tripped on my stairs and wrenched his back. Of course that's my fault. I'm liable. But he only wants five million."

"That's nuts."

"Of course. But the point is, you're a target. Haven't you had any of that kind of thing?"

Drake shook his head. "Not really. I mean, my dough's mostly in the foundation, so it's technically not mine. And I keep a low profile. Nobody really knows who I am. The groundskeeper here thinks I'm a dope dealer or something, I'm sure, because I'm always either surfing or hanging out. I mean, the only one who knows anything about me is Kyra next door."

"And you're not tapping that?"

"No. I mean, she's beautiful, but Allie and I…"

"What happened with her?"

Drake explained the situation as well as he could, and by the time he was done, Spencer was shaking his head. "Dude, that's deader than Michael Jackson. Time to play house with Miss Hollywood there."

"No, it isn't. Allie just needs time."

"How much?"

"She hasn't said. But in the end, I think it'll be worth it."

"In the end, we're all worm food. I say you go give blondie an oil massage and see what comes up."

"She's going to be here tomorrow, by the way."

"Who? Allie? Or Kyra? Do you need a cameraman?"

"Allie. Your buddies in the CIA came by for a talk today," Drake said, watching Spencer's reaction carefully. Spencer appeared genuinely puzzled.

"Really? What did they want?"

"They said if I told anyone, they'd have to kill him."

Spencer grinned. "At this point, I could use the life insurance payout. I'm broke, dude. That was actually one of the reasons I stopped in."

"Not because you miss me?"

"Hey, of course, but I need time…" Spencer laughed. "Seriously, though, I could use a loan."

"A loan? How much?"

"Enough to deal with the lawyers and all the bills."

"Which is…?"

"Fifty?"

Drake's eyes saucered. "Thousand?"

"I wish. No, million. That should last the year, until I can get the money back from the fund. It's crazy, but I had more money before I had money. You know?"

"Why don't you sell some stuff?"

Spencer began pacing. "I have both the plane and the boat up for sale already. The brokers were in shock – I mean, the ink's hardly dry. But they're probably used to it."

"Then your problems are solved. Or will be soon."

"Not really. Apparently there isn't a big market for planes right now. It's the economy."

"So you lose some money. Big deal."

"It's not that. They already told me I'll lose. It's just that there are no buyers. Planes don't sell like real estate. They said it could take a year or more."

"And the boat?"

"Those take even longer. Every big boat in the world's for sale."

"What about chartering it out? That would cut your burn."

"Right. Every other owner has the same idea. It's a cutthroat market. But right now, between the suits, the repairs and maintenance, the airport fees, the salaries…it's bad."

"That sucks."

"Three million a month, dude, and I'm not enjoying any of it."

"I can't believe…"

"Tell me about it. But apparently it's easy to buy, and really hard to sell. Go figure. They're brilliant at separating you from your money, but not so great at helping you unload your junk."

"So why fifty? Adds up to more like thirty-five, doesn't it?"

"Because the attorneys said it will get more expensive moving forward. It's like a protection racket – pay up or else." Spencer stopped moving and stared off into the distance at the shimmering blue Pacific. "You know I'm good for it."

"The problem is I can't just write a check, Spencer. It's the foundation's money, not mine. That's how I got around the tax issue. But it has an independent board of directors I have to run projects over a million past before I can get any cash. It's in the charter. So none of it's simple."

"How can that be? It's your money, not theirs."

"In the end I opted to keep only twenty out, and the rest is the foundation's, Spence. Sorry."

"How do they have it invested?"

Drake shrugged. "I think most of it's in bonds or cash. And I know ten percent's in gold. In Switzerland."

"What? Don't you know anything? The place to be is in stocks."

"Nah. I don't like the market. Too much I don't understand about it, and my attorney told me never invest in anything you don't understand."

"What are you doing with the twenty?"

Drake finished his water. "I'm thinking about buying a house. I'm just leasing this. But that's got to last me forever, Spence. I can't get more out of the foundation."

"Then I'm hosed."

Drake grinned. "Hey. Wait. Allie and I are going on an expedition. There's supposed to be a treasure at the end of it all."

"What? Where?"

"Laos. Myanmar. Thailand." Drake explained about the plane and the lost temple. When he was done, Spencer had fire in his eyes.

"Count me in. It's either that or wait around for someone else to sue me. When do we leave?"

41

"Really?"

"Absolutely. You had me at treasure."

"And you don't mind the whole CIA aspect?"

"Nah. Why would I? Their intel helps us find the green gargoyle, I'm all for it."

"Emerald Buddha."

"Whatever. When does Allie come?"

"Tomorrow morning. I'm going to call these guys and set up a briefing."

"I can help with the logistics. We'll want guns, you know. That area is heroin central. Some mean characters."

"You ever been there?"

"I spent a few months in Bangkok in my misspent youth."

"What were you doing?"

"What wasn't I?"

Drake moved to the phone, eyed the note he'd left by it, and dialed Collins' number. When the CIA man answered, Drake told him he'd assembled a team that would be available for briefing at noon tomorrow. Collins sounded grudgingly grateful, and promised to have someone come by.

"Now let me get the permits in motion. It'll take some doing, but we'll manage. And Mr. Ramsey?" Collins asked.

"Yes?"

"Thank you. From me, and from the senator. You made the right decision."

"I hope I feel that way next week."

Drake disconnected and turned to Spencer. "I'm starving. Let me shower off and then let's go for a ride in your land rocket. You can show me how to lose your license. We can hit a place I know on the coast for lunch, and then you can give me a tour of your new digs."

Spencer tossed him the keys. "You drive."

# Chapter Seven

*Santa Monica, California*

Drake waited by the charter terminal as the Citation X he'd booked for Allie taxied toward him, its turbines whining as they wound down. His heart was palpitating at the thought of seeing her again, and he realized as he watched the plane coast to a stop that he was more excited by her arrival than on embarking on an adventure in the Laotian mountains.

The fuselage door opened and the stairs lowered, and then Allie was standing at the top, her hair blowing in the wind, one hand shading her eyes as her gaze swept the tarmac. Drake waved at her and she smiled. His heart skipped a beat and he remembered why he was so smitten – she was nothing short of incredible; or at least, she was to him.

She descended the steps and approached him, and he marveled at how she seemed to glide, her grace natural and unconscious. When she was near, he moved to her and enveloped her in his arms, his hug anything but platonic. He moved to kiss her and she returned it with unmistakable longing. His spirits soared; and then the moment was over and she was pulling away.

"How was the flight?" Drake asked.

"Nice. The massage was a little amateur, but the caviar and cocaine were top shelf."

"Excellent. Glad to hear the foundation got its money's worth."

"Seriously, though, it was awesome. I could get used to that."

The ground crewman arrived with a single travel bag and carried it to Drake's FJ. Allie eyed the vehicle and smiled. "That is so you."

"What do you mean, me? Maybe I have a Lambo at home or something."

"Not hardly. No, this is exactly what I pictured you driving."

"You know me too well."

"I hear that happens if someone saves your life."

They were silent for an uncomfortable moment, and Drake opened the cargo door. The crewman set her bag inside and Drake closed it and escorted her to the passenger side.

"Such a gentleman. You must be a hit with the locals," she teased.

"I usually trick them into the back and then bind and gag them."

"That's right. We are in California, aren't we? Isn't that the national pastime around here?"

"When we're not busy with our cults or our macrobiotic juicing."

"Good to know." She studied him. "You look good. Sunburned, but I suppose that goes with the territory."

"I surf every morning."

She smiled. "No clichés here, dude."

"I like it. It's…peaceful. Kind of spiritual."

"Well, it definitely agrees with you."

They strapped in, and Drake negotiated the roads to Pacific Coast Highway. Traffic was headed in the opposite direction as high-net-worth commuters made their way from Malibu to the city, and they were able to make decent time. Drake pointed out landmarks as he drove, and they arrived at his house within forty minutes. Allie's response to the shabby exterior was only slightly better than Spencer's, but she warmed up when she saw the ocean stretching to Catalina and the Channel Islands.

"This is gorgeous, Drake."

"I like it. It's not like I haven't invited you out a million times," he said, and immediately regretted how it sounded. "I mean, you're always welcome. I've been dying to show it to you."

"Wow. Almost makes you want to give up cows and cactus," she said. "So you just run out to the surf there every day? How idyllic is that?"

"It's pretty cool," Drake said, setting her bag down by the dining table. Allie slid the door open and Drake moved to the gap. "Even with all the houses crammed together, it still feels kind of empty, you know? At least as long as you're looking out to sea."

"If I lived here, I'd never leave. I'd have food brought in."

Kyra's voice rang out from next door. "Drake? You there? Are you ready for that margarita?"

Allie's pupils dilated and then shrank to pinpoints as Drake blushed. "Um, no, Kyra. I have company. Sorry."

Drake began to close the door and Allie stopped him. She pushed past him and out onto his deck. Kyra was standing by a lounge chair, her hot pink thong bikini glowing against her copper skin.

"Oh. Hi," she said. "I'm Kyra."

Allie smiled and raised an eyebrow. "Nice to meet you. Allie."

"Hi, Allie." Kyra hesitated, out of words. "You guys are welcome to come by for a drink if you want."

Allie shot Drake a dark look and then met Kyra's with a grin. "Thanks, but it's a little early for me. Maybe Drake would like to get a head start?"

"No, I'm good," Drake stammered, flustered.

"Okay. Well, I'll just be lying out here if you change your mind." Kyra looked to Drake. "I missed you in the water today."

"Airport run."

"Right. Just holler if you want to come over."

"Okay," Allie said. "Wear sunscreen."

Kyra became animated. "Oh, I totally always do. Sunburns look gross on camera."

"Wouldn't want that."

Drake pulled the door shut and shrugged. "She's sweet."

"That's one word. Succulent might be another. And here I was worried about you becoming a hermit."

"Allie, it's nothing like that."

"Hey, it's none of my business," she said, walking to the kitchen. She opened the refrigerator and frowned. "Juice, a package of English muffins, and some butter? And enough soda to last a month. You ever eat real food?"

"Allie, she's just the neighbor. That's it."

Allie mimicked Kyra's surfer-girl tone. "Want to come over for a margarita and wrassle me?"

"She's an actress. They're dramatic."

"I'm not even going to ask what kind of movies."

"Her dad's some mogul in the business. She's harmless and bored out here all by herself."

"A pair of strong arms sounds like it might do the trick."

"Allie…"

"What time is the CIA goon going to be here?"

Drake looked at his watch, but was cut off before he could tell her by the sound of Spencer's car revving into the driveway. Allie looked to the door. "What's that?"

"Spencer, I presume. He likes to make an entrance." Drake had told her about his joining them on their adventure on the ride from the airport.

She threw open the door just as Spencer killed the motor and stepped from the car. He grinned and she returned his smile as he moved to her. Their hug seemed to last longer than the one she'd given Drake, he thought, and then dismissed the unexpected hurt he felt. Just as she was imagining things with Kyra, so too was he spinning scenarios that weren't accurate. Although it certainly looked more than brotherly to Drake.

Spencer held her at arm's length and nodded. "Wealth and a life of leisure agree with you, young lady."

"You don't look too shabby yourself, Spencer. What's with the pimpmobile?"

"I knew you'd love it. I built it on a VW chassis. A kit. I wanted a project. Idle hands and all."

"Drake was telling me about your trials and tribulations."

"Yeah, I dug that hole. Now I'm trying to climb out of it."

"Kind of fun to have everyone back together, though, huh? Like the old days."

Drake laughed, but to his ear it sounded false. "That was a whole three months ago."

Spencer smiled. "Is that all? And here little Allie is all growed up."

"It's the hormones. And the chain smoking," she quipped.

"You're a rebel," Spencer agreed, and looked at Drake. "Am I late?"

"Don't you own a watch?" Drake asked.

"Nothing that I could wear to Thailand."

"I think I've got an extra Casio," Drake said. "The most popular watch with terrorists, the guy at the store said—the Casio F91-W. How could I resist a sales pitch like that?"

"As long as it tells the time, I'm easy."

They settled in on Drake's couch and chair and talked about old times. Eventually the discussion shifted to Allie.

"So what did you do with all your loot?" Spencer asked. Drake had warned Allie about Spencer's loan request, so she was prepared for his overture.

"Oh, it's all in a savings account."

"What? Are you kidding me? What does it pay, like .0001 percent per year?" Spencer asked incredulously.

"Well, I don't really have time to learn the ins and outs of investing right now, and I've got my hands full with my dad's stuff, so I'll just let it sit until I find something to do with it."

"But you're leaving so much on the table…"

Allie smiled sweetly. "Yeah, I've had dozens of wealth managers fly in and try to talk me into going with them, but I never got a good feeling from any of them. They like to talk down to you, like you're an idiot or a child. Sort of that whole, 'Don't you worry your pretty little head over all that complicated stuff' thing. I frigging hate that."

Drake interrupted the discussion with the more pressing topic of the Emerald Buddha.

"As far as I can tell, it's all hearsay. The Khmer king never retrieved the treasure, either because the territory was too dangerous to mount a campaign in, or because he did and they simply couldn't find it. That's if the story's even true. For all we know, there is no treasure, and it's all an invention that got bigger over time. It's unclear where the truth lies."

"Sort of like every lost treasure, right?" Allie said.

"There's that. But one of the things that makes this particularly difficult is that the region was at constant war for so much of the following centuries. There are no records. It's all oral traditions and speculation."

"Too bad we don't have a handy journal to follow," Spencer quipped.

They were interrupted by a knock at the door.

"Come in. It's open," Drake called out.

Collins and a tall, serious-looking man in his late thirties entered, Collins carrying a briefcase, his companion empty-handed. Beneath his untucked blue striped dress shirt and jeans, the newcomer was clearly fit and athletic, his face all hard planes and sharp angles.

Collins introduced himself to Allie and Spencer and then held a hand out toward the other man. "This is Alex Banyon. He'll be your field liaison, and will accompany you into the jungle."

"Pleased to meet everyone," Alex said, his tone as gruff and as no-nonsense as his profile. "Mind if I sit? I've heard all this before."

"Sure," Drake said, and rose to get a chair from the dining table. When they were seated, Collins cleared his throat and set his briefcase beside him.

"Let's take the matter of the plane first. As I told you, Christine was on it when it went down."

"How do you know?" Allie asked.

Collins didn't blink. "We have our sources. She was flying from China to Thailand, and there were storms over Laos and Myanmar. Our working assumption is that the plane had to ditch due to a malfunction. Could have been due to weather. No way of knowing for sure until we find the wreckage."

"What was she doing in China?" Spencer asked.

"Some kind of spiritual retreat, as far as we know. Yoga,

meditation, that kind of thing."

"Isn't that usually something kids go to India to practice?" Allie asked.

Collins' eyes drifted to Allie and then back to Spencer. "Maybe she saw too many reruns of *Kung Fu*. I honestly have no idea about her motivations. I'm going by what her father has told us."

Spencer rubbed his hand along his chin. "How about the transponder?"

"For unknown reasons, it was turned off. Possibly because it didn't want to be tracked. It's fairly common with drug-running planes along that corridor." He opened the briefcase and removed a manila folder. Alex took it, quickly scanned the contents, and passed it to Spencer.

"That's the last snapshot from Thai radar. Laos doesn't have much reach in that region and it didn't show up on theirs, and Myanmar…Myanmar doesn't talk to us," Alex said.

Spencer put a satellite image on the coffee table and studied the red circle drawn on it. "That looks like it's partially over Myanmar."

"That's part of the challenge. We're working through a third party to get you permission to cross the border. To look for the temple, of course."

"Of course," Spencer said. "But how are we supposed to find a needle in that haystack? Says here that it was a Cessna 172. That's barely more than a kite."

"Why not use a drone?" Allie asked. "I see them all over the TV. Isn't that more efficient than having us go in?"

"Good question. The problem with smaller drones is battery time. Even the military models only go so long, and an hour is the outside max for the little ones. Anything larger tips our hand – both Myanmar and Laos would smell government agency all over it. Finally, the drug cartels that operate in that area would try to shoot down anything suspicious. So it's a bad idea all around." Collins frowned. "As to how you'll search for the plane, we're arranging for a helicopter. You'll perform a standard grid search at low altitude. It's doing it the hard way, but I don't see any other option."

"Why don't you zoom in with a super satellite? Like I've seen on the news?" Drake asked.

"Cloud cover, for starters. You can fly beneath it, but a satellite can't. We're of course doing exactly that anyway, but so far haven't turned up anything," Alex said.

They discussed the ins and outs of the plane search, and then turned to the temple.

"You mentioned you had intelligence for us," Drake began. "Let's see it."

Collins nodded and withdrew another file. "First, you'll all need to sign this security clearance. The file I'm about to show you is still classified." He set three forms down on the tabletop and handed Alex a pen.

They read the documents and, after a couple of questions, signed. Collins collected the forms and then set the file on the coffee table. "That's the transcript of an interrogation of a top Khmer Rouge commander who was operating in Cambodia and Laos. We captured him in 1970. The questioning goes on for hours. This is the relevant part."

Spencer read the four pages and handed them to Allie, who did the same, wincing in spots. Drake read it last and, when he was finished, set the pages in front of him. "That's it? A man who was being tortured spun some yarn about twin sisters guarding a hidden temple?"

"It's a little more than that. He claims to have seen the spot."

"Right, but it's gibberish. Twin sisters? What is that, trees? Rock formations? Mountains? Boulders?"

"Our analysts have narrowed it down to three possible locations. We know from him that it was in the western section of Laos or the eastern part of Myanmar. One of the things we did with our satellites was to look for likely suspects." Collins withdrew another satellite image from his case and laid it on top of the transcript. "The circles mark the three."

They all leaned in to look. The possible sites were all within the area they were going to be searching for the plane. Alex took over from Collins.

"You can see there are a pair of distinctive karst formations that might fit the description, and a third that's two conspicuously large boulder outcroppings – big enough that we believe they would have been plainly visible even six centuries ago. All three have valleys that match the legend, with streams, or in that case, a small river, running through them," Alex said, tapping the photos.

"Why hasn't anyone gone after the temple if you've known this for nearly fifty years?" Allie asked.

Collins smiled sadly. "The CIA isn't in the treasure-hunting business, young lady. We leave that to private interests like yourself. We've got our hands full defending the free world and faking moon landings."

The discussion went another hour, and when they were finished, Collins and Alex rose. Alex passed out airline tickets and told them to be at the airport by ten p.m. – the flight departed at one in the morning.

Drake eyed the ticket doubtfully. "Why don't we take Spencer's plane? He's got a G5."

"They're working on one of the engines," Spencer said. "Otherwise I'd be game."

"Give Alex here a list of anything you'll need, and he'll source it for you in Thailand," Collins said.

Allie wrote down some basic expedition requirements, and then passed it to Drake, who added a few items. Spencer read it slowly and then jotted down his own requests. When he was done, he handed it to Alex, who looked it over and stopped at Spencer's notes. "That's a lot of firepower," he said.

"That's drug-runner territory, right? You seriously expect us to go in with peashooters?" Spencer fired back.

"You could start a war with that."

Collins sighed impatiently. "Whatever they want, we'll arrange. Alex, we're running late. We still have a lot to do before the flight." He turned to Drake and Allie. "You have your passports? Everything's current?"

"Of course," Allie said.

Spencer nodded.

"Then I'll see you at LAX. Ten sharp," Alex said.

They watched the two CIA men leave, and Drake turned to Spencer. "What did you think?"

Spencer took a long breath and stood, rolling his head to work out a kink in his neck. "What I think is that Alex might be a problem in the field. He didn't seem to want us to have guns, or at least not anything worth mentioning. Other than that, I think the odds of us finding either a plane or a green Buddha in that jungle are about as good as my becoming a lingerie model in Milan."

Drake made a face. "I need eye bleach to erase that from my imagination."

Allie laughed. "We just might surprise you, Mr. Negative." She rose and eyed Spencer. "Now, are you going to invite me for a ride in that bumblebee you have sitting outside, or am I going to have to steal the keys?"

"Drake almost wrecked it yesterday. Man's a menace on the road," Spencer said.

"I did not," Drake protested, but he was smiling.

"Then let's race your FJ against my Lambo and get a decent meal, because once we're over there, it's all going to be monkey brains and bugs."

"I am not dining on monkey brains. Or bugs," Allie said with a frown of distaste.

"Don't worry. They won't tell you what you're eating. But if you find a carapace in your soup, just smile. It's considered rude to complain."

# Chapter Eight

*Chicago, Illinois*

Elliot London switched off the drive-time radio program he listened to every evening rush hour as he entered his neighborhood, a collection of single-story Midwestern homes in the sort of middle-class enclave typically given a name like Myrtle Cove or Arlington Ridge. Elliot's subdivision was Bel Aire Forest, with the closest things to a tree the two struggling spruce that had been planted at the community entrance. He'd lived there for eight years in relative peace and comfort with his wife, Diane, and twin five-year-old daughters.

He'd worked his way up at the newspaper from a cub reporter to a seasoned investigative journalist, and was used to irregular hours and constant pressure when running down a story. Elliot had been honored by several professional organizations for his coverage of local and national politics, and had broken stories that had forced a congressman to resign in shame, an attorney general candidate to decline his nomination, a high-profile priest to be charged with pedophilia, and numerous city councilmen to be hauled off in cuffs.

The hate mail came with the territory. As his father, also a journalist, used to say, if you weren't pissing people off, you weren't doing your job. Of course, his dad had operated in a different environment from today's corporate jungle, where only six conglomerates owned all the media outlets. Like it or not, Elliot had to tread carefully lest he be downsized in one of the endless reorganizations or mergers that were a constant in the business – he had a mortgage to pay and private school tuition to cover, as well as one of his daughter's special education needs and medications, so he tempered his zeal with what he viewed as sensible restraint.

Elliot eased into the driveway of his ranch house and sighed with relief when he shut the engine off. Another brutal day at an end, and his family to look forward to. He caught himself in the rearview mirror and shook his head at the middle-aged man looking back, puffy bags under his eyes, hair so sparse he bore almost no resemblance to his college photos, and jowls beginning to show the effects of time and gravity. Where had the good years gone? he wondered, and then shook off the introspection. No point in beating himself up over what couldn't be changed.

He walked up the path to his front door and took great pains to make sufficient noise unlocking it so his daughters would hear him. They delighted in greeting him at the end of every workday, and he cherished the experience as much as they did, painfully aware that soon they'd be grown, and he, older still.

The two girls came running down the hall toward the tiny foyer, and he smiled as they neared. "Daddy, Daddy!" they cried in unison, grime smudged on their faces from some unsupervised mischief they'd gotten into while their mother was preparing dinner, no doubt.

"Hailey, Casey, I swear you got more beautiful while I was gone. How is that even possible?" Elliot asked with feigned astonishment as he set his briefcase down and hugged them close.

"Hi, honey. How was your day?" Diane called from the kitchen. Diane was a third grade teacher and finished her workday hours before Elliot got home. It was a good pairing and had withstood the test of time.

"Not bad. Tilting at windmills. Bringing the powerful to their knees. Righting wrongs. The usual," Elliot said, releasing his offspring and standing.

"Oh, before I forget. Another one of those computer things came through the mail slot today. I'm guessing it's for you."

"Where is it?" Elliot asked, waggling his eyebrows at his daughters to delighted giggles.

"On the dinner table."

"Thanks. Speaking of dinner…"

"It's lasagna. Be ready in a half hour."

"Heart healthy, right? Extra cheese and sauce?"

"Why bother making it if you're going to skimp?"

Elliot entered the dining room and spied the small gray flash drive by his water glass. He was used to such clandestine drops – both here and at the office. For some reason whistleblowers tended to favor searching out his home address, which was readily locatable with even marginal computer skills, and he'd been receiving envelopes, CDs, photos, and now flash drives for most of his career.

He moved into his office and plugged the drive into one of his USB ports and, after scanning it with antivirus software, clicked on the menu and surveyed the contents. A screen popped up informing him that the drive was password protected. He squinted at the message. It made no sense: it asked for the last six digits of his mistress's phone number.

The only problem was he had no mistress. He'd always been faithful to his wife, and hadn't even had a flirtation of any note.

He scratched his head, and then an idea occurred to him. He sometimes joked about his boss, Lenny Cox, being his mistress, since work kept him from home so much.

Elliot entered the last six digits and pressed enter. An error message popped up.

"What? But that's the number!" he said out loud.

Another thought came to him. Lenny's extension was 408. He entered the last three digits of the phone number and then the extension and hit return.

The drive flashed several times and another screen appeared. He was in.

There was an introductory file in Word labeled "Read First." He opened it and did as instructed, taking in the contents rapidly, his reading speed triple that of a layman.

Fifteen minutes later he stood and called out to Diane. "Honey, I've got a hot one. Really big. I need to go into the office."

"Elliot! Come on. It's almost ready."

"I can't, sweetheart. I have to go."

"At least let me put a piece in some Tupperware. How late do you think you'll be?"

"Don't wait up. How long will it take for the lasagna?"

Diane appeared in the kitchen doorway thirty seconds later with a container. Elliot kissed her and took it from her. "Thanks. You're an angel."

"Remember to chew."

"Yes, dear."

Elliot practically ran to his car, so great was his excitement, and failed to notice the sedan parked at the end of his block – a perfectly natural oversight, since it was the first time he'd ever been under surveillance.

The passenger watched Elliot reverse out of his driveway and pull away from the house. He set down the high-power binoculars and turned to the driver. "Looks like it's game on."

The driver dropped the transmission into drive and eased from the curb. "I wish we could have intercepted the damned thing."

"Too many people around, and broad daylight. Not a chance. But we'll get the bitch's friend before the night is over. The reporter's the priority."

"Yeah. I got that. Let's just hope he didn't copy it."

"We'll do a break-in tonight. Sanitize his system."

"At least we know he didn't send it to anyone."

"He's too careful. No way would he share that until he's able to vet it. That's why he's going into the office. As predicted."

The driver smiled sadly. "It's good to be right, isn't it?"

"That's what we do."

"Damn straight it is."

Elliot's mind was redlining as he traced the familiar route to the paper. The implications of the data he'd received were staggering. It detailed a plot so complex, so Machiavellian and twisted, he could hardly believe it. Or rather, he didn't want to, because if it was true, everything he had known and believed was a lie.

That it would land on the front page was without question, if the details proved accurate. Elliot's gut said they would – the files contained detailed financial records with dozens of front companies, including at least ten that were subsidiaries of one of the largest insurers in the world, which had also been the beneficiary of a massive bailout during the financial crisis. He'd always believed it had been the recipient of the taxpayer's largesse because its largest creditor's former chairman had been Treasury Secretary at the time; but if the information on the flash drive was accurate, that was only the tip of the iceberg.

Elliot had no problem believing that what he'd just read was possible. He'd studied enough history to know that humans were capable of anything. But the average citizen would go berserk if they knew.

And he had been put in the position of being the one to break the story – for which he had no doubt he'd receive a Pulitzer and be looking at a book deal that would dwarf that of Woodward and Bernstein. That was the positive. The negative was that he'd make powerful enemies in the process and might have to move to Mongolia to feel safe.

But who was feeding him the gold? Someone had painstakingly obtained, probably illegally and likely in violation of national security, enough proof to cause a seismic schism. It troubled him that he didn't know who his leak was, but it wasn't essential to the facts. And he couldn't entirely blame the whistleblower – one look at how Edward Snowden had been pursued for baring the NSA's surveillance programs to the world would convince most thinking humans to forego the honor of landing in official crosshairs.

Traffic was light as he neared downtown, and the underground parking garage was almost deserted when he pulled into his usual slot. The paper's offices would be open, of course – the news never slept, and there would be a crew working to get the next morning's edition put to bed. Alas, sales were down markedly, as many turned to the Internet for their daily jolt of sensationalism rather than buying dead trees. The way of the world, he thought, as his shoes pounded on the concrete garage floor, echoing in the enclosed space.

The elevators required card keys to activate, and he retrieved his from his wallet and swiped it through the reader. A green LED blinked twice and the steel double doors opened. Elliot stepped inside and swiped his card again, and then punched the button for the seventeenth floor.

He ran a quick calculation as the car rose. It would take him a week, possibly two, to put out soft probes in order to verify the data. He'd need authorization for at least two research assistants, due to the volume of data information that would need to be sifted through. And he would have to swear everyone involved to silence. That the story was volatile was an understatement of epic proportions.

The indicator showed he was at the fourteenth floor when the elevator lurched to a stop.

"What the—"

The lights blinked and then shut off as a sharp metallic clank sounded from beneath the car.

Elliot's stomach somersaulted as the floor dropped away and the elevator free-fell a hundred and fifty feet, its emergency braking system disabled. The plunge lasted the longest few seconds of Elliot's life, which was extinguished abruptly when it crashed into the cement subbase, moving at well over a hundred miles per hour.

Hours later, firefighters pried the wreckage apart and found Elliot's mangled remains. Nobody noticed when one of them pocketed a flash drive from the victim's pocket, and immediately after left the site due to dizziness.

A glowing obituary honored Elliot's tireless work in exposing corruption, and within a week his death was forgotten by all but his family, who moved two months later, their home too filled with the ghosts of the past to ever be comfortable again.

# Chapter Nine

Spencer, Allie, and Drake sat on the deck, watching the sunset over the Pacific, cold beers in hand, a mild offshore breeze ruffling their hair. A few stragglers and beachcombers roamed the sand as the last of the diehard after-work surfers caught their final waves.

"How is it down in Laguna Beach, Spencer?" Allie asked, as the sun sank into the sea.

"Gorgeous. Not as many trust-fund kids and Hollywood hotshots as Malibu, but stellar views."

"Hey. Watch it – that's my hood you're dissing," Drake said, and held out a sweating bottle of Anchor Steam to clink against Allie's. She obliged with a happy sigh and went back to contemplating the salmon sky.

"Shame about the house. I hope you get that straightened out," Allie said.

"Yeah. Nothing's ever easy, is it? What about you? Sounds like you have your hands full with your dad's estate."

"I'm hoping to get the last of it settled in the next couple of weeks. I've got an excellent legal team out of Houston that's keeping the worst of the leeches at bay." She shrugged. "I can't believe how many there are when big money's involved."

"Tell me about it," Spencer said with a frown. "Are you planning to stay in Texas?"

Allie looked at a spot somewhere to the left of Drake's shoulder. "Depends. This is pretty sweet. I'm just not sure I could get used to the whole *Baywatch* lifestyle."

"Hazzle-whatever's a star in France. Like Jerry Lewis, without the telethon," Spencer said.

"Good to know I might have that to fall back on. Is that where unemployed treasure hunters go to die? Take up miming or painting or something?" Drake asked.

"It's sad. The bistros are lousy with them," Spencer said. "They'll usually leave you alone if you buy them a drink."

Allie nodded. "Or they start crying. I hear it's kind of like the island of misfit toys, only without claymation."

"Or the songs," Spencer agreed, and they all laughed.

"We should probably grab some dinner before the flight. There are some amazing restaurants nearby," Drake said, glancing at the time. "We have three hours to get to the airport."

"You'd think the CIA could whisk us through security. Like making us take our shoes off and X-raying us is going to prevent anything. I can think of a dozen lethal weapons you can make from crap you buy in gift shops on the jetway side of security. Do they really think terrorists don't have web access?" Spencer griped.

"I guess we just aren't special enough," Allie said. "Besides, Drake's hands are lethal weapons."

"Absolutely," Drake agreed. "Just put a gun or a Lambo in them, and bam, it's curtains."

Music flooded the quiet area from next door as the sliding door opened, and Kyra sashayed onto her deck, wearing spandex exercise shorts and a jogging top. She raised a beer and toasted them all. "Hi."

Spencer smiled like a Cheshire cat and Allie rolled her eyes.

"Hi back atcha," Spencer said. Drake gave an embarrassed wave.

"Are you going to be around tomorrow for the barbecue? You didn't forget, did you?" Kyra asked. The breeze carried the scent of vanilla and coconut from her as she neared the glass railing. Allie coughed.

"Oh, um, no, I can't make it," Drake said, flushing as Allie's eyes bored holes through him. "I've got to go out of town for a few days."

"That totally sucks. I guess it will be just me and my home girls, then. How boring."

"Drake hates to miss an orgy. Maybe a rain check?" Allie asked innocently in a low voice.

"What?" Kyra said. "Let me turn down my stereo."

"She said maybe a rain check," Drake offered. "Anyway, have a good time."

"I'll try."

Drake stood and went into the house before the conversation could go astray, and Allie and Spencer followed him in. "Let me change and we can hit the road," Drake said, and didn't wait for a response, opting to duck into his bedroom before being subjected to further torment.

At Allie's request they ate a delicious Italian dinner at Gravina on Pacific Coast Highway, and then returned to Drake's house to await the taxi to the airport. The ride south took an hour, and they were in the international terminal of LAX with ten minutes to spare. Alex was waiting for them at the Cathay Pacific counter, dressed casually, looking in his wrinkled safari shirt and cargo pants more like a midlife-crisis backpacker than a CIA field supervisor.

"Nice to see you made it," he said. "First-class check-in is over there. I'm in business class."

Drake noticed that his eyes never stopped roaming around the terminal even as he greeted them.

"No pampering for the wicked, I suppose," Spencer said.

"Not terrible, though. I'm a good sleeper. I suggest you try to get as much rest as possible, because we're going to hit the ground running. The only wait will be for the final go-ahead on the permits."

They checked in and left all but their carry-on bags with the friendly counter staff, and then moved to the security checkpoint. There was the inevitable line, where bored dullards were searching grandmothers and kids as though they were smuggling bazookas, making for a tedious half hour of shuffling toward the imaging machines.

The first-class lounge was lavish and half empty, and they spent their time online until the flight was announced.

Boarding began almost an hour before takeoff due to the size of the plane, and both Drake and Allie were asleep by the time the 777 trundled down the runway and lifted into the sky. Spencer watched the lights of Los Angeles disappear beneath its wings as it climbed into the heavens, the quest he was depending on to replenish his fortune about to begin.

# Chapter Ten

Jiao Long sat at the long rectangular conference table, facing his superior, Xiaoping Wu, the second-highest-ranking member of the MSS. Next to him was a nervous technician in charge of analyzing the servers that had been removed from Moontech's headquarters.

Xiaoping listened impatiently as Jiao gave his report. When he was finished, Xiaoping leaned forward, lit a cigarette, and exhaled a pungent gray cloud at the overhead light.

"So this Huang didn't know anything? He wasn't in bed with Liu?" he growled.

Jiao nodded. "I'm confident he wasn't."

"Will he make it?"

"No. He suffered a stroke during our interrogation. He's on life support now, but not expected to regain consciousness."

Xiaoping grunted and tapped ash from his cigarette into a porcelain ashtray, taking care to shape the ember with the side – a peculiar habit Jiao had seen too many times to count. "Then what does that leave us with?"

Jiao looked to the technician, who began speaking in a soft, almost feminine voice. "There's no question that the intrusion into our computers came from Moontech. But when we were going through the logs, I found an anomaly that was very interesting. It appears that the attack on our system was directed remotely, via a Trojan horse that was able to co-opt one of the Moontech servers and make it look like the operator was in the building."

Xiaoping waved an annoyed hand. "We know that."

"Yes, well, what was interesting was that we were not the only target."

"Don't play games. Spit it out."

"It looks like Liu was accessing the U.S. Department of Defense network. Their internal, most sensitive servers."

"What?" Xiaoping exclaimed. "Are you sure?"

"Positive. The signature is…let's just say that it's distinctive."

"How? We've been trying to crack that for years. We've never been able to do it," Jiao demanded.

"I'm not sure. That's the puzzling part. But he was able to gain access."

Xiaoping took another deep drag on his cigarette and his expression grew pensive. Nobody spoke until he stubbed the butt out and nodded. "We need to understand what he was doing. This significantly complicates matters. The Americans' DOD is the best-fortified network in the world. If Liu was fishing around in there, we need answers."

The technician cleared his throat. "There is one more thing."

Both older men stared at him. "What's that?" Jiao asked.

"It looks like I may be able to reproduce the protocol that enabled him to access their servers."

If the technician had levitated around the room, it would have had less impact on Xiaoping and Jiao.

Jiao's eyes narrowed and he gave the younger man an appraising stare. "The hell you say."

The technician nodded. "It's true. I'll need some time, but there still might be enough on the server to put the pieces together."

Xiaoping sat back. "If you can do that, I'll promote you to the highest possible position. You should be running our cyber efforts."

The technician smiled nervously. "I will do my best."

"Don't sit here any longer, then. Go do it," said Xiaoping. "Report to me at any hour of the day or night if you get through.

But…the Americans cannot know it's us. Under any circumstances. That would be disastrous."

"Oh, I'll bounce it through a half-dozen servers. They'll never suspect."

"I thought you told us that's what Liu did," Jiao said.

"He didn't know about the program I wrote that could trace it back through to the source. It technically doesn't exist. Except it does. And we have it." The technician smirked like a guilty schoolboy. "I could explain exactly how it works, if you're interested."

Xiaoping shook his head. "I care about results. Don't waste any more time with talk. This is the highest priority. Commandeer whatever resources you need. I cannot underscore its importance enough."

The technician rose. "I will report when I have a solution."

Jiao and Xiaoping watched as the slight man left the conference room, and stood for a moment without speaking, considering all they'd just learned.

"This could be an enormous breakthrough," Xiaoping said.

"Yes, but what troubles me the most is that we have no idea what this Liu was doing in the DOD servers to begin with. If you recall, we thought he was trying to sabotage our systems, which is why we took such…swift action."

"At your recommendation, as I remember it."

"Which perhaps was an overreaction, in light of his achievement. Our very best have been banging their heads into that wall for a decade, with no success." Jiao looked off into space. "Hard to believe a single rogue amateur could do what a team of a hundred top programmers couldn't."

"There was only one Einstein, too. Occasionally one man sees something the majority misses. I suspect that's the case this time." Xiaoping stood. "But we can't take back what is already done. Our best hope lies with our new prodigy, since we blew the old one out of the sky."

"At the time it seemed the prudent course. The penalty for

espionage is death. We simply saved the tribunal the effort of trying him."

"As with most things, nothing is ever completely black or white."

Jiao remained seated as his boss left the room, the only sound the faint hiss of the air-conditioning and the steady ticking of the wall clock. He rubbed his eyes, which constantly burned from the pollution that was a regular feature of China's large industrial cities. The rebuke in Xiaoping's tone had been as plain as a backhand, although delivered subtly, as was his way. Jiao had made an informed decision to sabotage the plane in which Liu had been fleeing the country. There was no way he could have been expected to second-guess that the dead man had posed no threat they could find, at least not to China. To the U.S.?

The first thing they needed to learn was what Liu had been doing in the DOD system. Once they understood that, then they could take appropriate action. But at the very least, having a clandestine window into the Americans' deepest military secrets would be of incalculable value to the MSS.

It could well shift the balance of power, wherein the U.S. presently held most of the cards. With ten aircraft carriers to China's one, and a military budget that dwarfed the next twenty-six industrialized nations combined, the U.S. projected its agenda through superior firepower as well as through its financial system. If China had access to its plans, it could take steps to block those most harmful to China's interests, and prevent the American war machine from dominating at least China's piece of the global pie.

*What had Liu been after?*

The question haunted Jiao as he rose and moved to the door, his tread that of a far older man than had entered the room only minutes before.

# Chapter Eleven

*Bangkok, Thailand*

The Airbus A330-300 jet banked on approach to Suvarnabhumi International Airport and slowed as the pilot cut airspeed. The flight from Hong Kong, the connecting point for the trip from Los Angeles to Thailand, had been mercifully calm compared to the uncomfortably rough slog across the Pacific. Allie yawned and peered out the window, and Drake tried not to be too obvious in his admiration of her charms, which were still holding his attention as they neared their twentieth hour of travel.

"How are you doing?" Drake asked.

Allie shrugged. "Okay. I wish we had gotten more sleep. That part completely sucked."

"Yeah, well, it is what it is. We'll be on the ground soon."

"I was reading about Bangkok on our layover. It's supposed to be pretty modern."

"Probably the last we'll see of running water or flush toilets until we're back out of the jungle."

"Still a romantic, huh?"

Drake was momentarily at a loss for words at Allie's ability to throw him with her abrupt shifts. By the time he'd decided on a response, he'd lost her to the Bangkok skyline glittering below in the morning sun.

The landing gear lowered into place with a thunk, and then they were dropping toward the ribbon of tarmac that stretched before them. The big plane seemed to float for an instant just above the runway, and then landed with a rough bounce before steadying as it slowed.

Spencer smiled at them from across the aisle as the aircraft neared the gate. "It's showtime," he said with a theatrical flair. "Bangkok awaits the great white hunter."

"If you're referring to me, it's not necessary to flatter," Allie said. "Although you can use 'Goddess' if you absolutely must."

They disembarked and filed to the immigration area, where stern clerks stamped their passports. Once finished with the formalities, they waited by the baggage carousels. Alex joined them, and after collecting their things, they moved out to where the drivers were gathered, holding signs and jabbering loudly. Alex turned his head toward Drake as he led them to the barrier that separated travelers from the waiting Thais. "We have a guide. I've worked with him before. He's a character, but knows the ins and outs of Thailand like the back of his hand."

Allie and Drake nodded, wondering what a CIA veteran would describe as being a character, and didn't have long to wait. A gaunt man of indeterminate late middle-age, with pecan-colored skin, his gleaming ebony hair slicked back with gel, and a Fu Manchu mustache that would have been the envy of any B-movie bad guy stood behind the barrier, watching them approach expectantly.

Alex's face relaxed for a split second as he neared the short Asian, who offered a crisp bow, the traditional *wai* greeting. Alex returned it and introduced them, and the guide bowed in turn to each.

"This is Uncle Pete. Uncle Pete, meet Allie, Drake, and Spencer," Alex said.

"Most honored," Uncle Pete said in heavily accented English, and then turned and snapped at a porter, who ran over and began stacking their luggage on a rickety hand truck. "My truck parked outside," he explained. "I have policeman watch it. About only thing they good for these days, besides take bribes and shake down innocent driver."

"Can you fit everyone?" Alex asked.

"Of course. I rent SUV just for you."

"Lead the way."

Uncle Pete marched briskly toward the departure terminal exit and then slowed so the porter could catch up. He nodded to Alex and grinned, revealing tobacco-stained teeth. "Been long time, no?"

"We can catch up later. What's the word on the permits?"

"Still wait. You know how that go. Someone holding out for more baht. But we promise we have tomorrow."

"Plan was to get into the field this afternoon," Alex said.

"Missionary man say, man propose, God dispose, right?" Uncle Pete said, his English suddenly improving. "In the meantime, I book you into top good hotel." He regarded Allie. "First time in Thailand?"

"Yes. I've heard lovely things."

Uncle Pete gave the porter and then the throng of locals meeting travelers a sour look. "Not from me. Lazy crooks."

Alex laughed, the first time he had since they'd met him. "Uncle Pete's a perpetual optimist."

"Bangkok full of snakes in grass," Uncle Pete snarled, and then cautioned the porter to hurry up.

"He's the hospitality committee?" Spencer asked in a low voice. "Couldn't they find a hungry crocodile?"

"Pete's charm grows on you," Alex said. "Like fungus."

The rental turned out to be a silver Nissan Armada, with just enough room for Alex to sit in the passenger seat and the three of them to cram into the rear. Spencer gave Allie a half smile as she tried to get comfortable. "You can sit on my lap if you want."

"I imagine I'm not the first girl to get that offer," Allie said. "Has it ever worked?"

"You might be surprised."

Drake chuckled. "Nothing surprises me after a ride in your Lambo, Spence. Although I still think that some orange shag carpeting would dress it up nicely."

"Maybe some fuzzy dice?" Allie quipped. "Ooh, how about one

of those 'Ass, grass, or cash, nobody rides for free' bumper stickers? We have them in every color of the rainbow out in cow country."

"I liked the car," Drake said. "Very Hollywood Eurotrash, if that's what you were shooting for."

"Screw all of you. It does zero to sixty in under three seconds."

Allie elbowed him. "Hey, at least it's practical for hauling groceries or lumber or whatnot…"

Uncle Pete might not have been the slowest driver in Thailand, but he was certainly in the running for the title. By the time they made it to the hotel, it was well past lunch time, and they were grateful to crawl from the cramped rear seat.

The hotel lobby was opulent, and two bellmen scurried to take their bags. Uncle Pete stayed in the car, obviously feeling out of place in the lavish digs. He had given everyone a card with his cell number on it and told them to call if they needed anything. After confirming that they were being attended properly, he pulled away at the speed of a geriatric snail.

"Want to try the hotel restaurant?" Drake suggested as he signed the register.

"Where's your sense of adventure?" Spencer asked. "Why not find a hole in the wall and try dining like the locals?"

Allie made a face. "Two words: monkey brains."

"I believe you can special order them if they're not on the menu," Drake said.

They took the elevator to the penthouse level after getting settled in their rooms, and had a delicious medley of Asian fusion cuisine, each dish better than the last. When they were finished, Spencer burped audibly and patted his stomach. Allie looked horrified, and he shrugged.

"In many countries burping is intended to express satisfaction with a good meal," he said.

"I can't wait to hear what other bodily emissions might be celebrated," Drake said.

"In Thailand, nose picking is also considered acceptable in polite company," Spencer added.

"How charming," Allie said. "I'm sure you'll feel right at home."

"It's important to understand the culture if you're going to get the most out of a trip to exotic lands."

"How about we find the statue and leave? Does that work for you?" she fired back.

"I can see you haven't gotten into the spirit yet." Spencer drained his water glass and raised it to the waiter, who nodded and rushed to retrieve a frosted steel pitcher. "What do you make of Uncle Pete?"

"He seems harmless enough," Drake said. "Although kind of a schemer."

"That's to be expected. He's making ends meet however he can. You get to know the type after a while. They get addicted to the easy money of being snitches and facilitators. The agency depends on that, I bet."

"I think he's sweet," Allie said. "I wonder what color Lambo he drives?"

"Definitely not mustard," Drake said solemnly.

"You just can't let it go, can you?" Spencer griped, but they could tell he was enjoying the ribbing.

"You should see if they have a lift kit for it, like my FJ. That would be radical. Off-road rubber. Mud and snows."

"Ha, ha."

A server arrived with the water and replenished their glasses. Another one spirited their plates away and was back moments later with a dessert menu. Allie waved him off with an eye roll. "I don't know about you two, but I'm going to take a nap. I forgot how much fun it was to miss a night's sleep."

"I'm with you there. Spencer?" Drake asked.

"Might as well. Doesn't seem like anything's going to happen until tomorrow, at the earliest, judging by what Uncle Pete said about the permits. I'll leave Alex a message and let him know we're going down for the count. We can check supplies tomorrow, and then if we're still waiting on the bureaucracy, at least make it to the border so we're ready to rock when we get the okay."

Drake's room was on the same level as Allie's; Spencer's was two floors above, and he said his goodbyes and left them in the elevator.

"Wild about Spencer's situation, isn't it?" Drake asked, making small talk so they didn't stand in silence.

"He's a big boy – he got himself into it. He can dig himself out. My money's on Spencer rebounding."

"Sounds like the hedge fund may have lost his money."

"What's the old saying about diversification? Pigs get slaughtered?"

"Ouch. But you're right."

The polished steel door whispered to the side, and they stepped into the marble-floored hall. "Allie, I wanted to tell you that…Kyra? She's just the neighbor. Nothing else."

Allie sighed. "I'm beat, Drake. Can we discuss it some other time?"

"I thought it was important to clear that up."

"I hear what you're saying. But I'm pretty overwhelmed by everything that's happening right now. Let's talk about it later."

Drake took the hint. There was no point pushing the subject. Fatigue, overload from responsibilities, adjusting to new circumstances, being in a strange country where she didn't speak the language and couldn't understand what people were saying, trepidation at going into the jungle again… Drake tried to imagine what was going on in her head, and sneaked a look at her as they walked together toward their rooms. He didn't have a clue.

"This is mine," she said, stopping at her door. "Sleep well. Maybe ring me around dinnertime."

"Okay."

Drake wanted to say more. Much more. He wanted to tell her about how she haunted his dreams, how he had imagined being with her, how much he wanted to hold her, to feel her lips on his, press her against him.

None of which he did, instead continuing to his room, feeling as alone and dejected as he could remember.

# Chapter Twelve

Uncle Pete arrived at the hotel the next morning looking like he had slept in his clothes, and waited while Drake and Allie gathered their things. When they returned to the lobby, he was standing outside the front doors, smoking and trading jokes with the valets in Thai. He spotted them emerging from the entrance and dropped his hand-rolled cigarette in the sand top of an upright ashtray.

"Good morning. Car over there," he said, motioning to the parking structure across the street.

"No cops to bribe today?" Allie asked.

"I on a budget," Uncle Pete replied with a wink.

They followed him to the SUV and were not so quickly on their way. Traffic was nearly stopped in the downtown area, a sea of brake lights stretching as far as they could see, tuk-tuks and motorcycles weaving through the coagulated morass of vehicles.

"Where are we going?" Drake asked.

"To office. We have all stuff you ask, but you need inspect while we still here, so you think of anything else, we buy before we go. Not much by border. Laos nothing but jungle, so this last chance."

"You have an office?" Allie asked.

"More like shop. It travel agency. Guide tours. That kind thing. Very popular with *farangs*."

"Farangs?" Drake echoed.

"Thai word for white people. It not insult," Uncle Pete lied.

"That's okay. I mean, we're the minority here," Allie said. "Is that your day job?"

"Yes. Do temple tours, city tours, beach tours…whatever you want." Uncle Pete looked slyly at Drake in the rearview mirror. "This very friendly, easy place. Anything you think of, I get. Anything," he repeated, his meaning clear.

"That's good to know," Drake said, uncomfortable with the direction the conversation was headed. "How far is it?"

"Over on other side Nana Plaza. Near river."

"Nana Plaza?"

"You never hear? It famous. That, Soi Cowboy, and Patpong."

"Dare I ask what it's famous for?"

Uncle Pete laughed. "Sex, of course! Millions farangs come for sexy tour. It big business."

"That's legal?" Allie asked.

"Gray area. It tolerated and regulated, so like everything Thailand, depend."

"Do you have any daughters?" Allie asked.

"No. Just two sons."

"How would you feel if you did, and they went into the sex trade?"

Uncle Pete frowned. "Most bar girl come from north, which very poor. This only way they make real money, send back, take care family. We don't judge – it financial, not moral question," he said, mispronouncing financial.

"So you agree it's immoral?" Allie pressed.

"If million farang want come and spend lots of money, I got no problem. We don't see same way you do. Lot of farang must like, 'cause they happy-happy customer!"

"I think it's sick," Allie said, obviously disgusted.

"So you no want special massage later?" Uncle Pete said, deadpan. "How 'bout you, Mr. Drake? Want meet nice ladies?"

"Um, no, thanks," Drake said.

"You no like girls?"

Drake sputtered a denial. "No. Or…damn, I mean, yes. I like girls just fine. I just…no, thank you."

Uncle Pete's eyes narrowed and he gave Drake a knowing glance. "Ah. Maybe you like meet ladyboys?"

"What? No. Of course not."

Allie couldn't resist the bait. "Ladyboys?"

"Oh, very popular. Most look zactly like girl. But with different…stuff." He rounded a corner and pointed at a group of youngsters in black miniskirts standing in front of a bar. "See? Ladyboys."

Allie and Drake gawked at the gathering. "Those are…boys?" Drake asked unbelievingly.

"Not boys. *Ladyboys*," Uncle Pete corrected.

Allie nudged Drake. "What's that song? 'Lola'? Don't worry, I won't judge you."

"I appreciate your tolerance in the matter, but no, thanks." Drake shook his head. "I would have thought they were female."

"If that's your story, hey…" Allie said, and Uncle Pete laughed.

"Sound like she got your number, Mr. Drake."

"It's all in fun," Drake said, blushing at the unwanted attention.

"Uh-huh," Allie said.

Uncle Pete's shop was close to the Chao Phraya River that snaked through the city, near the port in a run-down part of town. The exterior was painted bright red with gold lettering in Thai and English. Allie eyed it with a smirk. "Happy Time Tour Enterprise Company, huh? Sounds like you have your marketing down, Uncle Pete."

"Many happy customer. Lot of repeat. Everybody enjoy seeing sights, you know?"

"I'll bet," Allie muttered just loud enough for Drake to hear. "Sounds like we've got the Thai version of Caligula driving us around."

"Judge not, said the wise man," Drake said.

Uncle Pete held the door open for them and they entered the shop, which consisted of three desks, one obviously his, and the other two occupied by young Thai women. Uncle Pete didn't introduce Drake and Allie, instead leading them into the rear of the building, where there was a small storage room just large enough for a car. Stacks of Coach purses, Louis Vuitton handbags, and Tumi luggage were piled next to racks of Versace silk shirts and exotic furs, most of them protected species, from what Allie could tell.

Uncle Pete walked over to three backpacks sitting beside several cardboard boxes. "Here stuff. Tents, machetes, water pills, sun cream, first aid, flares, lighters, knives, whole deal. All genuine real, finest kind."

Allie came over to the gear and began inventorying it as Drake eyed the shirts. "I suppose these are all genuine, too?"

Uncle Pete laughed. "Almost. But silk. From China. Over there, everything pirate, you know? Even a Mercedes all fake. 500 SL. Look completely real. Made in China."

"I thought China cut down on piracy," Allie remarked from behind the equipment pile.

"That what news say. Now lots made in Vietnam and Cambodia. Same-same, different side border. But I only buy best kind."

"So only high-quality pirated fakes."

"Best kind," Uncle Pete repeated.

Allie smiled. "Of course. I'd expect nothing less. You're an honorable man."

Uncle Pete thumped his chest and offered her a yellow grin. "Zactly. Uncle Pete top shelf, no bad days. Don't worry, be happy. You see anything you like, I give you super special price. My cost. Practically free today."

"I don't think I'll need a Vuitton duffle in the jungle."

"Very styling. Popular. Make you look Richie Rich, for sure." He looked her over. "Maybe Rolex or Cartier? Look real. Best available."

"I don't think so."

"Maybe for friend?" Uncle Pete tried. Seeing he was getting nowhere, he turned to Drake. "You? Gold President, like Warren Buffet?"

"I don't think he wears a President," Drake said. "Drives a Buick, too, I believe."

"I go get. Maybe for your other friend?"

"No, thanks."

"Wife? Neighbor wife?"

Drake had to laugh at the little man's persistence. "Nope. But I appreciate it. Really."

"Okay. I got Viagra and Cialis, too. Make you strong like bull."

Drake moved over to Allie. "You look like you could use a hand with that."

She slid to the side and leaned toward Drake. "Irony is clearly not a big part of Thai culture. Although he would do well on a used-car lot."

"I suspect Uncle Pete is quite an entrepreneur," Drake agreed. "I hear he sells Buffet his Rolexes."

"I thought it was Chinese Benzes. Hard to keep up."

Ten minutes later they had inventoried everything and packed it all into the three backpacks. Uncle Pete hoisted Spencer's bag and they carried the other two to the SUV, and after loading the backpacks inside, the enterprising little Thai turned to them. "Headquarters say maybe you talk to girl mom. She here in Bangkok. Want see you."

"Christine's mother is here?" Drake asked, surprised.

"She crazy worried. Wanna be close by."

Allie nodded. "Makes sense. If my child went missing, I'd be on the first plane wherever she was last seen."

"Sure, let's go talk to her, then," Drake said.

~ ~ ~

Christine's mother was staying at the Mandarin Oriental Hotel, in a penthouse suite with a breathtaking view of the city. She greeted them at the door, a handsome woman with graying hair, still beautiful despite the stress of the situation and the accumulation of years. Allie and Drake could immediately see the resemblance to Christine.

"Thank you so much for coming to see me. I'm going out of my mind here with no word," Margaret said, after offering them coffee.

"I can understand," Drake said.

"When are you going in?"

"Tomorrow. We're hopeful we can find the…site," Allie said.

"It's just all such a blow. So tragic. Christine's so young, and although we don't always agree, she has a good heart."

There wasn't anything to say to that, so Drake simply nodded.

Margaret felt beside her for her purse and removed her wallet. She fumbled with the inserts, found a dog-eared photograph, and passed it to Drake. "This is her on prom night. She was gorgeous. So full of joy, of promise for the future. The picture doesn't do her justice."

Christine was radiant in a formal dress, looking older than a high school senior. Allie scooted closer to see, and Drake held out the snapshot.

"Oh, she's beautiful," Allie said.

"You have no idea. In person she lights up any room she's in. She's one of those special personalities. She could be anything she wanted, I always told her." Margaret fished another photo from the wallet. "And this is Christine on her seventh birthday." She held it out with trembling fingers and dropped it. "Oh, damn."

Drake recovered the photograph and studied the image. Margaret gave a muffled sob and quickly recovered, brushing a tear from her face. "I'm sorry," she said, her voice tight. "I promised myself I would be strong."

"You're doing fine. This has to be hard," Allie sympathized.

"You have no idea. After Arthur and I divorced six years ago, it affected Christine more than I like to think. I can't help but blame myself for this. Maybe if we'd stayed together, she wouldn't have gone off in search of whatever she was looking for, would have been more at peace…she took it really hard. That was the start of her wild period. Just the usual college stuff, but she drifted away from me as she grew up, until one day she announced she was going to China. Didn't ask. Just told me, like it was an afterthought. And now…"

Drake handed Margaret back the photos. "Mrs. Whitfield, we're going to do everything possible to learn what happened. If your daughter's alive, we'll find her and get her out of there. You can count on us."

"Blakely. Margaret Blakely now. I went back to my maiden name after the divorce." She gave a small smile that was hard to interpret. "I've heard the jungle is dangerous. Everyone says it's a snake pit," she went on. "I'm sorry. I didn't ask you here to watch me blubber." She stood and moved to the wet bar, poured herself three fingers of Johnny Walker Blue, and waved the bottle at them. "You want a cocktail?"

Allie and Drake demurred. "No, thanks."

Margaret nodded and took two healthy swallows. "I'm not a drinker, but...well, I can't sleep, can't eat. All I can think about is Christine..." She choked up again and finished the glass. When she turned to them, her eyes were brimming with tears. "Thank you so much for doing this. I just need to know for sure..."

"I understand. We won't let you down."

Uncle Pete caught their signals from his silent position by the door and gave a small nod. Allie and Drake rose. Margaret tried to smile, but the effect was brittle and her gaze unfocused.

"We'll show ourselves out," Allie said.

"Thank you again for coming. I...I just wanted to meet you and offer my appreciation. If there's ever anything I can do for you, just say the word. Or if you need something here – money, whatever. You know where I am. I'll move mountains to get what you need."

"We appreciate it, Mrs.... Ms. Blakely. And we'll keep that in mind," Drake said.

The elevator ride back to the ground level was somber. The reality of the emotional toll of Christine's disappearance had drained them. Uncle Pete was the only one who seemed unaffected, and when they were back in traffic, his attitude was as though nothing had happened.

"You want sightsee? Got time. Permit coming end day, soonest."

"No, thanks. Back to the hotel, I think," Drake said.

Uncle Pete gave Allie a sly look. "Maybe ping-pong show?"

"Like a match?" Allie asked, her mind elsewhere.

Uncle Pete cackled. "You look on web. Big deal here. Popular."

Allie gave him a puzzled look, not registering his meaning.

"I don't think we want to know," Drake said, processing faster than Allie and cutting Uncle Pete off before he could venture further down that road.

Allie's eyes widened and her mouth formed an O as realization of what the little Thai was alluding to dawned on her.

Drake shook his head and met Allie's horrified stare. "Some things are best left for the documentary."

# Chapter Thirteen

Alex and Spencer walked along the sidewalk in downtown Bangkok. Heat rose in waves around them; the air was muggy and tinged with the aroma of fried food, cigarettes, and exhaust. Pools of oily water glistened in potholes, the remnants of a morning cloudburst that had dropped a few inches of rain on the metropolis just after dawn. Street vendors hawked every manner of ware, from leather wallets and consumer electronics to illicit substances and sex shows where animals or children featured a prominent role.

They ignored all the come-ons and made their way toward the Chinese cemetery, past ornate temples layered in gold leaf and bright hues and into a residential district where every other building boasted a sign in neon red or green proclaiming the lowest prices in all Bangkok.

When Alex told Spencer the agency had secured weapons for them, Spencer had insisted on accompanying him to inspect them.

"You don't have to. I can handle it," Alex had said.

"No problem. If my life's going to depend on gear, I'd rather see it with my own eyes before we buy off."

"Suit yourself. But is it really a good idea to give civilians submachine guns? That's an accident waiting to happen."

"They know their way around weapons. They'll be fine after some basic orientation."

"If they shoot their foot off, it's on you."

"Appreciate the concern."

Spencer had let Alex's condescending tone go. He could see the agent's point. If the situation had been reversed, Spencer would have voiced the same concerns, and he didn't take it personally. Both were professionals, and neither was trying to make a new best friend. They had jobs to do, and might need each other to survive once in the jungle.

As they passed a restaurant filled with local diners, a comely young woman in a short red silk dress offered them a menu with a bright smile. Alex shook his head and Spencer noted his permanent scowl was back on display – like he'd just swallowed a shot of vinegar.

Three blocks down, Alex checked his smartphone and verified the address.

"It's that orange place," he said. They crossed the street and approached the building, which housed apartments above an antique store.

They entered the shop, and a wizened man with gray hair and steel spectacles peered up at them from his chair, which was surrounded by curios and furniture.

"Anurak?" Alex asked.

"Yes. How may I help you?" Anurak replied in good English.

"I'm looking for a baby carriage."

"We have several."

"Something in blue."

The old man's demeanor changed, and he pushed wordlessly past them to the entrance. He flipped the sign over so it read "Closed" through the glass door, and locked the deadbolt. When he returned, he was all business.

"In my warehouse," he said, and led them through a glass-beaded curtain to the rear of the building.

A dark green duffle bag rested on a wooden crate near a water dispenser. Chests, armoires, and tables filled the large space. At the far end a refinishing and sanding area sat empty, cans of stain and varnish strewn around the floor. Anurak unzipped the bag and removed a submachine gun. He handed it to Alex, who disassembled it with practiced familiarity and inspected the parts. Anurak watched with an impassive expression and then extracted another identical weapon and gave it to Spencer, who eyed it approvingly.

"Heckler & Koch MP5SD6. Very nice. Three-round burst mode, integrated suppressor, chambered for 9mm parabellum. Thirty-round box mag. Simple, easy to use, light, compact," Spencer said.

"No match for an AK," Alex observed.

"In the jungle? How close are we going to be? Fifty yards? Tops? Although I agree, which is why I requested a pair of AKMs for us. Bulkier, but a lot more stopping power and range." Spencer fieldstripped the ugly little gun with sure hands. "Didn't see any reason to saddle them with any more than they'll need."

"I have four Beretta 9mm pistols as well," Anurak said.

"Where did you get the H&Ks?" Alex asked.

"Pakistan. They manufacture them under license there. These, as you can see, are new. Only test fired to verify they're in good working order."

"And the AKs?"

"Chinese. Quite good, I think you'll agree. Accurate to at least three hundred meters." Anurak peered over his spectacles at Spencer. "Depending on the shooter, perhaps farther."

Twenty minutes later they were done with their inspection and had accepted the arms. Each pistol came with three full magazines and belt holsters, and the MP5s and AKMs with six full magazines each. They exited the shop, with Alex carrying the heavy bag, and retraced their steps toward the hotel. Spencer glanced at Alex as they made their way down the blistering sidewalk and noted the sweat beading on his forehead.

"I can take it for a while. We can trade off," Spencer suggested, and Alex nodded and handed him the duffle.

"We'll swap every couple of blocks."

"You want to grab a taxi? Or a tuk-tuk?" Spencer asked after another block, the swelter almost overwhelming with the heavy load, referring to the motorcycle-based tricycles that carried a pair of passengers in addition to the driver, ubiquitously used in Thailand for cheap transportation.

"Might as well."

The sound of a powerful motor roared behind them. They spun just in time to see the grill of a dark sedan bearing down on them, two of its wheels up on the sidewalk. Spencer threw himself out of the way; Alex was right behind him, but a split second too late. The car slammed into his legs, throwing him into the air like a rag doll as the vehicle accelerated and sped away.

Alex struck the ground with a sickening thwack, and Spencer could see in an instant that at least one of his legs was broken, and likely his pelvis as well. Spencer glared at the departing sedan, its license plate unreadable due to muck smeared across it, and then forced himself to his feet and ran to where Alex lay in the street.

"Can you talk?" Spencer asked, kneeling beside him.

Alex fought for breath. The pain had to be blinding, Spencer knew, and he recognized the signs of shock in Alex's pallid complexion. He stood and looked around and saw a woman on her cell phone, frozen in place.

"You. You speak English?" Spencer called out.

The woman nodded. "Little."

"Call the police and an ambulance. My friend's hurt. Please."

"All right," she said, and terminated her conversation and dialed emergency. After thirty second she hung up. "They coming."

"Thank you."

"Crazy man in car."

"Yes," Spencer said, suddenly remembering that he had a bag full of guns and ammo. Perhaps the police wouldn't be that understanding of his presence under those circumstances. He knelt beside Alex again and whispered to him, "Nod if you understand."

Alex managed a weak nod.

"Help's coming. You carrying anything that would give your cover away?"

A small shake of Alex's head, almost imperceptible.

"Okay. I'm going to get out of here. Hang tough."

Alex nodded again and Spencer stood, the wail of an approaching emergency vehicle all the warning he needed. He turned and, without saying another word to the woman, jogged to the corner and disappeared down the side street, and then sprinted as fast as he could manage with the bulky duffle toward the boulevard two blocks down.

By the time he made it to the wide street, more sirens were klaxoning toward Alex. There being nothing left he could do for the fallen agent, Spencer flagged down a tuk-tuk. He gave the driver the name of a hotel a block and a half away from his, and then sat back in the seat, the duffle beside him, his brow furrowed in thought as he tried to piece together what had just occurred.

# Chapter Fourteen

*Washington, D.C.*

Senator Arthur Whitfield looked up from his reading at the knock on his office door, scowling at the interruption. Dark rings lined his eyes, though as usual his full head of silver hair had been carefully styled to minimize the bald spot at the crown of his head. Behind him, oil paintings of Revolutionary War battles in golden frames adorned the walls, with the area opposite floor-to-ceiling bookshelves devoted to the War Between the States. He thumbed the sides of the hundreds of pages of the latest bill that was coming up for a vote and growled a command.

"Come in."

The heavy cherry-wood door swung open and his aide, Alan Sedgewick, stepped in, an apologetic expression on his face.

"Sorry to disturb you, sir, but the gentlemen from the agency you asked to see are here."

Whitfield nodded and checked the time. "Very well. Show them in."

Collins and the deputy director of the CIA, Edward Cornett, entered. Sedgewick showed them to two burgundy leather chairs beside a polished mahogany oval table. Whitfield rounded his desk and took a seat opposite them.

Sedgewick made to leave, but Whitfield stopped him with a curt gesture. "Pull up a chair. I want your input on this," Whitfield ordered.

Sedgewick did so, opting to sit near the door.

Whitfield addressed the newcomers. "What have you got for me? Tell me it's good news. I'm beside myself with worry."

Cornett shook his head grimly. "I'm afraid nothing definitive. We've deployed a team and will be commencing a search of the area. But the odds aren't good of finding anything but confirmation that she didn't make it. I'm sorry."

Whitfield exhaled noisily and stared at the ceiling molding before addressing Cornett. "Why has it taken this long?"

"Unavoidable, Senator. Laos isn't particularly friendly, what with the unexploded Vietnam conflict ordnance that's still scattered around the country, and Myanmar...well, you of all people understand the situation there."

"I want the details. How big a team, what methodology they're using, how long you estimate it will take...the works."

Cornett nodded. "As per your instructions, we're going in soft. We've obtained the cooperation of a civilian group that is a guarantee to get the necessary permits, working under the pretense that they're looking for a national treasure."

"Why would Laos and Myanmar grant them that latitude?"

"For Laos, it would be an important historical find," Collins said. "For Myanmar, we all know they're destitute, so they're motivated by self-interest. In both cases we've used some operational cash to lubricate the way."

Whitfield grunted. Among other things, Whitfield sat on several intelligence agency oversight committees, and knew all too well that the CIA had any number of undisclosed income sources it could leverage to achieve its ends.

"We've arranged for one of our most seasoned hands to accompany them," Cornett added, "and they'll have access to a helicopter we chartered in Thailand to perform the search. Only we will know their true objective."

"What's your take on the timeline?" Whitfield asked.

"Three to four days. Weather permitting."

"Why so long?"

"It's not a small area, Senator. They need to be methodical."

Whitfield sighed and looked over at Sedgewick. "Anything I left out?"

Sedgewick steepled his fingers and looked over them. "Why all the secrecy? Why not just ask Laos to do a search and rescue effort? I'm not sure I understand the need for subterfuge. The senator's daughter went down in a private plane. I'd think that would be enough."

All eyes swiveled to Cornett.

"The senator requested that we handle this subtly," Cornett said. "There are fears that Christine's absence could be used by hostile factions to exert leverage over him, or at least to capitalize on an unfortunate situation."

"Assuming she's alive," Whitfield said.

"But the odds go down every day the plane's not found," Sedgewick fired back. At twenty-nine, having graduated at the top of his class at Harvard with a JD from Harvard Law, he was a rising star, and brilliant, if somewhat abrasive.

"I've balanced that against the other issues in play," Whitfield said, "and frankly, the likelihood of her having survived a crash, given the terrain, the size of the plane, and all other known factors, is slim to none. After speaking to experts, I've resigned myself to that fact. But I want to be certain. It's one thing to think you know, another to have confirmation."

Sedgewick frowned slightly. "What other issues, sir?" he asked. "I can't offer a valid opinion without all the facts."

Whitfield eyed the two CIA men. "We've received some chatter from the Chinese end that implies that she fell in with the wrong crowd. She was dating a fellow over there who might, and I stress the word might, have been involved in…might have been up to no good."

"I had no idea," Sedgewick said, his voice low. "You mean something illegal? Smuggling? Drugs?"

"I don't have all the information yet, but apparently he was an undesirable. That's all we know." Whitfield paused. "We believe he was also on the plane."

"Then it might not have been accidental?"

"Anything's possible. We don't know. But it's a working theory I have." Whitfield stood, signaling the meeting was at an end. "Gentlemen, I will expect regular updates as this unfolds. And I appreciate your assistance in the matter. It's obviously deeply troubling, and the sooner I have answers, the sooner I will be at peace."

"We'll do everything we can, Senator," Cornett assured him. "This is a top priority."

"I appreciate it, gentlemen. Give my warm regards to the director."

"I will."

Sedgewick showed the CIA men out and then headed back to the chamber. Whitfield was behind his desk, poring over the bill. He would normally have had one of his aides write a summary for him, but he wanted something to take his mind off Christine's accident, and work was his favored diversion.

Sedgewick cleared his throat, and the senator fixed the younger man with a concerned stare. "Sir, don't take offense, but is there something you haven't told me about the Christine situation?"

"Why do you say that?" Whitfield deflected.

"Nothing. Just an impression."

"I suggest you get your antennae tuned, Alan. You're normally more on point than that."

"Yes, sir. Again, I meant no disrespect."

"None taken. This has been difficult for everyone involved. I know you don't see the wisdom of conducting the search the way I am, but you'll have to believe that I have valid reasons."

"Yes, of course, sir."

"I trust that puts the matter to bed?"

"Absolutely. Will there be anything else?"

"I'll need the notes for the meeting tomorrow on my desk by eight forty-five." Whitfield was chairing a Department of Defense oversight committee that was dealing with trillions that had gone missing from the DOD over the last decades. Tomorrow was the commencement of deliberations on whether there should be formal hearings on the matter. The morning before the 9-11 terrorist attack brought down the twin towers in New York, Donald Rumsfeld had announced that there were over two trillion dollars unaccounted for at the DOD. That investigation had ended abruptly the next morning when the section of the Pentagon that housed the staff researching the money trail had been killed by the plane strike. Following the attacks, the administration had been galvanized into action, and the missing money had been back-burnered as the country geared up for war.

But questions kept arising, and the press had grown more inquisitive as years had passed – and now the American public wanted answers.

Which made Whitfield's job all the harder, because there were national security issues at play, as well as matters that might affect confidence in the country's leadership.

Whitfield had a reputation as tough but fair, and was one of the few members of the Senate who was respected on both sides of the aisle. At some point, a presidential run wasn't out of the question, so he needed to be balanced in his steerage of the committee, showing no undue favoritism to any of the parties involved.

Tomorrow morning, he would be in the hot seat.

A position he was more than familiar with, but which weighed heavily on him with the loss of his daughter.

He sighed again and glanced wistfully at a carafe brimming with eighteen-year-old Scotch on his bookshelf, and then lost himself in his work, the complex nuance of the bill commanding all his attention if he was to absorb it in time for the vote.

# Chapter Fifteen

*Bangkok, Thailand*

Alex faded in and out of consciousness. The painkillers pumping through him blunted the worst of the agony from his injuries but left him in a fugue state, a Neverland of blurred images and confused impressions. The air smelled like industrial cleaner, astringent and laced with the peculiar medicinal smell particular to hospitals. Beside him, a monitor beeped with each beat of his heart, and he registered the pressure of a pulse oximeter on his finger as he shifted on the bed.

He cracked an eye open and saw daylight. So he hadn't been out that long. Assuming it was still the same day. He tried to bring his wrist into focus and then gave up when he realized his watch was missing.

Alex replayed the moments before impact again and again in his imagination, searching the impressions for anything that might hint at who had been driving the car that struck him. But it was no good. All he remembered was a glimpse of a grill, and then the world tilted as he flew through the air, pain overloading his synapses from his ruined legs and the impact of his landing.

He cursed the effects of the drugs, and prayed that he hadn't sustained any permanent brain injury that was causing the memory glitch. Bones they could always pin together, he knew from friends who'd taken bad hits while on their Harleys, but the old gray matter was an entirely different matter.

The door opened and a nurse entered. At least, Alex thought she was a nurse. For some reason he couldn't get his eyes to focus. Eye. His left lid seemed to be stuck shut.

The woman spoke to him in broken English, but he couldn't make out what she was saying. The words seemed to distort as she talked, sounding more like a vacuum cleaner's whine than conversation. Alex groaned and closed his eye again – he'd find out soon enough what she was going on about, if it was important.

When he came to again, he was moving. The harsh white glare of overhead fluorescent lights strobed above him as he was rolled down a hall. He could just make out two orderlies wheeling him along the corridor, a plasma bag connected to the gurney and draining into his arm. Maybe he was going into surgery? The throb from his legs was muted from the morphine, and he hoped that whoever was making the calls wouldn't amputate them. The thought of being legless sent a spike of fear through him, and he struggled to speak.

"My…legs…"

The effort was wasted, because the gurney's forward momentum didn't slow. He tried again, but what emanated from his mouth was a strangled moan in place of words. He decided to save his strength for battles he could win.

Eventually he felt the gurney slow, and then he was moving through a pair of steel doors. The chilled, relatively dry air changed to warm humidity, and he realized he was outside. The mechanism below his body made a series of loud clacks and pops, and then he felt himself lifted. He opened his eye again and saw that he was now in the back of a vehicle – an ambulance. So they weren't taking him to get his legs cut off. But if not, why was he being put through the trauma of a move?

Before he could muddle through the puzzle, the engine started and one of the orderlies closed the rear doors. Alex tried to move his arms to assess the damage, but all he managed was to flop his right one around like a beached smelt.

The ambulance began moving and he stopped trying. There would be time enough to learn how badly mangled he was. He suspected it wasn't pretty, but there wasn't much he could do about it now.

The ride was smooth, for which he was grateful, and he didn't even notice when he slipped from the present into the narcotic dream state in which he'd spent the last few hours. When he was jarred back to consciousness, he wanted to complain, and then realized that the ambulance had stopped.

The rear doors opened and two men lifted the gurney out. He heard them speaking to each other – but again it sounded odd, distorted. He drifted away as the opiate warmth washed over him, and this time dreamed of being a child, running through a field back home in Texas – he was five or six, he thought, because his family had moved to Ohio when he was seven, and the landscape had changed for the worse. Someone was running ahead of him, and he could make out his father, his gait confident and strong, his bristly hair thick against the vivid blue of the summer sky.

The scene darkened as the sun's warming rays changed to something more ominous, and then he was in a different place – another hospital room, but this time holding his father's hand, which was now frail as a bird's wing, the skin nearly translucent, the tremor in his desperately clutching fingers a byproduct of the poison the doctors had pumped through him in an effort to arrest the malignancies eating him alive. Alex's gaze roamed down an arm bruised beyond recognition from IV cannulas, shots, and blood draws, and he could almost taste the salty tear that worked its way down his unlined cheek, young and idealistic as his father's had once been; and then the scene seemed to accelerate away from him, down a long tunnel whose walls were closing in as his speed increased to a dizzy blur.

He came to with a start, pain lancing through his head. For an instant he didn't understand what had happened, and then he realized that something – no, someone – had slapped him. He forced his eye open and found an Asian man in street clothes glaring down at him. Alex fought to force his reluctant lens into focus and, in spite of the drugs, felt a chill creep up his ruined spine. The man's eyes were the color of lead, flat and uncaring, and Alex knew in an instant that this was no doctor.

Jiao nodded slowly at the realization he saw in the CIA man's stare. When he spoke, his accented English was musical with the singsong cadence of his native tongue.

"The pain meds will be out of your system within a few hours, my friend. Then we will have a talk, and you can share with me everything you know about your operation."

Alex's eye widened in horror at the words, which his brain had no problem deciphering, and realized with dismay that his ravaged body was now the least of his problems. There was no question about the man's intent, and Alex offered a prayer to a God he didn't believe in to spare him the torment that would surely come – before he told the Asian everything, which he knew he would eventually.

In the end, Alex died a hundred times before he finally stopped breathing.

# Chapter Sixteen

The mood at the hotel was glum as Spencer, Drake, and Allie waited for Uncle Pete to arrive. Spencer had called their guide after returning to the hotel and told him about Alex. The Thai was shocked, and explained to Spencer that he'd need to confer with his superiors before any action could be taken. An hour later, Uncle Pete left a message for them all to be in the lobby by no later than two – they were shipping out.

"Any idea how long it will take to get to Chiang Rai?" Spencer asked.

"I can look it up," Allie said, waggling her phone at him. She tapped in her query and waited for the answer. "Says here…hmm…once we're out of Bangkok, maybe eight to ten hours, depending on how fast we drive."

"You've already seen Uncle Pete's skills," Spencer said.

"So we'll be there about midnight," Drake guessed.

"Midnight tomorrow, more likely," Allie added.

"Why don't we fly?" Drake asked. "I wonder if we can get a charter that doesn't require us to go through a security scan?"

Allie checked her watch. "I can ask the concierge to make some calls."

Drake shook his head. "How are you going to manage that? You can't really say we're gunrunning and want to dodge the authorities, can you?"

"Let's ask Uncle Pete," Spencer suggested. "Not that I don't want to spend the next ten hours on the road. But it seems like we're wasting time we don't have. Whoever ran Alex down is out there, and for all we know, we're next."

"Why, though? It makes no sense," Drake said.

"Maybe someone recognized him? Someone with a grudge?" Allie speculated.

"There are only a few possibilities," Spencer said. "The first is that it was an accident – someone either drunk or not paying attention while they were texting, who lost control and freaked when they hit Alex. The second is that it was deliberate and they wanted to take him out, either because they recognized him or because of something we haven't been told about our little jaunt."

"Sounds like you think there might be a third possibility," Drake said.

"Yeah. If I hadn't gotten lucky, the car would have hit both of us. So it could have been that I was the target all along, and Alex was just in the wrong place at the right time."

"Why would anyone want to flatten you, Spencer?" Allie asked.

"God knows. I mean, I made plenty of enemies in past lives, but nobody comes to mind in Bangkok."

"Angry ex?" Drake suggested.

"I'm serious. I mean, it's a very low probability, which is why it's number three. I actually think it's likeliest it was an accident."

"Why?"

"Because if they wanted to off either one of us, they could have just shot us. Few pros would opt for a car as a murder weapon."

They mulled over Spencer's words until Uncle Pete appeared through the oversized entry doors, his face tight and his usual half smirk missing.

"We go now," he said by way of greeting.

"Uncle Pete, we have an idea, and you're probably just the man for the job," Spencer said.

Uncle Pete's face was unreadable. "What you want?"

"We were thinking it was a nice day to fly instead of drive."

"You crazy. Can't fly with stuff. Remember?"

"We were thinking you might know someone with a plane we could charter to take us there, including our luggage, without getting too curious about what we were carrying."

Awareness dawned in Uncle Pete's eyes. "Ah. I see. Maybe. But gonna be lot of baht."

"I'm not feeling price sensitive, in light of the uncertainty on the ground here at the moment," Spencer said. "Just get us a plane. We'll take care of the rest."

Uncle Pete busied himself with a flurry of calls, and showed up in the lobby with a triumphant expression half an hour later. "We got plane. Leave in two hours. Take maybe that long get to airport with traffic. Terrible. We go now."

"Which airport?" Spencer asked.

"Don Mueang. North side."

Uncle Pete whistled and a bellman ran over with his cart. Spencer refused to let the man take the duffle, and followed them out to the waiting SUV with it in hand.

The drive took just over an hour, and they were pleasantly surprised to discover that the private jet terminal was sumptuous and quiet. Uncle Pete guided them to one of the windows overlooking the runways and pointed to a Hawker 800XP being fueled by two airport workers. "That plane. We pay now."

"How much?" Drake asked.

"Dollars? 'Bout ten thousand."

Drake looked at Allie. "I only brought ten cash. Didn't want to have to declare anything."

"Me too."

"Split it with you?"

"I'm game."

Uncle Pete counted the money and then disappeared for ten minutes. When he returned, he was all smiles. "I tip security. They not interested look at bags. Say your face trustworthy."

"I get that a lot," Drake said.

"Not you. Her."

"Oh."

"How big a tip?" Allie asked.

"Five hundred dollars. You give on plane, okay?"

Spencer winked at Allie. "I could learn a lot from Uncle Pete."

"I have a feeling the lesson's not over yet. And it will no doubt be pricey."

They toted their bags to the plane, the security workers blissfully otherwise occupied with a judiciously timed cigarette break, and loaded onto the jet. After a smooth takeoff, Uncle Pete filled them in on the discussion he'd had with his control in the U.S., who had told him they would try to get someone to replace Alex as soon as possible, but that Uncle Pete should act as their liaison in the meantime. That made sense, given the amount of time that had already gone by and the sense of urgency implicit in finding the plane.

"And we get permits. So ready to go," Uncle Pete finished from his position in the bulkhead seat.

"Then we can start the search tomorrow?"

"You betcha. We use airfield at Chiang Rai as base, yes? Close to border. Helicopter waiting, start tomorrow morning."

"Perfect," Spencer said. "Any word on Alex?"

"In hospital. Many broke bones. But look like will make it, for sure."

"That's good," Allie said.

"Did headquarters have any thoughts on the incident?" Spencer asked.

Uncle Pete shook his head. "Say keep eyes open. Thailand dangerous place sometimes."

"That's helpful."

"Don't worry. I take good care of you."

The flight was smooth and they touched down without fanfare, only to discover that their hotel, the best in town according to Uncle Pete, was a rattrap. He apologized but pointed out that the town was mainly frequented by backpackers and hippies, so their choice of accommodations was limited. After dropping their bags off, they met him outside the hotel and went as a group to dinner, Uncle Pete in the lead, marching in his baggy pants and sandals as though on a mission from God.

Jiao waited in the shade beneath a banyan tree across the street from the hotel until the Americans had made their way down the teeming road, motorcycles and tuk-tuks buzzing at breakneck speed in what passed for the backwater town's evening rush hour. He drew a final drag on his cigarette, crushed it underfoot, and ambled toward the hotel, a black nylon backpack hanging from his shoulder, his clothes those of a casual tourist. He'd been alerted to their departure from Bangkok and on a charter flight of his own twenty minutes after they'd taken off.

The hotel was all one level, built around a parking lot, with the office at the front. He'd followed the group from the airport, but hadn't had time to reconnoiter the grounds properly. A glance at the office told him he'd be spotted if he entered that way, so he continued walking until he rounded the block, and stopped at an overgrown field that backed against the hotel perimeter wall.

Twilight cast long shadows as the sun dropped behind the mountains. Jiao took his time, and when it was dark enough that he was confident he wouldn't be spotted, he crossed the expanse until he was at the base of the wall.

A quick perusal convinced him that it was no good. There were no footholds he could use, and the razor wire coiled along the top would prevent him from climbing over, even if he contrived a way to scale the ten-foot-high wall. He cursed under his breath and moved back to the side street – he'd hoped to avoid his alternative plan, but would now have to implement it if he was to be successful before the farangs made it back.

The office door swung open with a creak and an attached bell tinkled. A short woman shaped like a brick emerged from the office and moved to the reception counter.

"Yes?" she asked, in a raspy voice seasoned by a lifetime of smoking.

"Do you have any rooms?" he asked in broken Thai.

"Yes. For how long?"

"Only one night. I'm off to see the temples tomorrow."

She pointed to a board behind her with prices in baht and dollars. Jiao nodded, removed a thick wad of currency from his pocket, and peeled off several bills. "A quiet room, if that's possible," he requested. "No parties. I'm up early."

"You want smoking or non?"

"Smoking."

She nodded and handed him a key and a towel. "Check out at eleven. Soda machine outside by the pool."

Jiao skirted the parking lot, pretending to look for his room. When he found it, he paused in front of the door and studied the lock. He was relieved to see that he could jimmy it in his sleep, the mechanism at least twenty years old.

Once in the room, he moved to the far window and pulled the dingy curtains aside, but it had corroding iron bars on the exterior, so using it to access the other rooms wasn't viable. He quickly unpacked his bag and removed a set of picks and a flat metal slim jim that he slipped inside his windbreaker. The picks went into his jacket pocket, and then he was ready.

The parking lot was still. He'd already confirmed on his walk that he wouldn't be visible to the office if he stuck close to the building. He pulled his door closed behind him and strolled unhurriedly to the closest of the Americans' doors.

Ten seconds later he was inside the dark room. He hurried to the backpack sitting on the bed and extracted a small disk from his pocket – a tracking chip with a built-in battery supply good for at least thirty days. He felt along the bag until he found a small flapped compartment on the inside lining, and then pulled a pocketknife from his jacket and sliced the stitching above it. When he had created sufficient space, he forced the chip inside and shook the bag until the disk fell to the bottom, between the lining and the outer shell. If the stitching was noticed, the instinct would be to dismiss it as shoddy manufacturing.

He powered on his phone and saw the orange blinking icon on a satellite image that confirmed the chip was transmitting. Jiao smiled in the darkness. Would that all his tasks were so easily performed.

At the door, he listened intently for signs of life outside. When he was confident he was alone, he slipped from the room and locked the door behind him, and then headed for the office to get a restaurant recommendation, his time now reduced to waiting patiently until the group located the plane.

Once seated in the outdoor dining area of a family-style restaurant several blocks away, he placed a call to Xiaoping.

"It is done."

"Very well."

"Any progress on our project?"

"He claims he should be in within hours. But that's what he said yesterday, so while promising, celebration would be premature."

"I will report in when I have something to share."

"Good luck."

He disconnected and stared at the phone, a knockoff iPhone manufactured on the northern border using the schematics of the genuine article. He personally thought that the tracking of the Americans was a waste of resources, but he understood Xiaoping's logic. It was possible that there was a hard disk or a flash drive that had survived the crash, and if so, there might be valuable data they could use to penetrate the DOD's network. While Jiao believed it to be a wild-goose chase, he hoped that he would be proven wrong.

That, however, wasn't how life worked in his experience, and he distrusted anything that was too easy. But he was willing to reserve judgment until he'd completed his mission and seen the wreckage with his own eyes, assuming it was ever located. Until then he would do his duty without question, and hope that the computer technician would be successful in his efforts. That days had gone by without any result wasn't promising; but the man was a genius, and if he thought it was possible, then perhaps it was.

Jiao ordered steamed fish over rice, foregoing the customary spices with which the Thais polluted everything, and sat back waiting for the server to bring him his beer – a small reward for a small success, but one he was looking forward to after hours enduring the humid heat.

# Chapter Seventeen

*Washington, D.C.*

General Brad Holt strode to his car, parked in the Defense Intelligence Agency's security lot, and after a sweep of the area, started his vehicle and pulled through the gate. Twenty minutes later he was changing from his uniform into sweats at the apartment he kept for dalliances, and ten minutes after that he was at the gym. Two other men with military bearings and the clipped hair of career officers sat in the dressing room. After a hard look from Holt, they followed him onto the outdoor terrace, where several tables and chairs awaited them, the area empty.

"All right. Let's make this quick. You're both up to speed with the train wreck in Thailand, correct?" Holt asked.

The shorter of the men, Colonel Sam Daniels, nodded. "Our sources at the CIA have no idea what went wrong. This came out of left field."

"They couldn't find their asses with both hands," growled the third officer, Major Henry Lorre.

"Be that as it may, we have to assume they aren't the only ones on the game board now. Until proven otherwise, we have to proceed as though there are unidentified hostiles," Holt said.

"Right, but it's not our play. What can we do differently?"

All three men were members of the Department of Defense

covert operations group: the Defense Clandestine Services, responsible for, among other things, the military's black ops and wet work – assassinations, torture, kidnappings, terrorist attacks against unfriendly regimes. While officially the group didn't exist, the reality was that the CIA often acted in its own best interests, for motives known only to its leaders, and the DOD sometimes needed to employ tactics that, if Congress had been aware of them, would have been shut down and their planners jailed. Their recently aborted mission in Pakistan was a classic example: word of it had been leaked online by a website that delighted in breaking top-secret information – information that in this case could have only come from one place – the DOD's own servers.

"I know we said we'd stay out of this one, but I think the situation has escalated to the point where we can't take a passive role anymore. We need to send our own people in."

"I thought the idea was to keep it deniable."

"That hasn't changed."

"I disagree. My vote is to watch and wait. We try to launch a concurrent effort, and it could blow up in our faces," Daniels said.

Holt considered the input. "What do you think, Henry?"

"Much as I'm inclined to want to take control, I don't see anything we can do that's not already being done. We have to trust that if there's something to find, the supposed experts will find it. Ferrying in a bunch of commandos is unlikely to end well, or we would have already done it."

"So we do nothing? That's the consensus?" Holt asked.

Both his subordinates nodded. Holt hated that answer, but knew in his gut it was the right one, even if his instinct was to commission outside contractors to go in. The DOD often hired third-party organizations to carry out more sensitive missions, especially when it wanted deniability, which was essential in this instance. But Holt would go with his group's advice – for now.

The men went back inside, where Holt would pump iron for an hour while the others returned to their offices. Holt moved out onto the floor without saying anything more to them, selected a chest press, and pegged the weights at the maximum. Even at fifty-three he was built like a bear and had the strength of two younger men, and he was fighting the inevitable ravages of time every step of the way.

He did three sets of twenty reps and moved to the next machine in his circuit, his mind working over the problem he was facing. What should have been straightforward had turned into a downed plane with a high-profile civilian involved. And now the CIA man on site had been taken out. If it could get any worse, he couldn't see how.

After a career in the military, Holt was a realist, under no illusions about how things worked or anyone's competence. He had more ugly secrets swirling around in his head than anyone should, but that was the life he'd chosen. Someone had to make the tough decisions – weigh the unthinkable and authorize the unmentionable. It went with the program. Civilians didn't understand it, and he didn't expect them to. Ignorance was bliss, and it was better for everyone if they focused on buying more unnecessary crap and voting for the talking heads of the professional liars who wrote their scripts. Holt had nothing but contempt for the population he was charged with protecting, and he did so without expecting their thanks. That they would have hated him for what he did in their name was immaterial. They were fat, dumb children, to be treated as such.

Holt moved to the barbell area and began his curls, his arms burning from lactic acid rushing to the damaged muscles. He forced himself to continue through the pain. That which didn't kill him made him stronger, and he would approach this latest challenge like he did all others – fighting. The hearings had been a major irritant, but the DOD had been able to stonewall the politicians sufficiently so that no irreparable damage was done.

But the situation in Laos was a wild card that bore watching. If there was damaging material that had survived the crash, and it fell into the wrong hands...

Holt shook off the anxiety that seared through his stomach and moved to the pull-up bars, where he would do a hundred, as he had every other day for the last thirty-something years. As he began his routine, he comforted himself with the thought that exercising restraint when there were as many unknowns as they faced was often more effective than going in with guns a-blazing.

That said, he would be monitoring the CIA-sponsored group's progress with interest, and planned to make a few calls once he was finished that would ready a crisis team from one of his military contractors and get it into position in Thailand.

"Just in case," Holt said to himself. "Better safe than sorry."

# Chapter Eighteen

*Chiang Rai, Thailand*

Dawn broke over the mountains east of Chiang Rai, painting the sky with a neon display of mango and pink, high streaks of clouds glowing as the sun rose. Uncle Pete sat in the front of a van with faded taxi markers on its doors, and Allie, Drake, and Spencer occupied the rear bench seat. The shabby vehicle bounced along a rutted road to the old airport, long out of use for anything but occasional charter flights, and the jumping-off point for their helicopter ride.

They rolled through an open gateway whose rusting barrier had been pushed to the side, and proceeded to where an ancient Bell 206B helicopter waited on the cracked pad, its mottled green paint peeling in spots. The logo of Thai Fantasy Air on its side looked as though a child had drawn it using crayons in the dark. Spencer looked skeptically at the aircraft and addressed Uncle Pete. "Are you frigging kidding me?" he demanded.

"It top shelf helicopter. Finest kind in area. Pilot famous," Uncle Pete said, but his eyes were glued to the aircraft, and the doubt in his tone betrayed his words.

"That thing's a relic."

"Means it work good for years."

"Uncle Pete, it's older than I am," Spencer fired back.

"You still got plenty good game, right? Same with helo."

The cab driver coasted to a stop and they climbed out. A middle-aged Thai man with a completely bald head approached, his mirrored aviator glasses winking in the strengthening sunlight. Uncle Pete said something in Thai and the man laughed good-naturedly before turning to eye Allie in a way that gave her the creeps.

"Welcome, welcome. I'm Daeng. Nice to meet you," the man said, offering a courteous wai to the four of them.

Daeng's English was orders of magnitude better than Uncle Pete's. He explained the grid approach they would use for the search, pointing to a map he'd ceremoniously unfurled. Each quadrant would receive a thorough inspection at a slow hover. When he was through with his orientation talk, he drew himself up. "Any questions?"

Spencer nodded. "I notice you avoided the section by the Myanmar border. Why?"

"Oh, we don't want to go there," Daeng explained. "That's controlled by the Shan State Army. They're as likely to take potshots as they are to ignore us. They have serious weaponry – .50-caliber machine guns, RPGs, you name it."

"But that's Myanmar. Isn't it controlled by the military?" Drake asked.

"No. There are a number of groups that operate there, each more dangerous than the other. You have the drug gangs, the Shan State, rogue militia, factions of the Myanmar Army that deserted or are working their own schemes, the works. All armed to the teeth."

Allie looked from Spencer to Drake. "Nobody mentioned that in Malibu," she said.

"It appears our friends might have left something out," Drake acknowledged. "Let's hope there's nothing more they forgot to tell us."

"So what good does the permit do us?" Spencer asked. "I thought it was essential to overfly that area. It sounds like we're flying into a combat zone."

"Well, my helo's known to most of them, so we'll be okay as long as we don't venture into this area," Daeng said, tapping his finger on the map. "We can work around it. I can get us high enough so we should be able to see across it."

"What's the point, if we can't go in to verify what we're seeing?"

"Don't worry. I guide on ground," Uncle Pete said.

"Wait. If you know the territory, you knew about all the armed groups. Why didn't you say anything?" Allie demanded.

Uncle Pete shrugged. "None of my business. I following orders. Loyal ant, Uncle Pete."

"How dangerous is it?" Drake asked Daeng.

"Since the U.S. invaded Afghanistan, heroin production there went from nothing to more than the total world demand, so the groups here in the triangle aren't growing nearly as many poppies as they used to. The drug gangs and the rebel armies have shifted to methamphetamine production, which is way cheaper and easier to deal with. So we're not in that much danger of accidentally overflying a poppy field, which might provoke an armed response." Daeng paused. "But that's still not a complete guarantee that someone doesn't take a shot at us."

Allie's eyes widened and she glared at Drake. "What did you get us into?"

Daeng patted the side of the aircraft. "The helo's got an inch of steel plate on the underside. Welded it myself. It'll stop most rounds, so it's not as bad as it sounds."

"How about the glass?" Drake asked.

"Bulletproof glass is too expensive. But I have yet to get shot."

"Then why the steel?" Spencer asked.

"Insurance. It cuts down on the payload I can haul, but it's like a seat belt – it's annoying until you need it, and then you're grateful."

"Your English is very good," Allie said.

"My father was American. GI. So I grew up bilingual until he left us when I was ten."

"I…I'm sorry," Allie said softly.

"Oh, don't be. If you knew my mother, who I love like my own blood, you'd think he was a saint for sticking it out that long. I would have been gone years before."

Spencer eyed the map. "Looks like a lot of the area they could have gone down in is on the west side of the Mekong River. In Myanmar. How do we search that section?"

"Very carefully."

"You're kidding."

"You asked," Daeng said with a shrug. "Like I said, there's no other way but to try to stay high enough so we're not in easy range. But look at the bright side – at least they don't have anti-aircraft guns or fighter planes."

"Sky's filled with silver linings," Drake muttered.

Spencer moved to the helicopter. "What year is this thing?"

"1977. A good year."

"Not for music," Spencer said. "Who maintains it?"

"I've got a guy. Ex-serviceman. Pretty good. It's been trouble-free, for the most part."

"Where did you get it?"

"Thai air force. They retired her when she turned twenty-five."

"How many hours have you clocked?" Spencer drilled.

Daeng smiled and removed his glasses. His eyes held no trace of humor. "Your people vetted me. They felt I was more than qualified. You want to look for someone else who'll fly that area, knock yourself out. I could use the extra sleep. Just say the word."

"He top good pilot," Uncle Pete declared enthusiastically, as though his pronouncement sealed the deal.

Spencer shook his head and patted the duffle. "At least we've got something to shoot back with, if it comes to that."

"Let's hope it doesn't. Nobody wants to start a war. Bad for business. I'm just telling you the risks, is all," Daeng said. He stared at Spencer for a long beat. "We through with the audition?"

Spencer nodded. "Looks like it. How long will it take to make it to the first quadrant?"

"Maybe twenty, twenty-five minutes." Daeng checked his watch. "Let's saddle up. Time's a-wasting. We'll burn an hour getting back and fueling up, so the sooner we're in the air, the more territory we can cover."

They followed him to the helicopter and climbed in. Drake

wrinkled his nose as he tossed his backpack onto the rear compartment floor and took one of the two front seats. "It smells like rot."

"Don't forget perspiration. I'm definitely getting sweat," Allie added from the bench seat in the passenger area. She laid her backpack next to Drake's and strapped in. "This is gross."

Daeng took the pilot's seat and slipped on a headset, and within two minutes they were rising into the air, the cabin trembling like a hobo with delirium tremens. Drake looked back at them over his shoulder with a concerned expression.

Daeng laughed when he caught Drake's discomfiture. "She'll smooth out soon. Just temperamental in her old age."

"Very reassuring," Spencer said as he unzipped the duffle and removed one of the AKMs.

Allie grimaced. "You really think we'll need those?"

"You remember how to work yours, right?" he asked, handing her one of the H&Ks after slapping a magazine into place. She looked at the fire selector switch and verified it was in the safe position, and nodded.

"I don't have to tell you this is doing nothing for my nerves, do I?" Allie said.

Spencer eyed Uncle Pete. "You know how to use one of these?" he asked, patting the AKM.

Uncle Pete nodded solemnly. "Like ride bicycle."

"Don't shoot our feet off," Spencer warned, and handed him the other Kalashnikov.

The angle of the Bell changed, and soon they were flying over banana fields, which transitioned into jungle as they traveled north. When they reached the starting point for the first quadrant, Spencer tapped Daeng on the shoulder. "Maybe we should start at the northern edge of their last known position?"

"Bad idea. I want to try to avoid the Myanmar side as long as possible," Daeng called over the sound of the turbine.

Spencer sat back as the helicopter slowed to a crawl. The altimeter read twenty-five hundred feet – which, given the elevations, put them no more than eight hundred feet off the jungle floor. Drake raised his binoculars to his eyes and began searching the area. Allie and Spencer joined him, peering through the cloudy glass as the chopper droned forward.

"We're looking for anything that might be a crashed plane – wreckage, a furrow in the canopy as it crashed, whatever. Call out if you spot anything, no matter how insignificant it might seem," Spencer said.

The first quadrant took four hours to cover, after which they agreed to try for another two hours and then return for fuel and a quick lunch. By the time they were back on the ground, they were more than ready to stretch their legs. Daeng walked over to a waiting fuel truck as Uncle Pete called the taxi driver they'd used to get there. Ten minutes later they were on the way to a local restaurant the driver assured them was the best in all Thailand, oblivious to Drake's and Allie's skeptical frowns.

The second half of the day went very much like the first, and other than several remote villages and an occasional hill tribesman on one of the innumerable trails, they didn't see anything promising. By the time they called it a day, the magnitude of their task was obvious, and they were quiet and thoughtful as they returned to Chiang Rai, grateful for the breeze through the half-open windows that passed for air-conditioning in the ancient helicopter, though it was still woefully inadequate under the relentless blaze of the tropical sun.

# Chapter Nineteen

*Washington, D.C.*

The streets of Georgetown were crowded with pedestrians on their way to dinner or heading home after a late day at the office. Early diners were already seated in the restaurants along picturesque M Street as Alan Sedgewick strolled along, slowing to admire the groups of female university students ambling in the warm breeze.

Sedgewick had changed from his business attire into a rugby shirt, jeans, and a frayed Baltimore Orioles baseball cap, and appeared to be almost as young as the students around him – perhaps a late bloomer working on a doctoral thesis. He looked nothing like a top aide on the Hill, which was the point; he was embarking on a dangerous course, he knew, from which there could be no turning back, and he wanted to avoid attracting attention.

At the corner of Thirty-First Street, he jaywalked along with a dozen others and continued along the block until he reached his destination – a popular French bistro well away from his usual haunts, where the possibility of being recognized was slim. He dutifully waited for the couple ahead to be shown to a table, and spotted his rendezvous as he shifted from foot to foot: a stocky male Sedgewick's age with black curly hair, nerdy glasses, and a pallor that spoke of long hours in front of a computer screen.

Sedgewick moved to the table, and the man looked up.

"Alan, good to see you. Please, sit."

"Larry, been too long," Sedgewick said.

"Yeah, well, life does have a habit of getting in the way, doesn't it?" Larry gave Sedgewick an appraising glance. "You look good. Being a parasite agrees with you."

"Long hours for crap pay."

"They don't really feature that in the sales material, do they?"

Sedgewick shrugged. "I knew what I was getting into."

"How long do you see yourself doing it, though? It's a young man's game."

"Another few years. Then it's onto the lobbyist gravy train. That's where the money is. Only way to make easier cash is panhandling or televangelism."

"Or working on Wall Street."

Sedgewick made a face. "I'd turn tricks in rest-stop bathrooms before I'd stoop that low. I have *some* morals."

Both men laughed. Sedgewick and Larry Burnell had gone to college together, Larry pursuing journalism while Sedgewick had gone into public service. Now Larry was a reporter for the *Washington Post*, trying to make a name for himself and dreaming of winning a Pulitzer for an earth-shattering story that so far had eluded him.

They studied the menu and made small talk and, after ordering, got down to business. Larry sipped his chardonnay and sat back. "So to what do I owe this pleasure? Not that hanging out isn't reward enough, but you mentioned on the phone you had a story?"

"Might have a story," Sedgewick corrected. "First of all, let's establish some ground rules, okay? Everything I tell you is off the record until I give you the go-ahead to run with it. Deal?"

"Sure. This must be pretty serious if you want to muzzle me. Why even tell me at all?"

"I want to bounce it off you and see what you think."

"Fine. Shoot."

"You know I work for Whitfield, right?"

Larry nodded. "It came up."

"His daughter went down in a private plane crash a few days ago. In Laos."

"What? That's the first I heard of it. But…that's the big secret?"

"Part of it. They've kept a lid on the news so far."

"Why?"

"That's where it gets strange." Sedgewick paused. "You know Whitfield's on the committee investigating the DOD, right?"

"Of course. The liar's club, we call it in the business."

"Well, a couple of CIA rankers showed up, and apparently Whitfield's got them looking for the plane wreckage on the sly."

Larry considered the information. "That doesn't make sense. It would be in his best interests to have a full-blown aerial reconnaissance over the flight path. Pull out all the stops."

"That's what I say. Something's fishy. There's more to the story, and I think I know what it is. And it scares the hell out of me, because we're talking about…treason."

"What? Who – Whitfield? He's as red, white, and blue as they come."

"That's what I've always thought, but now I have my doubts. I think we could be looking at something as big as Snowden. Maybe as big as Watergate."

The waiter arrived with their dishes, and they remained silent until he'd left.

"Do you have any evidence?" Larry asked, after confirming the adjacent tables were still empty.

"I'm collecting it."

"Care to tell me what you suspect?"

"Not until I have it documented. If I'm wrong…let's just say I don't want to say anything more. I just want to know whether this is something you could run with if I hand everything off to you once I've got definitive proof."

"Of course."

"And would you keep me anonymous? If word leaked, I'd be finished in this town."

"I'd treat it as a confidential source. Wild horses couldn't drag it out of me." Larry eyed him. "Dude, you look pretty stressed. This must be huge."

"You have no idea."

The two men ate quickly, and when they were done, Larry signaled for the bill. "What kind of time frame are we talking?"

"I'm hoping within forty-eight hours."

"Wow. That fast, huh?"

"It's the story of the decade, Larry. Total game changer."

"You angling for a slice of the book royalties? Because I'm a whore. Name your price."

"Nah. I'll be hiding on an island somewhere warm until it all blows over."

Larry paid the bill and they rose. Sedgewick led him to the front entrance, and they shook hands inside the waiting area. "How do you want to do this?" Larry asked.

"I'll call, and we'll do a handoff in person."

"My phone's always on."

"Perfect."


Outside the restaurant, a dark blue van was parked in a loading zone. In the rear, two men exchanged a glance.

"You heard it. We have it on tape," the older of the pair said.

"We do," his partner agreed.

"We have to neutralize him."

"Agreed."

"I'll get authorization." The older man placed a call on an encrypted cell phone and, when the line picked up, spoke softly: "We activated his cell remotely and recorded the whole thing. It's as we feared." He paused, listening. "No, nothing hard, but it sounds like he'll have something soon. He told the reporter about the daughter, but nothing else." Another pause. "Roger that. We'll take care of it immediately."

The older man hung up and moved into the driver's seat, leaving his partner to shut down the eavesdropping gear as he started the engine.


Sedgewick retraced his steps and made a right toward the Potomac, preoccupied with the road he'd embarked upon. Part of him felt guilty at betraying the senator's trust, but another part was exhilarated. He was doing the right thing in a town where that never happened, where people's actions were overwhelmingly dictated by self-interest and the accumulation of influence and raw power. And it felt good.

He reached the canal and some faint instinct caused the hair on the back of his neck to prickle. A city dweller, he'd developed a keen sense for urban predators, and even in Georgetown, a relatively safe enclave, there was plenty of crime – although nothing like the surrounding areas, many of which had higher murder rates than Detroit. He paused at the corner and glanced over his shoulder, painfully aware of how secluded the area was. All the traffic was on the main streets; the dirt path that bordered the canal was deserted now that night had fallen, even the most motivated joggers having returned home.

Two men in overcoats were walking steadily toward him; overcoats that were out of place on a balmy evening. He tried to resist the impulse to run, but his mind was screaming in protest, clamoring for him to bolt.

Sedgewick opted for a compromise; he turned onto the canal path and began jogging west. He was only a block from the next street, which hopefully would have more traffic. Halfway along the way, he dared a glance over his shoulder.

There was nobody there.

"Little paranoid, aren't we, buddy?" he muttered to himself as he slowed. His imagination was running away with him – he was jumping at shadows, seeing threats behind every tree.

When he reached the street, he took the stairs two at a time and, after a final look back at the empty path, shook off his premonition and grinned at a pretty girl walking by, who returned his smile before continuing along the sidewalk. Normally not a drinker, Sedgewick felt drawn by the Irish pub he passed, and it took considerable willpower to keep from going in and downing a few pints. That wasn't an option – he'd have to be in chambers by six a.m. to get everything he needed accomplished for the senator's morning. A hangover wasn't in the cards until the weekend.

Sedgewick hurried the six blocks to the townhouse he'd inherited from his father on Prospect Street, a quiet block of ancient, brightly colored three-story homes, and pushed his front gate open. Looking over the postage-stamp-sized front yard, encircled by a wrought-iron fence, he made a note to himself to do some necessary housekeeping on Sunday – the grass was overgrown and the place looked shabby.

Once inside the foyer, he switched on the lights and dropped his keys on a side table. He checked for messages on his cell phone as he mounted the steps to his bedroom on the third floor, his footsteps echoing in the empty house, and was reading a text from the senator when he entered the room.

A gloved hand clamped over his mouth, and he dropped the phone as he tried to twist free. He grunted and elbowed his assailant as hard as he could, and then convulsed as an electric shock seared through him from his scalp, short-circuiting his nervous system.

Sedgewick dropped to the floor, spasming, and barely registered a second man holding a stun gun, its prongs stuck into his scalp, the assailant's shoes covered by plastic bags cinched around the ankles with rubber bands.

"Not your lucky day, buddy," the first man said, and then they lifted Sedgewick and carried him into the bathroom.

Thirty minutes later the pair were back in the van, moving toward the Key Bridge.

"Think the coroner will spot the punctures from the stun gun?" the driver asked.

"Nah. We'll see to it that it'll be ruled a suicide. Poor guy. The pressure was too much for him, so he slit his wrists in the bathtub. At least he did it the right way – too many botch it by slicing across, instead of up."

The driver grinned. "Bet he had a hell of a headache before he went out."

"Should have stuck to fetching pencils and sucking up."

"The senator will be devastated."

"A tragic loss." The passenger flicked the red tip of a safety match against his thumb and lit a cigarette.

"Christ. Do you have to do that in here?" the driver complained.

"Sorry. I didn't get enough breastfeeding as a child."

"At least roll down the window."

The passenger complied and blew a stream of nicotine at the moon. He smiled in satisfaction and turned to the driver. "Nice work, Mr. Smith."

"Likewise, Mr. Jones."

# Chapter Twenty

Clouds darkened the night sky as a storm moved north, and the air was heavy with the smell of incipient rain. The airport was still and the surrounding homes in shadows as three figures ran from the brush toward the silhouette of the helicopter parked on the cracking tarmac. All wore muted clothing and moved like wraiths, their footsteps soundless as they neared the aircraft.

Two of the men stood by the fuselage, assault rifles in hand, as the third approached the turbine cowling, a satchel with tools in it hanging from his shoulder.

Fifteen minutes later the three returned to the brush, where their motorcycles had been hidden for a quick getaway. They started the engines and roared off, back toward the porous border from whence they'd come. Their leader, a prominent drug lord, had recognized the helicopter that was working its way toward his meth labs, and had ordered his best men to arrange for it to have maintenance issues. Word had gone out, a small fortune by Myanmar standards had changed hands, and an ex-Myanmar Army sergeant who'd worked on helicopters for four years had agreed to incapacitate the aircraft.

Tomorrow the annoyance would be ended, and the labs could return to normal, their production schedule back on track to meet the endless demand for the stimulant whose annual cash value was estimated to be greater than the entire legal Myanmar economy. With the vast majority of the country's population living in abject poverty, working in the drug trade was the only way for most to support themselves, be it from growing opium or trafficking narcotics, or on the manufacturing side. For all the effort to quash the trade, drugs remained the only viable solution to endemic impoverishment, and sustained most of the hill tribes that lived in the Golden Triangle.

~ ~ ~

Uncle Pete wiped his brow with a stained rag as he sat in the helicopter, waiting for Daeng to start the engine. Dawn had come and gone a half hour earlier, and the whole group had a sense of time passing by, no closer to their objective than they had been the prior day.

Spencer passed out the weapons again as the turbine growled to life, and soon they were hovering over the third of six quadrants on the Laos side of the border. Daeng watched the line of storm clouds over Myanmar with a wary eye as they began the grid search, coaxing the helicopter along ten stories above the tree line. They'd agreed to move in as close as possible the prior day, fearful of missing a telltale sign of wreckage, given that the canopy was so thick in places that they couldn't make out the ground.

"Didn't spend any extra money on the cushions back here, did he?" Allie muttered to Spencer, shifting on the bench seat.

"If I never see this miserable contraption again, it will be too soon," Spencer agreed from beside her.

Uncle Pete remained silent, and Allie's nose wrinkled at the sour smell of alcohol and cigarettes seeping from his pores. Apparently their guide liked a morning eye-opener after a night of festivities on the company account, though Uncle Pete's hangdog expression announced that he was regretting his celebratory enthusiasm today.

Daeng tapped one of the gauges and furrowed his brow.

Drake leaned toward him. "What is it?"

"Our oil temp is in the red. Something's not right," Daeng said, his voice tight.

"That's bad, right?"

Daeng was about to speak when the helicopter shuddered and the turbine groaned. Daeng battled the controls as they lost altitude, and then alarms shrieked in the cockpit as the rotor blades froze and the helicopter plunged at a sickening angle toward the earth.

Allie was screaming when the aircraft crashed into the surface of a tributary that fed the Mekong River, the force of the impact so jarring her gun flew from her hands. The windows shattered, spraying safety glass all over them, and water gushed through the gaps.

Uncle Pete was the first out, unbuckling his seatbelt and kicking what remained of his window free before climbing from the wreckage and plunging into the river. Spencer helped Allie get her belt loose, and she crawled through the opening as the helicopter sank. When she was clear, he leaned forward to where Drake was fumbling with his harness.

A glance at the unnatural angle of Daeng's head told him that the pilot had taken his last flight. Spencer wedged himself into the gap between them and freed Drake.

"You okay?" he yelled.

Drake nodded. "I think so. Bruised."

"Get out of this thing. It'll be on the bottom in a few more seconds." Spencer glanced at Drake's submachine gun still clutched in his hands. "Don't let go of that, whatever you do."

Water rose to chest level and Spencer fumbled for the duffle handle. After retrieving it, he launched himself through the cabin window as Drake scrambled out the windshield opening. The current was strong, and muddy water swirled around them as they pulled for the nearest shore.

When Spencer crawled from the river, he spotted Allie nearby, dripping wet but otherwise with no sign of injury. He made his way to her and she threw her arms around his neck and hugged him. He held her for a long moment, and then Drake's voice called from across the water. They both looked over at where he stood, Uncle Pete beside him, on the far bank. The frothing brown river rushed by as the helicopter settled on the bottom, leaving only the top of the rotor shaft and one blade jutting from the water as evidence of its existence.

"Are you okay?" Drake yelled.

"Yeah. You?" Spencer called.

"Sore and swelling. Allie?"

"Same here."

"Daeng?" Allie asked Spencer, and he shook his head.

"He didn't make it."

The still air exploded with gunshots, and the earth around Drake fountained as slugs pounded into the bank. Uncle Pete ducked and ran into the brush. More shots sounded from downstream, and Spencer squinted at a bend in the river, where a boat filled with gunmen was fighting the current, its outboard laboring as the shooter standing in the bow tried to steady his aim.

Spencer swung his AKM into firing position and squeezed off a burst to buy Drake time, and nodded in satisfaction when at least a few of his rounds thumped into the wooden hull. The men onboard all began firing at him as the bow shooter took cover. Spencer yelled at Allie as rounds sprayed the sloping bank a dozen yards short of him.

"Get out of here. Hurry," he ordered, and emptied half his magazine at the boat before he turned and sprinted for the brush line where Allie had disappeared. Ricochets whined off the nearby rocks, and then he was in the trees. He spotted Allie ahead and ran in a crouch toward her, the whistle of bullets shredding through the vegetation too close for comfort. She kept up her pace, and they didn't slow until they'd put a hundred yards between themselves and the river.

Spencer held his finger to his lips and pointed to a small clearing near a thicket of bamboo. She nodded and he took the lead, his pace as fast as the terrain would allow. When he reached the thicket, he slid his hand into the duffle and drew out one of the pistols. He handed it to her wordlessly before retrieving another and strapping the holster onto his belt. She did the same as Spencer groped around in the depths of the bag for a curved AKM thirty-round magazine.

When he found one, he swapped it for his nearly spent one and then gestured at the faint impression of a trail leading south from the edge of the thicket.

Allie nodded and they set off, not waiting to see whether the boatload of killers had followed them or gone after Uncle Pete and Drake.

Half an hour of hard pushing later, they slowed. Allie whispered to Spencer, "What do you think that was all about?"

"Probably one of the neighborhood drug gangs. They tend to take a shoot first, ask questions later approach. They were likely in the vicinity and were drawn by the helicopter going down."

"Were we hit by a missile or something?"

"No. Daeng thought it was a malfunction of some kind."

"Where does that leave us?"

Spencer looked up at the sky and then at their surroundings. "We're pretty much in the middle of nowhere, so nobody's going to save our bacon. Which means we're on our own. Let's head to our left. Eventually we should hit the river we crashed into, which will dump into the Mekong. Maybe we can find a shallower part where we can cross."

"What about Drake and Uncle Pete?"

"First things first, Allie. Uncle Pete strikes me as resourceful, and Drake still has his MP5. Let's get back to the river, and then we'll figure out how to find them."

"What if we don't?" Allie asked, her voice suddenly small.

"Allie, a lot of survival is about attitude. If you believe you're done for, you already are – might as well lie down and die. Allie, look at me," he said, and she tore her eyes from his gun and met his gaze. "We *will* get out of this, and we *will* find them. We just need to choose the best way. It may seem like a big jungle, but it's not as bad as the Amazon, and we walked out of that, didn't we?"

"Not all of us," she said, almost inaudibly.

"Well, *we* did, and we're going to do the same here. Now, come on. Let's find someplace to cross the river."

"What about the gunmen?"

"I doubt they're going to devote a ton of time trying to track us through rain forest. We don't have anything they want. They're just protecting their turf."

"They were pretty convincing."

He stared into the trees and then turned to her. "I want to put some distance between us and them before it starts getting dark."

"That's hours away," Allie said, but not disagreeing.

"It'll be here sooner than you think."

# Chapter Twenty-One

*Chiang Rai, Thailand*

Jiao watched the blinking icon on his phone from his position by the hotel pool, a cool soda in hand, a nearby oversized umbrella providing welcome shade. The Americans were flying a methodical search pattern he recognized from the prior day – about as exciting to watch as grass growing. He sighed and closed his eyes, reasoning that there was worse duty than the one he'd been assigned, even if he despised Thailand on principle; the place was little more than a den of inequity populated by barbarians.

His phone beeped and he opened his eyes. When he focused on the screen, he sat up, staring at it in disbelief.

The icon had disappeared.

He tapped buttons and rebooted, but still, nothing. Blinking rapidly as his mind raced, he was at a loss for what to do next. He called Xiaoping and told him what had occurred.

"How many men do you have there?" Xiaoping snapped.

"Three."

"We cannot lose the Americans. They're our only lead. Find them."

"How?"

"That is up to you. Use whatever resources you think appropriate. But do not fail."

Jiao hung up and stood. He understood what he needed to do.

What exact form that action would take eluded him, but he would figure it out. He fingered the screen and zoomed in on the last location the blip had been…and spotted a small river.

He would start there.

~ ~ ~

Spencer held up his hand and stopped walking along the track he'd been following. He cocked his head, listening. Allie's eyes narrowed and she looked back at the trail. Spencer motioned for her to get down and she did, taking cover behind a tree.

The snap of a twig sounded from down the trail and she froze. Spencer took cautious steps to her left as he removed another magazine from the duffle, and then set the bag behind a bush and raised his weapon, his hand steady as he flipped the assault rifle's collapsible wire stock into place. He stood unmoving, sweat coursing down his face, his attention laser-focused on the approach.

The bushes rustled thirty yards away, and he adjusted the aim of the AKM's muzzle a few degrees. Allie withdrew her pistol, flicked the safety off, and thumbed back the hammer.

Another rustle. Spencer squinted down the sights, ready to open fire.

A boar emerged from the brush and snorted before it took off at a run past them. Allie exhaled with relief and was standing when she heard something else.

The sound of men moving along the trail.

*Of course.* They must have scared the wild boar out of the undergrowth.

She caught Spencer's eye and he tilted his head, silently urging her to move toward him. She complied, her pulse pounding in her ears, her finger hovering over the trigger of her pistol, which seemed puny and insignificant now. He murmured in her ear, so softly she could barely make out his words.

"Follow me. We're going to try to hide. Don't shoot unless I do."

They crept off into the dense foliage. Spencer took care not to break any branches as he forged a new track, moving stealthily as he searched for the path of least resistance.

When they had made it twenty yards, they froze at the muffled sound of soft voices. Both slowly crouched down, and Spencer brought the AKM to his shoulder as Allie watched the trail.

A half-dozen gunmen came into view, walking single file and toting AK-47s. The lead man held his gun at the ready, the others' weapons were dangling from their hands or hanging from shoulder straps. They moved deliberately, their caution evident from their body language and the constant motion of their eyes.

The lead gunman abruptly stopped and the others fell still. The jungle was quiet, and Allie was sure she could hear the men breathing. The leader raised his rifle tensely, and then the errant boar exploded from the brush in front of them and tore off like the devil was after it.

Two of the men laughed nervously. The leader cut them off with a hand gesture, obviously unamused. He slowly swept the area with his gaze, and Allie instinctively shrank even lower, willing herself to be invisible to the gunmen.

After a seeming eternity, the column continued down the trail. Spencer and Allie remained immobile for five solid minutes, and when it was safe, he drew closer to her.

"Looks like they're more persistent than I gave them credit for."

"What do we do?"

"My gut says we backtrack."

"What? That's nuts."

"No, it's where they'll least expect us – behind them. They're probably following our footprints."

"Won't they stop once they see there aren't any more?"

"Depends. The ground was spongy earlier today from the morning rain. But it's getting firmer, so for the last bit we haven't left any."

"Then why are they still after us?"

"Because they know they're on our tail. We're just going to trick them."

"What about whoever's back at the boat?"

"We'll deal with that when we get there. They know this jungle. It could be there's an outlet further along, or even a camp. So their advantage is familiarity with the locale. Our only edge is to do the unexpected."

"I guess that doesn't include crying and praying for it to stop."

Spencer smiled. "Maybe later."

"I wish I'd held onto my machine gun when I bailed out of the helicopter."

"Hey, you're here in one piece. Daeng isn't. I'd say you were pretty fortunate by any measure." He stood to his full height and checked the time. "Let's get moving. Ideally we'll be across the river before dark. I don't like the sound of spending it in Myanmar with these guys nosing around for us, do you?"

She gave him a frown. "I gather that's a hypothetical question."

The slog back was slower. By the time they neared the river, its burbling surface visible through the leaves, the sun was setting. Spencer warned Allie to stay put and crept away into the brush. Allie resisted the urge to follow him when he'd been gone for ten minutes, but after twenty, she began to panic. The only thing that kept her rooted in place was that she hadn't heard any gunshots, which she was sure she would have if Spencer had encountered any gunmen.

When he returned, his face was grim. "The boat's there. Two shooters."

"Where were you?"

"Taking a look at the river to see if there's anywhere promising we can cross."

"And?"

"There is. Just around the bend from the boat."

"That's cutting it pretty close, isn't it?"

"We have no choice. It widens out and looks like it's no more than three or four feet deep."

"Maybe that's why the boat stopped where it did?"

Spencer shook his head. "No. That thing can't draw more than a couple of feet, tops. They stopped near the helicopter because they wanted to pick up our scent. And probably Drake and Uncle Pete's as well."

"Oh, Spencer…"

"Don't worry. But it'll be night soon. We should give it a try before it's too dark to see."

"You think there are crocodiles here?"

"They'd be the least of our problems."

"You wouldn't happen to have a sat phone in that bag of tricks so you can call in the cavalry, would you?"

"It's back at the hotel. Figured we wouldn't need it in the helicopter. My bad." He gazed at the river. "Follow me."

Spencer led her to the promising shallows. It was so gloomy by the time they made it that Allie could barely see the water. Spencer looked her in the eyes and took her hand in his, shouldering the duffle after stowing the AKM inside.

"You ready?" he asked.

"I can think of other things I'd rather do, but yes, I guess so."

"It's only bad until it gets worse."

"Ever the optimist."

Spencer moved into the water, which quickly rose to his waist. He felt with his hiking boots along the uneven bottom, scraping along the larger rocks that were gathered there as he searched for flat areas to maintain his footing. Allie cringed when the water reached her chest, but he kept pulling her along.

She slipped and went under, and Spencer pulled her to her feet. She sputtered a mouthful of water but didn't make any further sound, and Spencer squeezed her hand reassuringly and continued to edge through the current. After an agonizing section where the level reached Allie's chin, the bottom gradually began rising, spurring them on.

When they dragged themselves onto the far bank, Allie paused, panting, her eyes adjusting to the darkness that was now almost complete. When they had caught their breath, Spencer moved toward the brush.

"Where to?" Allie whispered.

"As far as we can get before we can't see anything more."

"Then what?"

"Then you'll get some rest and I'll stand watch."

"You need some, too."

"I'll rest when we're out of danger."

She stared out over the river towards where the boat waited with death aboard. "That could be a while."

"I've been through worse."

Allie studied his face and believed him. "Lead the way."

# Chapter Twenty-Two

*Five hours earlier, Southwestern Laos*

Uncle Pete hurried through the rain forest with the vitality of a teenager, and Drake struggled to keep up. The shooting had been all the warning they'd needed, and the wily Thai had made it clear that Drake would have to maintain the pace or be left behind. Drake couldn't discern any trail Uncle Pete was following, but he trusted that he knew what he was doing. In any case, Drake had no choice, the H&K in his hands slim comfort given the gunmen behind them.

When they'd been underway for two hours, Uncle Pete stopped, listening for signs of pursuit. After several minutes he grunted and sat beside a tree, cross-legged, and closed his eyes. Drake stared at him unbelievingly.

"What are you doing?" Drake hissed.

"Thinking."

"Unless it's about our funeral, shouldn't we keep moving?"

"Depend."

"That's helpful."

"It why I thinking."

"Should I wake you if an army of murderous drug runners show up?"

"Not sleeping. Thinking," Uncle Pete repeated, his tone annoyed. He cracked an eye open and glared at Drake. "Take five."

"You do remember that we just survived a helicopter crash and narrowly escaped being gunned down, right?"

"No talk. Think."

Drake gave up. He lowered himself to the ground and tried to occupy himself by inspecting his weapon, but quickly realized he had no idea how to break it down to clean it properly. He didn't want to take the chance of dismantling it only to discover he couldn't reassemble it correctly – the middle of the jungle while they were being pursued wasn't the right place to learn how difficult it might be.

He tilted the gun and a rivulet of dirty water trickled from the barrel. Drake didn't have an inkling whether the weapon could still fire, but figured Uncle Pete would. The bullets were watertight, he guessed, but he didn't actually know. After shaking the gun a few times, he set it down beside him and watched the area they'd passed through.

Minutes dragged by, and Drake was becoming increasingly impatient when Uncle Pete's eyes popped open and he fixed Drake with a flat stare. His gaze drifted to the weapon and he clucked his tongue. "Give me gun."

Drake obliged, and Uncle Pete quickly fieldstripped it and wiped down the parts with his shirt before snapping it together like he'd done it a million times. Which, for all Drake knew, he had. When he was finished, he stood and motioned to the left. "We go now. I keep gun."

Drake was in no position to argue, so he nodded and offered a silent prayer that the shifty Thai knew what he was doing. Based on his performance with the weapon, Drake would have said he did, but that was hardly the same as leading them to safety. Still, even though a slender reed upon which to hang his hopes, it was better than nothing, so Drake followed Uncle Pete without question or complaint.

As the day wore on, the heat climbed to a swelter, the air thick as syrup as they made their way further from the river. Drake busied himself with swatting away invisible insects and hoping that there were no snakes lurking nearby. Uncle Pete soldiered on as though he had a map in his head, his steps unwavering until they reached a gorge that dropped precipitously to a stream below.

"Now what?" Drake asked.

"Go south."

"How do you know which way that is?"

"Sun set in west," Uncle Pete explained, as though describing the earth's rotation to a none-too-clever child.

"How far do you think we are from the border?"

"Maybe thirty, thirty-five klicks."

"So in miles, that's…about twenty?"

"Maybe."

"Aren't there any villages between here and Thailand? Or maybe further inland?"

"Hill tribes. But maybe more men with guns. Not safe."

"Then how are we going to get out of here?"

"Walk. My wings all broken." Uncle Pete's face was a blank, and then he grinned. "You want adventure, right? This adventure."

"What about Allie and Spencer?"

"Have own adventure."

"Right, but what if they're in trouble?"

"Spencer seem good with gun. Know ropes, that right?"

"Possibly."

"Then worry 'bout us."

"But we have to try to find them."

"Can't do anything now. Bad men behind. Our job stay alive. Mekong to right. We get to river, maybe catch boat."

Uncle Pete's logic was difficult to argue with, Drake had to admit. Get to the river and follow it south. The Mekong was a major waterway, and there would be barges, ferries, and cargo vessels plying their trade. All they had to do was evade the drug-gang gunmen and any other threats the jungle threw at them and find the Mekong.

"How do you know it's there?"

"It downhill."

Drake didn't ask if that meant the river was at a lower altitude, or whether Uncle Pete was expressing a preference for following gravity because it would be an easier hike. In the end, Drake supposed it didn't matter.

Uncle Pete looked ready to say something else when he stiffened and stared off into the distance. "Hear that?" he asked in a whisper.

"No, what?" Drake whispered back.

"Someone follow."

"Are you sure?"

"Quiet." Uncle Pete stood stock-still for half a minute and nodded. "Not far behind."

"What do we do?"

"We go."

"Right. But how do we lose them?"

Uncle Pete spit into the bushes. "We don't. We kill."

"What? We can't go around murdering people," Drake protested.

"They kill you, then."

Drake swallowed hard, reality setting in. He was in another nightmare like that with the Russians in the Amazon, where only one party emerged alive. Suddenly the innocuous jaunt the CIA had described had become a killing field; and in his corner was a highly questionable Thai whose background was a complete unknown and who had the only weapon.

Uncle Pete set off at a fast trot and Drake hurried to keep up. They moved along the ridge, the drop to the stream steep and deadly, and then the trail forked. Uncle Pete took the uphill track, surprising Drake, but stopped after a dozen yards and broke a couple of branches before he turned on his heel and led Drake along the downhill slope. Drake understood his strategy without any explanation – it was possible their pursuers might believe they'd taken the high road, buying Drake and Uncle Pete a little additional time.

Ten minutes later, Uncle Pete stopped beside a clump of bamboo. He eyed several fallen stalks and selected two yellowed, desiccated lengths, and reached into his pocket and removed a butterfly knife, which he flipped open theatrically. He made short work of fashioning two jagged points, and then set to work on trimming the opposite ends so he had a pair of six-foot-long spears.

Drake watched him wordlessly and then whispered, "What are you going to do with those?"

"What you think?"

"Why not just shoot them?"

"Maybe. Depend how many."

"Can't we just hide?"

Uncle Pete nodded. "We will."

"Where?"

He pointed at a banyan tree whose branches shaded the trail. "In tree. They come, we jump, spear like fish."

"That'll never work. Just shoot them."

"Shooting make noise. Bring more bad men."

"Shooting's efficient. Something goes wrong, we're dead if all we have is spears."

"Still got gun. Spears better."

"It's insane."

"Come. We climb."

# Chapter Twenty-Three

A pair of oriental pied hornbills flapped into the sky as a trio of gunmen worked their way down the trail, having only been duped by the broken branches on the upper trail for a few minutes. They moved carefully, their sandals quiet on the ground, their AK-47s held at present arms, ready to fire. All wore the simple vestments of rice farmers, baggy long-sleeved shirts and loose pants rolled to the knee, and the skin on their exposed hands and faces was brown as pecans.

They came around a bend, and the lead gunman slowed near a banyan tree. He pointed at where the bark was frayed off a low-hanging branch and motioned for his companions to spread out, their weapons now trained on the tree's breadth. As they approached, the leader signaled for the man on his right to circle the tree; anyone hoping to ambush them was likely hiding on the back side. The gunman nodded and crept around the trunk, squinting up at where sun was streaming through the dense cover.

The gunman looked at the lead man and shook his head. The other two moved to where he was standing, puzzled expressions on their faces. Someone had climbed the tree. But to what end?

There was now nobody there.

~ ~ ~

Drake studied the raft that he and Uncle Pete had painstakingly

137

constructed from branches they'd gathered. The contrivance bobbed unsteadily in the current, and Drake shook his head.

"Not a chance."

"Only way end trail."

"It's the best way to drown, you mean."

"You no want kill anyone, so run like schoolgirls. Can't run forever."

"I don't think it'll support both of us."

"We try, okay?"

Drake regarded the fronds Uncle Pete had used to tie the collection of flotsam together. It was suicide to try to navigate the river, which at this point was easily thirty yards wide and obviously deep, but he could also see the resourceful Thai's point: they had to lose their tail if they were to avoid a gunfight. Getting a little wet was certainly preferable to being shot to pieces.

"You get on first. Let's see how it holds," Drake suggested.

Uncle Pete shook his head disgustedly and moved to the raft. He waded knee deep into the water and dragged himself onto the makeshift platform. The raft sank a good three inches, but remained afloat. Drake didn't know whether to be happy or sad.

"See? No problem." The raft shifted and creaked as though taunting Drake. Uncle Pete held out his hand. "Need help?"

"No, I think I can manage getting onto a raft."

Drake inched into the water, holding the vine they'd used as a tether, and crawled aboard the raft next to Uncle Pete. It was now barely above the water, but still floating, Drake had to admit. The current took hold and they began drifting south. The chocolate water frothed around them, the river swollen from rain runoff. They were running out of time before dark, and the sun was now sinking into the western mountains of Myanmar. Even though Drake was reluctant to give Uncle Pete credit, he had to admit that the raft was doing its job, as every yard they drifted put another between them and the abrupt end of the trail they'd left.

"You sure they'll give up once they see we're no longer on land?"

"Probably. Want to get home before night, if they smart."

"Sure. They probably have families."

"No. Scared of other killers in jungle. This place bad. Lotsa drug wars."

"But doesn't the same danger also apply to us?"

"One problem one time."

Several minutes went by, and the river curved so they couldn't see the spit of land from where they'd pushed off any longer. If nothing else, Uncle Pete's idea had done its job, and now, assuming he was right, all they had to do was float down the Mekong and they'd be able to find a barge headed south.

"Uncle Pete, I've got to hand it to you—"

Drake was interrupted by the sound of water splashing directly ahead of them. They turned to face downstream and Drake spotted a ledge no more than ten yards away where the river disappeared – a waterfall where the froth was spilling over.

"What do we do now?" Drake asked.

"Hang on."

They picked up speed as they neared the waterfall and then they were over it, landing hard in the froth six feet below the falls.

The raft gave a sickening lurch and split in pieces as the bindings let loose. Drake watched helplessly as a third of the branches drifted away, and then he was sitting in six inches of water, the raft breaking apart beneath them.

"Damn," Drake said, and then the rest of the bundled wood let go and he was swimming for shore, fighting the undercurrent and trying to keep his head above water. Uncle Pete was splashing a few yards ahead of him, pulling for the bank with all his might.

They made it to the rocky slope and dragged themselves out of the water. Drake spit a mouthful of brown to the side and made a face. Uncle Pete coughed and eyed their surroundings.

"You think we got far enough to lose them?" Drake asked.

"Know soon. Hope so."

They looked up at the peak of a green mountain towering above, and Uncle Pete forced himself to his feet, dripping but uninjured. He dumped water and mud from the barrel of the submachine gun and then moved back to the water to rinse it. Once finished, he stripped the weapon and wiped away the worst of the grit. Drake watched him and then gazed off at where the sun was dipping into the hills.

"Now what?"

"We close to Mekong. Road run along Laos side. Get to road, easier going. Follow nose."

"Not much light left."

"We camping, for sure."

"Would have been nice if we'd managed to grab one of the backpacks," Drake said, thinking about the equipment now underwater in the wreckage of the helicopter. He tried to imagine the senator's daughter's plane going down, at night, and realized that they really were completely out of their depth – the jungle was vast, and they were only a few amateurs. A wave of hopelessness washed over him, and he felt like an idiot for allowing himself to be talked into the search. His ego had gotten the better of him, and the CIA had played to that – Drake Ramsey, master treasure hunter, unstoppable force of nature, doer of big deeds.

"What's the saying? Never believe your own press releases..." Drake muttered, and Pete gave him a dark look. Drake tried a grin and felt grit between his teeth. "Nothing. Just thinking."

Uncle Pete finished with the gun and began walking along the bank. "We get away from water. They still after us, they walk down bank like me. No good."

"You really think we can find the Mekong without tracking the river?"

"Gonna give try."

They made it no more than a quarter mile before dusk surrendered to night, and stopped near a clearing. Drake took the first three-hour watch while Uncle Pete tried to sleep with the calls of nocturnal animals for a lullaby and the elephant grass and rocky ground for a bed.

# Chapter Twenty-Four

*Chiang Rai, Thailand*

Reggie Waters, former Georgetown halfback and now one of the CIA's deep-jungle field specialists, stepped from the jet and made his way to the arrivals area inside the airport, checking his cell phone signal as he walked. He'd been on planes for the equivalent of two days, with the connections and the time difference from Washington to Bangkok, and he was anxious to meet the treasure hunters, who headquarters had assured him were already searching for the downed plane.

Reggie had arranged with Uncle Pete to meet up after the day's helicopter flight, and he checked the time as he strode through the terminal to where a throng of sad little taxis and tuk-tuks waited outside in the shade provided by the roof overhang. He selected the least decrepit vehicle and gave the driver the address of the group's hotel as he blotted his brow, his skin the color of cappuccino from a Caucasian father and Jamaican mother. The low-horsepower motorcycle engine revved to life and the driver called out to his fellows, presumably announcing when he'd return.

The town had all the charm of a fungal infection, but Reggie felt at home. He'd spent more than his share of time in Cambodia, Laos, Vietnam, and Central America, so he was used to the conditions. Compared to some of those spots, Chiang Rai was Park Avenue.

The trip to the hotel took ten minutes, and by the time he arrived, he was ready to be rid of the tuk-tuk, the exhaust of which seemed to spew directly into the passenger seating area. He paid the driver and carried his bag to the office. He was accustomed to living out of a suitcase and, sometimes, out of a tent; it was often rough duty, but he did a job few could, and it was a necessary one, he believed.

At forty-three Reggie was old by field standards to still have an operational career, but he dreaded the prospect of a desk job – the inevitable future as an analyst, which would pay well but was about as exciting as getting his teeth cleaned. Reggie was an adrenaline junkie through and through, and the idea of sitting in a cubicle made him cringe, so much so that he'd begun exploring retirement to one of the islands he'd set his eye on. Belize, Honduras, Panama, all had the environment he enjoyed – away from his fellow man, living in harmony with nature.

The hotel was passable, and he killed time wandering the nearby streets. When his six o'clock meeting with the group didn't happen, he began to worry, and by nightfall he was sure something had gone wrong. When eight o'clock came and went with no Uncle Pete, he made a series of calls to headquarters, the last of which assured him that he would receive instructions as soon as anyone knew anything.

Half an hour later his phone rang, and he thumbed it to life on the second ring. "Waters," he answered.

"Big problem. Air traffic control shows their transponder in the middle of the Laotian jungle." The dispassionate voice gave him the coordinates.

"Maybe they located the target?"

"Negative – they're not answering their sat phone, and they didn't call, which they would have if they'd found the plane. The transponder signal is weak, but it looks like it's coming from the middle of a small river a few miles from the Mekong. We had a satellite overhead and there wasn't much cloud cover in that area, so we were able to pick them up on the historical footage from the bird." Reggie's control paused. "It shows the helo crashing into the river."

"Shot down?"

"Not that we could see. The rotor looks like it just froze up. It dropped like a rock."

"Crap. So how should I proceed?"

"We zoomed in, and four passengers managed to make it out."

"Then they're alive?"

"At least they were then. But it gets worse. Drug smugglers are operating in the area, and they went after our gang. So they're now either dead or stranded somewhere in the jungle. We want you to go in and verify which it is."

"I'm presuming there's been no communication," Reggie said, just to be clear.

"Roger that."

"Any backup?" Reggie asked.

"Negative. You're not to wait. Go in ASAP."

"It's already dark here. I'll have to line something up. Might take until tomorrow morning."

"Understood. Keep the line open and report in when you have the logistics confirmed."

"10-4. My phone will be on."

Reggie terminated the call and sat, thinking, for several minutes before retrieving a zipped satchel from the bag on his bed. He withdrew two stacks of currency – one dollars, in fifties and hundreds, the other Thai baht. He'd need to spread some money around to find someone willing to ferry him to where the helicopter had gone down, and that wouldn't happen instantly. If he was lucky, he could be underway by late morning, after locating a suitable craft with a captain who could exercise appropriate discretion. He checked Google Earth, entered the coordinates his control had given him, and then zoomed out to see where the nearest outpost of civilization was. He spotted what he was looking for and nodded. Surely there would be someone he could sway with his powers of persuasion and a fistful of hard cash. It would just be a matter of pounding the waterfront at dawn.

He peeled off a suitable slug of both denominations and stuffed the wads into the pocket of his Ripstop TDU cargo pants, and then repacked his bag and set off to find someone to drive him north to Chiang Saen, on the Mekong River – a charming little hamlet that was as close as you could get to the epicenter of the infamous Golden Triangle, where the borders of Laos, Thailand, and Myanmar converged. He wasn't worried about accommodations – there was sure to be at least one fleabag where he could find a room, given the town's prominent location as a trafficking stop. His only concern was getting up there. Chiang Rai didn't seem like the kind of place where anyone drove the roads at night if they could help it, and he fully expected to be turned down a number of times before locating a ride.

Reggie's most pessimistic expectations were more than met, and he wound up spending the better part of an hour being rejected by every working taxi in the city. Eventually he found a trucker in a bar who was willing to brave the road for a couple hundred dollars, and as they set off into the gloom, he wondered what the odds were that a collection of neophytes could survive in one of the most dangerous places in the world.

# Chapter Twenty-Five

Allie jolted awake. Spencer's hand covered her mouth, muffling her involuntary cry. She could barely make him out right in front of her in the darkness, but she could see the moonlight reflecting off the whites of his eyes. He moved his lips to her ear and whispered so softly she barely understood him.

"Something's coming."

She shivered and was instantly alert. He'd said something, not someone, reminding her that the jungle was filled with threats easily as dangerous as the upright biped variety.

"What do we do?"

"Move."

Spencer's hand enveloped hers, the AKM in the other, and he led her forward. Branches tore at their clothes as they fought their way through the dense vegetation. They had barely made it a dozen yards when she tripped over a vine and went down with a thud, biting back the yelp of pain her twisted ankle caused.

Spencer was helping her up when a flashlight blinked on from the other side of the clearing and a voice called out in Laotian, which bore some similarities to Thai. Neither of them understood what the speaker was demanding, but the sound of metal on metal from rifles being readied was sufficient translation. Spencer slowly knelt and laid the AKM on the ground and then stood with his hands over his head. Allie struggled to her feet and did the same, slightly off balance as she favored her hurt leg.

Three men approached in the flashlight's glare. Allie flinched as one of them searched her, his hands roving over every curve. Another man did the same with Spencer before calling out to whoever was holding the light. A response came instantly, and the third member of the trio scooped up Spencer's AKM while the other two trained weapons on them.

A push against their backs with gun barrels drove Allie and Spencer toward the flashlight, which blinked off as they neared. Their eyes adjusted to the gloom, and they could just make out two more men, also heavily armed, regarding Allie like they'd never seen a female before.

The one with the flashlight barked an order, and the gunmen behind Allie and Spencer prodded them with their weapons again. The flashlight bearer, clearly the leader, turned and led them into the night, the trees swallowing them up as they left the clearing and moved through the jungle.

Allie desperately wanted to speak, but held her tongue. She didn't dare provoke their captors, and didn't want to risk a gun butt slam to the head. She limped along, her ankle sending spikes of pain up her shin, but ignored the discomfort as her mind frantically searched for some way out of their predicament.

Eventually the heavy brush gave way to terraced fields, and the going got easier as they trod along a hard-packed dirt path. The cloud cover melted away and starlight shone through the remaining haze. It was obvious they were now in an agricultural area, the plots bordered by jungle, but large expanses of the land cultivated.

They drew near a collection of thatched huts grouped at the base of a mountain, and she saw firelight flickering in the near distance, where a gathering of men and women sat in an open area between the structures. Torches flamed around the perimeter, lending an otherworldly quality to the scene.

Several of the gathering rose when the group drew near, and Allie spotted at least a dozen armed gunmen in the shadows, guarding the village. A tall figure stepped forward, and Allie gasped in astonishment – it was a Caucasian man in his sixties, wearing an olive tank top and camouflage pants. She could see in the orange light that despite his age he was trim and athletic, with tribal tattoos snaking down deeply tanned bare arms. He moved closer and she could see intelligent eyes beneath a thicket of unruly dark hair, a goatee lending him the appearance of a devil in the firelight. After a brief glance at Spencer, his eyes fixed on her.

The man said something in the native dialect and then in Thai. Spencer shook his head, and the man tried again in English.

"Well, well, what have we got here? Backpackers lost their way?" He sounded American, but Allie remained silent, preferring to let Spencer do the talking. One of the members of the armed patrol held up Spencer's AKM, and the man's tone changed. "Not with that, you aren't. What's the story? Trying to make a connection in the Triangle?"

"Our helicopter went down a few miles from here," Spencer said.

"That was you? Scared the hell out of my people here with that racket overhead."

"That wasn't the intention."

"What happened to the helo?"

"Mechanical. We're lucky to be alive. The pilot didn't make it. Only reason we're walking is because we hit a river instead of the ground."

"Well, you're right about being lucky." The man looked Allie over and then turned to Spencer. "What were you doing in a helicopter out here? You're risking somebody blowing you out of the air in this area."

"The pilot said most around here knew the markings and wouldn't."

The man shook his head. "The pilot was stretching the truth. There are at least three groups battling it out for the Laos side of the Mekong at present, and on the Myanmar side you've got the Shans, a splinter group that hates them and is at war for their own slice of turf, several warlords with hundreds of men and nasty attitudes, and forays by the Myanmar military, which is as crooked as a silly straw."

"We have permits," Allie said, and the man's eyebrows rose.

He laughed harshly. "Look around here, missy. You think anyone I just described gives two shits about some permits? Did the head of the Shan army sign it? You see any drug lords mentioned as giving their blessing?"

Allie looked down, embarrassed for her naïveté. The man continued, his tone only slightly softer.

"Out here, the only permits anyone understands are bullets. It's the Wild West, little lady. The only rule is there are no rules."

"Then what are you doing here?" Allie fired back, bristling at his condescension.

"Saving your ass, for starters. If my men hadn't brought you in, you'd have likely been passed around like a joint by whoever captured you, and then tied over an anthill or fed to the crocodiles for sport."

The truth of the stranger's words stung. When she looked back up, a tiny tear was working its way down her cheek. "Who are you?" she asked softly.

"Name's Joe. Who are you?"

She sniffed. "Allie, and this is Spencer."

"And what brings you to my jungle?"

"*Your* jungle?" Allie repeated.

"This patch sure is. Now answer the question," Joe snapped. "You mentioned you got permits. Permits for what?"

Spencer cut in. "We're archeologists. We're looking for ruins."

Joe looked him straight in the eye. "You're about as much of an archeologist as my boot is."

"She's the real thing. I'm the hired help," Spencer explained, his tone neutral.

"And you're flying around one of the world's most infamous drug-producing areas, looking for ruins? You must be out of your minds."

"Yeah, that occurred to me about a minute after the chopper hit the water."

Joe grinned. "Sounds gnarly," he said, suddenly sounding more like a surfer than a renegade in the Laotian hills. "Oh, well, I suppose if I'm not going to sell you into slavery or cut you up and eat you, I might as well offer you some grub. How long you been wandering around out here?"

"All day," Allie said. She looked nervously back at the gunmen. "Do they have to point those at us? What if one of them sneezes?"

Joe nodded and said something in Laotian. The men grumbled but lowered their weapons. He shifted his attention back to Spencer. "If you don't mind, we're keeping your popgun, sport. Just in case you feel frisky later."

"You're the top dog here?" Spencer said, more a statement than a question.

"You could say that. Part sheriff, part rainmaker, part spirit guide, part entrepreneur." Joe called out in Laotian, and two of the women near the fire stood and moved to one of the huts. "Take a load off while they're fixing up some vittles. You look beat." He strode back to the fire.

Spencer and Allie accompanied him and sat on a log where Joe indicated.

"Do you have any water?" Allie asked. "I'm parched."

Another command, and one of the men entered a different hut and returned with a half-full five-gallon plastic water bottle and two clay mugs. "Have at it," Joe said. "It's safe to drink."

The man poured both mugs to the brim, and Allie took one with trembling hands and drained it greedily. Spencer followed suit. Joe said something else, and several of the nearby men laughed while the women averted their gazes.

"What did you say?" Allie asked.

"Nothing important. A little humor at your expense. But what you don't know won't hurt you."

After another refill, Joe poked at the flames with a branch. "So what kind of ruins would get you to risk your lives like this?"

"It's a legend. We're following up on it to see if there's any truth to it."

"A legend? I've been here for thirty years, and I've never heard of any legendary ruins."

"It's a temple. A temple that's been lost for centuries. In a hidden valley," Allie said.

"Well, don't that just take the cake. Here I've been eking out a living in these hills half my life, and nobody told me about the lost temple." Joe's eyes locked with Allie's. "Anything valuable in this temple?"

She nodded. "Could be. That's what we're here to find out."

"There a living in that? Really?" Joe asked skeptically.

Allie shrugged. "Sometimes."

"It pays pretty good, does it?"

"Depends," Spencer cut in.

"If someone was to help you find this hidden temple, you might be real generous, would you?"

Spencer's face was a blank. "Could be. Why?"

"What's your plan now that your helicopter's a submarine?"

Allie snorted. "We don't really have one yet. Probably try to get another helicopter."

"Good luck. One goes down, you think anyone else is going to sign up for that duty?"

"It was an accident," Spencer said.

Joe rolled his eyes. "Yeah. Right. Like anyone'll believe that." He sat back. "Trust me. You're grounded. There's nobody going to risk their lives ferrying your happy asses around."

"How can you be certain?" Allie asked.

"Easy. I'm a pilot." He looked up as the women emerged from the hut with some earthenware containers. "And I'm the only one crazy enough to be willing to give it a try – if the price is right."

"You have a helicopter?" Spencer asked.

"Nah. Those are for sissies. Got my own plane."

"Where?"

"Dirt strip about a quarter mile away. Comes in handy sometimes," Joe said, but didn't elaborate.

"We lost two others in our party," Allie said. "Before we could do anything, we'd need to try to find them."

"Where did you lose them, and how?"

"When we crashed. They wound up on one bank, and we swam to the other. Then the shooting started and we took off."

Joe's eyes darted to Spencer. "Shooting?"

Spencer told them about the chase and their night crossing of the river. When he was done, the women put the containers down in front of Allie and Spencer before moving back to where they'd been sitting.

"It's pretty good. Stewed fish. Spicy. There are some wooden spoons in there somewhere. I love the stuff. Goes down easy with some rice wine. You want some?"

"Oh, um, no, thanks," Allie said.

"None for me," Spencer echoed.

"Don't know what you're missing." Joe looked back over his shoulder and spoke a few words. The water bearer darted into the hut and returned with a jug. Joe uncorked the top and took three long swallows and then burped contentedly. "You want some grass?"

Allie and Spencer shook their heads in unison.

Joe raised an eyebrow. "Finest kind. Home grown. All organic. Give you a buzz like a mule kick to the head."

"Maybe some other time," Spencer said.

Joe shrugged. "Suit yourself. So, last you saw of your buds was on the other side of the river, and some unidentified baddies were shooting at them?"

"That's right."

"What would it be worth to find them?"

Allie let Spencer answer that. "You could name your price," he said quietly.

"Really? Like...ten grand apiece?"

"Done."

Joe took another drink. "Shoulda asked for twenty. Oh, well. Part of my journey on this plane of consciousness is to let go of the material. It's only money."

"Pays for fuel, though, huh?" Allie said, and then regretted the barb.

"Guy's got to earn a living, you know? Judge not and all that. Turn the other cheek. Be bigger than your hunger. But a word of warning – one of you stays with me until I get the money. That's not negotiable. I'm trusting, but I'm not stupid." Joe closed his eyes and then reached into his pocket and withdrew a joint. "Sure you won't partake? Loosen you up…"

"Not tonight," Allie said.

Joe poked the branch he'd been holding into the fire for a few seconds and then used the flaming tip to light the joint. He took a deep drag and held the smoke in, and then blew it through his nose, like a bearded dragon. "Whoo! Hot damn, that rules!" He blinked a few times and then called out to the gunmen. At least twenty of the men around the fire leapt to their feet and went to get their weapons.

"What did you say?" Spencer asked when Joe sat back down heavily.

"Told them your associates are out there, and whoever finds 'em will get the mother of all rewards. They'll put the word out to everyone we know, which is most of this territory. Even the warlords up the river will hear the tom-toms. It's your best shot."

"How much did you offer them?" Allie asked, curious.

"As much as it takes," Joe said, smiling enigmatically.

They sat in silence while Joe smoked his marijuana and drank. When his eyes were glazing over, Allie slid a few inches closer to him. "So what's your story? You said you've been here for thirty years?"

"Yeah. I came for the dope and stayed for the living."

"There's got to be more to it than that."

"Oh, sure. There was a girl." He grinned crookedly and for a moment looked a decade younger. "Isn't there always a girl in one of these stories? Anyway, I fell hard for her in Thailand and took her out of the life there. We moved here, to her village, and the rest is history."

"You still with her?" Allie asked.

"Nope. She's part of the cosmic dance now. Died in childbirth. Neither of them made it. So she's gone on to her next incarnation while my tired white butt is still here, learning whatever lessons I can until I get called away for my next chance to get it right."

"I'm so sorry, Joe," Allie said.

"It was a while ago, although I'd be lying if I said it didn't still hurt. But that's life, right? Bittersweet, and nobody knows when their clock runs out."

They were quiet for a long moment, and then Spencer spoke. "You've been here all that time?"

"Sure, off and on. You know, sometimes you get sucked into the world, whether you want to or not. But I like it here. It's simple. Real. People live, they struggle, they celebrate when they win and commiserate when they don't, they honor their old, and they don't fear death. What would I go back to that's better than that?"

"Sounds like you don't miss it."

"Part of the lesson I'm learning is that nothing is to be missed. It all happens for a reason. The good, the bad, those are just two sides of the same coin. Everything's an illusion, and our job is to see through it to the real stuff."

"Very existential," Allie said.

"Yeah, well, maybe so." Joe yawned, the alcohol and drug hitting hard, she could see. He gestured vaguely to one of the shacks. "You can crash in that hut, if you want. Or you can come keep me company. I'll show you my etchings. Or give it the old college try."

"The middle one there?" Spencer asked, saving Allie the embarrassment of answering.

"That's the one. We get up with the chickens, so see you when I see you. I'll be doing my tai chi at dawn."

"Seriously?" Allie said.

Joe stood unsteadily and grinned. "Depends on the cosmos. But that's the plan."

# Chapter Twenty-Six

Drake stirred as dawn broke over the clearing. He eyed the sky and noted sourly that it was gray with clouds, so he could expect to add rain to the list of indignities he was subjected to. He looked around for Uncle Pete, but didn't see him, and debated calling out before rejecting the idea. Last thing he needed was to draw enemies to their location – the little Thai was probably performing his morning ablutions.

He scratched the mosquito bites he'd acquired overnight and tried not to think about the illnesses that were endemic to the area. Malaria, yellow fever, dengue fever, and a host of other nightmare plagues lurked in the rivers and the parasites that swarmed the jungle, and with the way his luck was running, he'd come down with all of them concurrently.

Drake sat up and rubbed a tired hand over the stubble on his chin. He'd only gotten a few hours of sleep after his last watch; his imagination amplified every sound from the brush to be a portent of imminent doom. Eventually he'd drifted into a restive doze, replaying the seconds of the helicopter's drop over and over, the grizzly image of Daeng's head lolling at an obscene angle frozen in his mind's eye.

Movement drew his gaze to a nearby clump of bushes, and he gasped when he spied an undulating length of a snake, easily five feet long. He leapt to his feet and moved away, and the Malayan pit viper's menacing triangular head rose as its cold black eyes regarded him. The viper's tongue darted out, and it began to coil. Drake stepped back, giving it as much of the ground as it wanted.

Drake was about to yell for Uncle Pete when the Thai's head poked from around a tall fern.

"There's a really big snake–" Drake began, but he stopped mid-sentence when he saw the expression on Uncle Pete's face.

Uncle Pete took another step forward and Drake noticed his raised hands just as the barrel of a Kalashnikov appeared behind him. Drake stood rooted to the spot as Uncle Pete neared. "We got trouble," the Thai said, and three more gunmen stepped into the clearing.

Drake slowly raised his hands before dropping his eyes to the snake, which appeared to have lost interest in him and slunk back into the underbrush.

The gunman in charge of the group snarled an order, and Uncle Pete responded in the same tongue. The man said something else and Uncle Pete nodded.

"He say we go with them."

"Where?" Drake demanded.

"Where they want."

"Are these the guys in the boat?"

"Don't think so."

"Why not?"

"We alive."

"Ask them what they're after. Why are they taking us?"

Uncle Pete shook his head. "No. Don't want get shot."

Drake had no rebuttal for that, so he resigned himself to a forced march. "I need to use the bathroom."

Uncle Pete said something and the entire group exploded with laughter before the leader spat a few words. Uncle Pete translated. "He say make fast."

"What did you tell them?"

"That farangs make dirty pants easy."

"In this case, you may be closer than you think."

After relieving himself under the watchful gaze of one of the gunmen, Drake and Uncle Pete formed a ragged column with the rest, the leader walking swiftly ahead and his henchmen following with guns at the ready. Thunder roared overhead and it began raining. The water was a lifesaver for Drake, who caught what he could with his mouth, his head held at an angle with his tongue out. The pace up the long slope was brutal. After two hours Drake was struggling to make it, and his legs were rubbery from heat and hunger. He staggered several times, and the leader finally called a halt. After a twenty-minute pause they continued their journey, the men unruffled by the distance or the conditions even as Drake pushed himself to the limits of his endurance.

Uncle Pete bore any discomfort he felt with typical stoic calm, outwardly unfazed by the grueling trek. Drake's pallid complexion and shaky movement gave his effort away, and by the time they hit a particularly steep area, his stomach was churning with more than hunger. He thought of Allie lost in the wilds, and remorse slammed into him with hurricane force at convincing her to accompany him on what had become a suicide mission. His only hope was that Spencer's survival instincts would enable them to elude any pursuers and make it out of the rain forest.

Of course, Uncle Pete's ninja skills had proved less than effective, and now they were being herded like sheep to the slaughter. Drake tried speaking, but the gunmen shushed him. The leader's dark glare when he looked over his shoulder gave Drake all the warning required.

It was almost noon when the jungle fell away and they emerged into a wide clearing, a scattering of indigenous huts forming a semicircle around a primitive well. Hill tribesmen with assault rifles watched from the shade as the war party filed toward the little village. The poverty was palpable, and even the children who'd stopped their play were as serious as executioners at the sight of Drake.

The lead gunman barked instructions to his men and then abruptly stopped and turned to Uncle Pete. He said something low and fast, which Uncle Pete answered.

"What? What did he say?" Drake whispered, his heart trip-hammering in his throat.

Uncle Pete coughed wetly and spit to the side. When he looked at Drake, his stare held all the warmth of ice.

"He say we meet chief. Say he powerful and—"

Uncle Pete's translation was cut off by the gunman, who made a curt motion with his hand and patted his weapon. Uncle Pete shrugged and turned away, the tribesman's message clear.

Drake's apprehension grew with every step as they resumed marching along the central path, his worst fears now manifest in the cold gaze of a gunman who looked like he'd murder them without a second thought.

# Chapter Twenty-Seven

Allie stirred on the woven grass mat that had served as her cushion and reluctantly opened her eyes. The prior day's exertion had sapped her resources, and she was sore all over from the crash. She probed her ribs delicately and decided that they weren't broken, and then realized that she was alone – Spencer, who had spent the night across the floor from her, wasn't there.

She yawned and stood as the sound of women laughing reached her through the window opening. She stumbled to the gap and saw a group of females carrying gourds and buckets vanishing into the heavy ground fog as they moved toward an unknown destination. Allie pulled on her shoes and stepped outside from the raised hut floor and peered around in the white haze, the covering so thick she couldn't see more than thirty feet in front of her. She spotted Spencer nearing from the fog and sighed in relief. Even though Joe had agreed to help last night, there was a part of her that distrusted him automatically – something about the way he looked at her made her skin crawl.

Spencer grinned when he saw her. "Up already? I figured you'd be out for another few hours."

"I couldn't sleep any longer."

"How do you feel?"

"Like a piano dropped on me. But I'll make it. You?"

"More or less the same. I wish I had Joe's recovery time."

"Why? He's awake?"

"He's finishing up some kind of yoga, a tantric something-or-other exercise routine. Talk about an eccentric character, huh?"

"That's an understatement. But as long as he's on our side…"

"Keep your friends close, and your enemies closer," Spencer agreed.

"Where is he?"

"Over by the edge of the rice fields. There's an old banyan tree there. He says he draws energy and wisdom from it."

"Probably high as a kite."

"I didn't get that. I think he's really just into the Eastern mysticism thing. Kind of a burnout hippie fascination, for lack of a better description."

"What do you think he's really doing here?"

"With a plane and a private airstrip in the middle of the Golden Triangle? Three guesses."

"That's what I was afraid of."

"Oh, I'd say he's pretty benign compared to the alternatives we could have run into. And he did agree to help. That's a major positive for us, because I suspect he's right about the local pilots wanting to have nothing to do with us once news of Daeng's untimely demise spreads."

"Let's hope he can actually remember what all the controls do. He doesn't inspire a lot of confidence." She paused and looked away. "You don't think this is some sort of ruse?"

"Ruse? To achieve what?"

"I don't know. He just creeps me out. I don't trust him."

"Nor should you. But in a war zone, anyone willing to shoot at the guys you're shooting at is one of the white hats – until they turn on you."

"I'm not convinced."

Spencer nodded. "I'm reading that between the lines." He sighed. "Tell you what, let's see what he can do. What harm is there? If he can help us track down Drake, that would be major. He made it sound like he knows everybody and is on friendly terms with the local cutthroats. If he is, then things might work out after all. He can put the word out not to kill them, for starters. And with a reward being offered…" Spencer shrugged. "Just because you're crazy doesn't mean you're incompetent. I had an uncle like that."

"I'll believe it when I see it."

"Come to think of it, my uncle was just nuts, not really proficient at anything."

"That's very reassuring."

"He did know a lot of limericks and colorful sea shanties. But he was tone deaf. And he liked to sing them naked."

"You're making this up."

Spencer smiled. "I like to keep 'em guessing."

Joe's distinctive shape drifted through the fog, and Allie raised an eyebrow at his outfit – he was stripped to the waist, his body devoid of fat, his abs ridged, and the tattoos that adorned his arms carried across his chest and back. His orange drawstring pants were obviously homemade, and his feet were bare. Allie had to admit that he had a commanding bearing – that of someone to be reckoned with. She could see why the tribe deferred to him; to them he must have appeared to be some sort of divine sage.

"Good morning," Joe said, his tone calm and flat.

"Same to you," Allie said.

"You sleep well?"

"I did."

"Maybe tomorrow you'll wake up early enough to join me in my sun salutation."

"I don't see any sun," Allie observed.

"Like hidden treasure, the most valuable of nature's gifts are rarely immediately obvious," Joe intoned.

Allie and Spencer exchanged a glance that said maybe their host was high after all.

"Tell you what," Joe continued. "Let me get cleaned up, we'll have breakfast, and when this burns off, you can check out my plane."

Allie offered a small smile and studied Joe's face. If he was suffering from the prior night's excesses, it didn't show. "Sounds like a plan. Any word on our friends?"

"If you know how to listen, the wind whispers its secrets." Joe shook his head. "To listen is easy. To hear is a gift we must earn."

"So that's a no?" Spencer asked.

"In the land of the blind, the one-eyed man is king."

"Right," Allie said with an eye roll. "Good to know."

Joe made a gesture with his hands from his chest, thrusting them outward and then apart, palms raised. "Open your heart, invite the universe in, and all things will come to you effortlessly."

"Sounds great," she agreed, at a loss for any more words.

Joe's stare took on a faraway quality. "It is the beginning of true wisdom for the wave to recognize itself as part of the sea and not a separate thing. Real beauty is to be had in the belonging, in the acceptance and appreciation that we are all as one."

"Uh-huh," Spencer said.

Joe seemed to snap out of his trance. "Now if you'll excuse me, I'll rejoin you in ten minutes. You can wait for me here," he said, his tone businesslike. Without waiting for a response, he strode off.

Allie shook her head. "Tell me that wasn't frigging weird. He's completely spun."

"He's certainly spiritual."

"Schizophrenia and delusions of grandeur aren't the first qualities I look for in a pilot," she said.

"Maybe he's just feeling particularly metaphysical this morning."

"Right."

Joe reappeared, now wearing his tank top and camouflage pants, and smiled. "Hope you're hungry. We have a delicacy today: fresh rat tail soup with wild dog medallions."

Allie looked away. "I think I'm going to be sick."

"Don't judge our ways. Celebrate them," Joe said.

"I'm serious."

Joe chuckled. "Don't worry. I'm just playing." He turned from them and called over his shoulder as he made his way toward the well. "You don't mind beetle curry, do you? Tastes a little like chicken. If chickens were really big feathered beetles."

Allie leaned into Spencer and whispered, "I think someone

watched too many *Kung Fu* reruns during his childhood."

"All journeys begin with a single step," Spencer said, deadpan, eliciting a smile from Allie. "Although he had my mouth watering with the beetles."

"What do you think we're actually going to be offered?"

"Beats the hell out of me. But I'm starved. Hope it's not still wearing shoes, that's all I can say."

"You're almost as bad as he is."

"Something tells me you're underestimating Joe in a big way."

Allie stared after him. "If he calls me grasshopper, I'm going to scream."

After a reasonably palatable breakfast of rice and a thick stew, they followed Joe around a rise to where a large camo net covered a two-seat prop plane parked by a shack. Joe eyed the aircraft and called to Spencer.

"Give me a hand with the netting. Easiest if we go back to front and roll it as we pull it off."

Spencer moved to one corner, and they peeled off the cover. When they were done, they found themselves staring at a Cessna 150C that looked like it was held together with duct tape and bailing wire, its paint corroded off in more places than it still covered. Joe patted the side of the plane fondly.

"Don't let looks deceive you. This baby soars like a proud eagle."

"What year is it?" Spencer asked.

"1963. One of four hundred seventy-two built. A veteran that's never let me down. Her name's Bertha."

"Bertha," Allie echoed. "It actually flies?"

"Sure. One of the most reliable planes ever made. Carries a surprisingly decent payload, and sips fuel. It's the VW Bug of small prop jobs. You can't kill 'em." Joe grinned at Allie. "No time like the present. We can buzz around where your friends were lost and see if we can pick up their trail, and maybe take a look-see for your ruins. You know roughly where they're located?"

"Yes, but I don't have a map."

"No problem. Could you find it on a GPS with a satellite photo?"

"I think so."

Joe opened the pilot door and ferreted around, and held up a handheld GPS unit that looked no more than a year old. Spencer and Allie looked at each other as Joe powered the unit up.

"Okay, I'll zoom out," Joe said, moving closer to Allie. "Show me the river where the helo went down."

Allie studied the image and tapped the screen. "This looks about right. Daeng said we were around twenty-two or twenty-three miles up the Mekong."

"Oh. Wow. Yeah, I can see why you might have gotten a rude welcome. That's Shan Army territory on the Myanmar side. Pretty dicey customers."

"You sound like you know them well."

"Sure. I mean, when you live out here, you get used to breaking bread, you know? Everybody's friend, stay neutral, and run errands, whatever."

"Like flying medical supplies into Thailand?" Allie asked.

"I'm like Federal Express. If you tell me you have two hundred pounds of bandages in your package, who am I to question it?"

"That's very decent of you," Spencer said.

"Hey, life's short, and whatever gets you through the night and keeps gas in the plane." Joe looked around at the fog, which was burning off. "Looks like a lovely day for a tour. You ready?" he asked Allie.

She gave Spencer an uncertain gaze. "Why do I have to go?"

"You're the archeologist, aren't you? Or do you think Spencer here can do the same job you can?" Joe asked.

She frowned, but had to concede the point. "It's safe, right?"

"As safe as anything around here. Like I said, embrace the universe and you'll have a happier life."

"And a considerably shorter one," Allie mumbled under her breath.

"Let me start her up and we'll get busy. I've got binoculars and a radio in the plane, so we're ready to go."

"How about a fire extinguisher and a parachute?" Allie asked.

Joe eyed her. "You have a good sense of humor, I see. That's healthy."

"I'm not kidding."

The engine sputtered to life and Joe adjusted some knobs, and after a few minutes the rough idle settled into a purr. Allie climbed into the small cockpit and strapped in next to Joe. He pulled on a ragged headset, gave Spencer a thumbs-up, and taxied to the edge of the rutted dirt strip.

"Hope there are no mud cows on the damn runway," Joe said, and Allie shook her head. He grinned crazily again and chuckled. "Don't know why they like to amble onto the airstrip sometimes, but they do. Haven't hit one yet, but it keeps you on your toes."

"Tell me you're joking."

"We'll soon find out," he said as the plane eased forward. "Not very adventurous considering your line of work, are you?"

"After a crash and being chased by gunmen through the jungle, my adventure quota's full up for one lifetime."

They picked up speed, and the plane's tricycle landing gear hit a particularly ugly rut. The fuselage gave an ominous groan and the whole aircraft shuddered. Allie gritted her teeth, her sacroiliac aching from the pounding, and then they lifted into the fog at a steep angle. "Got to get over the trees or it won't be pretty," Joe explained. Allie closed her eyes, not wanting to see her death racing toward her at the hands of a stoned madman.

Thirty seconds later, they were over the canopy and bouncing higher through light turbulence. Joe tapped the compass with his finger as they continued their climb. Allie opened her eyes and stared at the device. "What's wrong?"

"Oh, nothing. I keep meaning to fix this thing. It sticks every now and then."

"The thing that tells us where we're headed? That thing?" she asked.

"I know these hills like the back of my hand. Have no fear."

"Does the altimeter work?"

"Mostly."

"That sounds like sometimes not."

"Glass is half full, little lady, half full. Just put out positive vibes. No need to fret."

At three thousand feet above the ground, Joe banked and headed north, and soon they were over the Mekong River. Joe pointed at a long barge straining against the current. "Slow boat there. Hell of a way to make a living."

"Daeng, our helicopter pilot, said that sometimes the drug traffickers shoot at aircraft."

Joe nodded. "That they do. But not usually, especially not at this altitude. Waste of time with anything but a .50-caliber machine gun, and why blow the rounds? Not like they don't know my plane."

"That's right. I keep forgetting you work for...who is it you won't work for, again?"

"So much disapproval. Live and let live, that's my motto." He pointed at the river coming up on their right. "That look familiar?"

"Yes. That's it."

"Let's go down some and see if we can spot your friends."

An hour later, after numerous runs along the river and the surrounding trails, they'd spotted nothing but an occasional ox and peasants working the terraced fields. Joe turned on the GPS and headed west. "Pick the first of your possible ruin sites and we'll take a gander. They're all in Myanmar, are they?"

"One is. The other two aren't."

"Let's look at the Laotian ones first, then. Even I get the heebie-jeebies flying over Shan Army territory."

"We do have a permit."

"From a government the Shans don't recognize as legit. Use it as toilet paper, because that's about all it's good for."

They buzzed the first of the locations and Allie shook her head. "That doesn't look promising, does it?"

"I don't see anything but jungle."

"Let's head for this spot," she suggested, indicating the second site. Joe nodded and made an adjustment to the controls, and ten minutes later they had completed two passes over the site, with the same result as the first.

"If there's anything down there, it's not obvious from the air," Joe said. "Looks like we're headed into Myanmar."

Allie nodded, lost in thought. When they crossed the Mekong, Joe turned to her. "What were you doing at that river? Not really that close to any of the sites, is it?"

Allie frowned as she debated telling him about the plane crash. After a few moments, she decided it couldn't hurt.

"Someone I know was also looking for the ruins, and their plane crashed. We were hoping to spot the wreckage – sort of kill two birds while we're here."

"A crash? When was that?" Joe asked, his eyes narrowing.

"About a week ago. At night."

He thought for a long beat and turned to her. "Might have heard something about that."

Allie regarded him. "Might have, or did?"

"Depends on who asks, and whether there's a bump in pay involved."

"How does double the money sound?"

"Not as good as triple."

Allie sighed. "Done."

"Seems I heard from the Shan Army folks that a plane went down maybe…five, six nights ago. I'll have to ask. It was one of my men who told me."

"Did he happen to mention where?"

"No, just somewhere past the Mekong. Let me radio and see if he's around."

Joe twisted the volume up on his radio and spoke into the microphone. After several minutes, an answering voice chattered back. Joe listened intently and asked something else. More jabber in the language of the hill tribesmen assaulted him, and he sat back and twisted the volume down. He turned to Allie.

"He's going to reach out to his buddy in the Shan Army. Unfortunately, it's not like picking up the phone. He needs to take a handheld radio and get within range, and then hail them on one of their frequencies. From there, it'll be a matter of how long it takes to find him and learn what he knows."

"Which could take how long?"

Joe pointed into the distance at a pair of hills that had been carved away by erosion, leaving tall, narrow spires reminiscent of the monoliths at Stonehenge – only ten times as tall. "There's your hidden valley."

She swung the binoculars and gazed at the area, following the river that ran through it, pausing along the top of the ridge the water had cut over time. "I don't see any ruins, do you?"

"I'm not the expert. What exactly are we looking for?"

"It's not clear. Something. Anything man-made."

They circled slowly for an hour, and when Joe pointed the plane back toward Laos, Allie's frustration was palpable.

"What do you think?" Joe asked.

"It could be. I mean, it matches the description we have. But I didn't see anything obvious, did you? Supposedly there's a cave, inside of which is the temple."

"Only way to know for sure is to go in on foot. That's one of the problems with overflying. There's a limit to what you can spot." He paused. "It's a big area. Maybe it doesn't seem that way in photos, but it's a lot of ground to cover."

She watched as the valley disappeared beneath them and nodded.

"Looks like we're going for a hike."

# Chapter Twenty-Eight

Drake and Uncle Pete sat on a log, drinking water like lost men at a desert oasis as their host watched, the barrel of his AK-47 making it abundantly clear that they were not to attempt anything. Drake finished with his jug and rubbed his stomach, his body slowly returning to normal after having been run into the ground.

Uncle Pete was taking in the rhythm of the village as the tribe went about its daily business, his eye following particularly attractive young females, Drake noticed with amusement. He was readying a barb when a voice called out from behind them.

"Drake! Uncle Pete! Well, I'll be damned…"

Drake twisted at the sound of Spencer's voice. He wondered if he was hallucinating when his friend sauntered over from down a trail, his gait easy and untroubled, and no evidence of a guard in sight.

"What are you doing here?" Drake sputtered as he leapt to his feet.

"We're the ones who organized the search party. Glad to see it was successful. We had a bet that you were eaten by a tiger," Spencer said.

"Where's Allie?" Drake asked.

"Oh, she's up in the air with our resident guru, looking for you."

"Guru?"

"An American. He has a plane. Runs this tribe, from what I can tell. A little eccentric. Or truthfully, more like a lot."

"She's flying with him? When are they going to come back?"

Spencer shrugged. "Later today, I'm sure." Spencer studied Drake's soiled clothes and disheveled appearance. "Tough night, huh?"

"You don't know the half of it."

"When did they find you?"

"Probably four hours ago, maybe five. Just after dawn." Drake stared at Spencer. "How did you lose the gunmen?"

"Led them astray and then doubled back. Crossed the river at a shallow point, and then got jumped by this bunch. Fortunately, we were able to work a deal with Joe, their shaman. He knows the area and has agreed to help us look for the temple." Spencer filled them in on the details. When he was done, Uncle Pete grunted.

"Maybe not good, work with stranger."

"We don't have a lot of options," Spencer said.

"Is the guy trustworthy?" Drake asked.

"Don't know. It's hard to get a read on him. You'll see what I mean."

The drone of a plane engine approaching echoed through the valley, and Drake and Uncle Pete looked to the sky. Their minder stood with his weapon, and Drake glanced at Spencer. "Any way we can get Mr. Trigger Happy here to stop pointing that thing at us?"

"Don't speak the lingo. Sorry. But sounds like Joe's on his way. He'll take care of it."

"What can you tell me about him?"

"He's kind of a burnout, spouts a lot of metaphysical crap, but he claims to know all the players here and get along with them. The hill people defer to him, and he's clearly the village leader. Beyond that, he's got the world's oldest plane, which he uses to run errands for a who's who of miscreants. And he *really* likes his booze and dope."

"Oh. Perfect, then. Just what the doctor ordered."

"That, and I think he might hear voices."

"A Joan of Arc. Great. And Allie's in a plane with him?"

"To her credit, she wasn't too excited about it."

The plane appeared over a hill and waggled its wings at them before coming in low and then pulling up in a steep climb. Spencer shook his head and began walking down the trail. "Something tells me Allie's not happy, if that's how he's flying."

"She's fine, though?"

"Looks like she was ridden hard and put away wet, but like you, she has youth on her side."

"I can't believe there's an airstrip here," Drake said as they followed Spencer.

"Not sure I'd refer to it in those glowing terms. More like a scar on the valley floor." Spencer kicked a rock off the path. "But apparently it gets the job done."

They neared the clearing in time to see the Cessna on a hovering approach, the wind dimpling the treetops as it almost sheared them with its landing gear, and then it was on the ground, bumping along as it slowed. The little plane roared to a stop next to the shack, where the netting was heaped on the ground, and Joe killed the engine.

Allie leapt from the plane when she spotted Drake and ran to him. Drake took her in his arms and held her as she trembled, and then crushed his lips to hers.

"You kids get a room," Joe said from behind them, breaking the spell. Allie pulled away from Drake, and a multitude of expressions flashed across her face.

"What happened? Are you all right?" she whispered.

Drake nodded. "Rough night in the jungle, and I thought we were toast this morning when your new friend's men found us. But overall, no permanent damage."

Allie nodded. "You'll have to tell me all about it. Do I ever have stories for you."

"Mine has a big snake in it."

Allie glanced at Uncle Pete. Drake shook his head. "No, a real snake. Big."

She smiled and turned to Uncle Pete, who was eyeing Joe. "Drake? Uncle Pete? This is Joe." Allie looked up at Drake's profile. "Joe runs the place. We were searching for you, and when we didn't see anything, we flew over the possible ruins sites. Only one seems like a decent candidate."

"Hey, Joe. Nice to meet you," Drake said, offering his hand.

Joe gave him a small wai instead of shaking it. "Pleasure's all mine, dude." Joe looked to Uncle Pete and said something in Thai after another wai to him.

Uncle Pete beamed at him and bowed, but Allie could see that his eyes were taking Joe's measure.

For his part, Joe appeared completely unconcerned by the newcomers. "Allie here owes me big for locating you, so it was strictly business. I understand you had some trouble after your helo took a dirt dive?"

Drake nodded. "Oh, yeah. We were tracked by some gunmen. Had to lose them by building a raft and riding the rapids." He shrugged. "No big deal."

Concern lit Allie's eyes, which made him happy. That, and the kiss, had demonstrated that her standoffishness had little to do with her interest in him. He wished he understood females better, but contented himself with his small win.

"Joe thinks he might have heard about Christine's plane," Allie announced, and Spencer's stare drilled through her.

"You told him?"

"He's going to put out feelers. Save us a ton of time."

Joe nodded. "Already in the works, Spencer. But if it's where I think it is, your troubles are just starting. It's in an area controlled by the Shan Army, which is occasionally challenged by the Myanmar military in pretty gnarly gun battles."

"So our permits mean nothing," Allie finished.

"Then how do we get to it?"

Joe smiled. "That's where I come in. I know the leader of the Shan Army. It'll cost you some, but I can arrange for safe passage."

Drake gave Allie a sidelong glance. "I'm sure you'll be more than fair."

"It'll be a bargain. But that's not your biggest problem."

"What is?" Spencer asked.

"That area is also being contested by a splinter group that wants a piece of the meth trade – the Red Moon gang. And they're meaner than a wet mongoose," Joe said. "Spencer, help me put the netting back after I fuel up, would you?"

Spencer tilted his chin at the shack. "I was going to ask you about gas."

"Got a couple of barrels out back. Won't take more than a few minutes to top her off."

Spencer followed Joe to the shack, and soon they were filling the tank with a hand-powered pump. When they were done, they unfurled the camo and pulled it into place.

Uncle Pete cleared his throat as Spencer and Joe approached. "Need call home," he said.

Spencer took his meaning. "Joe, I don't suppose you have a sat phone here, do you?"

"Funny you should mention it. I do."

"Can I use it?"

Joe grinned. "Hell, boy, you can have it." His face grew serious. "For five grand."

"What? They only cost a thousand bucks new!"

"Maybe back home. But I own and operate the only telecommunications franchise hereabouts. And sat phones cost five grand today."

"That's robbery," Spencer complained.

"Well, I do have another one that I would part with for twenty-five hundred. Older model. Special today only."

"But it works?" Drake asked.

"Of course. What would be the point of selling you a phone that doesn't work?" Joe asked, pretending offense.

Drake sighed. "Fine. Sold. Where is it?"

"Over in the village. I keep the batteries charged with a solar system."

"In case someone comes along and wants to pay a fortune for a sat phone in the middle of nowhere," Spencer added.

Joe laughed good-naturedly. "You'd be surprised."

Allie gave him a cynical smirk. "Not me."

Joe began walking back to the village, and Drake called after him.

"Can you tell your goon to stop holding his AK on us, Joe?"

Joe turned and spoke a few words. The gunman nodded and lowered his weapon. Drake could have sworn he looked disappointed.

When they made it back to the village, the phone turned out to be a scratched model that was at least a decade old. "Put it on our tab," Allie said.

Joe paused. "That reminds me. We need to work out how you're going to pay me."

"Once we're back in civilization, I can have a wire sent wherever you want. Or I can give you cash, if the bank has enough."

"Oh, wire's preferred. Wouldn't be cool to have a bag of hundreds lying around – might give the villagers the wrong idea. Just use your nice new sat phone to call it in. Twenty for finding these two, and half the sixty for the escort into Shan country. I'll get you the account details later."

Allie smirked. "Why does none of this surprise me? I should have asked if you take credit cards."

"Nah. Too much fraud." He snapped the battery into place, turned the phone on, shook it, and then removed the battery. "Gotta charge it again. Been a while. Give me a few hours, and it'll be good as new."

"You sure it works?"

"Or your money back."

# Chapter Twenty-Nine

Allie, Drake, and Spencer were sitting in the shade when Joe reappeared, obviously excited. Allie stood as he approached with a handheld radio in one hand.

"Looks like you're going to owe me that plane bonus sooner than we thought," he said. "Which reminds me. We never discussed the amount."

"Surprise us," Drake said, his tone dry.

"I'm thinking…if a temple's worth sixty, a plane's got to be worth…forty?"

Allie couldn't help but smile. "Seems like the lucky one today was you all around, huh?"

Joe gave a small shrug. "I keep telling you to open your heart to the universe, but I can only do so much."

"More like open your wallet," Drake said to Spencer.

Joe chuckled. "Or you can take your chances looking for it on your own. Let me know when you want to go in search of these ruins."

"You really think you know where the plane is?" Spencer asked.

"Within a kilometer or so. One of the Shan men was on night patrol in the jungle when he heard it crash. Said it started raining right after, but he's sure it was a plane. If so, we know where he was, so it's just a matter of calculating the flight pattern. Where was the plane coming from?"

"The north," Spencer said.

"Flying to?"

"Chiang Rai."

Joe's brow furrowed. "That's weird. Wonder why they were on that side of the border? Kind of out of their way."

"We heard there was heavy weather over Laos, so they probably detoured to avoid the worst of it."

Joe's eyes sparkled with understanding. "Oh, that was the night! Yeah, it was pretty messed up, even for around here. No wonder they veered west." He paused and gave Drake a hard stare. "Take your time thinking my proposal over. If I don't have to fly anymore today, I'm going to take a nap."

Drake checked his wristwatch. "We still have, what, four hours of light?"

Joe nodded. "'Bout that."

Drake made a summary decision. "Fine. You're now a hundred grand richer, if you can help us find the plane and the temple."

Joe held up a finger. "Hundred and twenty-two five. Remember the finder's fee for rescuing you, and your new-to-you phone."

Drake appraised him. For a hippy recluse, there was nothing lax about his math skills.

Joe grinned in victory. "Let's get into the air. Is it going to be you and me again, little lady? Only room for one passenger in the plane."

She shrugged. "Might as well."

"I'll go," Drake volunteered.

They returned to the airstrip, and Joe gazed at a line of angry clouds moving from the south. He sniffed at the air, held up a wet finger, and then gave a small wai to the sun. Drake and Allie said nothing. Spencer and Uncle Pete hung back as Joe walked to the dirt runway and knelt, touching the ground and massaging some of the grit with his fingers before standing and nodding. "Spencer? Little help for the old man?"

Five minutes later they were soaring above the jungle in a northerly direction. Joe filled Drake in on the details as they droned toward their destination.

"The Shan scout was near a waterfall on the western side of the

Mekong just after an area he describes as a dogleg. I know the spot. From there, we can skim the tops of the trees. If there's a crashed plane there, we'll find it."

"Wouldn't it be visible from satellite if we can see it from a plane?"

"Don't know anything about that. Sorry. Why? You know someone with a satellite?"

Drake backpedalled, realizing he'd come close to revealing too much. "Not unless you're selling one. Which wouldn't be a shock."

"Nope. Just the phones. There's a thriving market in them lately."

"Supply and demand," Drake said.

He reminded himself not to let down his guard with Joe. He appeared harmless, but there was definitely an edge to him, and Drake wouldn't have bet his life that Joe wouldn't sell them out if the opportunity came up—like the right buyers. Something had driven him into the Laotian jungle, living a life with killers and drug smugglers, his village fortified like a military base in a war zone.

When they reached the dogleg in the river, Joe corrected west and dropped to a thousand feet over the canopy. They cruised for fifteen minutes, and then he called out to Drake over the motor. "Off to your right. About two o'clock. See it? That's the waterfall."

Drake focused the binoculars, trying to steady them so he wouldn't feel sick, and spied the white water coursing over rocks. "Does it have a name?"

Joe shook his head. "Not much around here does." He pointed ahead and dropped closer to the treetops. "We should be coming up on the flight path in a short while." He switched on the GPS and thumbed through the images, zooming in and setting a waypoint where the falls were. "Okay. It could be anywhere around here. Keep your eyes peeled."

Drake concentrated on the areas of the mountainous terrain he could make out through the trees, which weren't many. Minutes went by as Joe circled and retraced their course, and before he knew it, they'd been in the area for two hours. Joe looked over to Laos as he made another graceful bank, and his lips tightened into a thin line.

"That front's getting too close for comfort. We need to head back."

Drake nodded, suddenly exhausted by the adrenaline leaving his system after sustained anticipation. "Maybe we'll spot it tomorrow." He looked off into the near distance and pointed to a pair of karst peaks. "Is that our valley?"

"Yep."

Two holes suddenly appeared in the left wing, and Joe cursed as he twisted the plane right. Drake stared at the holes as the turn's g-force pressed him back into the seat, Joe urging the plane higher as fast as it would climb. "Are those...did somebody just shoot at us?"

Joe nodded grimly. "Looks that way to me."

"I thought you said everybody knows you."

"They do. But not everyone likes me. Hang on," he said, and jerked the plane to the left as he continued to ascend. "Don't want to be an easy target."

Drake closed his eyes. The easy flight was now a nightmare as Joe twisted and turned the plane for all he was worth. When the plane steadied, he opened them and checked the altimeter – they were at six thousand feet.

"That should take care of that. They won't want to waste any ammo now."

"They actually hit us."

"Probably had to empty a full magazine to do it."

Drake took another fearful look at the bullet holes, and then his gaze drifted down to the canopy, obviously dangerous even from the air. His mind wandered to the memory of the helicopter plunge as his eyes traced a line, following the natural curve of the stream ahead. He was turning to speak to Joe again when something winked in the fading sunlight. His words caught in his throat and he sat up straighter in the uncomfortable seat. *There it was again*. It wasn't his imagination.

Drake stiffened and grabbed Joe's arm. Joe turned in surprise as Drake's grip tightened. Drake raised the glasses again as Joe pulled free of his hand.

"What is it?" Joe demanded.

Drake stared through the binoculars for a long beat and then lowered them, his eyes glued to the stream.

"I see something."

# Chapter Thirty

Allie paced near the airstrip while Uncle Pete taught Spencer some Thai words, delighted at the American's mispronunciations. Spencer was good-natured about the ribbing he was receiving, pausing to occasionally protest that he used to have a rudimentary command of things like greetings.

"Maybe brain soft? Drinky drinky? Or smoke?"

"No. I just didn't file it away in my permanent banks."

Uncle Pete's brow beetled. "You got bank?"

"Not like that. Memory banks."

"Farangs got bank for memory?"

"Never mind."

Thunder boomed as the storm neared and Allie looked to the sky, worried. The clouds, purple and gunmetal gray in the waning light, were almost on top of them now, pregnant with rain and pulsing with lightning. Another explosion echoed from the hills, and she shook her head. "They're never going to make it."

Their heads swiveled in unison as Joe's plane appeared from the west, buzzed over the runway, and then executed a tight turn before diving for the dirt strip. The Cessna was a flyspeck against the looming backdrop of the massive roiling clouds, and moments after it touched down, the near hills disappeared behind a gray curtain of heavy rain.

They ran to the plane as it coasted to a stop near the hut. The motor fell quiet and the air was filled with the sound and fury of nature. Joe and Drake jumped from the plane, and Joe jogged toward them.

"Never mind the netting. We can put it on later."

"Allie, we found it!" Drake cried triumphantly.

"The plane? You did?"

He nodded and said something that was drowned out by another deep explosion of thunder.

"What?" Allie yelled as the first heavy raindrops began falling around them, the sporadic drops almost instantly transforming into opaque sheets. Joe led them at a run toward the village and they struggled to keep up; the older man was considerably spryer than his age would suggest. Allie slipped and went down in the mud, and Spencer helped her up with an unceremonious pull on her arm.

When they reached the huts, they darted inside the one Spencer and Allie had slept in, while Joe continued on to his. All four of them stood dripping as the downpour intensified, the thunder now nearly continuous and the air crisp with ozone from nearby lightning strikes. Allie sank to the wood floor with a sigh. Drake flopped beside her and pushed a wet lock of her hair from her eyes, and she gave him a tired smile. Spencer sat across from them, while Uncle Pete chose to remain standing, leaning against a wall, eyes locked on the deluge outside.

"I said I found it. I saw it out of the corner of my eye. It was so weird. One minute we're doing evasive maneuvers and the next, there it is. I wouldn't have spotted it if we hadn't gone so much higher. From lower we'd have had to be right on top of it. So strange – I mean, if the sun hadn't been at that exact angle, and we hadn't climbed like we did…"

"Go back…evasive maneuvers?" Spencer asked.

"Oh. Yeah. We got shot. The plane took at least two rounds. Joe said he'd check it tomorrow, once it stops raining."

"Wait – someone shot at you?" Spencer demanded.

"Apparently it happens around here," Drake said. "We're okay, don't worry. The important thing is that we found the crash site. Joe thought the rain should fade by morning."

Uncle Pete looked to the sky. "Storm over in few hours, tops."

Drake mopped his forehead with a wet sleeve. "Hope you're right."

"I right."

"Where's the plane, exactly?" Spencer asked.

"It looks like it crashed in a small stream. Or maybe that's just where it wound up. Hard to tell. We had to get back because of the storm." Drake hesitated. "Joe set a waypoint. He said we could find it again."

"Is it near the Mekong?"

"Not really – more like forty or so miles, at least. But you can see our two peaks from it. The temple site."

"How far is it from there?" Allie asked.

"I don't know. Maybe two or three miles?"

Spencer eyed him. "Let's get back to someone shooting at you."

"Joe says this territory is in play. Being disputed by a new drug gang. They've carved out a chunk and successfully held off the Shan Army, who doesn't seem that interested in it, except on principle."

"I suppose you've seen one jungle, you've seen them all," Spencer said.

"Guess so. Joe says they've set up a meth factory and are pretty well armed. Hundreds of men. Most ex-Shan, so they know each other's tricks. It's a standoff right now."

Allie sat back. "Great. So both the plane and the valley are in this group's territory?"

"Joe thinks so, but he says the situation's fluid. It's more like they're in a no-man's land between the two areas. Shan to the north, the splinter faction to the south."

"And us in the middle. This just gets better and better," Spencer said.

They sat wordlessly as the storm tore at the thatched roof, and Allie and Drake dozed while Spencer joined Uncle Pete in watching the downpour. After an hour the intensity lessened, and in another half hour the rain had stopped completely. Uncle Pete grinned like he'd just won a marathon and gave Spencer a high five.

Minutes later Joe's voice called from outside the doorway. "Phone's charged."

Allie and Drake awoke and eyed the opening groggily. Allie stood and moved to the threshold. Joe approached, the phone in hand. "Hate to let this baby go. It's a vintage piece. Collector's item."

"You mean relic," Allie said.

"He means worthless pile of old junk," Drake corrected.

"Such a downer, man," Joe said. "Turn that frown upside down. Hey, I know. You want some weed? Put you in touch with your higher energy."

"Pretty sure I just need some sleep," Drake said.

"This stuff's killer. I mean, like, 'whoa, whose hands are these attached to my arms' kind of otherworldly high," Joe persisted. "Takes it to a whole 'nother level."

Drake shook his head. "I'm holding out for the heroin."

Joe made a face. "That's mean stuff, dude. Sledgehammer to the back of the head."

"I've heard."

"Oh, I get it. You're F-ing with me." Joe chuckled. "That's cool. Remember Buddha was always smiling."

"Maybe he was wincing because he had gas," Spencer said, and Uncle Pete snorted.

"The cosmos is absurd, it's true. But beautiful, man. You should take some time to appreciate it." Joe handed over the phone and battery. "By the way, when you power it on, might not want to talk too long. And once you're done, turn it off and remove the battery right away."

Drake frowned. "Why? Is the battery that much of a dud?"

"Nah, it's primo. More the phone. I mean, it's probably nothing. The dude I bought it from said it might be a little hot, that's all."

"Hot? As in stolen?"

"I wouldn't traffic in stolen goods, young man," Joe said, his tone serious. "No, apparently he had a disagreement with some government or other and narrowly missed being taken out by a drone strike. He thinks they triangulated the phone chip. But that was probably just a story, you know? Everybody likes a good story. I'm pretty sure it's fine."

Drake eyed the phone like it was a scorpion. "You *are* frigging joking, right?"

Joe shrugged. "You wanted a bargain, dude, and hot deals always have strings. Nothing in life's free, kid. Just don't stay on the call too long, and pull the battery as soon as you can – and just to be safe, might want to go down the trail a ways before plugging it in. Not that there's anything to worry about." Joe smiled. "And send positive vibes. Don't worry, be happy."

They watched Joe shuffle off through the mud, whistling to himself, and Spencer shook his head. "Drone strike? Can that be for real?"

"Who is this guy?" Drake asked. Allie slid the battery into place with a snick and powered the phone on. The signal was moderately strong. She handed the phone to Uncle Pete and told him to make the call from the airstrip. The little Thai stepped down into the mud and disappeared into the jungle. Drake turned to Allie when he was gone. "Once he gets back, I want to talk to Collins. This is not what we signed up for at all."

"What? You're going to let a little Shan Army and some drug lords keep you from the temple?" Spencer teased.

"I'm serious. They shot at the plane. We could have been killed."

"Well, let's see what he says, but remember that Christine – if she's alive – has now been out there for a week," Spencer said. "I have a feeling he's going to insist we investigate the wreckage immediately. We're her only chance."

"It's not worth risking our lives for," Drake insisted. He was looking at Allie, and it was obvious he was intent on protecting her from harm.

"True. Maybe our new best buddy Joe will have some ideas," Allie said.

Drake shook his head. "Right. Mr. Super Bong is going to lead us to victory."

"He did find the plane, and we narrowed the valley down to the one in Myanmar."

Spencer nodded. "I agree with Drake: it's dangerous. But I also know how the agency works. If we're this close, there's no way they're going to let us turn back. Remember that we're the only ones with the permits, and those are ostensibly to search for the temple. If we turn our backs on this, the girl's dead."

"She's probably dead already," Drake stated flatly. "We've gotten a sense of how bad the jungle is. She crashed in it at night. Let's be honest, at least among ourselves."

Allie sighed. "The difference between 'probably' and 'not' is the difference between thinking you're pregnant and being pregnant," Allie said softly. "Might not matter to anyone else, but it matters a hell of a lot to the baby and the mom."

Drake remembered the discussion with Christine's mother, and his tone softened. "Yeah, you're right. We gave our word to Ms. Blakely we'd see this through. I just don't want to risk anyone's life to keep that promise."

Uncle Pete returned. He passed the phone to Allie, who handed it to Drake. "Do what you think best, Drake. For what it's worth, I think you made the right call when you agreed to this."

Spencer stepped aside so Drake could pass. "I'm not big on altruism, but Allie's got a point. We didn't say we'd do our best unless it got dangerous; we agreed to the terms, and the CIA did its part and got us the permits. Seems like a deal's a deal, even if the deal sucks for us now. I bet that's what Collins says."

"Collins isn't risking his life."

"True." Spencer exhaled and met Drake's stare. "It's also true that I need the money this treasure could mean, Drake. So maybe I'm more motivated to make it work. I'm not dissing you in any way, but if you walk from this, you're still set. My life's more of a question mark, so I'm in, no matter what."

"You'd continue even if I pulled the plug?"

"Cornered rats fight harder."

"You're not a rat. And the hedge fund still has your money, remember?"

"That's what they say. But when you ask someone to hold your wallet, and they agree but then come up with fifty reasons you can't have it back? Not a good sign." Spencer looked at Allie. "Ever."

Ten minutes went by agonizingly slowly, and Allie's lids were growing heavy when Drake reappeared, his jaw set in grim determination. He removed the battery from the phone and sat down on the mat next to Allie, took her hand in his, and looked her in the eyes.

"They want us to get going at first light."

"And you said?"

Drake squeezed her hand, his gaze unflinching.

"We're going in."

# Chapter Thirty-One

Reggie Waters rolled over on the mat he was trying to sleep on and waved away a mosquito with a listless hand. The persistent insect ignored the feeble gesture and landed on his lip, the one spot Reggie hadn't slathered with insect repellent. Reggie stirred as the mosquito crept to a promising area and drove its long proboscis into the tender flesh. The sting of the forced entry woke Reggie fully and he sat up. The mosquito took flight, its search for nourishing blood aborted at the unexpected jarring.

He cursed quietly and his eyes drifted to where his bag rested on the flattened grass, his satellite phone atop it. Blinking, signaling that he'd missed a call.

Reggie swore again, this time audibly, and retrieved the phone. His Seiko dive watch showed that it was almost seven a.m. The sun was still too low on the horizon to really penetrate the overhead canopy, and his jungle encampment was still dark with shadows. He pushed away the rain poncho he'd jury-rigged over his head to shelter himself from the rain and checked the time of the call.

Calls.

Beginning at eleven the prior night, he'd received one call per hour thereafter. Reggie had set the phone to vibrate lest its warble draw the attention of predators – his Laotian guide had refused to stay with him overnight and warned him that he was in drug-gang territory, so to be discreet. They'd agree to rendezvous this morning at eight, but Reggie had his doubts as to whether the boat captain would reappear – even though he'd only collected half the promised money, he was alive to spend it, whereas the odds apparently declined the further north on the Mekong he pushed.

He thumbed the phone to active status and stood – he'd need to find a clearing for decent reception. He hurriedly dismantled his camp and shouldered his bag, the phone in one hand, an ancient Browning 9mm pistol the captain had sold him for five times the going rate in the other, and set off toward the river, which was a few hundred yards west.

Reggie had only made it thirty yards when he heard voices and smelled tobacco smoke. He crouched in the brush and stayed motionless, recalling the captain's words.

"Plenty bad guy working river. Not safe."

"Right, but on the Laos side, there's a dirt road that parallels the river, and enough traffic to and from the farms, so it's probably okay, isn't it?"

The captain had shaken his head. "No work that way. Drug gang run that part Laos. Bad news. Farmers pay protection. But druggies everywhere. Plenty guns. Shoot first, no ask questions. Many disappear there."

"What about the Myanmar side?"

"Worse. Even Laos druggies scared of Myanmar."

Reggie glanced down at the peashooter that was his only defense and then back to the trail ahead. The captain had explained that if the dirt road was dangerous, the trails were worse – that's where the caravans of beasts of burden laden with sacks of candy-coated methamphetamine tablets, referred to as *yaba*, worked their way south, accompanied by heavily armed traffickers who would kill anyone they encountered.

A procession of Laotians came into view, their AKs unmistakable even through the dense vegetation. They were leading a half-dozen mules carrying packs heavy with yaba bound for the metropolitan areas of Thailand, where the meth and caffeine blend was the most popular drug in the country, especially among sex workers and in the thriving nightclub scene. Reggie shrank back and willed himself to blend in with the darkened jungle – as lethal as he was, his odds against six automatic rifles were nil.

The men didn't seem to be expecting trouble, though, judging by their chatter and the cigarettes. Reggie wasn't sure whether to find it reassuring or troubling that they seemed so unconcerned. While it meant that they were less likely to have their antennae finely tuned, it also spoke to the security they must feel – reinforcing that, as the captain had warned, they were a law unto themselves.

Reggie remained still as the column filed past his hiding place, and was ready to issue a sigh of relief when one of the mules snorted in alarm, its eyes focused on where he crouched. Reggie silently did the math on the number of rounds in his pistol and, at thirty to forty yards, the likelihood of being able to hit all the men before they could turn their higher power weapons on him. Even though he was a marksman whose accuracy was far above the norm, one semiautomatic handgun against a hail of fully auto fire was suicide.

He controlled his breathing, forcing his heart rate lower in preparation for his last stand, his finger hovering over the trigger. His eyes darted to the side – a fallen tree, rotting, but possibly still solid enough to provide cover. He would take out the leader first, a straightforward kill shot, and then dive for the log and pick off as many of the men as he could before they nailed him. The prospect was grim, but Reggie had long ago resigned himself to death, and a small part of him believed that going out in a blaze might be preferable to a slow decline in the climate-controlled air of an office in Washington.

The lead man peered into the brush, now on alert, and then his companion raised his rifle. The leader said something in rapid-fire Laotian, and the man nodded and began an approach. Reggie steadily raised the Browning and drew a bead on the man's sweating face, and then dropped his aim to the center of his chest – a shot to the torso at that range was a sure thing, a head shot less certain.

The man kept coming and Reggie's finger tightened on the trigger. As he was squeezing it, the man froze, his eyes wide. Reggie let some pressure off as the gunman backed carefully away, his gaze fixed on the ground in front of him, not on Reggie. He returned to the column, and Reggie understood what had happened to save the trafficker's life when he pantomimed flaps opening at the side of his neck as the others laughed.

The group continued on its way and Reggie turned his attention to the brush, where he was sure one of the myriad king cobras that called the area home was lurking. He maintained his position for five minutes, eyes roaming over the jungle floor, before rising and making his way gingerly to the trail, giving the suspect area a wide berth. Aside from being deadly, cobras were fiercely territorial, and he didn't want to tempt fate twice in a handful of minutes.

He veered west and made it to a clearing near the river. After checking the satellite phone signal and altering his position slightly, he made a call.

His control answered in seconds. "What happened?"

"I had company. Some of the local rabble. But I can talk now."

"Is the situation stable?"

"As much as any around here."

"We heard from the Thai guide – they're moving into Myanmar this morning. They found the plane and will hit the trail at dawn."

"So too late for me to join them?"

"Affirmative."

"Why didn't they wait?"

"The guide said that it was a nonstarter. There's a warlord in control of the area, and a local is going to act as their envoy to ensure safe passage. He's got ties to the Shans. But the more unfamiliar faces, the more risk, so he didn't want to chance it. The local doesn't know this is an agency op, either, and explaining you would have taken some doing."

"I get it. How should I proceed?"

"We have the approximate coordinates for the plane. You should shadow them if you can pick up their trail to the wreck site." The control told him the longitude and latitude, and he fished an aluminum shaft pen from his pocket and wrote the information on a slip of paper.

"Should I make myself known?"

"Only if absolutely necessary. The guide understands he's to retrieve anything that looks pertinent: remains of computers, flash drives, CDs, that sort of thing. Although given the circumstances, it's unlikely there's going to be much besides wreckage."

"Why don't I just go through it if I arrive first?"

"You won't be able to from where you are. They've got a hell of a head start."

"Roger that. What can you tell me about the Shans?"

The control gave him a brief rundown, and when he was done, Reggie was silent for several moments. When he spoke, he chose his words carefully. "Any chance of getting me some backup? All I've got is a pistol. Sounds like I could use SEAL Team Six."

"We discussed it. We're putting out the word to see if we can locate any friendlies in Myanmar. But don't count on it. Best case, maybe we can get you some heavier ordnance."

Which meant he was on his own. Reggie knew how the system worked. They wanted to keep him deniable, and a larger presence would jeopardize that. At the end of the day, Reggie was expendable, as were all field assets. The mission always came first.

"I'll check back in once I'm across the river. Don't bother calling. I'm shutting the phone off to save battery. Sounds like I'm going to be out here a while."

"Understood."

Reggie powered down and considered his next step. He'd need to find a way across the Mekong, which was easily three hundred yards at its narrowest point in that region, so negotiating it on his own was out of the question. Which meant he'd need a boat. Of course, the captain was history now, Reggie having moved from his campsite, assuming the Thai ever returned.

He set off north, hoping that he could find a native who would exchange safe passage for a fistful of dollars. Reggie was confident he would – the only question was how much time it would take to find someone.

# Chapter Thirty-Two

Joe led the group to the Mekong River, where one of his men had arranged a pair of dugouts to ferry them across the sprawling span of muddy rushing water. They climbed aboard, one of the precarious craft carrying Allie, Drake and Spencer, the other with Joe and Uncle Pete, who was quieter than usual. Their captain was a reed-thin man whose face was etched by a lifetime of hardship, and when he grinned a gap-toothed greeting, he looked like a demonic carving from one of the Khmer temples.

The trip across the river took five minutes, the tiny motor mounted to the back of the canoe barely able to negotiate the current. When the first boat arrived at the far side, they disembarked while the man watched the bank nervously. Once on land they waited for Joe and Uncle Pete, whose boat was slower, and Drake adjusted the ratty backpack strapped to his shoulders – one of three castoffs Joe had offered to lend them. Surprisingly, he didn't charge them the price of a business jet to do so. They'd packed as many provisions as Joe could find them in the village, and each carried three curved thirty-round magazines for the AK-47s Joe had handed them.

"Chinese production, but reliable. You lose one, cost you a grand."

"How much per bullet?" Spencer asked, his face serious.

"On the house, up to the first thirty, so make every shot count."

Joe had grinned and explained that they would only need the weapons once they were in the disputed zone. While they were in established Shan territory, they'd be as safe as in their mother's arms. Spencer had looked at him doubtfully but remained silent, and Drake had shaken his head and gone to help Allie pack her kit.

Birds called from the branches of the tall trees as Joe led them forward. Earlier, they'd agreed to remain silent until he rendezvoused with his Myanmar contact – a lieutenant who reported to General Yawd Serk, who headed up the rebel organization. That group, officially called the Shan State Army – South, had risen to power when the original Shan State Army dissolved in 1995.

The members of the group, as Joe informed them, wore actual uniforms and were well equipped with weapons from the U.S. and China, and appeared to be prosperous from their drug trafficking as well as clandestine funding from the American government.

"Why would the U.S. support a drug cartel?" Allie had asked.

Joe had shrugged. "Wouldn't be the first time."

They began the trek through the jungle hills, sticking to the trails that snaked around the rises, the mud soon caking their boots with reddish-brown. After four hours of fast hiking, they arrived at a two-lane strip of battered asphalt running north to south, where a small Buddhist temple sat at the roadside, the sun blinding as it reflected off the curves of its golden dome. Three men, all in green camouflage uniforms, waited in the shade. Beside them were two of the sorriest tuk-tuks ever built and a motorcycle, all coated with a thick layer of mud.

One of the men detached himself from his companions and greeted Joe with a nod of his head. They spoke in hushed tones, and then Joe turned to Allie. "This is the welcome committee. They brought the vehicles for us – otherwise it would be a two-day walk, easy. He said the track is pretty decent, so we should be able to make it to their camp by nightfall."

"They aren't worried about an aerial attack from the Myanmar military?"

"It's been quiet for a few years. Everything's settled down, and there's a cautious truce in place, even if neither side officially acknowledges it." Joe walked over and inspected the tuk-tuks. "Two people will fit in each. I'll ride bitch on the bike."

Joe asked the Shan fighters a question, and they nodded in unison. Joe set his pack down, extracted a few mangos and a banana, and held them out to Allie and Drake. "Lunch time. They said we have ten minutes, and then we've got to get moving. Even they don't want to brave the trails after dark."

The company ate their fruit and were soon on their bouncing way. The tuk-tuks periodically slid in the mud, but the drivers were skilled enough to avoid disaster. The going was agonizingly slow, each slope posing a substantial challenge to the small engines, which buzzed like lawn mowers as the pilots gave them full throttle.

They stopped after three hours, and the drivers refilled the fuel tanks from plastic jugs. Then they were on the second leg, where the terrain became more treacherous with each mile. When twilight arrived, the men switched on their lights, and Joe called out from his position on the rear of the motorcycle. "Won't be long now. He says we're only a few klicks away."

Joe's optimism proved overstated, and it was pitch black when they pulled around a bend and saw fires glowing in a large clearing. Tents ringed the area, and they could make out soldiers patrolling the perimeter.

The vehicles drew to a stop in front of what looked like a command tent, the structure larger than those surrounding it, and the riders cut the motors. Everyone disembarked, and a short older man with a neatly clipped gray mustache approached, limping slightly as he neared. Joe nodded to him and offered a small respectful wai. The man mirrored the gesture and then studied the new arrivals. After a few uncomfortable moments, he said something Joe seemed to understand. Joe turned to them.

"This is Colonel Htut Leng. He commands this outpost. His word is law here. The only higher authority is the general, and of course, God." Joe grinned. "And I'm not sure that's the correct order."

Leng motioned for them to move to one of the fires, where two logs had been pushed near to serve as benches. Leng lowered himself onto one and Joe sat opposite him. Allie joined Joe, trailed by Drake and Spencer. Uncle Pete reluctantly sat at the far end of the colonel's log, appearing ill at ease.

Leng began speaking, offering what seemed like a monologue. When he was done, Joe waited as a sign of respect before translating.

"He says that while we are allies of sorts, your permits are meaningless to him, as they were issued by a rogue state he doesn't recognize. So he respectfully declines your request to go in search of the ruins."

Drake bristled, but Spencer eyed him calmly and he quieted himself before saying anything. "So that's the opening salvo? How long do you think this will take?"

"These people love to negotiate. It's like the national pastime. It could last hours." Joe winked at Allie. "But I brought a healthy supply of rice wine, so we might be able to shorten it up some. We'll see. It's my special bottling – probably forty proof instead of around fifteen."

"No weed? What's wrong with them?" Drake asked.

"Not their bag, man. But you'll all be expected to drink some. No way around it, or you'll seem rude."

"Where are we going to sleep tonight?"

"They should provide tents. If not, it's the stars for our roof."

"Meaning periodic rain," Drake said.

"No plan's perfect." Joe extracted a plastic jug from his pack and held it aloft, his eyes shining bright in the firelight. He said something to the colonel, who first refused, and then acquiesced.

"Oh, brother," Drake said, and Joe gave him a hard stare before taking a pull from the jug and handing it to Leng, who snapped his fingers at a nearby underling. Moments later a handful of tin cups materialized and Joe nodded gratefully. Leng took a deep drink from the jug and set it down so they could pour themselves portions, and then belched loudly and smiled in appreciation. Joe matched his grin and pointed to the jug.

"Fill everyone's up, but don't pour much. I have a feeling we're going to need all the firepower I can muster here."

Spencer rose and did as instructed, spilling an inch of the amber liquid into the cups before handing it back to Joe. Uncle Pete stood and took one, and Drake picked two up and offered one to Allie. She made a small grimace and took it. Leng chuckled. Joe held the jug aloft and offered a toast, and everyone raised their cups and took cautious sips as Joe chugged a healthy swallow, blinked twice, and passed the jug back to Leng.

Allie almost choked when the liquor hit the back of her throat, and it was all she could do not to gag. Drake's reaction was only slightly better, whereas Spencer and Uncle Pete could have been drinking tea.

Drake's eyes watered as he held the cup. "Wow. That's gasoline."

Joe ignored him, now in a hushed discussion with Leng. Allie elbowed Drake. "You want mine too?"

He shook his head. "Don't want to be rude."

"Bastard."

"Have I told you how beautiful you are when I'm drinking?" Drake paused. "Wait, that didn't come out right."

Her eyes became slits. "Oh, I got the message."

"No, I meant it's easier to say so when…never mind."

"If you can find anything attractive about me after three days in the jungle, you've got a more vivid imagination than even Joe does," Allie said, and took another small taste of the wine. "God, that's foul," she said, smiling like it was wonderful. "I wonder if I'll go blind."

Joe twisted toward her. "Leng says he likes you."

"I hope that's not a condition for us to go in," she replied evenly.

"It is now, but let's see how the night goes. At least we're horse-trading, not being blocked completely."

"It's charming to view me as a dumb animal to argue over," Allie said, the smile frozen on her face.

"Cultural. Nothing personal. Don't worry. I'll work around it."

"Do that," Drake said.

An hour went by, and then another, the jug level dropping steadily until it was empty. Both Joe and Leng appeared to be in fine spirits, but Joe seemed surprised when Leng called his lieutenant over and growled an order. The man ran to the command tent and came back with a clay bottle. Joe grinned, and Leng poured everyone another portion, and then tipped the bottle to his mouth and gulped a mouthful. He sighed contentedly and the drinking ritual continued, the only positive that this spirit was weaker than Joe's knockout potion.

Eventually that bottle was finished as well, and Joe sat forward, now clearly in his cups. Leng motioned into the darkness, and two young men with sergeant's stripes approached. Joe nodded and turned to Allie. "These are our escorts. Never mind their names. We can call them Dick and Harry."

"What? Wait. We don't want these guys to know where the ruins are, exactly – or the plane."

"Well, that wasn't an option. And I had to promise to cut him in on the booty. He wants an even share. I told him that's not a problem – a five-way split seems more than fair."

"You can't agree to that," Spencer protested.

"Too late. It was a condition."

"And it's not a five-way split. Uncle Pete isn't taking a cut," Drake corrected.

"Oh, I didn't think he was. I figured you'd want me to have a slice since I'm going so far above the call of duty."

"Absolutely not," Drake said. "It's not negotiable."

Joe shrugged, and when he spoke, his voice sounded less inebriated. "You want me to tell him you said he can suck it? He might not react well. Fair warning."

Drake looked to Allie and then Spencer. "It's your call. Neither of us has as much riding on the outcome as you do."

Spencer swallowed the dregs of his cup, tossed it in front of him, and stared into the dimming flames. He sat silently for a long spell, and when he spoke, it was barely more than a whisper. "Seems like it's screw Spencer year, huh? Hell yes, they can have it. Hundred percent of nothing's nothing, if my calculator's right."

Joe grinned and returned to Leng, who beamed at them all drunkenly when Joe broke the news. After much bowing and scraping, Dick and Harry escorted them to a pair of tents, while Joe sat with Leng, a third container of liquor having materialized in order to celebrate the auspicious alliance. Drake, Spencer, and Allie climbed into one of the tents, exhausted from the day's march, and after saying good night to each other, curled up and went to sleep, the morning rushing at them with the speed of a runaway train.

# Chapter Thirty-Three

*Mong Lin, Myanmar*

Jiao yawned and stretched as he bedded down on a rough wood-framed cot in the tiny farming village where he'd called it a night after a long journey from the river. His source had checked in the day before and alerted the Chinese about where the Americans were headed, and he knew he'd have to tread cautiously if he was to make it without being discovered. His men were camped out in a nearby field – he'd taken pains to avoid being seen with them as a group, as he didn't want to arouse any interest.

An offer of a few bills to the largest farm had yielded a cot in a rustic room adjacent to the barn, which was more than fine after the previous night in the jungle. Tomorrow he'd be going deeper into hostile territory and would be sleeping on a bedroll, so Jiao stretched and savored the relative luxury of four walls and running water nearby.

The source had told headquarters that the Americans had located the plane deep in Shan Army territory, and were going to attempt to work a deal with that group. Jiao's intent was to shadow them and, once they were at the plane, to make his move – or not, depending on what the source indicated they found. The informer had a sat phone, as did Jiao, so communications weren't a problem, although his source had made it clear that the phone would be off until he was ready to share information.

Jiao didn't like that arrangement, but the informer had been adamant, so he'd backed down and agreed to the terms. He could see the logic – the last thing the snitch wanted was to be found out, and Jiao shared that fear. The man would be of no use if the Americans suspected he was selling them out. That was to be avoided at all costs.

The irony was that nobody had any idea if Liu had been carrying anything, much less whether it had survived the crash. Likely not, he'd been assured, so this whole ordeal was probably for nothing. But even if the odds were only one in a million, they had to be sure – the stakes were far too high to leave anything to chance. The possibility of Liu being in possession of data the Chinese might want had been the only part of Jiao's final solution in sabotaging the plane that he hadn't factored in; but then again, he hadn't had all the information when making the decision.

Jiao tried to get comfortable on the canvas as his mind went over the next day's objective. They'd have to make better time than they had today, because they had to cover at least thirty miles. The hope was that he could find a willing driver who could cart them at least part of the way; otherwise it was looking like two full days to reach the site.

That part made him apprehensive. In spite of the impression headquarters had, the roads were little more than ruts. His superiors believed it wouldn't be difficult to make most of the trip by truck or bike, but Jiao wasn't so sure.

He and his men were dressed in local garb, the cheap shirts and pants worn by the farmers, and if stopped by the Shan army, they'd likely be ignored. That was the hope, anyway. If all else failed, he could buy his way out of trouble. The population's love for money was reliable anywhere in the world, just as his informant had been buyable. The only thing that ever changed was the currency and the amount.

~ ~ ~

Night creatures serenaded Reggie as he lay on the bank of a creek, his theory being that the flat gravel would act as a deterrent to snakes and other predators. He peered up at the glimmering stars and offered thanks for the lack of clouds. With luck he'd be able to sleep without getting soaked multiple times, as he had throughout the day.

He'd made reasonable progress toward the plane, but it had been a tough slog, and he'd ultimately stolen an ancient bicycle to speed his trip. His guilt had compelled him to leave a fifty-dollar bill in its place, easily five times what it was worth. But the theft had proved fortuitous, and he was now only twenty miles from the coordinates he'd been given – an easy ride, assuming he could continue to avoid Shan Army patrols.

Being obviously not Asian was an impediment operating in Myanmar, but he had no choice but to forge on. He'd do his best, and if captured, would have his control pull strings with the Shan troops, who were on a cordial basis with the CIA. That would blow his cover, but if it was either that or torture and death, he was sure the agency would understand. At least, that was his hope.

But it would be better to stay under the radar. They were so close now. The seemingly impossible had come to pass, and the plane would be inspected shortly – perhaps as soon as tomorrow. Then he could return to the world and leave the entire mess behind, his job done, another successful notch in his belt.

The nearby bushes rustled and he inched the barrel of his pistol over to face it. He wasn't worried about random drug gangs this far inland, but there were plenty of other menaces lurking in the hills, many of them deadly – and hungry.

A small furry form edged from the brush. Two glittering eyes spotted him, and the creature scurried away.

He smiled up at the night. A panther or, worse, a crocodile wouldn't be so easily spooked. He'd debated trying to find a tree to sleep in, but discarded the idea in favor of the bank.

Reggie could go days without rest if absolutely necessary, but as he'd gotten older, his stamina had flagged. He didn't want to test his endurance tomorrow, when things got real. What was possible and what was advisable were two different things, and the aches in his body were unmistakable signals that he was no longer the twenty-something dynamo he'd once been.

He opened his eyes and checked the time. It would be light in six hours. If he got two of sleep, he'd be happy.

# Chapter Thirty-Four

Joe marched toward the hidden valley at the head of a ragged column. Dick and Harry followed directly behind, and the rest trailed in a rough procession along the game trail. Joe gripped a machete in one hand and his AK in the other, and occasionally hacked his way through a tangle of vines and branches, the track only clear to knee level.

"Boar," Joe had explained when he'd found the path. "We'll follow it as long as it leads in the right direction. Better to stay away from any human-sized trails as we enter the contested zone. Don't want to draw enemy fire."

"That would be bad," Drake agreed.

"Total buzz kill," Joe said.

"How will we know when we're out of Shan territory?"

Joe held out his machete toward Dick and Harry. "Just watch their body language. When they look like they're going to piss their pants, we're in no-man's land."

That had been just after dawn, and they'd been hiking southwest ever since, the ground fog thick for the first three hours. The going was slow due to their choice of routes, but Joe had insisted on staying in the densest part of the jungle, using the GPS for guidance as they worked their way toward the twin spires.

They took a break for lunch by the bank of a brook that gushed down the side of a mountain, dining on a rice pudding that Joe assured them would hold for a week without spoiling. Once they were done, they continued plodding toward the valley, climbing steep slopes and traversing rocky outcroppings, the peaks barely visible in the distance when they reached high points above the canopy. It drizzled all afternoon, making an already unpleasant route even more difficult, and everyone was exhausted by the time they reached a stream several miles from the karst peaks.

They made camp with the last of the fading light, and Joe had a hushed conversation with Dick and Harry. Drake had discussed how to distract the pair so that they could sneak away and inspect the wreckage during the night, and Joe had agreed to take one for the team.

A fire was out of the question, given their circumstances, so after the tents were pitched, they sat in the moonlight, which was bright enough for them to see each other clearly, and munched on their dinner. Dick and Harry had some sort of foul-smelling fish concoction they spooned down with mess kits, and every time Allie got a whiff of it, her gorge threatened to rise in her throat. They seemed happy with their meal, though, and smacked their lips and burped continuously as they wolfed it down.

When they were finished, Joe held out a joint the size of a cigar, brandishing it like a magic wand. The men's eyes lit up at the sight, and after a token refusal they were passing it back and forth.

Joe leaned toward Drake and gave him a crooked grin. "I laced this with a little opiated hash for extra pop. You want a taste?"

"Um, no, thanks. I think, given what I'm going to be up to, I'd rather be straight."

"Total downer, man. Maybe it'll help you see in the dark. It definitely sharpens my intuition, you know?"

"Yeah, well, good for you. I'll pass."

Joe took a long drag and held it in as he handed the spliff back to Harry. "Smooth, daddy-o. Lemme know if you change your mind."

The three of them smoked the joint down to a nub, and soon Joe was yawning, his eyes glazed. Dick and Harry looked like they'd been shot with a tranquilizer dart, and were out cold within minutes of staggering to their tent, their snores a rumbling drone through the thin fabric.

Joe whispered theatrically to Spencer as he stood. "Good luck, dude. Watch out for gremlins."

"I need the GPS," Drake reminded Joe. Joe looked around and then stumbled to his tent. He stepped back out with the GPS in one hand and a pair of night vision goggles in the other.

"Leng lent me these in case we had to move at night. You ever use them?" Joe asked.

Uncle Pete stepped forward. "I know how."

Joe handed the goggles to him, and Uncle Pete slipped the strap over his head. Joe regarded Allie. "We're about three klicks from the wreckage. Take you a couple hours each direction if you're lucky. So no rest for the wicked tonight," he said, offering the GPS to her. "You know how to work it?"

"I can figure it out."

Uncle Pete led the way from the camp, and Spencer followed, Allie and Drake bringing up the rear. The valley was enshrouded with fog, and the moonlight lent the white blanket a ghostly glow as they ascended the rise. Joe's estimate of the time it would take to reach the stream proved overly optimistic, and the two hours had turned into three before they found the river where the plane had gone down.

They stopped at the water's edge, and Uncle Pete consulted the GPS. He pointed east. "That way. Maybe two hundred meters." He pushed the goggles up and blinked. "See good with no scope, huh?"

"Yes. Lucky it's nearly a full moon," Allie whispered.

Uncle Pete picked his way along the bank, moving slowly, the only sound the burble of the water rushing around occasional rocks. They reached a fork in the stream, and Allie peered at the GPS before pointing to their right. Uncle Pete nodded and they made their way around the bend and then stopped and stared at a shape in front of them. The twisted metal of a fuselage rose halfway out of the water. One wing was wedged into a tree, and the other lay fifteen yards behind the plane.

They stood transfixed by the sight of the mangled tail section, the cabin in surprisingly good shape. Spencer was the first to move and approach the wreckage. Drake and Allie followed, Uncle Pete hanging back as they neared.

The glass was shattered from every window, and the passenger door hung crookedly from a single hinge. Spencer walked to the prop and studied the engine section while Drake and Allie peered into the cabin.

The pilot's decomposed corpse grinned at them from his seat. Most of the flesh was gone, the jungle's predators having feasted on it and maggots having done the rest. Allie grabbed Drake's arm as her eyes adjusted to the grisly vision and she looked away.

"Oh, God, Drake..."

He drew her close and hugged her as he whispered in her ear, "The big surprise is that it's only the pilot. I don't see Christine's or her boyfriend's bodies. They aren't here."

"Maybe they got thrown clear?" Allie ventured. "It looks like the plane came apart when it hit."

Spencer's voice carried from the front of the plane. "Guys? I think I know what caused the crash." He rounded the fuselage and stepped toward them. "And it was no storm."

~ ~ ~

Jiao crept along, following the Americans after watching the Myanmar soldiers pass out in the camp. He'd arrived shortly after he'd received word from his source that they were at the base of one of the tall monoliths that framed the entrance to a remote valley.

He'd been able to secure a ride on a motorcycle with a young farmhand who had jumped at the chance to make the equivalent of a hundred dollars, and had made it near the camp after receiving the call. His hike from the road in the dark had rattled his nerves, given the inherent danger in the area, but he'd made it without any problems and had monitored the group until four of them had snuck off, presumably in search of the plane. Jiao had followed at a safe distance and hidden in the bushes when he'd seen the outline of the aircraft. The Americans were now having an animated discussion, but he couldn't make out what they were saying.

He watched as the tallest of them led the other three to the front of the plane and pointed to it. Whatever they had discovered had unnerved them. Jiao crouched motionless in the moonlight as they inspected the wreckage, his fingers on the butt of the pistol in his belt, waiting patiently as the Americans murmured unintelligibly by the twisted remains of the Cessna.

# Chapter Thirty-Five

"What I'm saying is that I've seen this kind of damage before," Spencer said. "Look. There was an explosion in the engine compartment. You can see here and here where the metal blew out. Only a blast from the motor would cause that. It's pretty distinctive," he finished.

They studied the area Spencer had identified. He was right. There was no other explanation, given the damage.

"So the engine blew up?" Drake asked.

"Or someone sabotaged it with explosives." Spencer's gaze swept the area. "What's most interesting to me is that there's no sign of either Christine or her boyfriend."

"I was thinking they might have been thrown clear on impact. They had to be going, what, a hundred miles per hour?" Allie said.

"Maybe less. And the water would have softened the impact some," Spencer said.

Uncle Pete walked down the bank a dozen yards and called out softly, "You come now!"

The three of them approached where the little Thai was standing over a collection of pale rocks. They were arranged into letters six feet long.

"S.O.S.," Drake whispered. "There's your answer to whether they were thrown free. At least one of them had to be alive to collect these stones and spell this out."

"Then they're alive," Allie murmured.

"Were. We don't know whether they still are, or how badly hurt they might be," Spencer corrected.

"So where are they?" Drake asked.

Spencer's eyes roamed along the bank and the surrounding jungle. "That's the million-dollar question."

Uncle Pete returned to the plane and climbed in. By the time they made it back to the wreckage, he was stepping out. He flipped the goggles up and shook his head. "Nothing in plane but dead guy. But someone else been here. Radio stolen. Same-same with other gear."

"Are you sure?" Spencer asked.

"Course."

"It has to be the drug gang – they're the only ones in this area. Remember the intel Collins provided? There aren't even any hill tribes around."

"Then it's possible they have them," Drake murmured thoughtfully.

"What do we do now?" Allie asked.

Drake's jaw tightened. "We call home," he said through gritted teeth. "Uncle Pete, you have the satellite phone?"

"You betcha," Uncle Pete answered, and dug the device from his satchel and handed it to Drake.

Drake inspected it and squinted at Uncle Pete. "The battery?"

"Oh. Yeah. Here."

It took a minute to acquire a strong signal. Drake called the number Collins had given him, and it was answered on the second ring.

"We found the plane. Looks like Christine and the boyfriend were alive after it crashed," Drake said, his voice low.

"What!"

"Yup." Drake told him about the S.O.S. and the plane being looted.

"Any sign of where they went?"

"No."

"Did you find anything in the plane?"

208

"Nope. Just the dead pilot. Or what's left of him. Everything that was worth anything has already been stolen." Drake hesitated. "Spencer says that it looks like the plane was sabotaged."

Collins' voice turned cold. "How?"

"He thinks explosives."

"Is Uncle Pete there?"

"Yes."

"Let me speak with him."

"Did you hear me? The crash was no accident. What haven't you told us?"

"You know as much as I do. Let me talk to Pete."

Drake's voice hardened. "Collins, we have our asses on the line here. We're in hostile territory, everyone's got a gun, it looks like this Red Moon gang knows about the wreck and could show up any time, and we just get the surprise of the century. I think we deserve an explanation."

"Damn it, Ramsey. Hand the phone to Uncle Pete. You're wasting valuable time," Collins snapped.

Drake shook his head in frustration and tossed Uncle Pete the sat phone. "Wants to talk to you."

Uncle Pete spoke softly as he walked away. Drake turned to Allie. "I think Collins knows something he's not telling us."

"So we've been had?"

"I don't know. I mean, he did sound surprised, but he recovered too quickly, like it wasn't that big a shock."

"What do we actually know about Christine besides that she's the senator's daughter?" Spencer asked. "What was she into? Exactly? Why was she on the ass-end of the planet, for starters?"

"You heard the briefing. Some kind of religious thing. Finding herself."

"What about the boyfriend?" Allie asked.

"Again, I don't know anything more than you do. He was Chinese. Possibly into some shady dealings."

"Then isn't it likely she was collateral damage? Maybe he crossed the wrong people and this has nothing to do with anything more than taking out a problem," Spencer said.

Uncle Pete circled back to them. "He say go back to camp, look for temple. They check around."

"That's it?" Drake demanded. He eyed the sat phone in alarm. "Take the battery out. Last thing we need is a missile landing on us."

Uncle Pete shrugged, removed the battery, and slipped the equipment back into his bag. He dropped the goggles into place. "You ready?"

"How are we supposed to continue like nothing happened?" Allie whispered to Drake.

"Easy. We found the plane. We did our job. If Christine and the guy are alive and have been captured, that's not our problem. It's the CIA's."

"You know it's not going to be that easy," Spencer said from behind them. "It never is."

"Maybe not, but I'm finished with this. Let's go find the Emerald Buddha, and let Collins play spy. We got him the info he was after. We're done."

The trek back to the camp was interrupted by a cloudburst that soaked them with warm rain, making the trails more treacherous and slowing their progress. When they eventually arrived, Drake checked the time and sighed.

"Only two hours till dawn."

Allie took his hand and led him to the tent. Spencer murmured that he was going to use the little boys' room and wandered into the brush as Uncle Pete opened his tent and crawled inside. Allie lay down on her bedroll and closed her eyes, and Drake hesitated before kissing her. The connection was electric, and Allie's breathing deepened as the intensity built. She squirmed beside him and Drake pulled his lips from hers.

"Oh, Allie–"

She held a finger to his lips. "Shh."

The mood was broken by Spencer lifting the flap and entering.

Drake moved a few inches from Allie, but Spencer didn't seem to notice he'd interrupted anything. Drake squeezed Allie's hand and whispered in her ear, "Good night."

He could sense her smile in the dark. "To be continued."

# Chapter Thirty-Six

*Five days earlier, 14 miles west of Mong Lin, Myanmar*

Christine shook off the haze that clouded her ability to think and forced her eyes open. Bare cinderblock walls wept moisture, feeding the mold that streaked everything dark green. Consciousness had come and gone in waves, and she struggled to recall how long she'd been in the chamber. It might have been hours, or months. Time had ceased to mean anything to her ever since she'd collapsed by the plane after dragging Liu from the cockpit and crafted her pointless attempt to signal for help out of river rock.

Blurred memories tortured her during her few waking hours – that of Liu's brutalized face, gashed from the broken windows, bright arterial blood staining his shirt. She'd done her best to fashion a tourniquet from one of the cables she'd salvaged from his laptop bag, but had drifted off, the shock too much for her system.

When she'd come to, she'd found herself baking in the harsh glare of the sun, and then a flat Asian face with a nose like a losing boxer's had blocked it. And…and then everything was a blank.

But something had just awakened her.

A scrape outside the rusting steel door.

Voices drifted on the light breeze that wafted through what passed for windows, really nothing more than gaps below the ceiling where every second block had been skipped. She blinked and tried to sit up, but something was stopping her.

Her wrists were lashed to the frame of a wooden cot.

No. They were bound to something beneath it.

The door creaked open on its corroded hinges and two men entered. One, a short, squat man in his thirties, carried a leather bag. The other, tall and fit, also about the same age, stood back where she couldn't get a good look at him.

The squat man adjusted his rimless glasses and eyed her with a small frown, as though she'd done something to disappoint him. She was reminded of her father's similar expression, which was his customary response to most of her efforts, and felt her abdomen muscles tighten at the thought. The man opened his bag and removed a stethoscope, and she relaxed. He was a doctor.

She tried to speak, but the only sound that came from her mouth was a dry croak. The doctor shushed her and proceeded to examine her, probing her chest and then her shoulder, which sent a flare of pain shrieking through her skull. She moaned like a strangling animal, and everything went black.

~ ~ ~

Christine regained consciousness sometime later. The first thing she noticed was hunger. That was good. Hunger meant she was alive. Hunger meant her body was healing. The second thing she registered was the tattoo of rain on the roof. Corrugated steel, like a Quonset hut, she thought absently. And it was really coming down.

Her shoulder felt numb. No. All of her felt numb. Dreamy.

Maybe this was all in her mind, and she would wake up soon, and Liu wouldn't be bleeding all over her as she held him helplessly in her arms, sobbing to the dark heavens, promising any bargain he wanted to a God she didn't believe in if Liu survived.

The numbness washed away her concerns, and she was floating behind closed eyes, the world now filled with warmth, well-being...and...sleep.

~ ~ ~

An old woman spooned gruel into Christine's mouth. The doctor was back, the same look of professional detachment on his face, his chubby hands gentle as they probed her. The warm sense of euphoria was less than…when? When had she last been conscious?

The doctor finished his examination and nodded with satisfaction. This time when he left, the other man remained, standing just out of her line of sight, in the shadows. The crone finished with her feeding and tottered off with the empty clay bowl and a sack filled with rags she'd used to clean Christine, and the man stepped forward. The first thing she noticed was that he had a cruel mouth. The second was his skin, so badly pocked from acne it looked like a shotgun had blasted him in the face.

He approached Christine and said something in what she guessed was Laotian. She looked at him with incomprehension, and he switched to broken English.

"You speak?"

Was he asking her to talk, or whether she spoke English? She tried to nod, but her neck refused to cooperate. She wet her lips and forced a few words.

"Yes. English. And Cantonese." Her throat felt thick, and her speech sounded clumsy, like her tongue was swollen or coated with tar. "Where am I?"

The man nodded and switched to Chinese. "We rescued you. You're in Myanmar at my…facility. My name is Lee. I run this place."

"My friend…"

"Didn't make it."

She absorbed the news and everything went gray. Moments, or perhaps minutes later, she returned to her body. Lee was staring at her impassively. Even half out of it, she felt revulsion, as though he was violating her with his gaze.

"You are very beautiful for a round eye. Many will pay a top price to have you. Your clavicle is broken from the crash, and you have some other wounds, but they are healing. When you are presentable, I will sell you to the highest bidder. After I have verified your skills, of course." Lee paused, studying her. "When the bruising goes down on your face, I will come for you. I prefer it if you fight me. I will enjoy it more."

"You have no right."

Her words clearly enraged him, and he moved closer, his proximity menacing. "No right? I take what I want, do what I want. I have every right. I am the law here, which you will discover, and now you are in my debt. You will pay as I wish, when I wish." His lip curled into an ugly sneer. "I own you. I found you, and you are my pet, like a fat white dog that eats too much and soils itself. Look at you. You sicken me. And you dare to tell me what I have the right to do?"

The fury drained from his expression and his customary placid calm settled over him. When he next spoke, it was as though he were discussing the weather, and he reached out a grimy thumb and ran it along her jawline. "You will clean up well, and once the stink of your Western diet burns out of your skin, I think you will be serviceable. I don't see the attraction, but my tastes aren't important. There are many who will pay to abuse an imperialist princess. Now rest, because you will be popular."

Christine's scream echoed off the walls as Lee left her to visions of unmentionable degradation at the hands of sweaty men willing to pay for a chance at forbidden fruit. She'd been rescued to serve as a sex slave in a country with no law, and her savior was the devil.

She sobbed until her chest hurt, her throat burning with impotent rage, and when she exhausted herself, she began calmly calculating how she could end her life before it became a living nightmare in hell.

# Chapter Thirty-Seven

Edward Cornett and Collins waited patiently for Senator Whitfield to arrive. Cornett had asked for a special meeting before the business day got underway on the Beltway, and Whitfield had instantly agreed. All parties knew better than to say anything on the telephone – the NSA's eavesdropping extended to everyone, including elected officials, and caution was the natural state of affairs.

When Whitfield entered he was like a supernova of energy, the aura of power palpable as he strode into his office with a nod at the CIA men. Nobody else was working yet; the building was quiet at six thirty, which was why Cornett had asked for the meeting at such an early hour.

Whitfield set his briefcase on his desk and shrugged off his suit jacket. He beckoned to Cornett as he carefully hung it on a coat rack behind him, and then adjusted the blinds so that they were fully closed. Cornett and Collins took seats where indicated and waited for Whitfield to finish.

The senator sat down and folded his hands in front of him on the desk blotter. "Gentlemen, you mentioned that you had news? I gather it's important, judging from the hour."

"Yes, sir. We located the plane. Your daughter's body wasn't in the wreckage. Neither was her boyfriend, Liu."

Whitfield's eye twitched. "What does that mean?"

"We're not sure, sir." Cornett told him about the S.O.S.

"Then they're alive?"

"Possibly. It's too soon to make that determination. There's a distant chance that they weren't on the plane at all, and this was some sort of ruse."

"A ruse? What are you talking about?"

"Sir, there's a troubling aspect to this. Our people tell us that it looks as though the plane was tampered with. Sabotaged. In which case the crash was intentional." Cornett met the senator's stare. "Can you think of a reason anyone would do that?"

"It sounds preposterous. Of course I can't think...unless it was the damned boyfriend. It has to be something he was involved in. Organized crime? Terrorism? Drug smuggling?" Whitfield hesitated. "Did your people find anything in the plane?"

"Negative. Although it had been looted."

"Then someone beat you to it."

"Yes, and it's possible they have your daughter and Liu."

Whitfield sat back. "Have?"

Collins took over for his superior. "Sir, we don't want to get your hopes up. In all likelihood your daughter didn't make it. But there's now a better chance that she did, and that one of the rebel organizations in the area rescued her...or took her captive."

Whitfield looked shocked. "To what end?"

"Kidnapping isn't unknown in that region, sir. Again, it's too early to speculate, but if one of the armed factions has her, it's likely because they intend to make money with her. One way or another. There have been reports of tourists being abducted near the border. Usually Caucasian females." Collins let the statement speak for itself.

Whitfield pushed himself to his feet and began pacing in front of the window. "Gentlemen, if Christine's alive, you must do whatever is necessary to get her out of this. Whatever the cost, in dollars or in human assets, it has to happen. There cannot be even a whiff of my daughter being held captive, or serious questions would arise as to my motivations and whether I can be influenced. We are at a delicate time in the DOD hearings, and I don't need to tell you what a story like this could do to the proceedings."

"Yes, sir. Of course."

"So break down for me exactly what steps you're taking. Short of sending in an aircraft carrier and invading the country, it better be impressive."

"We have an experienced field agent monitoring the situation as we speak. We've authorized him to put out the word that he's interested in locating the occupants of the plane, regardless of the circumstances. And he's indicated he's not price sensitive."

Whitfield's intake of breath was a hiss. "Wait. You only have one man handling this? That's it? Did I not make clear how important this is?"

Cornett nodded. "Of course, sir. However, more bodies won't achieve anything but run the risk of driving whoever has them to ground. If they get spooked, their captors could be as likely to put a bullet in them and bury them in a ditch as get involved with something that smacks of covert ops. Better to handle this surgically."

Whitfield sat back down, his shoulders slumping as he did. He glared at both men, and when he spoke, his tone was arctic. "If something goes wrong and we don't get her back, I will hold you both personally responsible. This is your area of expertise, so I won't meddle, but I want it on the record that I'm highly concerned that the agency isn't putting sufficient resources behind this."

"Message received," Cornett said. "As of right now, all we know is that her body wasn't at the crash site. We're only guessing as to why." He paused and checked the time. "We hope to have more information as the day progresses. But we figured you'd want to know everything we do, as soon as we know it."

"Yes, yes, of course. I'm sorry. I don't mean to bite your heads off. But this news is so unexpected, and the ramifications…well, you can imagine what I'm going through."

"I can. One other thing, though. It wouldn't be wise to share this latest bit of news with your ex-wife, sir. Not yet. We don't want civilians complicating matters."

"Yes, I understand. She was ready to put posters up on every light pole until I talked her down."

"If your daughter and Liu are alive, we'll find them and extract them. You have my word," Cornett said. "And if they aren't, we'll obtain definitive proof that they didn't make it."

"Very well," Whitfield said with a glance at his watch. "You better get out of here before the staff begins arriving. Wouldn't do to have questions raised about why I'm meeting with a pair of agency personnel."

Cornett and Collins stood and shook the senator's hand. When they left the office, they walked wordlessly to their car. Once inside, Cornett turned to Collins.

"What's he hiding?" Cornett asked.

"Don't know. But you picked that up too?"

"Of course. He's good, mind you, but not that good."

"Well, he is a politician, so all he does is lie all day."

"True. Something's rotten, though."

"Can you speak with the director, off the record, and see if there's another layer to this request we're unaware of?" Collins asked.

"I'll give it the old college try, but don't expect much. If the chief wants to run an op for reasons only he's privy to, that's his call."

"Right. But I don't like being the pawns in this game. What we don't know could come back to bite us. Hard."

Cornett put the transmission into gear and nodded. "We don't need any more disasters."

"Coffee?"

"I'm way ahead of you."

# Chapter Thirty-Eight

Reggie shook his head as he hung up the sat phone. He understood the logic, but his control officer clearly had no understanding of the logistics involved in putting the word out that he was on the hunt for the plane passengers. For one, he was in the middle of nowhere, and it would take him all day to make it anywhere close to civilization. For another, it wasn't like you posted an inquiry on the web and waited for an email. The villages where members of the drug gangs might have contacts were remote, and any direct interaction with their representatives could be fatal.

But he had his marching orders. His trek into the jungle had been for nothing. He'd pushed himself to the limits of his endurance to reach the camp, only to fail to make it in time to join the foray to the plane. It had been midnight by the time he'd had the tents in sight, and he'd been surprised when he'd turned on his phone to discover that he had a missed call from HQ. When he returned it, he'd been told that the girl and her companion hadn't been on the plane, and to stand by for further orders.

That had been in the wee hours of the morning. Now it was light, and he'd been handed another virtually impossible task.

Welcome to government work, he thought, as he eyed his stolen bike with a sour expression. His ass hurt from the seat, and every rut in the trail felt like a proctology exam gone horribly awry. Now he'd be pedaling all the way back to the nearest real town, which was…Tachileik. A good thirty miles on the world's worst bicycle. Assuming he didn't get gunned down for sport.

He looked back over his shoulder at the peak of the nearest karst formation and groaned quietly. Maybe a desk job wouldn't be so terrible after all.

An idea occurred to him. He powered on the phone and called his control again. "Do we have anyone in Bangkok who could handle the urban part of this? I'm in position, in deep cover."

"Not really. I mean, yes, of course we have people on the ground there, but this is a delicate situation. We were hoping to rely on your expertise. Can you not make it?"

"It'll be this evening, more than likely, at the earliest." He gave the man his coordinates and suggested he look at a map.

"Stand by."

Reggie waited for five minutes while his precious battery power drained. He was about to hang up and hope for a return call when his control came back on the line.

"Negative. We want to keep this a closed circle. Do the best you can."

"Roger that."

Reggie disconnected and swore under his breath. Closed circle indeed. Easy for some faceless wonk to wave his hand and send Reggie into perdition. It wasn't he who was trying to make it cross-country in Injun country.

He trudged over to the bike and, after pulling on his backpack, began wheeling the ungainly conveyance down the game trail, the nearest dirt road that he could safely ride it on many miles away.

~ ~ ~

Drake poked his head out of the tent as the sun climbed into the sky and spotted Joe chatting with Dick and Harry, whose green complexions spoke volumes about the aftereffects of inhaling a drug cocktail. The pair moved far slower than they had the prior day, whereas Joe's gestures and voice were animated and crisp. In spite of being at least double their age, Joe couldn't have looked better if he'd just gotten a massage and a facial.

Joe saw him and gave a cheery wave. "Yo! Youngblood. Time's a-wasting."

"Yeah. I see that," Drake said as he stepped into the open. "You take another taste of the magic potion this morning?"

"See, that's the kind of question that makes you seem like a small thinker. I was up before anyone, did my yoga, and ate. You're mistaking being in touch with the world's energy for something drugs can bring."

"So you ate the roach?"

Joe offered an impish grin. "Waste not…"

"That's what I thought."

"How did it go?"

Drake eyed the two Shans. "You positive they don't speak any English?"

"Look around, boy. Your secrets are safe."

"We found the plane. Nobody was in it. Which is somewhat of a mystery."

Joe nodded as though he'd expected the news. "Now what?"

"We continue in our search for the Emerald Buddha."

"The what?" Joe finally registered surprise.

Drake ground his teeth – that was a stupid slip. "The ruins."

"That's not what you said."

"I only got an hour or two of sleep. I don't know what I'm saying," Drake deflected.

"I heard you. First you mentioned anything about emeralds. Or a Buddha."

"Can we just drop it? We'll find the place and see what's in it. End of story."

"Little testy, aren't we? You need a big shot of mellow-the-hell-out. So agro. Unbecoming in a youngster."

"I really appreciate the life lessons, but maybe some other time? I feel like crap."

Joe gave him a sly look. "I might have something that could pick you up."

Drake gave him an incredulous stare.

Joe shrugged. "Hey. No biggie. Let me know if you need anything."

"Regular corner drugstore, aren't you?"

Joe smiled and moved back to Harry and Dick. Harry looked like he was about to vomit. Drake suddenly didn't feel quite as bad, the Schadenfreude helping somewhat. He ducked back into the tent and almost collided with Allie.

"Oh. Sorry. Good morning," Drake said.

"If you say so."

"Ready to pack up and hit the road?"

"I suppose."

Half an hour later they were filing through the jungle. Uncle Pete cleared the way with his machete, their good fortune in finding trails having fled when they'd left the camp. The way toward the valley was thick with vegetation, and the morning passed with slim progress as they hacked a path through the rain forest.

Lunch was a hushed affair while a cloudburst drizzled on them, offering a welcome cooling from the humid swelter. Joe and Uncle Pete consulted with Spencer on the best way to proceed, and by the time the rain abated, they'd agreed that Joe and Spencer would trade off leading the way for the afternoon, giving the little Thai's tired arms a rest from wielding the machete.

After two hours, they arrived at a small clearing.

Allie pointed north. "There they are."

In the near distance, two towering karst peaks, their rocky sides sheer as cliffs, rose into the azure sky from the surrounding jungle.

"The two sisters," Drake said.

"And the valley between them."

"My hunch is there isn't going to be a Holiday Inn at the base, so let's search for a spot to make camp once we're in their shadow," Spencer said, noting their position on his compass. "If we can find another game trail, we'll be there in a few hours. Maybe even early enough to root around and locate our cave."

They picked up their pace, inspired now that their objective was in sight, and were fortunate enough to find a swollen stream that led straight to the half-mile-wide gap between the two peaks. When they reached the entry to the valley, Drake's watch read three thirty, so they had at least three solid hours of light to go before they'd need to pitch their tents.

Allie adjusted the worn straps on her backpack as they eyed the valley. "We're looking for a cave. But after five hundred years, it might blend into the landscape or have caved in. Keep your eyes peeled."

"You mean there isn't going to be a big stone gate or something?" Drake asked innocently, and Allie smiled.

"Wouldn't that be nice?" she replied, and then they began methodically scanning their surroundings, Joe and Spencer taking turns with the binoculars Joe had brought.

After fifteen minutes, nobody had spotted anything. Spencer shrugged and unsheathed his machete. "Looks like we do this the hard way. Any preference on where we start?"

Allie pointed to the nearest of the two peaks. "Any cave is likely to be close to the base, so I'd suggest we begin at the bottom of the right one and work around it, then go across to the other."

"Fair enough," Spencer said, and headed into the brush.

Two hours later they'd been over the entire base, spread twenty feet apart in a sweeping pattern to ensure they didn't miss anything. The sun was low in the afternoon sky, and its blistering glare had faded to a diffused glow. Ghostly tendrils of ground fog began drifting through the peaks as the air cooled with dusk's approach.

Spencer called over to them. "I think we're done for the day. Let's find a decent place to camp, and we'll finish this tomorrow."

They made their way down to the steep bank of the stream and found a flat area behind a thicket of bamboo fifteen yards from the water. Uncle Pete busied himself setting up the tents with Drake and Spencer, and Allie excused herself to freshen up at the stream before it got completely dark. Drake was finishing up driving the final tent post into the ground when Allie came hurrying toward them from the stream.

"I think I found something," she said breathlessly, her face shiny from the heat.

"What is it?" Drake asked. Spencer raised his head, and then he and Uncle Pete moved to join them.

"There's an outcropping of rocks on the far bank that looks unusual. It could be a cave entrance."

"I'll get some flashlights," Spencer said, and went to the tent to retrieve them. When he returned, he handed one to Allie, and they all set out down the stream to the suspect area.

Sixty yards down the bank from their camp, she stopped and pointed. "That's it. What do you think?"

They stared across the water at a mound of rocks overgrown with vegetation, with another pile next to it that looked cleaner – as though the stones had been placed there.

"Could be. Definitely suspicious. Maybe we can get across around here?" Drake said, eyeing the rushing water.

Spencer shook his head. "Looks too deep. It's wider by our camp. Let's cross there, and we can work our way back along that side."

They made their way back to the wider, shallower part of the stream and stepped across, the water rising to their knees. Once on the far bank, they made their slippery way toward the outcropping as the last of the sun's rays surrendered to the blanket of fog settling over the valley. When they reached the rocks, Drake flicked on his rugged aluminum flashlight and moved to the fresher-looking pile of stones.

"It's definitely not a natural formation. Someone stacked these here," Drake said. "Allie, hold the flashlights for us. Spencer, give me a hand. Let's see if we can budge a few of these and find out what's behind them."

Allie moved beside Drake and took his light, and the two men selected one of the smaller rocks at the top as Joe and the pair of Shans looked on. "Ready? On three. One. Two...three!" Drake exclaimed, and they both heaved. A vein bulged on Drake's forehead as he strained. The stone shifted and tumbled down the face of the slope with a crash, and then settled in the mud by the side of the stream.

"There's a space behind them," Drake said, peering into the gap. "If we get a few more out of the way, we should be able to squeeze through."

Spencer nodded. "This one looks like it could be dislodged relatively easily. Allie, hand me a light. I can use it for leverage."

She gave one of the lamps to Drake, and he wedged it into a crevice between the two stones and pushed. The rock inched forward with a scrape. Spencer joined him, and together they got it free. It rolled down and joined its mate by the stream, creating an opening barely large enough for a child to squeeze through.

"If we shift this one too, that should do it," Allie said, motioning to another medium-sized stone.

"You heard the lady. Third time's a charm," Spencer said, and they both wedged their lights behind the stone and rocked it back and forth until it gave. It dropped into the opening with a thud, creating an aperture twenty by thirty inches.

"That ought to do it," Drake said, and then switched his lamp on and directed it into the opening. "You want to take it from here, Allie? You're the expert."

Allie took a final look at the twilight fog and the near-dark of the remaining visible sky, and crawled up the rocks into the space beyond. Drake went next, followed by Spencer. Joe contented himself with watching from outside while Harry scrambled through, leaving Dick with Joe.

The cave was narrow at the front and widened as it stretched deeper into the slope. Allie's beam was transfixed on a carving near shoulder level – the unmistakable visage of a smiling Buddha with some stylized figures beneath it. She reached out and ran her fingers along the stone. "This is Khmer. It's very distinctive," she whispered.

"Then this…"

"Unless there are multiple caves between the 'two guardians' with Khmer carvings, I'd say this is our spot," she said, and swung her beam toward the far chamber created by the cave's irregular walls. She took a hesitant step, and then another.

Drake swept his light around them, alert for scorpions or snakes – caves being a favorite hiding place. Allie edged nearer the chamber as Spencer and Harry brought up the rear, and together they moved into the second area.

She stopped abruptly at the threshold, her breathing shallow. When she turned to face them, she was white as a sheet.

"Looks like we're too late. But that's the least of our problems."

# Chapter Thirty-Nine

Drake pushed by Allie and squinted into the recesses of the cave. There were more carvings on the rock face, matching the Khmer Buddha behind them, with alcoves cut into the stone walls and elaborate pictographs framing them – but any trace of treasure was gone. His beam hit something brown near the floor, and when he fixed the light on it, he understood Allie's reaction.

At least twenty Kalashnikov AK-47 assault rifles lay in an open wooden crate, with several more containers of ammunition beside it, and a lump of material covered by a large camouflage tarp. Spencer approached it and lifted one edge of the fabric, then dropped it – he'd seen enough.

"It's drug-refining equipment and another two crates of rifles. And at least a pallet of cellophane-wrapped blocks of white powder." Spencer paused. "Looks like grave robbers got here a long time before we did, Allie. But I agree, we've got a bigger problem. These weapons look like they're in good shape." He leaned over and picked up one of the Kalashnikovs and ran a finger over the breech. "Oil. No rusting. So whoever owns them stashed them here relatively recently. And they'll be back to collect their heroin, I'd bet. This must be a drop-off point. By the looks of it, a regularly used one."

Drake's eyes widened as he made the connection. "So this is a frequent stop for them. A lot of them. Because it would take more than a couple to get those stones back in place…"

"Correct. They're too heavy for one or two people to manage, as we just saw," Spencer agreed.

Allie blanched. "Which leaves us camped footsteps away from a major drug hub…"

"The owners of which will probably want to have a chat with whoever found their stash," Drake finished for her.

"Maybe we can get out of here before anyone sees the displaced rocks," Allie suggested hopefully.

Spencer nodded. "It's night. These gangs know these jungles like their backyard. If they show up, they'll be pretty annoyed and scour the area for whoever crashed their party before they can notify the authorities. Which means we need to make tracks. Now." Spencer set the rifle back down. "Let's load up a few of these and pray we don't have to use them. Grab a handful of shells."

"Give me a minute so I can take some pictures. Joe – you have the camera?" Allie called over her shoulder. Joe had packed a cheap digital camera in his bag, along with the binoculars, when they'd readied for their hike back in the village.

"Sure thing," Joe's voice answered from the cave opening, and a few moments later he arrived with it in his hand. He stopped short when he saw the crates and shook his head as he handed it to her. "Whoa. This is bad juju, kids."

Drake nodded. "Yeah, we got that."

"So where's our treasure?"

"Looted a long time ago," Allie said.

"Are you sure this is the right spot?" Joe asked.

Spencer grunted. "Look at the carvings on the walls. Khmer." He sighed. "I'm afraid someone beat us to it. No telling when."

"If this area belongs to the drug gangs, anything worth finding would have already been, and the gold melted down long ago or sold on the black market," Drake said. "Sometimes you win, sometimes you get hit in the face with a brick. That's how it goes."

Joe eyed Uncle Pete. "I say we put some serious miles between us and this cave. We stick to the stream and avoid any trails – traffickers will use the trails. We don't stop until we make it back to where we camped yesterday, even if it takes all night."

Spencer nodded. "He's right. Let's fold up shop and get going."

They crawled out of the cave to find themselves in another world – a white one with ten yards of visibility. Fog thick as cotton blanketed the valley. Drake led the way back to the stream, and he was getting ready to step into the water when he heard the distinctive sound of metal on metal somewhere behind them.

"Was that you?" he whispered to Spencer, ears straining in the fog.

Spencer shook his head, and Joe mouthed a 'no.' Uncle Pete and the two Shans looked spooked, telling Drake everything he needed to know.

"Move. Follow me," Joe hissed. He pushed past Drake and stepped into the stream, taking care to do so silently. The rest of them followed a few yards behind. Spencer made it to the far bank and was turning to help Allie when Drake misstepped. His eyes saucered like a frantic deer's, and he tumbled to the side and landed in the water with a splash and a grunt of pain. Everyone froze, and then they heard the pounding of running feet approaching from near the cave.

Drake forced himself to his feet and bolted for the shore as the rest pushed past him. He was scrambling up when a figure materialized out of the fog, an AK-47 clutched in his hands; but unlike Drake, looking like he more than knew how to use one. The gunman was swinging the assault rifle at them when Uncle Pete loosed a burst. The man's chest exploded as rounds tore through him, and he fell face forward into the stream and dropped the gun.

Spencer screamed at Drake, "Move! Now, or you're dead."

Drake took off at a run as shouts from further upstream drifted through the heavy fog. They reached the camp and grabbed their backpacks as Spencer, Joe, and the Shans waited for the pursuers. The remaining gunmen had no way of knowing their prey had crossed to the other side of the stream, but they weren't counting on it – and now that the traffickers knew they were chasing armed quarry, they would be as silent as they were deadly.

Drake could barely make out the stream from his position, and he thanked Providence for the fog – if it weren't for that, they'd already be dead. Allie sidled up next to him and tapped his shoulder, pointing at a column of armed men who were creeping along the far bank. He nodded and crouched low, but one of the gunmen spotted them and cried out.

Rifle fire chattered and bullets whizzed through the surrounding vegetation. Joe and the Shans dropped flat beside where Uncle Pete and Spencer had dived for cover and returned fire, carefully squeezing off burst after controlled burst. They were rewarded with at least four of the attackers going down, but it was obvious neither time nor ammunition were on their side.

Another gunman emerged from the fog, and Uncle Pete's rifle barked once. The gunman's head exploded and he fell backward onto the bank, which was now littered with bodies.

Spencer rose and backed up, his weapon pointed at the stream as his feet felt their way, and whispered to Joe, "We're making it too easy for them. We need to keep moving."

"10-4, good buddy." Joe leaned toward the pair of Shans and murmured to them. They nodded and stood.

"We go," Uncle Pete said. More rounds shredded the leaves to their left at the sound of his voice, and he fired another burst at the stream as he scurried away.

"Follow me," Joe whispered. He stood and ran, dodging between the bamboo and the trees, racing to put distance between them and the gunmen. Once they were away from the stream, the traffickers would still have the same issue as before – their advantage of superior numbers would be largely equalized by the fog and the dark of night.

They ran for five minutes, stopping occasionally to listen for sounds of pursuit, and then Joe veered right and they were back at the stream. He paused, listening, as the rest of them stood motionless. Spencer edged close to him.

"What do you think? Do we try to outrun them, or find high ground and settle this where we'd have an advantage?" Joe whispered.

"Problem there is that they can flank us once we're stationary. It's what I would do," Spencer said. "Any advantage would be temporary. I say we keep moving. That's our only hope. Because come morning, our chances go way, way down when the fog lifts."

"There's another problem," Joe said. "They probably have radios. So they can call in reinforcements to ambush us."

"True. But what options do we have?" Drake asked from behind them.

Spencer frowned. "Right now? None. But I'd strongly suggest we get off this stream as soon as we can, because if I was them, I'd have some of my colleagues waiting along the water up ahead. The stream's the easiest way out of the valley, and that's what they'll be expecting. So we do the opposite."

Joe nodded. "Then let's recross as soon as it looks shallow enough, and find a game trail leading away from the water."

Uncle Pete didn't wait to hear anything more, and began working his way along the bank, the current rushing beside him.

Four hundred yards downstream, they found a stretch where they could see the water breaking over shallow rocks. They carefully picked their way across and worked south until they came to a promising gap in the underbrush. Joe and Uncle Pete set off toward it and then plunged headlong into the jungle, mindful that at any moment the shooting could start again.

The party pushed themselves hard, Joe periodically checking their position on the GPS. Hours later, he slowed and drew the device from his backpack again as the first dim glow of dawn burned through the fog. After studying the small screen and memorizing their coordinates, Joe turned to the rest.

"There's a river about a half mile away. From there we can cut inland and be at our old camp within an hour."

Allie nodded. "You think it'll be safe there?"

"It's the no-man's land between the clear boundary of the Shan territory and Red Moon's," Joe said. "Even if they pick up our trail, there's probably a limit to how badly they'll want to test us. Remember, they lost more than a few at the cave. My hunch is they'll head back to their base rather than risk being slaughtered. For all they know, there are dozens of us waiting in the trees."

Drake glanced down the trail they'd followed and then at Joe. "I hope you're right, for all our sakes."

Joe nodded. "So do I, man, so do I."

# Chapter Forty

Uncle Pete shifted the AK-47 strap from his left shoulder to his right as he watched the perimeter of the clearing. He and Harry were standing sentry for the first three hours as the rest slept. He'd be relieved in another thirty minutes, and after getting a few hours of rest, they would push on to the Shan encampment.

Uncle Pete made a gesture to Harry – he had to relieve himself. The Shan nodded and Uncle Pete disappeared into the brush. When he was a hundred yards from the camp, he stopped and waited. He'd made a surreptitious call on the satellite phone an hour into his shift, and his rendezvous should have shown himself by now.

Jiao stepped out from behind a tree. When he was close enough so they could hear each other's whispers, he studied the little Thai before speaking.

"So?"

"There was no temple. Just a store of weapons and some drugs."

"I don't care about that. What about the plane? What's their plan?"

"We're going back to the Shan base and then probably returning to the crazy American's village. There's nothing out here for them, no further reason to stay," Uncle Pete said.

"And the CIA has no idea what happened to the girl?"

"No. But they said they'd get back to us when they had more information."

Jiao gave Uncle Pete a dark stare. "You must remain vital to them.

If they discover anything, you will tell me immediately. Is that clear?"

"Of course, but there's only so much I can do. Now that these fools found the plane, their part in this is over. If the people in Washington don't want me involved any longer, I can't force them."

Jiao frowned. "I hope you haven't forgotten that your family's lives depend on your performance. One word from me, and your beloved granddaughter will meet with a horrible accident. I will not tolerate failure."

"How can I forget? It's all I think about."

"That and the money we're paying you."

"I have done my part. I am keeping you informed. If I learn anything, you will be the first to know." Uncle Pete waved in the direction of the camp. "Now go. I will call when I have more."

"Is there any reason to shadow you to the village?"

"None I can think of. Unless you're enjoying Myanmar's charms."

"Very well. See to it that you call. Remember your granddaughter. She's a little miracle. It would be a shame if misfortune befell her."

Uncle Pete's face was a cold mask. Only his eyes betrayed the hatred that simmered behind them. Jiao nodded in satisfaction at the man's glare. "I see you understand. Good," he said, and then turned and strode back into the tangle of plants, his boots silent on the moist soil.

Uncle Pete relieved himself quickly and returned to the camp, barely containing his fury at the Chinese intelligence officer's threat. He shouldn't have been surprised when his seemingly harmless subterfuge turned on him and the gloves came off, the promises of more cash replaced by threats he knew the Chinese were fully prepared to carry out – but it still shocked him how callously Jiao discussed murdering his granddaughter, who was only four years old.

His sideline, working all ends against the middle, had seemed savvy when he'd first been introduced to the Chinese through a mutual acquaintance in Thailand. Uncle Pete didn't mind that his friend was employed by the enemy – the truth was that anyone whose desires ran counter to what was best for the corporations that ran America was their enemy. It wasn't his fight, and he viewed his allegiance as that of a player on a sports team, who might be traded the following season and be wearing a different jersey.

The U.S. was the largest exporter of weapons in the world, so it was obviously in its best interests for the planet to be at constant war or fearful of imminent war; otherwise, there would be no demand for its wares. Uncle Pete completely understood the logic. It had been that way for generations and would likely continue long after he'd passed on. And the Americans paid well, and asked for little – that is, until this foray, when they'd become reliant on him. Which was largely due to the Chinese taking out Alex so that Uncle Pete's star could ascend in his absence.

No part of Uncle Pete had been troubled by that act. It was business. The Chinese had wanted him joined at the hip with the search party, with a minimum of outside interference – and had been banking on there being something salvageable in the wreckage. If Alex had been part of the group and there had been a surviving data storage device, Uncle Pete wouldn't have been able to snatch it and turn it over to Jiao. Plus, Alex had treated Uncle Pete like an underling, inferior, which made it easy to betray the arrogant CIA agent. Uncle Pete hadn't wished ill on the man beyond that, and had actually been surprised at how extreme the Chinese agents had been in dispatching him. He'd believe they might mug him and bonk him on the head, not run him down.

And now the same savages were threatening his family.

He shook his head to clear it; the fatigue from being awake for thirty hours settled on him like a heavy weight as he made his way back to where the Shan waited.

Upon his reappearance, Harry eyed him disapprovingly. Uncle Pete gave the frowning Shan a pained half smile and a shrug. "Stomach not what it used to be."

Harry nodded; and then the jungle exploded with gunfire, and the top of his skull blew apart.

# Chapter Forty-One

*Tachileik, Myanmar*

Reggie wiped a thin coating of beige dust from the window of the café where he'd arranged to meet his newest best friend, and squinted as he peered inside. There were three women sitting at a circular wooden table, and that was it. Reggie straightened and checked his watch. The man was ten minutes late. Annoying, but not necessarily indicative of anything, he told himself, other than that flakey characters tended to fit certain stereotypes.

He'd made it to the border town, whose two-lane bridge spanned the Mae Sai River that delineated Thailand from Myanmar, and had spent most of the prior evening spreading money around and letting it be known that he was a willing buyer for information on a white woman who'd gone missing in the jungle. Of course, he'd been offered a plethora of Thai or Burmese girls, and been assured that they were vastly superior to anything a farang could muster in the way of sexual skill, but once it became obvious that he was only interested in the lost woman, his audience in the squalid watering holes moved on.

At close to midnight he'd hit pay dirt when a slight man named Tam had offered that there might be such a woman. Tam had the disposition of a chronic yaba abuser, most of his teeth rotted away, his eyes darting constantly like a frightened rat, his frame whippet-thin with lean muscles that resembled knotted rope beneath his rawhide skin. A chain-smoker as well, he sidled up as Reggie was preparing to leave the bar, and held up an empty bottle of the local cheap beer.

"You buy me 'nother, we talk-talk, yeah?" Tam said in halting English.

"What do we have to talk about?" Reggie asked, trying not to recoil from the sour tang of dried sweat and tobacco that seeped from Tam's clothes.

"You look for someone. I know lotsa people."

"Yeah? So what?"

"You buy beer, we make talk."

Reggie signaled the bartender by pointing to Tam's bottle and held up two fingers. The only redeeming quality of the dive was that the beer was ice cold, although it had to be drunk quickly or it warmed in minutes.

The drinks arrived, and Reggie eyed the sweating bottles without comment. Tam lifted the nearest to his lips and gulped half the contents in a couple of swallows. He burped loudly and lit a cigarette, and Reggie reluctantly took a sip of his own beer while he waited to hear what Tam had to say.

"Up there, one man run everything. If girl there, he know," Tam began.

Reggie nodded. "Okay. What's his name?"

"He have many name. But General Lee now."

"General, huh? Is he Myanmar military? Or Shan Army?"

Tam laughed, and Reggie's eyes watered from the stench of rot that emanated from the man's mouth. "He general of own army."

"I see. Do *they* have a name?"

"They Red Moon. Bigtime now. Serious."

Reggie digested the information before continuing. "And what makes you think he'd know anything about the girl?"

"His business know everything."

Reggie stared at Tam. He was dog tired and in no mood for a protracted courtship. Tam seemed to sense he was losing Reggie and picked up his pace.

"I talk-talk to Lee people. They know something, you pay."

Reggie shook his head. "You introduce me. I don't pay unless I meet them."

"You no trust me?" Tam asked, aping indignation, and then brayed another laugh and finished his beer. "Okay. I talk-talk. Bring man. You pay then, right?"

"How much?"

"I want tousand dollar."

It was Reggie's turn to laugh. "And I want to live forever."

Tam's gaze combed the bar, and he rubbed a callused hand over his dry lips. "You pay...hunred dollar."

Reggie nodded slowly. "I pay when I meet someone who can help me. Find me someone, and I'll give you a hundred dollars."

"You give some now," Tam tried, his tone emphatic.

Reggie shook his head again. "I pay when you deliver, not before." Reggie fixed him with a deadpan stare. "So get busy. Chop-chop."

"How I reach you?"

Reggie drew one of several dozen cards he'd filched from his hotel and handed it to Tam. "Ask for Rick. If I'm not there, leave a message. I'll call you back."

"You no bullshit, right? You pay?"

"Tam, there's nothing I'd rather do than give you a hundred bucks. But you have to perform. Got it?"

"I call tomorrow. You wait, yes?"

"Better hurry up before somebody else earns the money."

"One more?" Tam asked, pushing his beer toward the bartender with a raised eyebrow.

"Nope."

Tam patted his chest. "I Tam."

"Good luck, Itam."

Tam shook his head vigorously. "No. Tam. Jus' Tam."

The hotel told Reggie that he had a message when he emerged from his room the next morning, and handed him a slip with a local cell number on it and 'Tam' scrawled in barely decipherable script.

Reggie phoned the barfly and they agreed to a meeting at noon at the café.

Five more minutes crawled by. Reggie was preparing to leave when Tam rounded the corner with another local in tow. Reggie took in the newcomer at a glance – expensive clothes, shoes, and sunglasses; well-groomed; and as friendly-looking as a barracuda.

Maybe Tam had delivered after all.

Tam neared and gave a slight bow. His companion inclined his head, Reggie did the same, and the man said something in Laotian. Tam coughed and nodded.

"We go in," he translated.

Reggie nodded and followed the pair inside. They ordered drinks, and Tam's associate waited until they were served before speaking. He went on for a full minute, and when he was finished, Tam took over.

"This Jun. He say maybe general have girl. How much you pay for her?"

Reggie absorbed the news. Christine was alive. Or might be, if the slickster wasn't lying. "I would pay a fair price. But I would need proof she's alive, and that she's unharmed."

More translation, and the gang member spat out a few sentences. Tam blanched and was obviously considering how to phrase things when Reggie leaned forward.

"Just tell me what he said," Reggie said, his voice low.

Tam swallowed hard. "He say girl alive, worth half-million dollar. You no like, they sell her twenty dollar a time."

Reggie kept his expression neutral. "Prove it."

Tam told the man, who smiled. He spoke so rapidly even Tam looked like he had a problem keeping up, and then sat back, watching Reggie.

"He say can video on phone. How you prove you got price?"

"Tell him to get the film, and I'll worry about the money."

Five minutes later their discussion was over, and Reggie had given the gangster the number of the burner cell phone he'd acquired that morning. Reggie waited until the pair left, and then called his control officer to report his progress. His control told him to keep his phone on and he'd ring him when he had further orders.

Reggie debated another cup of tea but decided against it. Maybe a few more hours of sleep instead.

After the grueling jungle ride and the eight beers last night, he'd more than earned it.

# Chapter Forty-Two

Uncle Pete hit the ground hard as he fired into the brush. The attackers' orange muzzle flashes winked like a carnival come-on from the jungle across from him, and bullets whistled through the air above his head. His third burst was rewarded by a tortured scream as his rounds found home.

Spencer rolled from his tent, his AK already in play, and then Joe and the Shan they called Dick joined the fray. Drake and Allie were the last to emerge from their tent, struggling into their backpacks as slugs shredded the plants around them. They swung their guns up, and then the clearing was a cacophony of gunfire as they emptied their weapons at the attackers.

After several long seconds, Joe ejected his spent magazine, slammed another home, and called out to them, "Fall back to the trail. I'll hold them off with Dick."

Spencer nodded and Drake nudged Allie. "Go with him. Get out of here."

"Drake…"

"Move!"

More gunfire erupted from the underbrush, and fountains of dirt sprayed into the air around them. Spencer grabbed Allie's arm and pulled as he dog-crawled toward the tree line. "Come on."

They vanished into the foliage as Joe and the Shan gunman laid down covering fire. Joe rose from his position and ran in a crouch past Drake, making for the trail. Drake caught a glimpse of movement from his right and blasted at it, and a heavy form fell in the brush with a strangled cry.

Uncle Pete was the next to retreat as the Shan continued shooting, and was passing Drake when Dick gurgled as three rounds pounded into him. Uncle Pete whirled and let loose another salvo, buying Drake his chance to dash for the jungle.

Then they were running, side by side, branches swatting at them as they sprinted along the track. Drake pulled away slowly as he poured on the speed. The gunfire receded behind them and then stopped, and the pounding of his boots on the moist ground gave the only sound. Drake rounded a bend and pushed himself even harder; Joe's back was just visible fifty yards ahead of him.

Uncle Pete cried out as he misstepped and slid off the edge of the slick trail, flailing for balance before tumbling down the steep slope. He slammed into a boulder at the base and groaned in pain as his shoulder dislocated. He tried to roll over onto his back, but his pack hampered him. His arm jutted from his torso at an impossible angle, and his AK lay useless halfway down the drop. He struggled and this time managed to right himself, but almost blacked out from the agony of the effort.

The air was still, and Uncle Pete blinked away mud and sweat as he evaluated his condition. He needed to get to the rifle. He reached over with his right hand and tried to pull his left arm so it would pop back into the socket, but froze when he heard a rustle from above.

"Drake?" he called softly.

A face appeared at the top of the trail, the features those of a hill tribesman. Uncle Pete's eyes met his as the man raised his rifle, a malevolent grin on his face. Uncle Pete flinched and closed his eyes, and jerked instinctively when a shot rang out from above.

The gunman's body rolled several meters down the slope, a bullet hole in the center of his forehead, and Drake's voice whispered urgently, "Uncle Pete. Can you make it up here?"

"I...no."

"Hang on."

Several moments passed, and then a coil of nylon line snaked down to Uncle Pete.

"Tie it around your waist, and I'll help you climb the slope."

"Gun…"

"Leave it. Just do as I say."

Uncle Pete fumbled the cord around his waist and seemed to take forever to cinch it with a crude knot. When he was finished, he nodded to Drake, who was dividing his time between watching the trail and the fallen Thai. Drake took up the slack and began winding the rope around his own waist by turning, since the gun he was holding prevented him from hauling it hand-over-hand.

Uncle Pete scrambled for footing against the pull, and slowly, inch by painful inch, ascended the steep grade. When he reached the top, he looked down at the dead Red Moon gunman and scooped up his AK. Drake grimaced when he saw Uncle Pete's shoulder, and was about to say something when Joe appeared on the trail, his gun pointed at Drake's head.

Drake's eyes widened in shock at the sight. He sputtered as he brought his weapon to bear, but he was too late.

Joe's weapon barked twice.

Another Red Moon gunman dropped behind Uncle Pete. Drake's heart skipped when he realized how close he'd come to being killed, and then Joe opened fire again as he yelled at Drake. "Run. There's more of them coming."

Drake and Uncle Pete made for Joe, but the rope binding them together slowed them. When they reached a grove of trees, Drake untied the knot and unwound the line from Uncle Pete's waist as Joe continued shooting behind them. "Can you make it?" Drake demanded as bullets whined around them.

"Maybe. Pull arm."

Drake nodded and grabbed Uncle Pete's forearm. The Thai winced, took a deep breath, and closed his eyes. Drake set his gun down and, using his right foot against Uncle Pete's chest, pulled as hard as he could. Uncle Pete screamed as the shoulder joint popped back into place, and then fainted, falling to the ground as Joe arrived.

"Hand me your gun. Mine's empty," Joe said, and contemplated the limp form of Uncle Pete. "Pick him up, or he's dead meat."

Drake gave Joe his rifle and gathered Uncle Pete in his arms. The Thai was surprisingly light, little more than skin and bones. Joe retrieved Uncle Pete's dropped AK and handed it to Drake. "Looks like at least a dozen more moving up the trail," he hissed through clenched teeth. "I'll hold them off as long as I can to give you a running start, but we're going to have to make a stand eventually."

"Why not here?"

Joe shook his head. "Our odds will be better the further we get into Shan territory. If we all open up on them at once, they might rethink how badly they want to continue the chase. Look out." Joe leaned out from behind the tree he was using for cover and fired again, and a man grunted no more than fifty yards away. "Get going."

Drake pushed through the brush, avoiding the open trail, as Joe continued shooting. A branch struck Uncle Pete in the shoulder and he stirred. His breathing deepened and he moaned, and then patted Drake's back. "Put down. I run okay."

"You sure?" Drake asked, continuing without slowing.

"I try."

"Okay."

Drake veered right around a banyan tree before stopping and bending over to let the guide down. The shooting was still sounding from behind them, and Drake leaned into Uncle Pete. "Follow me."

They set off at a good clip, and in a couple of minutes were back on the trail. Drake stopped near a rock outcropping and eyed Uncle Pete. "Did you see Spencer and Allie?"

Uncle Pete shook his head. "No. Think they ahead."

"Right, but where?"

The guide shrugged. More gunfire rang out from where they'd left Joe, and then it stopped. Drake heard footfalls hurrying toward them and raised his rifle. Joe appeared from around the bend, moving fast. When he reached them, he was breathing hard, his shirt soaked with sweat. "Let's get moving," he whispered.

"Where are Spencer and Allie?" Drake asked.

"I thought they'd be waiting for us."

"So you have no idea?"

The sound of shooting greeted them from their right. Drake caught Joe's eye. "If that's Spencer, we need to help them, Joe."

Joe nodded just as the shooting stopped. "Question is, where are they?" He cocked his head, listening. "And how do we avoid getting killed in the process of coming to the rescue?"

Drake pointed in the direction where the last shots had rung out. "We need to do something."

Joe tilted his head at Uncle Pete. "He's not going to be a lot of help, so it's really just the two of us. And we've got, what, one more magazine between us? Not trying to be a downer, but that's not much firepower."

"They're my friends. If you won't help them, I'll do it alone."

Joe sighed. "You're stubborn. Anyone ever tell you that?"

"We're wasting time, Joe. You in or out?"

"Crap. Fine. Let's do this." Joe set off in the rough direction of the last shots. The going was tough, there being no trail, and they were forced to press through the tangle of vines and branches until they came to a small open area. A dead gunman lay on one side of the clearing. Joe darted over and retrieved the man's weapon, his eyes on the surroundings, and then froze.

Drake did the same when he followed Joe's gaze to where a crimson smear of blood colored a thicket of bamboo. Uncle Pete moved slowly to the spot, knelt down, and then rose with something in his hand. Drake looked at it and his heart sank. It was Allie's green bandana.

Drake moved to where Joe was still scanning the brush, his gun at the ready, and leaned into him. "They've got Spencer and Allie."

Joe's face was unreadable, his eyes continuing to sweep the tree line. "If they took them prisoner instead of just killing them, it's because they want to know what we're doing on their turf."

"We have to find them."

Joe nodded. "Right. And how would you suggest we do that? It's a big jungle, and worse, right now there could be a rifle lining up on your head."

Drake frowned. "Where do you think they'd be taking them?"

"Probably to their headquarters for interrogation. That's what I'd do."

"And where's that?"

Joe spit by his boots and shook his head. "Beats me."

"I thought you knew this area like the back of your hand."

"I do. But there are still some things I don't know, and that's one of them. Rumor is they have a meth factory south of here, deep in their territory, but that's all it is – a rumor."

"A factory? Would it be big enough to spot from the air?"

"Maybe. Why?"

Drake turned to where Uncle Pete was crouched. "You have the sat phone?"

"Yes."

"Hand it over."

# Chapter Forty-Three

Spencer clutched his wounded arm as Allie trudged alongside him. The gunmen who'd taken them prisoner were silent as ghosts as they made their way through the jungle. Spencer had given up the fight when he'd seen that the shooters were preparing to gun down Allie, and had tossed his weapon aside and told her to do the same.

The bullet had torn through his shoulder, missing the bone and exiting cleanly, but the wound ached with each step, the flow of blood staunched from a crude pressure dressing one of the captors had rigged.

He had no idea where they were being led, but they seemed to be headed south, judging by the position of the sun whenever the canopy gave way to blue sky. Spencer wanted to reassure Allie, but he knew better than to risk the gunmen's wrath – the hike would be even harder after a rifle butt to the skull.

Two hours later they arrived at their destination: a crudely built cinderblock warehouse with easily fifty gunmen watching the perimeter of the clearing. Their captors guided them to a door and pushed them through. Inside was a pill manufacturing line, complete with conveyors; pill-making machines; a coating system; rolling steel shelves lined with jugs of muriatic acid, acetone, ammonia, and other chemicals used in manufacturing meth; and in the far corner, rows of large vats with hoses tangling from them.

At the opposite end of the building was another door. The gunmen herded them to it, and one of them slid back the bolt. The lead man pointed, his meaning clear – they were to go in. Allie walked into the gloom, and Spencer followed. The door slammed shut behind them, and they waited as their eyes adjusted.

A woman's voice from the corner startled them. "Welcome to hell."

Allie squinted to make out who was speaking, and gasped when she saw Christine Whitfield on a cot. She rushed to her and stood over her. "Oh, my God. It's you!"

"You speak English, obviously. How do you know who I am?"

"We've been looking for you since we found the plane."

"And who exactly are you?"

"We're…friends of your mother," Spencer said, before Allie could speak.

Christine peered at him. "Looks like you took a bullet."

"Yeah."

They were interrupted by the bolt sliding open and Lee entering with two gunmen. He sneered at the new captives and barked at Christine in Chinese, "You translate. Ask them who they are and what they're doing here."

Christine blinked and shook her head. "They don't speak English. I already tried."

Lee looked annoyed. "What nationality are they?"

"I think they're German. That's what they sounded like."

Lee looked them up and down and then stalked out, his gunmen following. The bolt slammed home and Christine looked to them. "Either of you speak anything besides English?" she whispered.

Spencer nodded. "Spanish."

"Me too," Allie confirmed. "What did he say?"

"He wanted me to translate for him, but I said you didn't speak English. I figured I'd buy you some time while he's trying to find a translator."

"Why?" Allie asked.

Spencer turned to her. "Because once we answer their questions, they'll have no reason to keep us alive."

Christine sighed. "Oh, they'll keep her around. They're going to sell me into sex slavery. I imagine she'll bring a pretty penny, too."

Allie's expression turned to one of horror. "Oh, God…"

Spencer moved to her side. "Don't worry. Drake and Joe will be looking for us."

"You saw how many are here. What can two do against a hundred?" Allie murmured.

"They're resourceful." Spencer looked at Christine. "How badly are you hurt?"

"Broken collarbone. Bruises, maybe a few broken ribs and a concussion. And they've been shooting me up with something for the pain – heroin. But they're decreasing the dose, so something's up. They filmed me yesterday saying my name and that I was okay."

"What happened with the plane?"

"One minute we were flying, the next we were crashing. Something exploded in the engine compartment. I'm lucky to be alive. My boyfriend didn't make it."

"I…I'm sorry," Allie said. "But you're right that you're lucky. The wreckage looked like nobody could have walked away from it."

"Yeah, I know what you mean. I still can hardly believe it myself."

Christine appeared to tire from the effort of speaking, and closed her eyes. Allie and Spencer moved to the wall and slid down, facing her. Allie glanced at the dressing on his arm. "You need some antibiotics so that doesn't get infected."

"I doubt they're planning to keep me around that long."

That simple truth seemed to reverberate in the cinderblock chamber, and Spencer joined Christine in closing his eyes. Allie stared numbly at the door, her stomach churning with bile at what was to come.

~ ~ ~

Reggie waited in the shade for Tam and his gangster friend to show.

He'd received a ten-second video time-stamped the day before from a burner phone, and had immediately forwarded it to CIA headquarters for analysis. His control had told him to agree to the trade, but to stall for time so they could bring a surveillance plane to bear and see if they could identify the building where she was being held. Now that they knew it was Red Moon that had her, they could narrow the search down to the gang's territory and were actively looking for any cinderblock structure in the southern Myanmar jungle that bordered the Shan state and Thailand, using a high-altitude reconnaissance aircraft equipped with sensitive infrared, thermal, and imaging gear. While it wouldn't have been able to spot wreckage of a plane, given the absence of a thermal signal, a factory would have personnel and a power source, and would therefore theoretically show up relatively easily.

This time Jun led the way to the café, Tam trailing him. When they were inside and seated, the establishment's only customers, he got straight to the point. He rattled off a few sentences, which Tam translated.

"He say you get movie. Girl alive."

Reggie nodded. "I did."

"You pay now."

Reggie frowned. "He wants half a million dollars. I don't carry that around in my wallet. I have to make a wire transfer and wait for it to arrive; then I can send it to him. But I need to understand the swap mechanism, because I'm not giving him money until I have the girl in my possession. Translate that for him."

Tam did, and the man grunted. He offered a solution, and Tam nodded as he listened. When Jun had finished, Tam began translating. Reggie cut him off mid-sentence. "No. That won't work. Too many ways he can screw me. So here's what I'll do. Give me twenty-four hours. When the money hits Thailand, I'll have the bank arrange for cash. It will fit in a briefcase. He brings the girl to a destination of our agreement, I bring the cash. We both come alone. Anyone but Jun and the girl shows up, the deal's off and I walk."

They went back and forth, and eventually agreed on a transaction they could both live with. They would do the exchange by the close of business the next day, and Tam would call to verify that Reggie had gotten the funds and was ready before they chose a location for the handover.

Jun and Tam left the café, and Reggie watched them turn the corner, and then an unremarkable-looking middle-aged woman did the same – a CIA asset in the area who'd been charged with shadowing them in the hopes of discovering Red Moon's base in town.

Reggie was back at his hotel when his phone rang. The news was as he'd expected. Jun was staying in a cheap tenement near the river, but it wasn't cinderblock, so that wasn't where the woman was being held – which made sense. She'd been captured in the jungle, and there was no reason to move her to an urban setting. Still, they'd had to rule out the easier option.

So they were back to waiting for the reconnaissance plane to score a hit. Once it did, depending on the location, Reggie would lead a group of commandos in to rescue the girl. A jet was already on its way, scheduled to arrive the next morning, with a dozen of the toughest special ops fighters in the world; hence the need for a delay. The plan was for Reggie to stall again at the end of the day, citing an issue with the bank, and arrange a later meeting so the team would have time to retrieve her.

Nobody believed that Jun would actually deliver Christine. Instead, it was a virtual certainty, given Red Moon's reputation, that Reggie would be ambushed and killed, the money stolen, and the girl sold into prostitution. Red Moon were ruthless, comprised of a new generation for which no abomination was unthinkable; they had risen to power by slaughtering their foes, including whole villages in their territory, without hesitation.

Reggie would be picked off by a sniper as he made his way to the rendezvous, the analysts predicted, and a motorcycle rider or the like would snatch his payload and vanish before he'd hit the ground. It was just the way things operated in the region, and Reggie didn't question the intel. Now all he could do was wait for the call that would tell him where Christine was being held prisoner, so he could mobilize and bring the war to her captors.

Something he would relish.

# Chapter Forty-Four

Drake stood in the sunshine, palm fronds stirring around him as the phone acquired a satellite and the signal bars lit. He dialed Collins' number and was relieved when the man answered in seconds.

"Collins."

"It's Drake. Allie and Spencer have been captured by one of the local gangs. An outfit called Red Moon."

"What? How?"

"The temple was a bust, but it had a bunch of guns and heroin in it. They didn't like us nosing around, so they came after us, and now they've got them – and one or both are wounded." Drake described the blood and the shoot-out. When he was done, Collins was silent for several moments.

"This group is the same one that has the girl. Our agent has been working another lead, and they're offering her to us for ransom."

"Where are they holding her?"

"We've located a facility in the deep jungle on the Myanmar side, which looks to be their headquarters. There are a lot of men around, heat signatures from generators, and a small dirt airstrip."

"Then you can go in and get them."

"That's the plan. But it won't happen immediately. That's not how we operate. We want to be successful, not lose the girl to a hurried mission. We have personnel on their way."

"What about Spencer and Allie?"

"Obviously, they'll be a priority."

"When are you going in?"

"To be determined, but probably tomorrow."

"That's too late. My contacts on the ground say they'll be questioned and killed. Red Moon have no reason to hold them."

"I understand your concern, and we'll front-burner this. But there are logistical issues. It's not like we pull the trigger and guys are parachuting in the next hour. That only happens in movies."

"You got them into this."

"I realize that. I'll call you when I know more."

"Where exactly is this facility located? Maybe I can nose around…"

"That would be a bad idea. If you're caught, it could jeopardize everything."

When Drake hung up, he was angry at the cavalier manner with which the CIA man had dismissed his concerns. He suspected Collins didn't particularly care whether Spencer and Allie made it – his objective was, and always had been, Christine; and anything else was a distraction.

Drake strode over to where Uncle Pete and Joe were sitting beneath a tree and relayed the substance of the discussion. When he was finished, Joe frowned. "You never told me you were working with the CIA."

"We weren't working with them so much as keeping our eyes open and tipping them off if we found the plane," Drake deflected.

"But you have the private number of someone you can reach at any hour of the day and night," Joe stated flatly.

"Joe, it's not relevant, okay? Who cares who got our permits for us? That's all it was."

"It matters to me. I hate the bastards. They're responsible for more misery than any other group in history."

"It was just a convenience. I'm not with them. I'm a private citizen. So are Spencer and Allie. We just agreed to help them out." Drake sighed. "But it doesn't sound like they're going to be able to do much for the time being."

"They'll be dead by the time they get around to doing something,"

Joe said, his voice low.

"Right. You already said that. But what can we do?"

"Tell me again about where they think this place in the jungle is?"

"Near the Mekong. South of us. Why? What can the two of us do? He said there was a small army there."

Joe nodded and rose. "Come on. Let's make tracks. Time's a-wasting."

"What are you thinking?"

"I'm betting that our friend the colonel would love the opportunity to take out his greatest rival in a surprise attack."

"The Shan?"

Joe smiled. "The enemy of my enemy is my friend."

"You serious?" Drake asked doubtfully. "You really believe he'd risk it?"

"Dead serious. He'd have single-handedly eradicated the biggest threat to Shan dominance in the area. I just need to convince him."

"And why would you risk it?"

"You and your girlfriend owe me over a hundred grand. Hard to collect if she's dead, am I right? And you look like you're stupid enough to try to find this place on your own, so we can make that you'll be dead too. So, simple: I want my money." Joe spit again and glanced up at the sky. "Now we going to sit here jawing all day or get busy? Sooner we make it to the Shan camp, sooner we can come up with a plan."

Drake handed the phone back to Uncle Pete, who removed the battery and slipped the phone into his backpack. Uncle Pete hadn't said a word during the exchange, and now seemed to be having trouble meeting Drake's eyes. Drake raised an eyebrow. "What do you think?"

Uncle Pete looked down. "Think they dead soon."

Joe nodded and made for the brush. "Come on. Nothing ventured…"

Three hours later, the first of the Shan outposts spotted them and radioed ahead. Colonel Leng was waiting for them when they entered the camp, his face hard. He growled questions at Joe, who did his best to explain what had happened, and after a tense discussion, he and Joe moved out of earshot, leaving Drake and Uncle Pete to replenish their water stores. Drake helped the Thai guide with his bottle, his injured arm still out of commission, and by the time they were finished, Joe had returned.

"Well?" Drake asked.

"He wasn't happy he lost two men, but he got over it pretty quickly when I told him I had the solution to his Red Moon problem."

"What does he propose?"

"He'll give us men, armed to the teeth, as well as AKs, RPGs, grenades, the works. In exchange, he takes over the factory and the trade. Simple deal. Oh, and I promised him a cash bonus from you since the temple was a big fat nothing."

"Right. But we don't know exactly where the headquarters is, and they're likely to have guards posted, aren't they?"

"These guys are jungle fighters; they're not worried about guards. The problem with where the factory's located is a little bigger, but I think I have a way to narrow that down some. You said it had an airstrip?"

"Correct."

"Then it would have to be a relatively flat area, and the terrain on this side of the river's mostly hills." Joe withdrew his GPS and powered it on. Once he had a lock on a signal, he zoomed in, starting at the disputed zone, and studied the imagery.

Drake checked the time and exhaled in frustration. "They could be getting tortured while we stand around here, Joe."

"Remember what I said about positive vibes, dude."

"Didn't do Allie and Spencer much good, did it?"

"Remains to be seen, my man. Now let me concentrate on this."

"What are you looking at?"

"Elevations. A flat area. It would probably be camouflaged to avoid detection from the air, and these images are probably so old it hadn't even been built yet, but you can't change the lay of the land. We find a decent-sized clearing that could handle an airstrip that's no more than a day's march from the temple, and that's our spot."

Ten minutes later, Joe was huddled with the colonel and his second-in-command, going over a paper map. Joe had identified a likely spot, and they were discussing how to best approach it without being detected. When they were done, Joe moved to where Drake and Uncle Pete were sitting. "He's going to give us twenty men. He wanted to bring everyone, but I argued for stealth – so he'll get into position, and his scouts will radio when we've taken the factory." He eyed Drake. "Time to saddle up. Leng thinks it's a five-hour march. That'll put us there around dusk, which would work in our favor."

"How do we avoid Red Moon killing the hostages?" Drake asked.

"We've got five hours to figure that part out. Now grab as many magazines as you can carry, and let's hit the trail."

"I should call the agency…"

"No way, dude. They'll just tell you not to do this. They're pencil pushers. By the time they get anyone in, your girl will be worm food."

Drake looked over to where the men were collecting their weapons and filling satchels with grenades. "How many night vision goggles do they have?"

Joe smiled. "Enough."

"You really think we can pull this off?"

"Positive vibes, dude. You really have to lose the cynicism."

Joe turned and called out to Leng, who grinned and gave him a thumbs-up. Drake asked what he'd said, and Joe shrugged. "I told him that you'd double his bonus if we got everyone out alive."

Drake's faith in the aging hippie increased as he watched him slide magazines into his cargo pants. There was a palpable sense of both excitement and purpose among the Shan soldiers, and whatever Joe had said had clearly lit a fire under them, whether it was the lure of financial gain or the prospect of eradicating their hated adversaries once and for all. The men packed their kits with efficiency, their expressions serious, and for the first time since Drake had seen the blood in the elephant grass by Allie's bandana, he felt a stirring of optimism.

He just hoped they'd make it in time.

# Chapter Forty-Five

Joe took careful steps along the trail. Uncle Pete beside him brandished a pistol, a rifle out of the question given his infirmity. The Shan gunmen moved soundlessly behind them, all obviously on high alert. Drake brought up the rear, his feet blistering from the hiking of the last few days in wet conditions, his face drawn as he labored forward, refusing to submit to the urge to quit. Visions of Allie being tortured, or worse, raced through his imagination during the silent march, and his abdomen was a rock-hard knot of tension as the afternoon light slowly began to fade.

His watch told him they'd been on the move for almost six hours. If they didn't reach the suspect site soon, they'd be further handicapped by nightfall. Only half the men had night vision equipment, Joe's assurance that there was an adequate supply as optimistic as his take on the duration of their trek, and Drake was afraid that the Red Moon guards might be better equipped. If they were, any element of surprise would be overwhelmed by superior firepower, and then it would become a bloodbath whose outcome couldn't be predicted.

Drake did his best to think optimistic thoughts, but what kept repeating through his mind was silent cursing at their predicament. He'd been suckered into a game that he was unprepared for, and now his love and his friend might pay for his poor judgment with their lives. It wasn't lost on him how quickly things could turn from good to bad, and he couldn't shake the feeling that they were headed toward disaster.

He stumbled over a vine and a flash of pain flared from his ankle, adding to his sour mood. He'd need to be more careful – preoccupation could get him killed. All he'd need to do was miss one telltale warning sign, and it would be over. His rifle felt heavier than it had when they'd started this jaunt, and he tried not to think about the gunmen he'd killed. Drake might have fancied himself an adventurer, but the truth was he knew he'd be haunted by the vision of his victims for a long time to come. That they were trying to kill him, so it had been self-defense, didn't mitigate his guilt at having taken human life. He wondered how men like the ones he'd surrounded himself with could eagerly go in pursuit of death, and he shook his head. They were almost a different species, Joe included. The aging hippie showed no remorse at having shot more than his share, and Drake was willing to bet he'd sleep well tonight even if he killed a dozen more.

The procession slowed as Joe held up a hand, his focus on the area ahead absolute. Drake filed past the waiting Shan and drew near. Joe turned to him and whispered, his voice so low Drake could barely make out his words.

"There's a booby trap just ahead. A trip wire. So we're getting close." Joe pointed to an almost invisible length of monofilament strung across the trail. One of the Shan nodded and pushed past them and, after a brief study of the device, snipped the line. Drake realized he'd been holding his breath and exhaled in relief. The rest of the men seemed unfazed.

Their progress slowed to a crawl as they picked their way along the trail. Joe spied one more trap, which the same Shan rendered safe. The gloaming's light was fading as they arrived at the edge of the clearing, and Joe nodded in satisfaction at the sight of the building in front of them. At one end hummed a generator providing power for the interior, but only a few lights illuminated the exterior, which made sense given the illegal nature of the operation. Still, it was easy to make out dozens of armed men in the shadows; at least five times as many as in the Shan force.

Drake murmured to Joe, "We need some kind of diversion. There are way too many to take on. Looks like the CIA underestimated their strength."

"Yup. More like a hundred men, easily. Idiots."

"So what do we do?"

Joe gestured at a shack well away from the main building. "See that? My bet is that's where they keep all the flammable material they use to manufacture the meth. If we can get to it, that would create a hell of a distraction."

"Yeah, but it's got at least twenty men guarding it. What are you thinking? Fire an RPG into it?"

"Problem is, those aren't very accurate at this distance, so it's just as likely to miss as hit." Joe shook his head and then gave Drake a small smile. "Maybe something more dramatic to get their attention?"

"Like what?"

"See the airfield over on the far side?"

Drake nodded. "Yes. And?"

"Is that a plane sitting at the edge?"

"Looks like it."

Joe nodded. "Then here's what we're going to do…"

Darkness now enveloped the jungle around the manufacturing plant. Drake, Joe, Uncle Pete, and two of the Shan fighters crept through the brush, skirting the clearing as they made their way to the plane – a Cessna 208 Caravan with pontoons for water landings. When he'd first seen the floats, Joe had theorized that the Red Moon traffickers were flying payloads of drugs offshore, where they could be smuggled onto boats for shipment to different locales, evading the customs inspections that were routine in Thai ports.

Although the buildings were heavily guarded, the dirt strip only had two men watching it, neither particularly vigilant, judging from their postures. Both were slouched on a log, chatting in low tones, with their guns resting beside them.

The two Shans moved like phantoms on soundless feet toward the guards as Joe edged toward the plane, keeping to the brush. Drake watched with Uncle Pete as the Shans reached the sitting men at the same time, muffled their cries with their hands, and plunged knives into the bases of their necks, instantly severing the guards' spines and ending their lives. Drake winced as the bodies slumped to the ground, and then his attention was drawn by Joe running to the plane, a satchel of grenades around his neck.

"Come on…come on…," Drake whispered impatiently to himself as Joe fumbled with the plane door. Drake glanced back at the factory, where the guards milled around, and then to the aircraft. Joe had disappeared into the ungainly fuselage and pulled the door closed behind him.

Moments later the groan of the plane's starter sounded from the runway, but the racket from the heavy generator powering the factory drowned it out. When the Cessna's motor roared to life, the guards at the large building froze at the unexpected sound. It was clear from their confused yells that nobody knew whether it was an unscheduled flight or a problem, and by the time someone had sounded the alarm, Joe was accelerating down the runway, whose beige dirt was barely distinguishable from the grass that framed it.

The seaplane lifted into the sky and climbed. A tall man emerged from the factory door and screamed an order, pointing at the departing aircraft. The guards began firing at it, but the plane was well out of range of the rifles, and their bullets missed by a wide mark.

Confusion reigned on the ground as the Cessna banked in the dark sky and returned, its lights extinguished so it was almost invisible against the partial overcast. Drake watched in fascination as the plane reappeared at almost stall speed, no more than a hundred feet above the trees, and a half-dozen orbs dropped toward the storage shack.

Four of the grenades detonated wide of the mark, but two exploded just above the roof. The shack blew in a massive fireball as the flammable agents inside ignited, throwing debris and a scorching wave for fifty yards.

The tall man, obviously the leader, roared commands as he ran toward the shack, and most of the surviving men accompanied him. The chatter of automatic rifles was constant from the building; and this time, due to the plane's elevation, some of the rounds found home. The tone of the engine changed when Joe attempted to climb to safety as he jettisoned the remainder of his grenades at the men below, but as the Cessna moved over the tree line, the motor coughed several times…and then quit.

Flames licked from the engine cowling as the aircraft disappeared over a rise, and twenty seconds later, another explosion shattered the night where it had vanished.

"Oh no…Joe," Drake murmured, and then his focus was drawn back to the building as Uncle Pete and the two Shan rose beside him. Gunfire encircled the Red Moon guards as the Shan force opened up on them, and what might have been a pitched battle became a massacre. Most of the gunmen were caught out in the open with no cover, led by their leader, who dove for a rocky outcropping as plumes of earth geysered around him.

A Shan soldier sprinted toward the generator housing and almost made it when two rounds stitched into his chest. He dropped face forward, and the grenade in his hand rolled the final yards before detonating by the power plant. The lights blinked off as the electricity died, and the grounds and structure were plunged into darkness.

"Let's go," Drake said. He flipped his night vision goggles down and activated the power switch, and the stygian landscape blinked neon green, the muzzle flashes from the defending Red Moon shooters bright flares. The Shans and Uncle Pete did the same, and he ran toward the manufacturing building as the gun battle played out around him. Drake was firing at the now-blind Red Moon gunmen as he zigzagged to the main door, and heard the Shans' guns barking behind him as they followed, picking off obvious threats with disciplined shots as they conserved ammunition.

Drake threw the steel door open and stopped shooting – the chemical smell was almost overpowering, and Joe had warned everyone that a spark could easily blow the entire place. He stepped inside of the empty production area and spotted two doors at the far end. Uncle Pete entered behind him, trailed by the Shans, who ducked into the entrance before slamming the door shut. Rounds pummeled the steel slab, but none penetrated. Drake led Uncle Pete to the pair of doors and pointed to the one that had a bolt on the outside. Uncle Pete nodded and moved to it, and Drake raised his rifle as Uncle Pete slid the bolt free.

"Allie? Spencer?" Drake called as the door creaked open.

"Drake!" Allie's voice rang out from inside. Relief flooded through him as he approached the entry.

"Are you hurt?" Drake asked as he peered into the room. He stopped when he realized that they couldn't see him. "Can you walk?"

"I've got an arm wound, but Allie and I can walk. What about you, Christine?" Spencer's voice answered.

"Maybe with some help," she said.

"I'm here at the door. I'm coming into the room with Uncle Pete. We'll lead you out – we have night vision gear," Drake warned. "Stand still until I reach you."

"Okay," Allie said, the intensity of the gunfire outside easing as the Shan men mopped up the Red Moon survivors.

Drake moved to where she was standing by the wall and whispered to her, "Take Spencer's hand and follow Uncle Pete into the warehouse." He raised his voice a fraction. "Christine?"

"Who are you?"

"Name's Drake. We're here to rescue you."

"Sounds like a war out there. Might be safer in here."

"Let me help you," Drake offered. "Take my hand," he said, holding his fingers out until he touched her arm.

"I can't. They've got me tied to this damned cot."

Drake inched closer and saw the bindings. He withdrew the knife he'd been given as part of his gear and slashed both wrist and arm bindings. "There. You're free."

Christine's legs were wobbly from a week on the bed, and she was unsteady as a toddler as Drake led her to the door. "Wait. They have my notebook computer from the plane. I can't leave without it," she whispered.

"You're going to have to," Drake said.

"No. You don't understand. It's got data on it that can't fall into the wrong hands."

"What are you talking about?" Spencer asked from beside Uncle Pete.

"Just look around. Please. It's got to be here somewhere. They took it when they captured me."

Drake led her over to Uncle Pete and the others. "Help them out. I need to look around."

"I help too," Uncle Pete offered.

"No. They can't see. You need to stay with them."

Uncle Pete grumbled his assent, and the group shambled to where the Shan soldiers waited by the entry, the sound of shooting outside now only occasional. Drake pulled the second door open and looked inside. There was a desk, several file cabinets, a shortwave radio, a bottled water dispenser, a weapons rack with at least twenty guns, and a massive safe. Drake slowly scanned the room, and stopped when he saw a laptop computer sitting atop the desk beside a large flat-screen monitor. His gaze followed the cable from the monitor to a CPU on the concrete floor, and he edged to the table.

A minute later he was at the entrance, his friends beside him.

"Did you find it?" Christine murmured.

"I took the only laptop in there. A Dell. Is that it?"

"Has to be."

Drake looked toward the pair of Shans and nodded as he took a deep breath and swung the door open.

The air outside stank of burning chemicals, and the conflagration at the shack belched black smoke into the night sky. Drake surveyed the exterior, the ground littered with the bodies of fallen Red Moon shooters, and whispered to Uncle Pete, who called a warning to the Shan soldiers so they wouldn't open fire.

The two Shans emerged first, guns sweeping the area, followed by Drake and Christine. Uncle Pete led Spencer and Allie out next, and let go of Allie's hand once they could see by the firelight flickering from the ruins of the supply structure.

Shots rang out from the corner of the building, and rounds ricocheted off the concrete. Drake spun and fired as the tall Red Moon leader tried to duck for cover, but one of Drake's rounds hit him in the chest and he flew backward, firing into the air as he dropped. Drake continued shooting until his magazine was empty, and then ejected the spent one and slid a fresh one home. He continued toward the corner and only stopped when he saw the man gasping, his rifle a few feet away.

Drake toed the weapon out of reach and watched wordlessly as the Red Moon leader struggled to breathe, the chest wound burbling with each effort. Christine limped to where he stood and stared down at the man, her face an ugly mask of hate.

"He was going to sell me into slavery after he and everyone here raped me. The only reason he hadn't yet was because of my injuries." She spit on Lee's face. "Burn in hell, you bastard," she hissed in Chinese. Drake's fingers on her arm seemed to startle her, and then her expression softened.

"He's not going to make it," Drake said.

"Good. Or I'd put the final bullet in him myself. I just hope he suffers for a long time."

Drake lowered his gun and nodded. "Let's get out of here. Think you can manage a hike?"

"Try stopping me."

Drake took her to where Allie and Spencer were standing. "Where's Joe?" Allie asked.

He told her about the plane. She gasped when he described it crashing into the jungle over the rise. "Oh, God…so he sacrificed everything for us?"

"Yes. Without his distraction, we might not have been able to get you out alive," Drake said.

Another shot rang out from near the airfield. The last of the stragglers were being dispatched by the Shans, who were showing their adversaries no mercy.

"Where's Uncle Pete?" Drake asked.

"He ran off toward the jungle over there. Maybe he's going to go look for the plane?" Allie said.

"I don't know about you, but the faster we're out of here, the better I'll feel," Spencer said. "I don't want to learn the hard way that there are more of these Red Moon characters lurking around, do you?" He paused. "Or that the Shan aren't much more honorable and might start thinking about ransoms rather than rescues?"

Drake nodded. "Point taken. But in a few hours, the whole Shan army will be here."

"Then let's agree that we won't be."

"What about Uncle Pete?" Allie asked.

"He's the expert tracker. He'll find us," Spencer said, moving to a dead guard and scooping up his AK. He handed the gun to Allie and then walked to where another rifle lay abandoned and snagged it before turning back to Drake. "Any idea where we are?"

"Yes. According to Joe, there's a dirt road that leads to a small town, Mong Tum, about nine miles south of us. From there we should be able to make it to the Thai border. We can stop and rest whenever we get tired, and still probably make it by morning."

"Sounds like a plan."

Drake eyed Christine. "You ready?"

She stared at the fire dancing from the smoldering ruins and then at Drake's face, her expression determined.

"Lead the way."

# Chapter Forty-Six

The journey south, even with the night vision goggles, was brutal with two injured travelers, and it was obvious by the time they'd arrived at the halfway point that Christine wasn't going to make it in one go. They found a spot by a stream and decided to wait until morning, when the danger of a misstep was lessened – she'd almost gone down twice on the trail, which would have been incapacitating with her clavicle broken.

Allie inspected Spencer's wound, which, as she'd feared, was showing signs of infection. They had no medications and couldn't even use the stream water to clean it due to its questionable origins, so all she could do was commiserate.

Spencer put a brave face on it, but they all knew that time was of the essence in reaching anything remotely resembling civilization, because in the jungle the progression from infection to sepsis could be all too rapid.

Spencer lost the hushed argument with Drake about who would stand watch while they slept, and soon was dozing, his breathing deep and regular. Christine was slumbering with her back against a tree, and Drake sat up the bank, where he could spot any threat before it reached them – at least, that was his hope.

After half an hour, Allie rose and joined him. They sat side by side in wordless communion, exhausted from the events but relieved to be safe, their ill-fated adventure hopefully nearing its end. As time wore on, the clouds dissipated and the stars came out, and Allie inched closer to Drake so her voice wouldn't wake the others.

"No Uncle Pete," she observed in a whisper.

"He's a big boy. I'm sure he'll be along, if he wants to."

"If he wants to? Why wouldn't he?"

"Beats me. I gave up trying to understand anything about this place about three days ago."

"Horrible about Joe, isn't it?" Allie said.

"He pretty much saved us all. Just goes to show you can't tell how anyone's going to react when it comes down to the clinch. I would have bet he'd sell us out in a blink."

"Not me. Uncle Pete, on the other hand…"

"He's not so bad. Little gruff, but hey." He turned to her. "What about you, Allie? How are you holding up?"

"Pretty good, all things considered. But if you're asking whether I'd do it all over again, that's a no."

"Me either. Hope Spencer's going to be okay."

"We need to pick up the pace tomorrow and get him to a doctor as soon as possible. Even in the moonlight I can see it's going the wrong way."

"What about Christine? What do you make of her?"

"She's not super talkative. Then again, I think if I had a bunch of broken bones and was strung out on heroin, I might not be all that chatty, either."

"Good point. Did she say anything while you were in with her?"

Allie shook her head. "Not much. She told the Red Moon thugs we didn't speak English, so we didn't want to risk much discussion."

"Quick thinking. Wonder what her deal with the computer is?"

Spencer moaned in his sleep, and they exchanged a worried glance. "How long until first light?" Allie whispered.

Drake looked at his watch. "Four hours."

"You going to make it with no sleep?"

"After what we just went through, I'll be lucky if I ever sleep again."

"It was pretty ugly."

"My ears are still ringing from the shooting."

Allie laid her head on his shoulder and sighed. "At least we made it."

"No Buddha, though."

"Least of our worries." She closed her eyes. "You still have the camera?"

"Uncle Pete gave it to me. Wish he'd done the same with the phone. I could use a helicopter lift right about now."

"You and me both."

~ ~ ~

Jiao looked up as one of his men returned from where he'd been watching the Americans by the stream. The Chinese had stayed out of the battle at the factory, preferring to let the Shan soldiers spill their blood to free the senator's daughter. Now that she was no longer protected by a contingent of armed guards, it would be child's play to snatch her, interrogate her, and bury her in a shallow grave.

"They haven't moved," the man said.

Jiao looked into the brush with an annoyed expression. They were waiting for Uncle Pete to appear so he could assist them with the woman – if they had someone on the inside, the likelihood of her being killed too soon was reduced, and the Thai could learn whether she had anything that would help them without her suspecting anything. The forced interrogation would only work to a point with someone who was already badly weakened, as she clearly was.

They'd tailed the group from the factory, keeping a safe distance, but Jiao was growing impatient. He was sick of the constant rain, the heat, the insects…in short, he was done with the whole damned jungle and wanted to finish his mission and return to civilization for a decent shower and meal.

For all the Chinese technician's confidence, the man had yet to penetrate the DOD's network, and tolerance of his continued failure was eroding with each passing day. If the woman possessed information that would enable them to penetrate it, Xiaoping had made it painfully clear on the last call that Jiao was to obtain it and return, wasting no further time.

As if it were that easy. Jiao glanced at his wristwatch and made a decision. He stood, and his three men joined him. "We won't wait any longer. Something must have happened to the Thai. Maybe he was wounded, or he couldn't pick up the trail. Remember what I said – the girl must not be harmed. The rest? Kill them, but try to do so silently. We don't want to attract attention if we don't have to."

The men checked their silenced weapons while Jiao screwed a suppressor onto a Ruger 9mm pistol. While the danger from the Red Moon group was now neutralized, they were getting closer to populated areas, and there were other predators in the jungle. Prudence dictated that they carry out the operation with a minimum of fanfare, so as not to invite the curious to investigate if they could help it.

Jiao shouldered his pack and nodded to his subordinates. This would be a lightning strike, in and out in seconds, leaving nobody alive but the target.

~ ~ ~

Drake blinked away his drowsiness while trying to avoid moving, lest he wake Allie. After days without sleep, he was near the end of his rope, but he comforted himself that soon they would be safe, at which point he could rest for days if he wanted. His thoughts turned to his situation with Allie – once they were home, he wanted to spend some serious time with her, renewing their connection and establishing a relationship that was more than sporadic phone calls.

He tilted his head at a sound from up the bank. It was faint, almost inaudible with the tinnitus still plaguing him from the gunfire, but unmistakable. Part of him wanted to dismiss it as the burble of the stream, but after living in constant danger, he resisted the urge and murmured to Allie.

"Get your gun and wake Spencer. I heard something."

Allie opened her eyes and gave him an unfocused stare; then realization spread across her face and she reached for the AK by her side. "Spencer," she whispered, and crawled toward where he was sleeping.

She shuddered when a voice called out from the dark tree line in broken English: "Drop guns. Now, or I shoot."

Allie locked eyes with Drake, and he nodded. They both lowered their rifles slowly, with careful movements so as not to trigger gunfire. Spencer started awake at the sound of Allie's rifle striking the stones and groped for his gun, but a warning shot, hardly more than a spit, whined off the rocks near his head and he froze.

Four black-clad forms emerged from the brush, their weapons trained on the group. Christine stirred and opened her eyes, and then cried out when she tried to rise and her shoulder bumped the tree.

"You have given me quite a bit of difficulty, young lady," Jiao said quietly, his Chinese melodically hypnotic. He looked at Drake and Allie, and frowned. "Kill them."

The staccato pop of rifle fire rang out from the jungle, and rounds thwacked into the two nearest Chinese. Jiao dived for the bank as the other gunman twisted and fired at where Uncle Pete stood, shooting a Kalashnikov one-handed on full auto, brass arcing in the moonlight as he fired. A bullet caught the third man in the throat, and he gave a strangled cry as he spun.

Jiao squeezed the trigger of his pistol as fast as he could, and two shots struck Uncle Pete, who fell backward and dropped the gun. Jiao brought his pistol to bear on Drake, but he was a split-second too late. Drake's rifle barked three times, and the handgun clattered onto the rocks as Jiao clutched at the spreading red stain on his abdomen.

Spencer was up in a blink, rifle in hand, moving to where the fallen Chinese lay. He kicked their weapons away after confirming that they were dead, and stopped at Jiao, whose eyes were screwed shut with pain.

"Who is he?" Spencer asked Christine.

"I don't know. Chinese intelligence, probably. He's a native speaker."

"Why would the Chinese be trying to kill us in the Myanmar jungle?" Drake demanded as he moved to Uncle Pete. The little

Thai's unblinking gaze was fixed on the new moon, and Drake knelt beside him and shut his eyes with a trembling hand. Drake bowed his head over his body for several seconds and offered a silent prayer, and then reached into his backpack to retrieve the satellite phone and camera.

"Damn," he muttered as he pulled the ruined handset from the bag. It had split open when Uncle Pete fell and was now junk. The camera had fared better, and he pocketed it before turning to Christine. "Well? Why are the Chinese after you?"

She sighed resignedly and met Drake's stare.

"It all started with a boy named Liu."

# Chapter Forty-Seven

Reggie threw the thin sheet from his legs and groped for the phone as he eyed the LED clock readout on the hotel nightstand: twelve thirty a.m. His fingers found the call button, and he punched it to life.

"Hello?"

"Wake up. Something big just happened at the Red Moon factory." The control officer's voice was tight, which woke Reggie as effectively as being doused with ice water.

"What?"

"We picked it up on satellite. Blasts. Big explosions."

"Damn. What do you think? An accident with the chemicals?"

"Anything's possible, but we need to know for sure. How long will it take you to get there?"

"Right now?" Reggie considered the distance he'd need to travel, first by car and then on foot. "Probably...six hours."

"By dawn?"

"Correct. When will the team arrive?"

"Right around then. I'll arrange for them to rendezvous with you. Get moving, and report back as soon as you understand what we're looking at."

Reggie cleared his throat. "Are we the only player on the field on this one?"

"Of course. Why do you ask?"

"Doesn't it strike you as a little coincidental that the site gets blown up right before we go in?"

"We don't know that it got blown up, just that there have been explosions," the control officer corrected.

"You get my point, though, right?"

"I do. We're not aware of any other group in the mix."

"Fine. I'll be on the road in ten and will call as soon as I'm in place."

Reggie disconnected and glanced at his bag. The sat phone was charged, he had weapons, he had a car he'd bought – probably stolen from Thailand, but he didn't care – so all that remained was to dress and drive north. Of course, what his control hadn't taken into consideration was how actively dangerous it was to drive after dark in that area of Myanmar, more so once he was on the dirt road that ran to the top of the peak overlooking the clearing where the factory was situated. But that was par for the course. It was up to Reggie to figure out how to get there in one piece.

Four hours later he was slogging through rain forest, his night vision goggles lighting the way, his submachine gun clutched in one hand and a razor-sharp machete in the other. His GPS had told him that he was only a half mile away, and he slowed his pace as he neared.

Reggie smelled the reek of smoke before he came over the rise and saw the building. He moved as close as he felt was prudent and watched as Shan Army fighters collected bodies and tossed them onto a pile – a funeral pyre. The work went on by torchlight, and after observing for thirty minutes, Reggie powered his satellite phone on and called his control.

When the man's nasal voice came on the line, Reggie spoke in a hushed whisper.

"The place is crawling with Shan Army. I mean, hundreds of them. Looks like there was a full-scale war down there. They're dragging bodies to the perimeter, and I count at least fifty."

"Any sign of the woman?"

"Negative. It's a killing field, though. The outlying building's just a smoking crater, and there are corpses lying around everywhere. If I

had to bet, I'd guess that the Red Moon organization is history."
Reggie paused. "I wouldn't send the team in. There's no way they can
go up against hundreds of Shan. They look well equipped, and they're
obviously on alert."

The control officer sighed. "Continue monitoring the situation
while I get feedback."

"Will do. But I'd rather not be here come first light, in case these
guys come looking for stragglers."

"Roger. Stand by."

The phone went dead and Reggie frowned at it. Another desk
jockey caught with his pants down while Reggie waited in purgatory.
That was always the way it seemed to go down. He was in enemy
territory with no backup, and his superior wanted him to wait while
they had a meeting back at the ranch.

As the minutes ticked by, Reggie's self-preservation instinct
battled with his loyalty, and he was considering disobeying his orders
when the phone vibrated in his hand.

"Yes?"

"Stay in position until the team's on the ground and we can get
better intel. We can't risk that the girl is still inside and we didn't do
everything we could to rescue her."

"All due respect, the jungle will be crawling with hostiles shortly.
If this was a rout of the Red Moon group, they'll be looking to finish
it – and I'm at ground zero."

"Understood, but word came down that leaving is not an option.
Take all necessary evasive steps, but stay on site until you get word
from us."

Reggie hung up and watched the activity below anxiously. The
orders were idiotic, in his opinion. Then again, nobody had solicited
his views. He was just the field talent and would be expected to put
himself in harm's way unquestioningly.

That may have been the job, but at the moment Reggie was
seriously questioning his continued commitment to his choice of
careers. His superiors were safe in an office where the biggest risks
were a paper cut or catching a chill from the air-conditioning, and

Reggie's ass was hanging out while death roamed the field below.

Reggie grumbled an oath and settled in for what he was sure would be an agonizing wait. He just hoped that headquarters came to its senses before he paid for their cavalier attitude with his life.

~ ~ ~

Christine swallowed hard as three pairs of eyes bored holes through her.

"Liu was my boyfriend. We met through an acquaintance at my meditation center. He was Chinese, a couple years older than me, and the smartest man I've ever met. He was easily a genius – anything having to do with computers or technology, he was like a fish in water." She winced as a flash of pain shot through her shoulder, and gasped as it took all her effort not to cry out. When the spell had passed, she continued. "Anyway, to make a long story short, it was boy meets girl, both fall head over heels. Fairy tale, except that he was also kind of a radical. Turns out he blamed the U.S. government for a lot of the world's misery, and he had been working with a group of hackers to, as he put it, expose them for what they are."

Allie nodded an understanding she didn't feel, encouraging Christine to continue.

"So we're together for three months, and one day he announces that he cracked the code. I didn't know what he was talking about, but when he explained it, I was scared witless. He'd somehow penetrated the Pentagon's files and downloaded a ton of top-secret evidence – information he said would make the whole Snowden revelations about the NSA read like a greeting card. And then he gave me an example, and I realized instantly that what he had was dynamite." She sniffed back a tear. "That's when I made my first mistake."

"Which was?"

"I called my dad."

"You told him what Liu did?"

"No, I just asked him some questions. Told him I'd seen some stuff on the web, where I was in China. I asked if he had any way of confirming it was true – I mean, he's like a bigwig in Washington and chairs a committee that deals with the military. I know my father – there's no way he would be a party to the kinds of atrocities Liu had told me about. I mean, it's beyond criminal stuff. Terrorism. False-flag attacks. Assassinations. Massacres. Lies about some of the biggest events of the last hundred years that are accepted as gospel."

"And?"

"My dad told me that he had no idea what I was talking about, but that there were a lot of people who hated America because of our prosperity, because of our freedom, and they would invent lies, but not to believe them."

Spencer's face could have been cast from bronze. He raised an eyebrow. "But you didn't buy it, did you?"

"Something about his voice. It was like, all of a sudden he was really distant-sounding. I don't know if he was afraid someone was listening in or what, but no, I didn't believe him." She sat up straighter and wiped away the tears that were streaming down her face. "Liu was out of town. I…I didn't tell him I'd talked to my father. I should have, but I didn't want to think…" She choked up and couldn't continue.

Drake asked gently, "What happened then?"

"One of his cyber-buddies posted an alert about an impending attack in Pakistan. It never took place, so I thought he'd gotten it wrong, and I relaxed some. Next thing I know he's back home and telling me we need to run, that something went wrong, that he'd also been snooping around in the Chinese defense department's servers, and somehow they'd caught on. So we leave in the dead of night, and…and you know the rest. The plane went down, he's dead, and now the Chinese are after me."

Spencer shook his head. "Why?"

"They probably think I know more than I do."

Allie rose. "We should get moving. We're assuming these four were the only ones. There could be more."

"Do you think you can make it?" Spencer asked Christine.

"I'll do my best."

Drake let out a breath he hadn't even realized he was holding and asked the question that was nagging at him. "Do you think…do you think you'll be safe if you go home?"

The look she gave him was bleak. She held his stare and then looked away. "I don't know where home is anymore. But if you're asking whether my father would actively conspire to have me silenced?" Christine struggled to her feet. "The truth is that I have no idea. I'm not sure what to believe anymore."

"And the computer?"

"Liu's. It's encrypted, so nobody but me can access it. I'm the only one who knows the password."

Spencer stood without speaking for a moment, his attention on Jiao, whose lifeblood was draining from him. "The Chinese would gladly kill you to get their hands on it."

"Sounds like they'd have to stand in line, doesn't it?"

"What are you going to do?" Allie asked softly.

Christine tried to smile, but the effect was more of a grimace. "Try to stay alive."

# Chapter Forty-Eight

The bridge from Myanmar to Thailand wasn't a viable option for anyone traveling without documentation, so after arriving in Tachileik at mid-afternoon, Spencer and Drake spent several hours trying to find someone to take them across the Mae Sai River, which served as the border between the two countries. Eventually they were able to work a deal with a local fisherman, who ferried them across at dusk for a hundred dollars.

A taxi spirited them south to Chiang Rai, where they checked into a small hotel that catered primarily to the backpacker community, judging by the other guests, who were uniformly shaggy, unshaven, and almost as filthy as Drake and his companions were. After showering, Drake and Spencer set off to find a doctor who would be working at such a late hour. They didn't have to look far: the first pharmacy they came across featured a physician who lived upstairs, who cleaned Spencer's wound and gave him an injection of antibiotic without comment.

"Do you have a feeling he's seen more than a few bullet wounds in his time?" Spencer asked, as they descended the stairs from the doctor's home office.

"In this area, it's probably his main source of revenue. At least he's had a lot of practice."

"Now we need to buy a phone. Let's hope there are some shops open this late."

Luck was with them, and they found an electronics store at the night market in the city center, which was teeming with humanity, mostly bored youths killing time without spending anything, groups of them wandering the lanes and eyeing the young girls, who pretended to be oblivious to their interest.

When the phone was activated, Drake called Collins, who sounded surprised to hear from him.

"Where are you?" Collins demanded.

"We just crossed into Thailand."

"We?"

"Yes. I was able to rescue Allie and Spencer. Oh, and Christine. But Uncle Pete didn't make it."

"What? Where precisely are you in Thailand?"

"Chiang Rai."

"Give me all your information."

"Like what? How I was nearly killed by the goons that captured them? Or how the CIA did nothing to rescue them before they were murdered?"

"Ramsey, this isn't a game. Tell me exactly where you're staying so I can get agents there to debrief you."

"Fine." He gave Collins the hotel information. "Now what?"

"Wait for our man to arrive."

"When?"

"Probably tomorrow morning."

"That really narrows it down."

"My next call is to the local office. Expect visitors shortly."

Drake hung up and tossed Spencer the phone. "I can't believe these guys. They would have left you for dead, and he sounds pissed that everyone made it out alive. He didn't even ask what happened to Uncle Pete."

"That's the agency for you. Not all that great a bedside manner."

"Well, screw them." Drake looked both ways, and they crossed the street to where a vendor was selling steamed food from a cart. "Think this is safe to eat? I'm starved."

"After the shot the doc gave me, I could probably eat a fistful of maggots and they wouldn't hurt me."

"That's reassuring."

Spencer rolled his eyes. "You asked."

They ordered skewers of something resembling chicken chunks slathered with a brown sauce, and sat on the curb, which was littered with discarded paper plates. Drake tried a tentative bite and smiled. "Not terrible."

"I don't want to even guess what part of the dog this came from."

"What do you think will happen with Christine?" Drake asked as they wolfed down their meal.

"I have no idea. It's out of our hands. We did our job, so we're off the hook. Let Collins and whoever figure out their mess."

"Now you're starting to sound like me. What happened to the whole 'You don't want to say no to the CIA' line?"

"Getting shot and almost killed gave me time to reconsider."

"I hear it'll do that."

~ ~ ~

Reggie worked his way along the ridge, his night vision goggles fading as the battery waned, and cursed his control officer for the thousandth time that day. He'd had to play a running game of hide-and-seek with the Shan patrols that had circled the production facility, and was soaked through with sweat, as well as exhausted. When the call had come in ordering him to stand down and find his way to Chiang Rai immediately, with no explanation of what had happened to the team of commandos that had been winging their way to Thailand, he'd been both relieved and furious. His anger had changed to disbelief when his control had told him the reason for the urgency.

"So the amateurs rescued the girl?" he'd repeated, his tone deliberately flat. That civilians had been able to find her and break her out of a heavily fortified location left him dumbfounded. "You're kidding me."

"You heard me loud and clear. We've got people on their way from Bangkok, but we'd prefer to have you handle the girl."

"Handle? In what way? She's safe, isn't she?"

"It appears so. But we'll want you to take her into protective custody until we can get her out of the country."

"I see. You want me to take an American citizen, the daughter of a senator, into custody..."

"It's for her own good."

"Right. And who am I turning her over to?"

"We'll let you know. How soon can you be there?"

"Not until dawn, best case."

"That isn't acceptable."

"I'm deep in the jungle and have to hike out. Then I have to drive the night roads in a country that hates Americans and that's swarming with drug traffickers and rebel forces, cross an international border, and make it to Chiang Rai. The only way I can be there faster is if you send a helicopter."

"Let me see what I can do."

That had been three hours earlier, and he was still a half mile from his vehicle. The phone buzzed again, and he stopped on the trail to answer it.

"Yes?"

"No go on the helo. Where are you?"

"I should be at my car shortly."

"Report in when you're in Thailand and you have her."

"What about the field office personnel?"

"They're on their way, but there was a glitch on their end. You might arrive first. Just call when you arrive."

"Will do."

Nothing about this operation had gone according to plan, and now it seemed to be running further off the rails with each call. Reggie's goggles were all but dead by the time he reached his car, but he kept them on with his headlights off for another twenty minutes, preferring to chance colliding with an ox than alerting anyone to his presence on the road.

He didn't dare risk taking the car across to Thailand, given how he'd come by it – the last thing he needed was to be jailed for driving a stolen vehicle – so he jettisoned his weapons and walked across under the watchful eye of the Thai military. Once in Mae Sai, he found a working taxi and was soon on the road south. He arrived at his destination at five a.m., dizzy from sleeplessness, and woke the proprietor of the hotel to rent a room. The old man seemed annoyed at the imposition until Reggie flashed his wad of baht, at which point he was all smiles.

Reggie stowed his gear and rinsed off in minutes, and felt marginally human by the time he knocked on Drake's door. When Drake opened it, his hair was matted to one side from sleep, and he looked disoriented.

"I'm Reg. Where's Christine?" Reggie announced as Drake glared at him with red eyes.

"She's two rooms over. Number seven. Like I told Collins."

"I tried that. Nobody answered."

"Maybe she's asleep," Drake said with a shrug, and began closing the door. Reggie blocked it with his boot.

"Why don't you be a sport and help me wake her?" Reggie asked, a smile in place, but his tone dangerous.

"Who the hell do you think you are?" Drake spat, looking down at Reggie's boot.

"I'm your new friend. Let's see how Christine's getting along and I'll be out of your hair, okay? Sound like a deal?"

Drake didn't say anything. Reggie waited while he retreated into the room, pulled on a new T-shirt with the name of a Thai chewing gum emblazoned across the back, and stepped outside.

Reggie knocked on Christine's door again with the same result. Eventually Allie opened her door, which was adjacent to Christine's room, and eyed Reggie and then Drake.

"What are you doing?" she asked.

"Where's Christine?" Reggie demanded.

"How would I know?"

Something inside Reggie's head snapped, and he growled an expletive and kicked Christine's door as hard as he could. The flimsy lock gave and the door sprang open. All three of them looked inside, and Drake shook his head.

"Looks like she's gone."

"What do you mean, gone? Why didn't you stop her?"

"You mean why didn't I, a private citizen, stop another person, who's over twenty-one, from doing whatever she felt like? Um, because I haven't slept for two days and was catching up on pillow time, for starters. That, and I'm not a cop," Drake said sarcastically. "And neither are you, Reg, are you? Because if not, it looks like you've got some explaining to do," Drake finished as the proprietor neared them, carrying a baseball bat, two of his sons trailing him.

Reggie's pulse throbbed in his temples while the owner glowered at him and jabbered in outraged Thai. Allie smiled at Drake and paused in front of her room. "Breakfast in maybe…six hours?" she asked.

Drake returned the smile and, after a wave at Reggie, winked at Allie.

"It's a date."

# Chapter Forty-Nine

Drake and Allie sipped tea after their meal in a local restaurant while Spencer drank what passed for coffee. Ten hours of solid rest had more or less revived them after their jungle ordeal. Allie was studying the photographs of the temple cave on the little digital camera as Drake and Spencer chatted about the CIA thug who'd kicked in the door.

"What do you think happened to Christine?" Spencer asked.

"She probably bolted once we'd gone to sleep," Drake said. "If she's even halfway correct about the Chinese and the DOD, can't say as I blame her. I mean, they blew up her frigging plane, for starters. Would you stick around to see what their next trick is?"

"With no money or passport, it's going to be tough to hide for long," Spencer observed.

"Thailand's a big place, and she might have access to resources we don't know about."

Allie smiled knowingly at Drake and returned to her perusal of the images. Spencer caught the look.

"Did you give her money?" he asked quietly.

"Do I have to explain what I do with my cash?" Allie fired back, continuing to eye the camera.

"I'd have thought you didn't have any, after being taken captive."

"How do you think we're paying for the hotel? I called my attorney when we were with Joe to transfer the fee to him, and had him send a few extra bucks here," Allie said. "Western Union to the rescue. They were open while you boys were out on the town."

"So you did give her money?"

Allie smiled sweetly at Spencer. "I have no idea what you're talking about."

"I guess a lady always has her secrets," Drake agreed.

"It does make you wonder what the incriminating evidence was, though," Spencer said.

"Not my problem," Drake said, pointing to his cup for more tea. The server nodded and hurried to refill it.

"Speaking of problems, with nothing in the temple, I'm still kind of hosed," Spencer grumbled.

"Funny you should mention that. Drake, look at this picture. Specifically, check out the angle of the back wall." Allie handed Drake the camera. He studied the photo and shrugged.

"It's a cave. Carvings. What am I missing?"

"We rushed out of there, or I'm sure I would have spotted it in person."

"Spotted what?" Spencer asked.

"Look at the geometry of the back wall. Specifically where it meets the ceiling," Allie said.

Drake offered the camera to Spencer and they both peered at it. Spencer saw it first. "It's a right angle. Ninety degrees."

"And how often does that happen in nature? Specifically, in the tops of caves?"

Drake nodded slowly. "Would the correct answer be 'never'?"

Allie smiled. "Right. That's a man-made wall that was crafted to look like a natural surface."

"A false wall," Spencer said.

"That would be my hunch."

"Then there might be a treasure after all..." Spencer murmured.

"Only one way to know for sure," Drake said.

Spencer's hand moved to his shoulder. "Can't we just take a helicopter or something?"

"That didn't go so well last time, did it?" Allie said.

"When do you want to go?" Drake asked.

"It's really up to Spencer. He's the one with the boo-boo."

"It's a mere scratch," Spencer said. "Let's get some supplies and head out – at least we won't have to worry about the Red Moon crew anymore."

"Why don't we hit Joe's village first and see if his second-in-command wants to be our guide? It might help to have someone on friendly terms with the Shans. Before, we had Joe. But now... Let's just say I wouldn't want to wind up being taken hostage again," Allie suggested.

"Kind of out of the way," Spencer said.

"Not if we wind up running afoul of a Shan patrol," Allie said. "We made a deal with their colonel, and he might interpret it as reneging if we're nosing around the area without his blessing. You really want to risk it?"

"Put like that, you make a compelling argument," Drake agreed.

"Then let's assemble whatever we need and do this right."

"The lady has spoken," Spencer said, tossing a few baht onto the table and rising. "Time to go shopping. How much did you have your attorney send you, anyway?"

Allie smiled again. "Enough."

The day went by quickly as they bought rugged backpacks and filled them with camping gear, a first aid kit, pry bars, a pick, camp shovels, and insect repellent. At the largest electronics store in town they bought a portable GPS and a satellite phone, and after topping up with prepackaged meals, they made their way back to the hotel.

Drake's burner cell rang as they neared the office. When he answered it, Collins' voice sounded furious.

"What the hell do you think you're pulling, Ramsey?"

"Mom? Is that you?"

"You think this is some kind of game?"

"Oh, Collins, nice to hear from you. Might have been nicer if you'd shown up with SEAL Team Six to help me rescue my friends, but I can understand if you were busy..."

"Where is she, Ramsey? Stop screwing around."

"As I told your charming representative this morning, I have no idea."

"We left her in your care."

"No, I rescued her from certain death, and she willingly came with me. We checked into a hotel, and she apparently decided she wanted to leave. I'm not a junior G-man, Collins. I found her, brought her to safety, and she took off. How am I involved anymore?"

"I can have you arrested for aiding a fugitive."

"A fugitive? Is she really? What's she done?"

"That's none of your concern."

"Wait – you threaten to arrest me for helping a fugitive, but you can't tell me why she's a fugitive? Good luck with that. Want my lawyer's number? He could probably use a good laugh."

"You're messing with the wrong people, Ramsey."

"Collins, you suckered me into helping you. I did what you sent me to do, and my friends and I almost died in the process. You've obviously kept information from me, and now you're threatening me. Why are we still talking?"

"I need to know where she went."

"I have no idea. I was asleep. She could have gone anywhere."

"Not without help."

Drake sighed. "Is there anything else?"

Collins' voice turned coldly menacing. "I won't forget this, Ramsey. I can make things difficult for you. Remember that."

"Sure. And next time you want some help, I'll remember the charming thanks I got for a job well done. I'd say we're about even."

"You little bas–"

Drake punched the off button and tossed the phone in the trash. Allie raised a questioning eyebrow, and he grinned. "Wrong number."

Spencer edged closer. "You might want to temper the go-screw-yourself with them, Drake. You don't want the CIA as your enemy."

"Right. Because having them as my buds has done so much for my well-being." He looked at Spencer's arm. "Think of that bullet you took as a greeting card from them."

"I'm just saying. If you have a choice, keep them on your good side."

"He threatened to have me arrested for aiding a fugitive."

"He what?" Allie gasped.

"I told him to pound sand. The call didn't go so well from there."

"But Christine isn't a fugitive...is she?" Allie asked.

"Not that he could articulate. I asked him what the charge was, and he deflected. I'd say it's BS. He's just trying to scare me. But after being shot at, crashing in a helicopter, and being in combat for a few days, I guess you could say I'm all out of scared." Drake's tone softened. "Let's head to the border and see about getting a boat first thing in the morning. We'll need to take the backdoor route, since we don't have passports."

"Damn. That's right." Allie shrugged. "I guess we've been okay without them so far..."

"We can get new ones from the embassy when we return to Bangkok, but Drake's right as far as keeping a low profile goes," Spencer said. "And I think we've figured out that we'll need weapons if we're going into bad-guy territory again."

"Seems like everyone over five years old has at least an AK," Allie agreed.

Drake grinned. "And some of the toddlers look pretty shady, too."

# Chapter Fifty

The boat dropped them off as close to the area they recognized from their last trip as it could get, and once in Laos, after a brief consultation with the GPS, Spencer led the way inland. They each carried a Kalashnikov with four extra clips in their packs, and had Browning 9mm pistols in belt holsters – all courtesy of the boat captain's cousin, who turned out to be one of the top police officials in Chiang Saen. Apparently the market for slightly used fully automatic weapons was thriving, and the cousin had no problem procuring guns for friends of his cousin from his store of confiscated firearms.

It had rained that morning as they'd made their way north on the Mekong, and they were soaked, the only relief provided by their wide-brim hats. Spencer was managing the trail at a good pace in spite of his shoulder, which he claimed didn't hurt, but which Drake and Allie could see was causing him grief.

When they neared the village, a voice called out a warning to them, and after slipping their rifle slings over their shoulders, they stopped and raised their hands. One of the sentries stepped into view and lowered his weapon when he recognized them. He said something in the local dialect and offered a hint of a smile, and then signaled for them to follow him up the slope to the village.

They marched behind him to where the remains of a fire smoldered in the central pit, the drizzle intermittent as the perennial fog burned off. A few of the gunmen they passed bowed wais in greeting, which they answered with similar gestures.

They froze when they reached the huts.

Joe stepped from his dwelling in his orange pants, a camouflage T-shirt topping the ensemble, and grinned. "Whoa. Look who the cat dragged in. I thought I'd seen the last of you."

"But…the crash…" Drake sputtered.

Joe shrugged and made a face. "Takes more than a few bullets to keep me down."

"How did you survive?" Drake said.

"It was pretty hairy. I managed to put the plane down in a clearing. Tore the wings off, but hey. I got out just before it went kabang." He grinned again. "Positive vibes, dude. Can't underestimate them. Oh, and the colonel told me you made it out, so all's well."

"You weren't hurt at all?"

"Stubbed my toe. Stung like a bitch." Joe's gaze moved to Allie. "Funny you should show up. I just made it back this morning. Like kismet or something." Joe motioned to the log. "Pull up a chair. What can I do for you? You seen the error of your modern ways and decide to go native?" He eyed Allie appreciatively. "Or was the power of our mutual attraction too much? We're both adults. We don't need to play games."

Allie laughed. "No, we need to go back to the cave."

Joe grew serious. "Why?"

"We think we missed a false wall."

"Bummer." Joe frowned. "That could be a problem."

"Why?"

"Leng told me they're hearing rumbling about the Myanmar Army making a push into that lower area. I guess all the commotion at the factory got their attention."

"But that's fine! We have permits from the government."

"Right. But you have to avoid getting shot in order to show them. You don't want to be in the middle of a firefight between the Shan and Myanmar Armies."

Spencer nodded. "So we can't talk you into going with us? We were thinking you could smooth the way with your buddy Leng."

"He's still a little touchy that you bugged out without paying him."

"That's why we came back! You can explain we're honorable, and we wanted to keep our word," Drake said.

Joe registered Spencer's bandaged shoulder. "What happened there?"

"Cut myself shaving."

Joe scowled and glanced around. "Where's Uncle Pete?"

Spencer told Joe about being ambushed, and Joe shook his head. "I could tell he wasn't long for this world. It was his aura. The universe knows."

Drake rolled his eyes at Allie. "Right. But back to our little project..."

Joe got a faraway look in his eyes. "You want to go back into no-man's land, in the middle of an active military offensive, where there could still be drug traffickers roaming around, after almost being killed...too many times to count?"

Allie pursed her lips. "Put like that..."

"Then you're not interested?" Drake asked.

Joe slapped his knee and stood. "Hell yeah, I am. When do we leave?"

"No reason we can't go right now."

"Let me pack some gear. Figure what, a week, tops?"

"You mentioned you knew other pilots. Anyone with a plane big enough to fly into an area close to the tomb?" Allie asked.

Joe's eyes narrowed. "I might – it'll be expensive."

"There's a shocker," Drake said.

Allie glared at him. "In for a dollar..."

"I'll need to look at the terrain some. And not to be a buzz kill, but there's always the chance the Myanmar Army shoots us down. They might think we're a Shan scouting flight or something."

"You think that's likely?"

"Not the way I fly!" Joe laughed, his eyes wild. "Let me check out the images. I still have the waypoint on my GPS."

"We have a new one with a bigger screen," Spencer offered.

"Cool. Hand it over."

Five minutes later, Joe grinned like a crazy man. "Let me get on the radio. I know a dude up the way who has a little Piper Comanche we could squeeze into. Looks like there's a dirt road we could land on that's only a few hours of hard march from the cave," he said, and strode back to his hut, mumbling to himself.

Spencer whistled softly. "He's completely out of his mind. You do know that, right?"

"He's going to help. So maybe having friends that are out of their minds isn't such a bad thing," Drake said. "I never held that against you."

"Touché. But if what he said is right, we might be better off waiting until the Shans and the Myanmar regulars settle their differences."

"We're here now. We came for the tomb. Let's get this over with. Besides, I've heard that some of us could use a slug of treasure..." Drake said.

"You had to remind me. As though the bullet wound doesn't sting enough."

Joe reappeared, carrying a different aluminum-framed backpack. "Lost the other one when the plane blew. I'll add that to your tab. You need another sat phone?"

"I don't think we can afford one," Allie joked, and Drake shook his head.

"We got one in Thailand."

"Okay, then. Plenty of ammo?"

"Yes."

"I talked to my bud. He's fueling up and should be here in an hour. Probably fifty-fifty that he shows. He's usually drunk by now."

"It's ten in the morning," Drake said.

Joe nodded sagely. "We all have different demons, man."

Drake whispered to Allie, "Guess that answers any questions about whether he's kicked his habits."

Allie shrugged. "Whatever he's on, I want some."

Drake took another hard look at Joe. "Let's just hope it burns off before he gets behind the wheel."

"Hasn't stopped him before." She gave him a commiserating smile.

"Did I mention I hate small planes?"

"So far they've been better to you than helicopters."

"Good point."

Joe led them to the airstrip when the Piper appeared over the hills, and they waited as the single-engine prop plane touched down uncertainly, bounced twice as it struggled to stay on the uneven, muddy runway, and then taxied toward them. Joe gave the pilot a wave as the plane coasted to a stop, and Spencer snorted in disgust.

"What?" Allie asked him.

"The thing's a piece of garbage," Spencer griped. "Look at it."

"We're not flying to London," Drake said.

"We'll be lucky if we make it over the river."

The door opened, and a thickset man with a full white beard stepped down heavily. As he approached, they got a strong whiff of alcohol. "Joe, you old bandit. Good to see you," the pilot said.

"Graham, always a treat. These are my passengers. Is she fueled up?"

"Might want to top her off."

Joe moved to his barrel and pumped as Graham held the nozzle, and soon they were in the plane and ready for takeoff. Graham had agreed to accept payment via wire, on Joe's word that he'd vouch for his passengers, and they were now ten thousand dollars poorer for the transaction. Drake and Allie squeezed into the rear seat, with Spencer in the copilot position, and they were sweating bullets by the time the aircraft hurtled down the dirt strip. Allie caught the look on Drake's face and took his hand, and for the first time that day he relaxed, all now right with the world, at least for a fleeting moment.

# Chapter Fifty-One

General Brad Holt walked in measured steps along the Potomac River, whose jogging path was nearly empty at three in the afternoon. The wind ruffled his jacket as he stopped and looked across the river at where the center of the American government lay. After checking the time, he continued along the stretch until he reached a lone bench, where he sat, watching the breeze dimple the tall grass.

Colonel Sam Daniels appeared two minutes later from the opposite direction and sat next to him. Neither man spoke for several moments, and then Holt twisted to look at Daniels.

"We should have sent our team in. This is a disaster," Holt growled.

"Hard to argue that in hindsight. But the odds were almost nil that she would have survived the crash, much less the rest."

"You know how I feel about luck. There's bad, and there's worse. We just got both in one helping."

Daniels nodded. "Yes, we did."

"Who have we got in-country?"

"Several specialists are on their way."

"If she goes public with what the damned boyfriend downloaded…"

"I know. So the question is, do we scuttle everything now and begin throwing up a smokescreen, or do we wait to see what happens?"

"There's too damned much at play here. We can't just pull the plug on some of these operations. They've been years in the planning, as you know."

"Perhaps we should begin leaking our own snippets, to prepare the media for what's to come? Diffuse the situation before it gets any worse? If we can control the spin, stay ahead of it..."

"How do we control the spin on domestic assassination, Sam? 'They needed killing because they were onto us' won't wash, and we both know it."

"In the end, it's our word against hers. I'm thinking we need to discredit her before she can go live."

"What did you have in mind?"

"Maybe rumors of a drug problem? Orgies? Roommates that said she was taking antipsychotic meds?"

"Sure, but many won't buy it. Those are the ones I'm worried about. Good Lord, think about how it will look if some of those documents were leaked in the *New York Times*? It could bring down the government."

"We'd just deny they were genuine."

"Right, but some of this speaks directly to what even a controlled press will construe as criminal. We won't be able to play the national security card. There will be too many questions." Holt turned to look directly at Daniels. "Questions we can't answer. She's got it all, Sam. The entire money chain. From the DOD, to the Saudis, to Wall Street, to you know who...we're talking almost ten trillion. People will pay attention."

"Then we'll need to set up some fall guys. It worked with Iran Contra. We'll find someone willing to take the heat for it who ultimately refuses to testify, who claims he was following orders. He'll get a token sentence and then retire somewhere tropical with a ton of dough. It's not like it hasn't worked before."

"There are too many enemies out there now – it's a different world. Nobody's buying most of our spin these days." Holt shook his head. "We may have stepped on a real mine this time."

Daniels frowned. "There's always a way out of any trap. We both know that. The question is how we proceed from here. Hell, as complacent as most of the population is, it might not even matter that much. If the right talking heads say it doesn't, then most of the country will believe it doesn't. Look at what they've swallowed so far."

"The problem isn't just our own people. Think about the international repercussions. We'll lose Latin America right off the bat if the truth about Venezuela slips out. And Europe won't be far behind when the French learn about the magazine bombing. There's only so much the market will bear. Christ, the Russians will go berserk once they have definitive proof about Ukraine. And eventually, even the dimmest taxpayer's going to want their money back or someone's hide nailed to a wall. I think we both know that we're candidates for that honor."

"Then obviously priority number one is to find her and neutralize her."

"Obviously." Holt stood. "I want you to personally supervise this. Get on a plane if need be. Do whatever it takes, pay off whoever we need to. She can't hide forever, especially in that part of the world."

"What about domestic loose ends?"

"I think we need to start sanitizing, don't you?"

"It could get messy."

"I'm sure it will. But put it in motion. There are some whom we simply can't have testify."

"I'm on it."

"Keep me informed. You understand the stakes."

Holt stood and marched away from the bench, his shoulders square. Daniels waited until Holt was out of sight to check the sound on the tiny voice recorder he'd used to tape the discussion. Daniels knew how the DOD operated, and he wasn't about to be collateral damage. This tape would be his insurance policy. Better to see Holt hang for high crimes against the nation, after all, than himself.

If it really came down to it, Daniels could vanish in South America until enough of the shit storm had blown over. Assuming it ever did. There were some things that could cause seismic shifts in the globe's underlying power structure; the knowledge that most of the industrialized world's truths were actually lies propagated to benefit an elite coterie of super-rich was one of them. The sheep were complacent and apathetic, but history had shown that during times of great stress, that could turn on a dime.

This could be one of those times.

If it was, Daniels didn't want to be within five thousand miles of ground zero.

The nation would forgive a lot in the name of patriotism, but some things were unconscionable no matter what the explanation.

"If only she didn't have the money trail," Daniels muttered as he stood. That was the most damning. There was no way to interpret it other than that the U.S. was being operated for the benefit of foreign and, in some cases, hostile interests – or rather, transnational interests that knew no allegiance to any country or ideology besides the accumulation of power and control.

Daniels walked slowly back to the parking lot where he'd left his anonymous sedan, just another man in a gray suit, unremarkable and uninteresting except for the hard gleam in his cobalt blue eyes and the way he carried himself, the years of drills and training impossible to hide even had he cared to.

He would do what he had to in order to protect his ass. Daniels hoped it didn't come to that, but he wasn't about to become a John Doe pulled out of the river, which was where it was all heading, barring a miracle.

# Chapter Fifty-Two

The Piper bumped through rough air coming off the Myanmar hills as it headed west. Joe hummed to himself as he changed altitude to stay below any radar but above easy shooting range from below. He'd warned them that he might have to take drastic evasive measures at any moment, so they'd stayed strapped in for the trip. The only positive was that he'd estimated a total flight time of less than thirty minutes, and they were now nearing their destination.

"There they are," Allie said, pointing to their right at the pair of karst formations. "The twin sisters."

Drake nodded beside her, his complexion slightly pale from the jostling of the plane.

Joe dropped another five hundred feet as they approached the road they planned to use as an improvised airstrip, and after several tense minutes, he called out, "Thar she blows!"

Spencer eyed the narrow beige ribbon dubiously. "You can land on that?"

"It does look kinda tight, doesn't it?" Joe acceded.

"What's the wingspan on this? Thirty-something feet?"

"'Bout that."

"That's narrower."

"Hopefully it widens some."

"If not?" Drake asked from the rear seat.

"Then we set down wherever we can. Just means we'll need to

walk more." Joe wet his lips as he scanned the terrain. "Positive vibes, remember?"

"That might work," Spencer said, indicating a stretch where the trees pulled back from the road.

"Little short. We still have to be able to take off again."

They banked and overflew the area again, but after ten minutes of widening circles it was obvious that the short area was their best shot. The sky above them darkened, and it began raining on approach. Drake shook his head. "Great. How does this get any worse?"

Spencer's expression was dour as they dropped toward the earth, and he flinched when Joe came down hard and immediately fought to slow the plane on the mud, the bald tires refusing to grip as they hydroplaned forward, the plane yawing slightly as they decelerated. The section where the road narrowed came up fast, and Allie cried out when the left wing tip smacked against a tree trunk and shredded as though it were made of tinfoil.

They ground to a stop, and Joe shook his head. "Graham's not going to be happy about that."

"How do we get out of here now?" Spencer asked.

"Not many ways besides walking that I can see. Damn. We almost made it," Joe said.

"Kind of like being almost dead, huh?" Drake asked.

"Let's get our gear. No point hanging out jawing. We're exposed here," Joe said and threw his door open.

They climbed from the plane, and Spencer surveyed the fuselage as Joe retrieved their backpacks and distributed them. Branches had torn some of the remaining fuselage paint off, and the wing looked like it had taken a grenade blast. He shook his head as he studied the damage and turned to them.

"This thing's definitely not going to fly again."

"Probably not," Joe agreed. "Hope we can find Graham another one for a decent price."

"Be hard to find an older one," Spencer replied.

"Got the job done," Allie said.

"Or half of it, anyway," Drake grumbled.

Spencer checked the GPS and shouldered his backpack, and then chambered a round in his AK. "We're a good four miles. No question we'll be camping out."

"At least we've got tents," Allie reminded him. "Positive energy, remember?"

"Right. I forgot about the vibes." Spencer sighed in resignation. "Let's get moving," he said, and moved down the road as rain fell around him.

The walk turned ugly once they veered off the road and were forced to cut their way through the undergrowth until they could find a promising trail. Joe did most of the hacking, Spencer's shoulder in no shape for exertion, and he traded off with Drake and Allie every half hour. Eventually they came across a track, and Joe knelt and studied the ground while they took a breath. When he stood, his easy grin had been replaced by a scowl.

"These are footprints. Judging by how fresh, maybe, two, three hours old."

"How do you know?"

"The water level and the depth of the impression. The ground was dry when they were made. You can barely see them; but here, and here, it was spongy and they left marks," Joe explained, pointing to the footprints.

"What do you think?" Spencer whispered.

"I think the flight in was the easy part."

"But you know all the Shans, right?" Drake asked.

"Sure. But why would the Shans be traipsing around here?" Joe shook his head. "I'd bet this is some of the remaining Red Moon gang. Or maybe an independent group. But whoever it is, it's not good. I figured we'd have the area to ourselves with all the action at the factory. Guess not."

"Any way to tell how large a party?" Allie asked.

"Large enough that I don't want to be on this trail. Looks like we keep cutting our way through." Joe held the machete aloft and simulated a sword fight.

The journey took hours longer than they'd estimated, due to the circuitous route, and by the time they arrived at the base of the outcroppings, fog was creeping between the towering formations, enshrouding the valley. They paused at the gap between the peaks, and Joe scanned the surroundings.

"Maybe this time it would be a better idea to make camp a decent distance from the river? Just in case we have more visitors," he suggested.

"Sounds good to me," Drake replied.

They followed the stream to the cave and then climbed the slope above it until they were perched a hundred yards beyond the rock pile that marked the opening – which they noticed had been rebuilt in order to conceal the cavern. They pitched their tents out of sight of the river, and by the time they were done, the sky was darkening.

Drake and Allie sat together as they ate their ration of energy bars, and he managed a smile when she was done with hers. "Hey, it could be worse, right? I mean, we're in a tropical wonderland on a unique adventure, and with any luck tomorrow we'll find our second treasure," he whispered as they watched the sunset.

"Exactly. And the company could be worse, too," Allie said, and leaned over to kiss his cheek.

"What happened to the 'to be continued' part? I was looking forward to that."

"Let's get out of the jungle first, okay? Not that a long day's sweat and a layer of trail grime isn't appealing," she said, rising.

"On you it looks good."

She beamed at him and shook her head slightly. "Good night, Drake. There really will be a 'to be continued.'"

He watched her walk to her tent and nodded. "I'm banking on it."

# Chapter Fifty-Three

"This is unacceptable," Xiaoping's superior snarled, slamming the table with his hand. "You assured me that our systems were bulletproof."

Xiaoping nodded, taking measured breaths, commanding himself to remain calm. "Yes. I was relaying what I was told. As you're aware, I am not a technological expert. I must rely on their assurances, which it appears were…overly optimistic."

Xiaoping paused and surveyed the room, which was a who's who of government ministers – all demanding answers. Xiaoping stalled for time by taking a sip from his water glass, and then sat forward, his hands folded.

"So far what has leaked is embarrassing, but not disastrous. Our record on human rights has never been our strength, so that portion of the revelations won't matter to our allies. Our intention to ramp up our defense spending? Again, relatively predictable, given that the U.S. has encircled us with bases and aircraft carriers. So far there is nothing that will change our position on anything, except perhaps the speed at which we move forward with our investments, and our official announcement of our precious metals reserves."

China was the largest manufacturer of gold in the world and exported exactly none of it. It was also the largest buyer of foreign gold through a network of shell banks as well as through legitimate channels. The propaganda it advanced to outsiders was that its population had a long tradition of hoarding gold – that it was a remnant of primitive habits, of a lack of sophistication in an era where Western financial groups referred to the yellow metal as a barbaric relic from a bygone age.

The truth was that in order for China and its allies to escape the U.S. dollar's grip, a superior solution needed to be advanced; and throughout history, when paper currencies failed – which they ultimately did, with one hundred percent regularity – the new global standard that was used for trade and for settling debts was always backed by gold in some manner. That had been true of the prior reserve currency to the dollar, the British pound, and it had been true of the dollar when the greenback had replaced the pound as the world's reserve currency. But the U.S. had made the classic mistake that all others before it had – namely, to reject the discipline that backing its currency with gold enforced – and instead turned on the printing presses, after declaring that the quasi-gold standard was inadequate for the modern world.

China and Russia had quietly begun amassing gold, all the while nodding along with the U.S. agenda. That the dollar was doomed to be relegated to a lesser role than the one it had played since the Second World War was not only predictable, but inevitable. China's policy had been to support the U.S. central bank's efforts to keep the price of gold artificially low, all the while shifting its dollar inventory quietly to gold without moving the price higher – taking advantage of the hubris of the nation's bankers and their belief that they could mislead the world indefinitely.

The amount of gold in China's government vaults was one of the country's most jealously guarded secrets, and in the last twenty-four hours, a report had been posted on the Internet detailing precisely how much it held, and where. The Chinese response had been typical – no comment – but they could only stonewall for so long.

"It is intolerable that our secrets are displayed for all to see," the defense minister said. "If you can't guarantee that they are safe, why did you put them where they could be accessed by some hacker?"

"With all due respect, Minister, I did no such thing," Xiaoping corrected. "The decision was made by a collective, and I was not invited to offer my opinion to that esteemed group."

"What steps are being taken to ensure this never happens again?" the chairman's deputy asked, his voice deceptively quiet.

All eyes moved to Xiaoping, including his superior's – the man was a veteran of the byzantine infighting of the party and had survived many crises during his career. Xiaoping had no doubt that he'd be thrown under the bus if a scapegoat was necessary, so when he responded, he did so with great care.

"As you know, our agent Jiao is missing and presumed dead. So are his men. There has been no communication for days, so that is the safe assumption. Our sources tell us that the woman survived somehow, and that she has made it her mission to broadcast the information her cursed lover was able to amass. But let's consider what the likely focus will continue to be: the Americans. The information that has been made public in the last day is devastating to their credibility, and there are already calls for regime change, as well as prosecution of past leaders for treason. I'd argue that given that damage, we have been fortunate." Xiaoping paused.

"Yes, we know all that. The question is what is being done so we aren't victimized again?"

"I would propose that our sensitive information be stored on a set of failsafe systems which can't be connected to the outside world, even via protected networks, as ours was believed to be. The only way to ensure nobody is ever able to hack it is to ensure it is physically impossible to retrieve information from outside the vault where it is located."

The discussion of the pros and cons of Xiaoping's solution were debated for thirty minutes before he was excused while the powerful continued to confer. He was under no illusions that his future was assured, but he was breathing more easily than he had been when he'd climbed the steps that led to the conference room. The penalty for failure was usually extreme, and even though the failure wasn't his, he would share the blame.

Xiaoping moved like an older man than he was. When he emerged from the building, the wind cut through his coat, chilling him. He'd always favored philosophy over fear, and if he was to be spirited away in the dead of night, a bullet to the skull his reward for thirty-six years of loyal service, then so be it. He'd lived a full life and wouldn't flinch if his destiny was an unmarked grave.

Of course he'd miss this world, but he also believed that, like his ancestors, when his time came, he would face the unknown bravely – the alternative pointless in the face of eternity.

The thought gave him comfort, so much so that he barely noted the pair of hatchet-faced men approaching fast from behind, or the van that trailed them, his destiny rushing to meet him with imminent finality.

# Chapter Fifty-Four

Drake cracked his eyes open as Spencer's voice whispered to him in the darkness of his tent. "Someone's on the move down by the stream."

Drake looked at the time – two a.m. He sat up and nodded to Spencer's outline and then crawled to the opening. A thick layer of fog blanketed the area, so dense that he could barely make out Joe and Spencer crouched motionless, listening. Drake strained to hear and was rewarded by the sound of rustling from the cave mouth. Minutes went by, and metal on stone drifted to them, followed by the thunk of rock shifting.

Joe murmured to Drake, "Someone's going into the cave."

Drake nodded. "Good. Maybe they'll take their stuff and leave."

"Doesn't seem like we'll have to wait long to find out."

Allie's head poked from her tent and Drake held his finger to his lips. Her eyes narrowed and she moved to his side. They listened as the sound of men laboring beneath them floated through the mist, and Allie leaned her head against Drake's shoulder and snuggled closer.

They stayed like that until dawn, by which point all signs of life had quieted from the cave. Joe rose, gun in hand, and headed down the slope. The others remained still until he reappeared.

"They're gone. Looks like they came for their dope. Makes sense if it's Red Moon – they probably lost everything at the factory, so all that's left is whatever they have stashed."

"How big a gang were they?"

"Hard to know for sure, but I'd guess at least five hundred active members, not counting all their contacts in the border towns."

"That's not that big," Drake said. "I mean, the Shans number in the tens of thousands, right?"

"Right, but this area is an easy one to dominate because of how remote it is. So it doesn't take that many men to protect it – and the Shan power base is way further north, which is why they let Red Moon have it in the first place. Not worth fighting over."

"What will they do now that they lost their production facility?" Spencer asked.

"Some will probably try to start new gangs, but most will just join up with whoever the new master of the area turns out to be," Joe replied. "If it's the Shan, great. If the Myanmar Army, super. The hill tribes are flexible in their loyalty. They have to be."

"But they're gone for now?" Allie asked.

"Looks that way. All the dope's cleared out. The only things left are a few guns and some grenades – and they probably have more than they can carry already. They didn't bother to replace the stones right, so it looks like they're done with the cave. At least for now." Joe paused. "They came in the dead of night because they're afraid of being spotted moving during the day. That tells me they won't be back while it's light out, if at all. So I'd say we're in the clear."

"Are you sure?" Drake asked.

"See? Negativity flowing from you. You've got to change your evil ways, young man." Joe grinned. "I'm as sure as we can be about anything. Then again, I was sure we had enough road to land on, so it's an imperfect world."

"What if they find the plane?" Spencer asked.

"What if they do? It's a long ways away. They'll probably assume it's another smuggler who ran into trouble and had to ditch. Happens all the time. They'll just strip the plane of anything they can sell and move along." Joe crouched down. "I'd give it an hour just to make sure they don't come back, and then have at it."

Time crawled by, and when they didn't hear anything more, they broke camp and moved down the hill to the cave. Allie and Spencer fished out their LED lights and scanned the interior while Joe and Drake maintained a vigil outside. When it was obvious that they were alone, they climbed through the gap to where the pallet sat empty. Allie moved to the back wall and tapped on it with her pry bar before gesturing at the base.

"See? Right angles. It sounds solid, but that's probably because they carved limestone blocks to wall it off."

"So where do we start?" Drake asked.

"Let's try the bottom."

Spencer joined them, and they scraped at the rock, which came away in chunks. Within minutes it was clear that Allie was right – the outline of a large block appeared beneath what now was obviously mortar created from local stone dust. They continued working through the morning, and by the time the fog had pulled back, a large section of man-made wall was exposed.

Spencer and Drake worked at the most promising block with their pry bars, but the stone was so brittle it broke off in chunks. They continued chiseling away at it and broke through just before noon. Widening the gap sufficiently for a human to crawl into the space beyond took only a few minutes, and when they sat back, sweating from the effort, Allie moved forward with her light and shined it into the cavity.

"Look at this," she whispered. Drake moved next to her and peered into the opening. "It's a door."

"Look at the seal on the handle. Clay and rope. It's never been broken."

"Pretty elaborate. Why wall it off like this?"

"I'd guess to avoid detection."

Joe joined them. "Well? Not like we've got all day. Are we rich?"

"Remains to be seen," Spencer said, and looked at Allie. "After you. It's your discovery. You were right about the wall."

Sudden movement in the antechamber drew their attention to a corner, and Allie drew back at the sight of the flared hood of a king cobra, its eyes glinting in the unexpected light, weaving slightly and hissing as it prepared to strike.

"That can't be good," Spencer whispered, but Joe just shook his head.

"Poor thing's probably scared."

"Poor thing?" Drake said.

"We're all made from the same stuff. You just need to be respectful of it, and it shouldn't hurt you. Show no fear, but honor it," Joe assured him.

"Honor the deadly snake. With positive vibes, no doubt," Drake said.

"Let me by. I'll show you."

"Are you nuts?" Allie asked, and then bit her tongue.

Joe chuckled. "Depends on who you ask."

They moved aside, and Joe fished a flashlight from his pack and scrambled through the gap. The snake reared back as he entered, and Joe stared at it, holding its gaze. He bobbed his head as he muttered something in Laotian. The cobra's eyes followed the movement, and Joe slowly held his gun out until the barrel was almost touching the snake.

Allie gasped as he pushed the creature's head aside with the muzzle and grabbed its body near the tail and then rose, holding the squirming six feet of angry reptile before tossing it to the base of the wall. The cobra slithered away and disappeared through a hole.

Joe grinned at them. "See? Honor it, and it won't hurt you." He motioned to Allie. "Come on. But be careful when you open the door. Could be a whole room full of the critters."

Allie reluctantly climbed into the six-foot-square area, her light focused on the snake hole. She took a deep breath and shined the beam on the seal. The orange clay bore a seated Buddha stamped into the molding, affixed to an ancient leather cord that was wrapped through a handle and secured to a peg driven deep into the wall. She tried to pull the peg free, but it wouldn't budge. She knelt in front of the seal and studied it carefully before flipping her pocketknife open. "Take a picture of it before I cut it," she whispered to Drake, who snapped several, the flash blinding in the small space.

"Got it," he said, and she nodded and slid the blade under the cord. The material crumbled to dust at the touch and dropped to the stone floor. She nodded to Joe and reached for the handle, and then stopped as her gaze drifted to the area above it.

"Stand back," she said.

"Why?" Joe asked as he did so.

"See the irregularity in the ceiling?" she asked, directing her flashlight beam at the suspect area.

"Yes."

"I'm thinking the Khmers might have been trickier than we give them credit for," Allie said. She rooted in her backpack and found a coiled nylon rope. She tied a slipknot to the handle, inspected the crude hinges, and stepped away from the door. "Ready? Drake, can you set the camera to video and shoot this in real time?"

"Way ahead of you," Drake said. The device was already blinking an indication that it was filming.

"Okay. Here goes nothing."

Allie pulled on the cord, but the door didn't budge. She gave it another jerk, but still nothing happened. Spencer's head appeared in the opening. "Pass it to me. Let me give it a try."

He wrapped one end around his waist and then leaned his body weight against it. The door groaned and began to shift, and he drove his legs against the wall to get additional leverage.

The ancient wooden slab swung wide, and a tumble of stones dropped from above, any one of them large enough to crush a human skull like a walnut. Dust filled the space, and Joe and Allie coughed. Allie held her sleeve to her mouth to breathe through, and Joe did the same with the bottom of his crusty T-shirt.

Joe's flashlight beam cut through the haze and flashed against something beyond the door. In spite of the sediment cloud, Allie moved forward, her lamp shining on the floor, the memory of Joe's close encounter of the cobra kind still vivid. Drake moved through the opening behind them and reached her in three quick strides, a bandanna held over his nose and mouth, his gun still in the cave, the camera in his other hand.

"Your instinct was right. You could have been killed," he said, eyeing the scattering of stones.

"I thought it was too easy," she said, blinking as the dust settled.

They walked together to the doorway and stood at the threshold. Allie swept the chamber beyond with her light and smiled, her eyes bright with excitement. "Looks like we did it."

"I'll never get tired of this part," Drake said, and they stepped into the room together, Joe following them as Spencer remained by the gap in the wall.

Carvings adorned every surface in the cave, and piles of gemstones and gold icons were piled in cubbyholes sculpted from the raw stone. Hammered gold and ruby emblems leaned against the bases of the walls, and fistfuls of ancient gold coins were overflowing from long-deteriorated sacks. At the far end of the chamber, in a position of obvious honor, sat a green Buddha draped in a gold cloak, its jeweled eyes twinkling in the light. Allie stepped forward and Drake filmed as she stopped in front of the statue.

"It's...it's breathtaking," she whispered.

Drake nodded silent agreement. Joe stepped forward and eyed the treasure.

"There must be thousands of coins," he murmured.

"Yes. But the Emerald Buddha was clearly the most revered of the stash," Allie said as she regarded the statue.

Joe moved closer and reached out a trembling hand to touch the icon, but froze when Spencer's voice hissed from the doorway.

"Better get back out here. We've got company."

Joe whipped around and was halfway to the gap when the still of the cave was shattered by the deafening bark of Spencer's rifle.

# Chapter Fifty-Five

Bullets ricocheted off the rock entrance as Spencer fired at a group of gunmen near the stream. Joe reached his side in time to see an Asian man fall, hit in the torso by Spencer's last burst. Orange muzzle flashes winked from the trees as the shooters concentrated on the cave mouth. Spencer spent his last round and ejected the magazine as he reached for another, while Joe replaced him at the cave mouth and began firing.

Drake and Allie arrived in time to see Spencer cry out and clutch his face – a rock chip from a stray bullet had sliced his cheek, missing his eye by an inch. Drake hurried over to Spencer and handed him his bandanna, which he gratefully took to blot the gash.

"I need a loaded gun," Joe screamed over the chatter of his weapon, and Allie handed hers to him as he emptied his and tossed it aside. She reached for it and changed out magazines before setting it next to him, keeping low to avoid the incoming rounds.

Drake spotted a crate at the base of the nearest wall with half a dozen grenades inside and crawled to it. "You want some grenades?" he called out.

Spencer nodded and Drake dragged the crate to the entrance.

Joe turned to him, keeping his head down, and frowned, his face covered with a patina of dust. "We're sitting ducks here. Just a matter of time till one of them starts chucking grenades. We know they have 'em," he said, eyeing the crate.

"What do we do?" Drake asked as Joe returned to the fight and loosed another burst.

"You know how to shoot that thing?" Joe yelled.

"I'm no marksman, if that's what you're asking."

"Who's the best shot?" Joe asked after his weapon ran dry.

Drake glanced at Allie. "Spencer."

"So we trade off until they either get us, or we finish them," Joe growled. "You able to shoot?" he asked Spencer.

"Yeah. Give me a few minutes so this can clot. I'm fine," Spencer said. "Although it hurts like a bitch."

Joe grabbed the loaded AK Allie had set by him and slid his empty one to her. "Keep putting new magazines in these. How many do you have left?"

Drake patted his pockets, as did Allie and Spencer. "Maybe a dozen including what's in the rifles."

"That's three hundred sixty rounds. We should be able to make those last a while. Problem is, they only have to get lucky a few times and we're toast."

"What's the range now?" Spencer asked.

"Most of them are by the river, so maybe a hundred, hundred fifty yards," Joe answered. "We mopped up the closer ones. They aren't taking any chances now that they know we can shoot."

"So it's a standoff?" Allie asked.

Spencer held the bandanna away from his cheek and eyed the blood on it before shaking his head. "No. They'll circle around before much longer and come in from above with grenades. We won't see them until it's too late."

"Then we need to do something," Allie said.

"Like what?" Joe asked, and squeezed off another burst.

"Get out of here," Drake said.

"We show ourselves, they'll gun us down," Spencer said.

"So what do we do? Wait here to die?"

"I'm thinking," Spencer said.

"Crap," Joe exclaimed, and emptied the rifle in a sustained burst.

"What?"

"A bunch of 'em just crossed the river. They figured it out."

"Then we have to surrender," Allie said.

Spencer sighed. "I doubt they've got a copy of the Geneva Convention. Joe's right. Second they see us, they'll shoot."

"It's worth a try. The alternative's certain death," Drake said.

Spencer looked to Allie. "See if there's another way out through the temple chamber. You never know."

She nodded and hurried into the depths as Drake ferreted through his pack. He found what he was looking for near the bottom and held it aloft. A mostly white T-shirt.

"I say we give this a try," Drake said. "Hang it on the end of a rifle and see what happens."

"I can tell you what the reaction's going to be. Better get down," Joe said as he draped the shirt on his muzzle and dangled it out the opening.

A barrage of gunfire answered. Joe retracted the shirt, which had a half-dozen holes in it, and tossed it to Drake.

"There's your warm Myanmar welcome."

Allie returned from the temple area and shook her head. "No way out."

"Then we need to take cover back in the temple and fend them off as long as possible. It's going to be raining grenades pretty soon," Spencer said, his tone hard.

"Will that work?" Allie asked.

A metal orb clanked against the rocks and rolled next to Joe, whose eyes bugged out of his head as he scrambled to toss it outside. The grenade detonated five yards from the entrance, showering them with dirt as they ducked, the shrapnel from it slamming harmlessly against the boulders at the cave mouth.

"Damn. That was quick," Joe said, as though commenting on a surprise in a sporting event. "Let's go. Won't be long now."

"But…" Allie said.

Drake took her hand. "I'm sorry, Allie," he whispered. He crushed his lips to hers as Joe emptied the magazine at the gunmen, buying them precious seconds.

"Move. We're out of time," Spencer barked. They rushed to the temple gap and scurried through the opening as Joe lobbed one of his grenades out of the cave.

"Just to give them something to think about," he said, and then turned and ran to the temple when the grenade exploded. He threw the crate through and followed it in, and he and Spencer took up position with their guns, waiting for the final assault.

Spencer looked at Drake. "Get her as far from here as possible, and hold your hands over your ears. When the first grenade goes off, the shock could rupture your eardrums."

"What about you?" Allie demanded.

"I'll roll with it."

Joe and Spencer exchanged a resigned look, and Joe nodded. "Leave your magazines here for us."

"No," Allie protested. "There has to be another way."

Spencer shook his head. "We'll do the best we can."

Allie's face froze in horror at the finality of his words, and she followed Drake numbly into the temple. Joe moved to the door and pushed it closed as far as it would go with the rocks blocking it, and then settled down into his position by Spencer's side.

"What's that line from that old movie?" Joe whispered. "The Indian chief on the mountain, with Dustin Hoffman? 'It's a fine day to die' or something?"

"Before my time," Spencer said. "What happened to positive vibes?"

"That's all the positive I have right now."

They focused their attention on the cave opening, weapons at the ready, and waited with grim determination for the onslaught that would end their lives.

# Chapter Fifty-Six

Another explosion shook the cave floor, and Spencer eyed the opening. "That came from above us," he said, and then automatic weapon fire rattled from outside the mouth of the cave.

Joe's expression turned puzzled as he listened to the crescendo of chattering assault rifles from beyond the gap, and grew into astonished when a projectile whistled across the river and blasted into the rocks where the Red Moon gunmen were concentrated.

"Sounds like some help arrived," Joe said. "Positive energy, dude."

"Who called them?"

"The universe."

Spencer shook his head, pushed himself through the gap, and moved back to the cave opening. Outside it sounded like a full-scale war was being waged, but now the object of the shooting wasn't the cave. Joe crawled to where Spencer was peeking from the opening, and nodded as though he'd planned the entire thing.

The shooting and explosions lasted a good half an hour, and when the valley grew silent, Drake and Allie pushed from the temple and joined them at the cave entrance.

"What happened?" Drake asked.

"Somebody took out the bad guys," Joe said.

"Who?" Allie asked.

"That's a mystery; but whoever it is, I hope they're friendlier than the others were."

"Maybe the Shan?" Drake suggested.

"Could be."

Their speculation was cut short by a guttural yell from outside. Joe listened intently and then called out in Thai. Another cry greeted his declaration, and he answered and then set his rifle down.

"We're to come out with our hands up."

"Can we trust them? Who is it?" Spencer demanded, obviously reluctant to drop his gun.

"Don't think we have a choice," Joe said and raised his hands over his head.

They filed out into the sun, blinking at the glare, and found themselves facing several hundred soldiers in the green camouflage uniforms of the Tatmadaw – the Myanmar Army. The river basin was littered with dead gunmen and a handful of soldiers. The fighters trained their weapons on the four of them until an older Asian man stepped from the group and approached.

The man's uniform was adorned with the insignia of a general, and he looked like any sense of humor he'd once had was a distant memory. He glowered at them and demanded something in rusty Thai, and Joe offered a soft answer. The man's expression changed from furious to something more like he'd just eaten a handful of scorpions, and he thrust his hand out in demand.

"He wants to see your permit," Joe said to Allie.

"Really?" she said in relieved surprise, feeling in her pocket.

Two of the nearest soldiers stiffened and Spencer whispered to her, "Easy. No fast moves. They seem excitable."

She pulled out the dog-eared, water-stained permit, unfolded it, and then stepped forward and presented it to the general like it was a holy relic. He snatched it from her and read the text, his eyes squinting as he came to the signature. He grunted and handed it back to her, and then rattled off some rapid-fire directions to his men before turning back to Joe. He said something more and then waved a hand in the direction of the cave. Joe's face revealed nothing as he translated.

"He says that this area is now under the protection of the Myanmar Army and that he will take over the temple discovery."

"What?" Spencer blurted. "I mean, that's good, but what about our cut of the treasure? Never mind the historic value – how do we know it won't just disappear?"

Joe shifted from foot to foot. "You really want me to ask that?"

"Maybe rephrase it so it's softer."

Joe spoke slowly, and when he was done, the general barked a harsh laugh and said something. Joe nodded respectfully and leaned toward Spencer. "He says you can apply to the Republic of the Union of Myanmar Archaeological Commission for any reward, but that we're not to set foot back in the cave or he'll shoot us."

"Did you ask his name?" Allie said.

"I will. Is there anything else?"

"How about finding out how we're supposed to get out of here? Can we at least get an escort to the Thai border? The area's got to be crawling with Red Moon and Shan," Drake said.

Joe nodded and spoke to the officer. He looked Allie over as Joe talked, and then nodded once and called out a curt order.

"What did he say?" Allie asked.

"He said he has a daughter about your age, so he'll take pity and have some of the soldiers take us to the river. From there we're on our own."

"I need my backpack," Allie said. "It's in the cave. The phone's in it."

"I'll ask, but he doesn't seem like he's in a good mood, does he?" Joe asked.

"Camera's in my pocket," Drake said. "Worst case we can always get a new phone."

Nobody was surprised when the general denied the request. After a brief inspection of the temple while they remained outside, the general emerged and called out to his men. Ten soldiers approached and he gave them direction. The oldest, whose uniform bore sergeant's stripes, saluted and snarled an order at Joe, who relayed it, although no translation was necessary.

"He says to move. He wants to be in town by evening. They have trucks a four-hour march from here, and it'll take another three to get to Tachileik." Joe nodded agreement and wiped his brow with the back of his arm. "Time for another hike."

Drake tried a grin, but his face wouldn't cooperate. "I never thought I'd be this happy to hear those words in my life."

"Positive vibes, my man."

"I'm a believer."

# Chapter Fifty-Seven

*One week later, Washington, D.C.*

Senator Whitfield strode through the crowded restaurant to his customary table, a lacquered wooden booth in the rear of the eatery, well away from prying eyes, where more matters of state had been decided than in the Oval Office. The skin on his face hung like that of a tired dog, although his two-thousand-dollar suit was crisp and his burgundy tie radiated quiet authority.

The last week had been brutal – easily the worst he'd seen in his long years on the Hill. Every day brought new revelations that threatened to topple the power structure of the Beltway, and his phone rang from dawn to well after midnight as an unending litany of atrocities appeared online, with no obvious rhyme or reason.

Whitfield had long ago parked his ethics at the door, and he wasn't so much surprised at the level of criminality that was the norm in government work as he was that the idiots at the DOD would keep records. It was mind-numbingly stupid, an invitation to exposure, and not a minute went by that he didn't curse the worldview that insisted that everything be documented – including the sins.

That morning had been another shocker for the fourth estate – the record of a domestic assassination of a liberal journalist with a Milwaukee newspaper who'd been digging around money that had gone missing in Iraq. There it was, in black and white, as the operation had been described in detail, and now the bastard's family was calling for an exhumation so the suicide ruling could be reviewed in light of the new information. Even though the apparatus had a chokehold on the press, some things couldn't be ignored, and even the most pliant editors had to approve articles breaking the news and calling for heads to roll.

Whitfield ignored the veiled stares of the other power brokers in the room and waited for his ex-wife to appear. She'd flown back from Thailand two days earlier and had demanded the meeting. Margaret was a wonderful woman, but she had no idea how the real world worked, and the naiveté that had been charming when they'd been students in the idealistic sixties had been her downfall when he'd taken up public service and bowed out of practicing law. She'd been unable to accept the compromises that were called for, and by the time Christine entered high school, their marriage had been a tense cease-fire rather than a partnership of any real sort.

They'd gone their separate ways and hadn't spoken for months at a time; when they did, it was to sort out some aspect of their property, which had been distributed equitably. The divorce had lacked the typical acrimony and more resembled a negotiated surrender of two tired armies, where it was largely unclear even after the victory parade who had actually won the encounter.

Her voice had been terse on the call, and he'd had to park his impatience at her demand when she'd mentioned Christine offhandedly. Margaret might have been unsuited for the Machiavellian schemes of Washington, but she'd learned a trick or two while they'd been married, and Whitfield knew better than to underestimate her. So he'd agreed to a late lunch, and now found himself staring bleakly across the restaurant as he waited for another in a seemingly unending parade of unpleasant shoes to drop.

A server approached in a white vest and matching bow tie, and smiled a welcome with a nod of his head. "May I get you a drink?" he asked, and Whitfield nodded. "Gin and tonic. Light on the tonic. And the ice."

"Yes, sir. Of course, sir. And how many are we expecting today?"

"Only one."

"Very well. One gin and tonic on its way. I'll bring water and bread in a moment."

Whitfield waved him away, wondering for an instant whether bread and water was a crack at the rumors swirling around the town about investigations into his chairing of the defense department committee, but decided that it wasn't. Not everything was about him, he reminded himself. His complicity in the crimes being aired on the web would be impossible to prove – at least, he hoped so. God help them all if his role had also been memorialized on the compromised servers. He'd be finished. But he'd take others down with him if he was disgraced; he'd see to that.

Whitfield had always believed that the lessons that had served the country well during the Cold War were valid in every walk of life. Mutually assured destruction kept everyone honest and reduced the tendency to view cogs in the machine like himself as expendable. Nobody was going to throw him to the wolves, he was certain – because if he began opening his mouth, the news on the web would seem like a trip to Disneyland compared to what he could recount.

Margaret entered the restaurant and made her way to the table, her expression as placid as a mountain lake – her 'moon face,' Whitfield had teasingly called it in the early years, before the term had taken on the aura of a ritual insult intended to demean. As so many things had. For an instant he wished he could take it all back, start over, and be the young firebrand who wasn't afraid to tilt at windmills, Margaret at his side.

The server arrived with his drink and set it down in front of him, the glass carefully draped with a napkin to preserve its chill and conceal the amount of active ingredient the senator was having with his lunch. Whitfield waited until the man had left to unpeel his treat and take a healthy slurp, and wished it was reasonable to gulp it through a straw as he registered the look in Margaret's eyes as she neared.

She slid in across from him and delivered a frosty smile. "Hello, Arthur. Oh, dear, you do look like you've been through the wringer, don't you?"

"Nice to see you as well, Margaret." He took another appreciative sip and set the glass down. "To what do I owe the pleasure?"

"I wanted to let you know that our daughter is alive and well."

Whitfield leaned forward. "You saw her?"

"No. I had an all too brief call while I was in Thailand. She was trying to explain why I'd probably never hear her voice again." Margaret swallowed back a small sob.

"Why did she run?"

"You want to sit across from me and pretend that you don't know? After all the news that's broken, you're as puzzled as I am?"

Whitfield's expression hardened. "She's in way over her head," he warned. "I can protect her."

"I tried to sell that. She wasn't buying. She is, after all, our daughter, so she's naturally suspicious." Margaret studied him, and her gaze reminded him of a lab technician eyeing a specimen on a slide. "She doesn't trust you. Which, based on the look on your face, makes two of us. You've never been able to hide your nature convincingly from me, you know. For years I told myself that it wasn't you, but it is, and I accept that I made a mistake."

"You don't have any idea what you're talking about."

"No? What's funny is that when she was telling me why she was going to see through Liu's work and ensure that it saw the light of day, she reminded me just a little of you. Stubborn, committed and, above all, fearless." Margaret paused. "What happened to you, Arthur?"

"Do you know where she is?"

"No. Not that I'd tell you if I did. But she asked me to deliver a message. So here I am."

"Fine. What is it?"

"That when you keep company with demons, you become one yourself."

"You must enjoy saying that very much," Whitfield said softly.

"It gives me no pleasure." Margaret checked something on her phone. "I'm afraid you'll be eating alone, Arthur. I thought I could manage it, but I seem to have lost my appetite." She slipped from the booth and stood. "I hope all this was worth it. Your daughter. Me."

Whitfield clutched his glass as she made her way to the entrance and left, his mind racing. He struggled to rise, but his chest suddenly cramped, and the most incredible pain he'd ever experienced shrieked through his synapses as his heart seized. He fumbled for the edge of the white linen tablecloth and then sat back, his breathing so shallow it resembled that of a baby bird fallen from its nest.

The server returned and took the senator's drink off the table and walked unhurriedly to the kitchen. He didn't stop until he was out the rear service door, where a van waited with its engine idling. He climbed into the passenger seat and dropped the glass into a garbage bag, and then peeled off his latex gloves, taking care not to handle their exterior, and tossed them in as well. The neurotoxin he'd used wouldn't show up on any autopsy report, and the good senator's passing would be mourned for the loss of his moderate voice and Solomon-like judgment.

The server removed the mustache he'd affixed that morning and pulled the putty from his nose – just a small amount was sufficient to alter his appearance, he'd found through trial and error. He looked at the driver and nodded once.

"Drive."

~ ~ ~

General Holt watched the Potomac rush by, the moon silvering its surface. A few late night joggers pushed themselves along the riverside path as the last balmy breeze of autumn stirred the trees around them. He'd spent the day in a series of panicked meetings with anonymous men whose deeds were now making headlines, and he was bone tired. Of everything. The subterfuge, the denials, the palpable fear in the rooms he drifted in and out of, unable to offer reassurance. The excrement had hit the fan good and well – with remarkable vigor, as one wag had said on television that morning.

And now he'd been summoned like a schoolboy for a clandestine conference with a man whom nobody said no to, presumably to have his ass chewed out and his future threatened. Holt would take it stoically, as was his custom, and assure him that damage control was being undertaken, and that they would all survive this, as they had so many other calamities. That Holt was expected to act as a lapdog to the most influential figures in the world didn't strike him as odd at all – in his experience, the hubris that inflated them with grandiose importance was always the first to dissipate, leaving them demanding that he, little more than a foot servant, do something to protect them from the antiseptic of sunlight.

He glanced over to admire a young woman who was approaching on the path, obviously athletic even in a hoodie and shorts. Holt might have been in the twilight of his years, but he could still appreciate beauty for its visceral pleasure. In his mind he wished her nothing but well, as she aged, became a parent, wrinkled and stooped as the unforgiving years had their way, and ultimately, turned to dust.

The pop of her suppressed pistol could have been mistaken for a distant backfire. Holt stared at her through fading eyes as her expression never changed and she fired three more rounds into his skull, the second one extinguishing his life, the rest for grisly show.

Another robbery gone wrong in an area beset by crime would go unremarked. The woman's long legs glided along the pavement, leaving the husk of Holt lying ruined by the water, his lifeless gaze staring accusingly into nothingness.

~ ~ ~

A week later, Daniels watched the CNN coverage of the unfolding train wreck in Washington with a bitter smile as steel drums pulsed from the beach veranda, the mild surf luminescent in the starlight. The bartender strode over and tilted his head at Daniels' drink – a blood-red fruit punch concoction that had enough rum in it to lay an infantry platoon low.

"'Nother one, mon?" the islander asked in his musical accent.

"No, Cliff, I think I've had enough. See you tomorrow."

"You bet, mon. Take it slow, you hear?"

"Is there any other way?"

Daniels' voice sounded slurred, even to him, but he didn't care. His life had fallen apart, but like the proverbial phoenix, he'd been reborn. Over his career it had been child's play to secret away enough money in offshore locales to be able to run – so much cash sloshed around in the system that you had to be a fool not to see the possibility. The trick had been to avoid being greedy, and to shave off a sliver at a time, which was never missed. "Shrinkage," he muttered to himself, smiling at the retail term for pilferage. "Just a little shrinkage, mon. T'aint no thang."

He'd covered his tracks sufficiently and was enjoying his fourth night on Ambergris Caye, Belize's best kept secret, as far as he was concerned. It was a country that boasted more spottings of fugitives on the FBI's most wanted list than any other, no doubt a function of labile borders and English as the official language, as well as a reputation for discretion from a populace that had its own affairs to contend with.

He padded along the beach to his hotel, the reef in the near distance glowing from abundant marine life with each surge, and didn't register the two islanders who darted from one of the darkened bungalows that lined the strand until it was too late.

Neither man spoke, letting the steel in their hands do the talking for them. When they ambled away thirty seconds later, Daniels had been stabbed eighteen times. The terminal stroke had penetrated his skull through his eye. The tallest of the pair slid a wad of hundred-dollar bills from Daniels' wallet and threw the empty billfold far into the water. Neither looked back at the dead man lying half in the surf, his blood staining the white sand inky in the moonlight. Violence against tourists was an increasing problem as the beleaguered country battled drug gangs intent on moving in from Honduras and Mexico, and the headlines would meet with disapproving head shakes over breakfast as the vacation spot ramped up for another long day under the tropical sun.

# Chapter Fifty-Eight

*Malibu, California*

Drake reclined in his Herman Miller Aeron chair and eyed the blue Pacific stretching to the horizon. Spencer shifted on the sofa and gave an exasperated sigh.

"Are you sure?" he asked.

Allie's voice on the speakerphone sounded equally impatient. "Positive. There's no such thing as the Myanmar Archaeological Committee, and the government is stonewalling us. There's no official statement about the find, no return calls, nothing. It's been the same thing for, what, coming up on three weeks?"

"My contact at the State Department said we're screwed through official channels," Spencer said. "As to the general, apparently the Myanmar dictatorship isn't big on publishing the names of its ranking officers. Or anything else, for that matter, so that's another dead end."

"There has to be something else we can try. What they're doing is criminal," Drake griped.

"The good news is we bought another lot of icons and coins, this time through a dealer in Hong Kong," Allie said. "That makes the third lot so far. They're really wasting no time, are they?"

"I can't believe there isn't a way to shut it down. It's not theirs to sell," Spencer said.

"Possession is nine-tenths, apparently," Drake offered. "The

Cambodian Government has filed formal complaints with everyone that will listen, but it's had no effect. Oh, it also expressed its continued gratitude for our generosity." Drake and Allie had been taking turns buying the temple treasure when it appeared at private auctions and gifting it to the Cambodian people. So far, the lots had run a couple of million dollars, and they'd set aside five apiece to restore the treasure to the rightful heirs of the Khmer Empire. It wouldn't begin to buy everything, but the hope was that it would go a long way into shaming the Cambodian bureaucracy into creating a fund to finish the job.

"Still no word on the Buddha?" Allie asked.

"Nope. Silent as the grave."

"A relic of that significance won't stay hidden forever. When it comes on the market, we'll hear about it. I've got all the usual suspects putting out word of our interest."

Their foray into the world of illegal antiquities had been eye-opening. There was a thriving market for illicit statues, parchments, and relics of all shapes and sizes, from Sumerian to Aztec to Greek and Roman – wherever there was big money looking to be deployed, mansions to furnish, friends to impress, there was demand for the rarest of the rare: one-of-a-kind artifacts unavailable to the great unwashed. A network of specialized outlets ringed the world, and live auctions were conducted by invitation only – or, in some cases, items were just sold outright when a match between buyer and seller could be arranged.

Allie and Drake had established contacts in that black market through legitimate art and antique houses, and had let it be known that they wanted first right of refusal for any of the Khmer items. They'd believed it might take a year for the initial buys, and had been surprised by how rapidly the general – or the Myanmar government – had been selling off the temple contents.

"But as of now, I'm hosed on any chance of a finder's fee," Spencer grumbled.

"Yeah, looks that way. That's how the ball bounces. We'll make it up on the next one," Drake said, ignoring Spencer's eye roll.

"How's your financial quagmire going, Spencer? Getting it all figured out?" Allie asked.

"The hedge fund says they can account for every penny, but so far they haven't delivered anything in writing," Spencer said glumly.

"And no money?" Allie said.

"Nada."

"That sucks."

"Tell me about it. I'm accepting donations. I'll paint your house, whatever you want."

Drake laughed. "He's got a cardboard sign: will work for spare millions."

"You should consider televangelism, Spencer. You'd be good at it," Allie said.

"Get a tent and take it on the road," Drake agreed. Spencer gave him the finger and Drake picked up the handset, taking the call off speaker. He walked out onto the deck and shielded his eyes from the sun with his free hand. "How much longer are you going to stay in Texas?"

"The depositions should be done within another week or so."

They'd spent three days in Bangkok, waiting for new passports to be issued by the embassy, during which time Allie had been badgered by her attorneys, who insisted she needed to be back immediately to deal with the lawsuits. The return to civilization had been jarring, and she'd grown distant almost immediately as her energy had gone into multi-hour conference calls to discuss strategy and new hurdles.

Joe had returned to his village a millionaire, taking the seven figures they'd offered him as thanks over the chance at more from the treasure. He'd been in the region long enough to understand the odds of ever seeing anything more in payout, and had taken the bird in the hand. His parting words had been typically cheerful.

"Dude, you ever want someone to hang with on another one of these, you know where to find me. Hut's always open for business. Stay positive."

"I'm not sure we can afford any more wisdom, Joe."

"Some things are priceless."

Drake spotted Kyra inside her house and waved. She returned the wave and gave him a 'hang loose' hand sign. "What's that?" he said, distracted and not catching Allie's last sentence.

"I said, hopefully I won't have to be here until these go to trial, although my team says I'd be smarter to settle. That's all these parasites want, a few bucks. Their attorneys are banking on me caving just to get them off my back."

"Maybe that's not such a bad idea," Drake said.

"Over my dead body. I'll spend my last dime fighting them – I'm not going to reward anyone for trying to take advantage of me."

"Sounds like your lawyers have job security for a long time, then."

"Maybe the suits will go away when their guys figure out there's going to be no easy payday."

"Hope's always good." Drake paused. "Have you thought about what we discussed? Moving out here for a while, seeing how you like it?"

"Of course. It's on my mind a lot."

"Spencer's got a condo in Malibu now. We could all be neighbors."

"What happened to his house?"

"Construction. Place is falling apart. They're ripping out the foundation piece by piece. He got robbed. It's unlivable, and he says he can't stand to look at it anymore."

"Poor Spencer."

"I can't believe you're feeling sorry for a guy with a Lambo and a private jet."

"Don't forget the boat."

"Right." Drake had to laugh. "So are you going to come out?"

Allie sighed. "Yes."

"When?"

"No more than two weeks from now."

"That's awesome," Drake said, trying to keep the excitement to a minimum. "You want me to start looking for a place?"

"I'd rather pick my own. I can stay on your couch or something while I look, can't I?"

"Of course."

After a few more minutes, Allie signed off, and Drake went back inside. Spencer grinned at him from the sofa.

"What was that all about?"

"She's going to be here in a few weeks. Said she'd give California a try."

"Sweet. Do you get to keep Kyra on the side?"

"What's wrong with you?"

"Just asking."

"When are you going to get the car out of my garage?"

"Still waiting for parts. Damned thing won't even start now."

"Handmade," Drake reminded him.

"Italian. I understand they can be temperamental."

"And expensive."

Spencer reached for his soda can and shrugged. "You don't say."

"I know what will cheer you up. Boat ride!"

"It's in the yard."

"Take the plane up and buzz around?"

"On charter this week."

Drake thought for a few seconds and then smiled. "Then there's only one thing left."

They both smiled and cried out at the same time.

"Pizza!"

# Epilogue

Two nubile young women in thongs and skimpy tops, their bodies glistening with oil, danced to the languorous techno beat throbbing from hidden poolside speakers. Several young men floated on inflatable rafts in the Olympic-size pool, its glass tiles translucent in the late-afternoon sun, creating the illusion that the depths continued to infinity. A bartender stood behind a granite station in a full tuxedo, staring into nothingness, seemingly impervious to the heat.

The men laughed at a ribald joke at the expense of one of the women, both of whom smiled, not understanding the language. They were Czech and communicated in English with the men, although they hadn't been hired for their conversation skills. Part of a rotating retinue of hospitality provided by the host, they spent a month in Dubai at a time, earning six figures before returning home. The agency that specialized in providing the entertainment could arrange for whatever the guests' tastes ran to, be it a Parisian model, a Russian dominatrix, Vietnamese twins, or a Venezuelan beauty queen. In a world where there was no limit on cost, anything was possible – for a price.

The swimmers were the scions of wealthy Saudi royalty, their petro-dollars incalculable, and as such they were accustomed to their every whim being instantly met. Weekend gambling trips to Monte

Carlo, shopping sprees in London or Milan, heli-skiing in Alaska, African safaris for endangered species – nothing was off-limits, resulting in the ennui only apparent in the super-rich, a perennial boredom in a world where, because cost was no object, nothing had any value. Two of the three men had been in rehab in a private Swiss clinic more times than most rock stars, and the other had criminal charges awaiting the customary acquittal after sufficient money had changed hands. They were on break from their studies in Europe, enjoying their fathers' offer of diversion with one of the wealthiest men in Dubai.

Sheik Ahmed Suliman was infamous for his sybaritic pursuits; his hedonism was whispered about in royal courts and scandal sheets the world over. An invitation to his forty-thousand-square-foot villa was a rare treat, and the men had been enjoying it for the last few days. They spent their mornings jet-skiing in the Persian Gulf, their afternoons skeet shooting, and their evenings dining on the offerings of a Michelin chef while swigging Château Pétrus like mineral water.

Inside the villa, Suliman lay on a massage table in a specially designed room, its temperature and humidity controllable to within a tenth of a degree, the light adjusted to a warm glow. The room was silent, as he preferred it after spending an hour in his isolation chamber, where he floated weightless as he meditated.

His corpulent form spilled over the edges of the table. A towel with his initials and family crest embroidered on it covered his hirsute lower back and mountainous buttocks. A statuesque blonde in a white silk kimono entered, carrying containers of heated, scented oils, and placed them on a rolling table by his side. He cracked open an eye and grunted.

"My back is at it again," he said in accented French.

The blonde nodded. "I know just how to fix that."

His porcine cheeks quivered as he smiled. "You are a miracle, Yvette."

She smiled warmly, if not entirely sincerely, and he closed his eyes; but not before he eyed the green statue sitting in one of the backlit niches that lined the room's walls, and snuffled in satisfaction. His latest acquisition, there was only one other like it in the entire world – in Thailand, where it was revered by royalty as a national treasure.

The Emerald Buddha's countenance regarded him impassively as the Swiss masseuse began her ritual, its timeless eyes beaming as she shed her clothes and reached for the oil, the bruises on her thighs and abdomen a small price to pay for the riches her benefactor regularly bestowed upon her.

# About the Author

Featured in *The Wall Street Journal*, *The Times*, and *The Chicago Tribune*, Russell Blake is *The NY Times* and *USA Today* bestselling author of over thirty-five novels, including *Fatal Exchange*, *The Geronimo Breach*, *Zero Sum*, *King of Swords*, *Night of the Assassin*, *Revenge of the Assassin*, *Return of the Assassin*, *Blood of the Assassin*, *Requiem for the Assassin*, *The Delphi Chronicle* trilogy, *The Voynich Cypher*, *Silver Justice*, *JET*, *JET – Ops Files*, *JET – Ops Files: Terror Alert*, *JET II – Betrayal*, *JET III – Vengeance*, *JET IV – Reckoning*, *JET V – Legacy*, *JET VI – Justice*, *JET VII – Sanctuary*, *JET VIII – Survival*, *JET IX – Escape*, *Upon a Pale Horse*, *BLACK*, *BLACK is Back*, *BLACK is The New Black*, *BLACK to Reality*, *BLACK in the Box*, *Deadly Calm*, *Ramsey's Gold*, and *Emerald Buddha*.

Non-fiction includes the international bestseller *An Angel With Fur* (animal biography) and *How To Sell A Gazillion eBooks In No Time* (even if drunk, high or incarcerated), a parody of all things writing-related.

Blake is co-author of *The Eye of Heaven* and *The Solomon Curse*, with legendary author Clive Cussler. Blake's novel *King of Swords* has been translated into German by Amazon Crossing, *The Voynich Cypher* into Bulgarian, and his JET novels into Spanish, German, and Czech.

Blake writes under the moniker R.E. Blake in the NA/YA/Contemporary Romance genres. Novels include *Less Than Nothing*, *More Than Anything*, and *Best Of Everything*.

Having resided in Mexico for a dozen years, Blake enjoys his dogs, fishing, boating, tequila and writing, while battling world domination by clowns. His thoughts, such as they are, can be found at his blog: RussellBlake.com

# Books by Russell Blake

## Co-authored with Clive Cussler

THE EYE OF HEAVEN
THE SOLOMON CURSE

## Thrillers

FATAL EXCHANGE
THE GERONIMO BREACH
ZERO SUM
THE DELPHI CHRONICLE TRILOGY
THE VOYNICH CYPHER
SILVER JUSTICE
UPON A PALE HORSE
DEADLY CALM
RAMSEY'S GOLD
EMERALD BUDDHA

## The Assassin Series

KING OF SWORDS
NIGHT OF THE ASSASSIN
RETURN OF THE ASSASSIN
REVENGE OF THE ASSASSIN
BLOOD OF THE ASSASSIN
REQUIEM FOR THE ASSASSIN

## The JET Series

JET
JET II – BETRAYAL
JET III – VENGEANCE
JET IV – RECKONING
JET V – LEGACY
JET VI – JUSTICE
JET VII – SANCTUARY
JET VIII – SURVIVAL
JET IX – ESCAPE
JET – OPS FILES (prequel)
JET – OPS FILES; TERROR ALERT

## The BLACK Series

BLACK
BLACK IS BACK
BLACK IS THE NEW BLACK
BLACK TO REALITY
BLACK IN THE BOX

## Non Fiction

AN ANGEL WITH FUR
HOW TO SELL A GAZILLION EBOOKS
*(while drunk, high or incarcerated)*

16265068R10202

Printed in Great Britain
by Amazon